THE REVELATION

Toni turned the cartridge slowly in her hands, then gave it a hard twist, but the plastic didn't give. She weighted it down with a book, pressed a screwdriver firmly against the plastic seam, and slammed it sharply with her fist. The cartridge exploded across the room, spooling the ribbon onto the floor. "Thank God," she muttered.

She rolled it up and held the film to the light. The typewriter had left a series of transparent impressions on the ribbon. There were no spaces between them. She grabbed a notebook and began to transcribe them.

Forty-five minutes later, she combed the jumble, marking any words that stood out. Toni hurried along the pages of dates and comments on the condition of the scroll. Then she came to it, a quotation from Matthew. "Tell people his disciples came by night and stole him away while we were asleep."

Toni scanned on. She came to the bottom of the last page of Buchmeunster's final entry, with the current date. She marked it off, starting at the end. "Were the chief priests right? Could two men have rolled the stone away? How could they have managed to fool his friends?"

Toni's hands were shaking. "My God!" she whispered.

THE
NICODEMUS
CODE

GRAHAM N. SMITH
AND
DONNA SMITH

An L/A House Novel

PINNACLE BOOKS
WINDSOR PUBLISHING CORP.

PINNACLE BOOKS

are published by

Windsor Publishing Corp.
475 Park Avenue South
New York, NY 10016

First printing: November, 1988

Printed in the United States of America

Judea—1988

The contest had begun with a burst of energy, driven by pride. But it was different this time. A recent earthquake had transformed the face of the cliff into a network of deadly traps. Familiar toeholds crumbled without warning, and each meter gained risked heart-stopping cascades of dirt and rock. By the time the Bedouin boys were halfway up the rock, it no longer mattered who was the victor. The tremors had destroyed any chance of retreat; the only route down was the path near the summit. They were in a race against the rock itself. They were in a race for their lives.

The boys climbed in silence, each alone with his thoughts, each consumed with a prayer for survival.

When Hassan, the older, reached the ledge a hundred and twenty meters from the desert floor, there was no cry of triumph. He scanned the Jordanian wilderness that stretched before him. The yellowish smudge that had been on the eastern horizon when they started the ascent was now a cloud of wind-borne sand, a *simoom* sweeping toward them out of the desert.

He spun and reached for his brother, who clung doggedly to the rock below. Their hands touched, then

5

locked, and Hassan pulled. But the young boy's grasp was slick with perspiration.

He slipped loose.

He slid, eyes wide with horror, until his feet caught on a projecting rock five meters down. He buried his face against the rock to hide his fear.

"Hurry!" Hassan yelled over the rising wind. "Come to me!" He stretched out a hand.

The younger boy glanced toward the base of the cliff. He stiffened and looked back upward, shaking his head. "I can't!" he sobbed. "I can't!"

"Ahmed! You must!" The taller boy glanced at the boiling sandstorm. It would be on them in seconds. "There is no other way! Come!"

His brother breathed deeply, resigning himself to the final climb. With a reluctant nod, he began to creep up the rock face. Slowly, he closed the distance.

"That's it! Hurry!"

Ahmed pushed, levering himself upward against the dusty clefts. A gust peppered his eyes with grit. He turned away from the wind, but his eyes burned. Unable to see, he froze on the rock. "Allah," he cried. "Allah!"

"No!" Hassan pulled his *keffiyeh* across his face to shield it from the scouring sand. "Climb! Do your praying later!"

The wind tore at the younger boy, flapping his caftan like a riped sail. He clawed at the crevices, inching upward. He was almost within reach of safety.

"Here!" Hassan lay flat on the shelf and stretched an arm downward. "Reach for me!"

Ahmed rocked with the wind as he looked at the

6

offered hand, just above him. He shook his head, afraid to let go.

The older boy pressed himself against the rock and leaned his chest over the edge, grabbing for his brother.

He missed. The effort loosed a shower of gravel and dirt into Ahmed's face.

On the second try, Hassan grabbed the climber's wrist and pulled. Ahmed clutched with both hands and shoved against his footholds.

The rock crumbled under Ahmed's feet and he dangled free, a pendulum in the violence of the storm. He screamed, sure of imminent death.

Hassan squeezed the wrist he held, tightening his grip to cut through Ahmed's panic. "Stop it! Listen to me!"

The younger boy grimaced from the crushing pain in his wrist. A stream of urine trailed off his legs into the wind, a spray of terror. He felt his hands slipping against Hassan's grasp.

"Ahmed! Push against the rock!"

The dangling boy worked his feet furiously, clawing at the cliff face.

On the ledge, his brother whispered. "Now, Allah! Give me strength!" He closed his eyes and heaved.

Ahmed lurched upward, clearing the ledge, and scrambled to safety.

The brothers embraced, pressing against the rock wall behind them. A gust ripped across the ledge, carrying away the older boy's *keffiyeh*. "We must find shelter," he shouted over the roar of the storm.

"Follow me!"

They picked their way along, huddled against the *simoom*'s fury. The path bent along a fold in the cliff, and the sand swirled in eddies around them. There was a cave ahead, three meters above the ledge. It hadn't been there when the boys had scaled the cliff during their tribe's encampment last year. The earthquake had probably opened it, but it looked stable and large enough to shelter them both. Hassan boosted Ahmed onto his shoulders, and the younger boy disappeared into the entrance.

Hassan waited for his brother to reach out and pull him up. Instead, there was the sudden rumble of falling stone and a choked-off, piercing cry.

"Ahmed!" Hassan tore at the rock. "Ahmed!!" There was no response, only the flat sound of his own shouts against the storm.

And the wind.

Chapter One

In a cool arcade near Jerusalem's Western Wall, Yigal Zorkin shifted uneasily and checked his watch again. It was getting late, and there'd been no instructions on what to do if the appointment wasn't kept. His beard began to itch and his scalp turned nervously damp under the woolen *yarmulke*. Breakfast, greasy herring and a bagel, festered in his stomach like a ball of phlegm. Beginnings had always been like this for him— anticipation, revulsion, nausea.

Zorkin closed his eyes and tried to lose his thoughts in the breeze from the fan overhead. The cafe was open to the outside, but the shade of the old stone and the fan's gentle whisper made it feel at least fifteen degrees cooler than the street.

He watched the steady stream of pilgrims who'd come to the wall. Some would pray; the ones who didn't would take pictures of the ones who did. Zorkin wondered how, in a city where theology walked hand in hand with commerce, Jerusalem's religious community had kept the fast-food chains a respectable distance away from the holy places. Hungry tourists were left to forage among the trinket stands until they found a place to eat.

A silhouette appeared in the entryway, starkly contrasted with the glare from the street. The newcomer brushed the dust from his cloth cap, then pardoned his way down the aisle, limping slightly. He wore standard issue for tourists—shorts and a tan shirt—but there was no camera, just a small drawstring bag from a souvenir shop slung over one arm. He was sandy-haired, perhaps in his late twenties, Zorkin judged. There could have been another ten years in the deep worry lines that framed his eyes.

"Who are you?" the man asked, cradling his cap between them like a shield.

Zorkin's response was automatic. "I am Esau, your firstborn. I have done as you told me."

The inquirer stiffened with surprise and struggled to keep his voice even as he began the second exchange, another verse from the ancient tale of how Jacob had betrayed his twin brother. "Two na—two nations are in your womb, and two peoples, born of you, shall be divided."

Zorkin could feel relief flooding through him, washing away his anxiety. " 'The one shall be stronger than the other, the elder shall serve the younger.' *Shalom*, my friend."

"*Shalom*. I'm sorry to be late, but it was a very long walk." He sagged into a chair and pulled a fat brown envelope from his bag. "I have been told to deliver this."

Zorkin took the envelope, measuring its thickness between his thumb and forefinger. "Thank you. The arrangements?"

10

"Done. Exactly as you said." The younger man glanced at the tables around them, then leaned toward Zorkin and spoke quietly. "Except—"

"There are no excepts when you deal with me!" Zorkin's voice was a cold lash. "The only changes made are those I choose to make. I survive because I trust no one. No one!"

"But we ha—"

"Least of all, you!" He shoved the envelope across the table.

The other man fidgeted, rapping his knuckles on the formica. "If you . . . We can't cancel now. It's all in place! It's already under way!" His words came unevenly, an edge of barely restrained anger tingeing them. "The only change is that you'll be met. There'll be a car waiting with my personal driver. Otherwise, we'll play hell getting you inside."

Zorkin stared hard at the courier, weighing the odds of a fatal deception. "This driver. You trust him?"

"With my life. He knows nothing, except to pick you up." He nudged the envelope back toward Zorkin. "You know, it isn't just me you'll be disappointing. My . . . investors . . . won't be pleased if you renege now. They have very long memories."

Zorkin looked at the envelope for a moment, then picked it up. "So they do. But you'd be wise to remember that I don't forget, either. I'll accept the driver, but no more changes. None."

"Agreed." The man across the table stood and smiled coolly. "I must be going."

"If you must, then *shalom.*" When the courier had left, Zorkin finished the last of his breakfast and rechecked his watch, a habit that had become a reflex.

Time was the one irreplaceable commodity. Every moment of his day would have to be carefully meted out.

He split the envelope at one end and pulled out the air ticket to check it. The flight would leave at 1:15 P.M. He would have to hurry. He replaced the ticket, then strapped the envelope into an outside pocket of his small bookbag, paid his check, and left.

Across the street, an unshaven one-eyed Arab stood in the shade, rattling his cup halfheartedly for alms. He saw Zorkin come out, then melted into the crowd and pursued him like a grubby shadow.

Zorkin's steps wove a cross-stitch down the thoroughfare as he dodged through the throng near the Wall. There was a side street that looked less crowded and he turned into it, hoping for easier going. The beggar paused at the intersection, reluctant to leave the camouflage of the main road's heavier pedestrian traffic. After letting Zorkin build up some distance, he followed.

Zorkin was walking quickly now—and paying for it in the heat. His beard was becoming a sponge. His eyes burned, and he fought the temptation to toss his sweltering *yarmulke* over the nearest wall.

A fruit vendor was nearly blocking the narrow passage ahead with his hand cart. He smiled as he saw a potential customer approach, filled both hands with oranges, and stepped quickly into Zorkin's path.

"Fresh from Samaria, my friend, none better than these."

The cloud of garlic from the vendor's breath nearly brought Zorkin's breakfast back up. He tried to force his way around, but the unyielding salesman moved with him.

12

"Please, I must—" Zorkin began, pushing harder.

"Come, look," the vendor persisted, smiling even wider to reveal a set of very bad teeth. "Perfect oranges, my friend. Picked only last night. A dozen for—"

Zorkin's shove sent the man sprawling against the wall, spilling his oranges into the dust. A torrent of curses followed Zorkin up the lane.

The street narrowed and wound through a *yeshiva*. Zorkin strolled along and nodded to a group of students who were chatting with an elderly Hasidic rabbi as they lounged against a wall.

There was a crash and a new barrage of abuse behind him. In the distance, Zorkin saw the vendor and a tall Arab with an eyepatch disentangling themselves on the ground as fruit from the overturned cart rolled toward all points of the compass. The one-eyed man glanced in Zorkin's direction, then apologized and began to pick up the oranges.

Zorkin took the steps ahead two at a time. The road headed uphill here, then through an arched tunnel. A small knot of sightseers stood near the War of Independence Monument, posing while their photographer gave them orders in French. North African Jews, thought Zorkin, judging from the swarthy faces under their skullcaps.

He walked past them, into the portico of a large building to get his bearings. He lit a cigarette and inhaled deeply, closing his eyes as he tried to drive the tension from his mind. When he opened them again, the one-eyed Arab was there by the monument, anxiously scanning the street.

Zorkin tensed.

The Arab was talking into a clenched fist.

A radio!

Zorkin took another deep drag on the cigarette. When he was certain the Arab would be looking his way, Zorkin stepped out of the shade and began to walk up the street, away from the monument. He gave the cigarette one final puff, then casually tossed it away, giving no sign that he'd seen the surveillance.

The Arab paused to ask the family at the monument for the time. He waited until his target had a discreet lead, then he slipped into the portico and followed along the front of the building.

Zorkin measured his speed. Experience had taught him that somewhere between a dead run and a normal walk, there was a comfortable pace for shadowing someone on a crowded street. But there weren't many people on this route today, and the Arab, if he knew his craft, would be well aware that it was only a matter of time before his presence became obvious. Zorkin would play on that anxiety, working it until the hound became the hare.

When he reached the shade of an old Turkish wall near the Zion Gate, he stooped down, under the pretext of retying a boot, and smiled to himself. There, a prudent distance behind, the Arab still followed.

There was a large archaeological excavation just ahead. He came abreast of it and shambled down two thousand years of decayed strata onto the floor of a Roman temple. It had been carefully unearthed, leaving walls of dirt and stone that were ten feet high in places. The floor was dotted with deep rectangular holes four or five feet across, where the archaeologists had probed even deeper. In the midday heat, the site was deserted. Zorkin pulled a small camera from his shoulder bag and began to take pictures of the carved script on a stone tablet as he waited for his prey.

The Arab lay watching atop a mound of dug-out dirt. When Zorkin walked around a bend in the excavation, the Arab scrambled down a work path to follow. He crept around the turn Zorkin had taken, only to see him consult a small notebook and disappear up a flight of crudely hewn earthen steps to ground level.

Zorkin headed down into another dig, where one of Jerusalem's ancient water systems had been discovered. At the surface, it was a twisting corridor in the earth with several deep holes scattered along it.

The Arab slipped down into the gash and eased along the wall, taking care to avoid one of the access shafts the archaeologists had left. He moved across the trench to stay on the blind side of the turn.

He stepped over another shaft and crept around the next curve. The excavation bent back on itself in a hairpin. He came around the bend and walked into a dead end of solid rock.

The Arab spun, but Zorkin's steel arm closed in a vise around his neck, catching him in mid-turn. A handkerchief with a smell like acetone clamped over his mouth, choking back a scream as he faded into icy blackness.

Zorkin eased the slackened body to the earth, face down. "Fool," he muttered. "Didn't anyone ever teach you to look down a hole before you step over it?"

The Arab was completely under, his breathing steady and deep. Zorkin emptied his pockets, finding only cigarettes and a few Israeli lire. The radio was tucked against the small of his back, with its antenna and audio wires taped to his skin. Zorkin disconnected them and took it out for a closer look. It was a small multichannel UHF transceiver, a recent model manufactured by Geloso in Milan.

As he rolled the man back over, Zorkin felt a solid object against his chest. He ripped open the caftan and found a leather thong around the man's neck. It held a piece of hollow red jade about two inches high, shaped like the Greek letter *tau*, with crisscrossed gold bands at the letter's junction.

"Damn them!" Zorkin exploded. He tore off the cross and threw it against the rock wall. It rebounded with a sharp, clear tone that was snuffed when the cross hit the dirt floor.

Zorkin hurried to cover his trail. He stuffed the radio and its cables in his shoulder bag, pocketed the money, and scattered the cigarettes on the ground. It would look like just another robbery when the body was discovered.

Zorkin dragged the Arab to the nearest shaft. He reached into his boot and pulled out a stiletto, not the best weapon for this job, but one that would have to do.

The Arab stirred. This needed to be done quickly. Zorkin slashed at his arms to leave signs of a struggle and pulled him to his feet on the edge of the hole.

Ripping the carotid was out of the question; he didn't need to be walking about spattered like he'd just slaughtered a chicken. Straight through the heart, then, quick and clean, and the body disappears . . . for several days, he hoped.

16

He steadied the Arab, drew back, and put all his strength behind the thrust.

And slipped.

The stiletto laid open the Arab's right cheek as he tumbled from Zorkin's grasp. He landed at the bottom of the shaft with a fleshy thud. Then there was silence.

"Merda!" Zorkin pounded his fist on the rock floor. He'd have to go down and make sure the man was dead. There was a wooden ladder up against one wall of the trench, but he didn't know if it would reach. He got up and started over to get it.

There were voices around the bend, very close.

Zorkin froze.

It was a tour group, almost on top of him.

He scrambled up the ladder to the surface and broke into a dead run.

When he reached the Zion Gate, he hailed a cab and gave directions to head up the Nablus Road.

The driver picked his way quickly through the traffic, past the Jaffa Gate and Jerusalem's commercial center. Soon they were speeding past the ramparts of new high-rise apartments on the north edge of the city.

The ribbon of pavement wound out ahead of the taxi through the rolling Judean hills. They swerved around a donkey-drawn cart, then cut back in behind an excursion bus. It turned off into the olive groves outside the Arab enclave at Beit Hanina. With the road clear, the driver sang to himself and accelerated into a narrow decreasing radius curve.

Zorkin lit a cigarette and closed his eyes, trying to ignore the squealing tires and the steep drop beside the road.

In a few minutes, they topped a rise and Jerusalem's

new Atarot airport lay ahead, cutting a tan swath through the green landscape. The driver shot a mock salute at the soldier outside the airport gate and dropped his passenger at the main terminal.

The schedule wouldn't be loose, but there was some time to spare. Zorkin stopped at the newsstand and bought a copy of the *Jerusalem Post*, then took a table in the airport restaurant and ordered a roast beef sandwich and coffee.

While he ate, Zorkin scanned the newspaper, then folded it and placed it on the floor next to his shoulder bag. When he'd finished the coffee, he bent to pick up his belongings and slipped the stiletto out of his boot into the folds of newsprint. He left a large tip with some of the Arab's lire, then walked out, heading for the men's toilet. The newspaper went into a trash bin along the way.

Zorkin sat down in an empty stall and retrieved the envelope from his bookbag. He leafed through the contents and put them back inside, except for a small key. Then he stood and tugged at the corners of his beard. It came off easily, and he tossed it into the toilet and flushed it down. He threw in the brown wig, then held his palm under his eyes and blinked out the darkened cosmetic lenses, first left, then right, and dropped them into the bowl. He flushed again, left the stall, and washed his hands.

Zorkin walked into the shower changing room and found the locker that matched the number of his key. He opened it and exchanged his *yarmulke*, shirt, trousers, and boots for the black suit and conservative shoes that were inside. He transferred the contents of the envelope, putting the passport and air ticket inside his

18

jacket and the billfold in his hip pocket. That done, Zorkin placed his shoulder bag in the locker, latched it, and dumped the key in the wastebin. Finally, he washed the last traces of makeup off his face, combed his hair, and nodded approvingly at the transformation in the mirror. The man who stared back was several years younger, had jet-black hair, and had eyes that carried the blue chill of sea ice.

He turned and headed for security to board El Al's flight to Rome.

The bored *Guardia di Finanza* sighed and motioned the next of the arrivals forward. "Name, please."

"Craig Durant," said the traveler, handing over his passport.

The customs officer opened the folder and checked the photograph against the face of the man in front of him. A good likeness, even though the camera had guessed wrong about the pale hazel eyes. It had also missed the early grey that ripped through the dark brown curls and put highlights above the man's temples. The final product was a tiny image, with brown eyes and hair that was almost blond.

"*Gràzie,* Signore Durant," said the guard. "From New York?" He ran down the list of questions on the form, then stamped the date in the passport and handed it back.

"Welcome to Rome, signore. Will you be staying long?"

"Probably. I'm a television reporter, and I'm going to be working out of a new bureau here."

"Ah! *Si, cronista!*" The officer's face lit up. "*Bene.*

19

You will need a residence permit from the Aliens Office. It's in Via Genova. Your hotel can give you directions.''

Durant thanked the officer, collected his bags, and stepped into a bright yellow taxi for the long ride into the city.

"Albergo Nazionale," he told the driver, and leaned back to enjoy the trip. He was immediately thrown forward as the driver slammed on the brakes. A black Lancia had been trying to shoehorn into the traffic, but the driver misjudged the distance and got caught when the cars ahead suddenly slowed to a crawl. For a moment, the Lancia and the cab were only inches apart, and the passenger, a priest with black hair combed straight back and the coldest blue eyes Durant had ever seen, gave them a withering stare. The traffic began to move again, and the Lancia pulled ahead and sped on, revealing a red license plate numbered SCV-206.

"Cafone!" the cabbie swore. "Idiot! Give them a red hat and they think they're God!" He saw Durant's perplexed face in the rearview mirror and explained. "That car is registered in the Vatican, and from the plate number, it belongs to someone *importante!"*

Chapter Two

Durant chewed the last of his breakfast roll and watched the morning traffic choke its way through the Piazza Montecitorio. An endless swarm of Fiats, Vespas, and an occasional black Mercedes crept by, their exhausts painting a faint haze over the weathered stone that housed the Chamber of Deputies across the square.

Durant strolled toward the hotel lobby as he catalogued his impressions of the Albergo Nazionale. It was profoundly masculine, full of heavy leather chairs and Renaissance portraits of minor dukes, and devoid of any female guests. Its proximity to the seat of government gave it a sense of quiet power. He'd overheard conversations in five different languages by the time he'd finished breakfast, and the cadences of one more floated back from a group of black men in bright *daishikis* who were walking just ahead. This was a grand hotel in the old style, its marble floors and paneled walls as polished as the diplomacy practiced in the hushed tones of its salons.

A damp wind hit Durant's face as he left the hotel, the promise of autumn coming wet and early. The parliament buildings across the *piazza* wore a baroque assuredness, the credo of architects who'd believed that when the world's other cities all turned to dust, Rome would still endure. A large column jutted up in the middle of the traffic. There had once been a statue of Marcus Aurelius on top, but the Apostle Paul had been substituted late in the sixteenth century. It had probably worked out best that way, thought Durant as a truck roared by in a sooty, choking cloud. Commuters in that snarl needed a saint to look after them.

The traffic took Durant back to the streets of New York, where he'd been scrambling as a local reporter less than a month ago. This was the kind of job he'd often dreamed of then, foreign correspondent in a European capital.

The squeal of brakes and a horn blast broke his reverie. A burly, unshaven cab driver jerked open his door and planted a threatening foot on Via del Corso, then directed a torrent of insults at another driver who'd dared to cut him off at a stoplight. The target, an elegantly dressed middle-aged woman, never acknowledged him until the light cycled back to green. Then, her gloved hand appeared from the window, retracting the two middle fingers to wave the cuckold's salute.

The cabbie was left speechless. Horns blared behind him, and the pedestrians who'd gathered to watch laughed as he slammed the door and flooded the taxi's engine.

Durant chuckled and walked on. In the Rome of the Caesars and the Borgias, even rush hour had a touch of style.

Diesel fog from a tourist bus caused him to cough.

When his watery eyes cleared, they focused on the smile of a young signorina who was watching from the doorway of a small shop. Embarrassed, he smiled back, and the girl's smile got even wider. He hurried on, hating his bashfulness and feeling her eyes follow him until he turned the corner.

Global News Service had taken space on Via Sabini, a short canyonlike street caught between the intrigue of multinational finance, in the shadow of government, and the peddlers who hawked souvenirs by the Trevi Fountain. Its landscape was dominated by a bank with a cavernous pedestrian mall cut through it, one small newsstand, and a swarm of leather shops. It was one of those happy commercial neighborhoods where the proprietors sent out for espresso for the tourists to sip while they bought overpriced wallets for the folks back home.

The bureau was two flights up in what had once been a *pensione*. The premium on office space had been too tempting, so the sightseer quarters had been turned into small suites for business tenants. They were more stable renters, kept the place full, and were far less likely to come in singing at two A.M.

Durant walked in to find a large room with three metal desks, several chairs, and two teletype machines chattering away behind an open closet door. Another teleprinter clanked from the direction of what appeared to be the bathroom. After chiming its bell a few times, the printer stopped, and a tall broad-shouldered man in his early forties came out into the main room.

"Ah, you must be Craig Durant," he said, sticking out his hand. "Mike Sibille, bureau chief, and at the

23

moment the entire Rome contingent of Global News. Sorry I couldn't meet you when you arrived. Hotel okay?''

"Very nice. I didn't expect that kind of treatment, from what I've been told about our budget.''

Sibille laughed. "That's one of my little jokes on the accountants. I told them it was the closest decent place to stay and that it was a good spot to pick up all the latest scuttlebutt on Italian politics. It's also got the best damned bar in town.''

He sat on a desk and motioned Durant to a chair. "We're a little cramped for now. You probably heard the TWX in the bathroom. I've been trying to get a few things straight with the producers in New York.'' He waved a fistful of flimsy message paper. "They keep asking if there's any way to get someone into Kabul and I keep telling them we can't get a visa.''

Durant smiled. It was the same kind of single-minded treatment he'd gotten from assignment editors for most of his professional life: Don't tell me problems, show me results. "I see,'' he said as his eyes took in the office. The battered desks and manual typewriters didn't look inviting.

Sibille caught his look. "Sorry about the accommodations. We're sort of a shoestring operation.''

That was putting it kindly. The place was cramped, its drab green paint was peeling, and it was dimly lit. It was the kind of place that made for short tempers; cheap but definitely depressing, thought Durant as he propped his feet on a tattered vinyl chair.

Sibille stuck a pipe in his mouth and held a flaring lighter to it. "Well, I planned to send you out on a story this morning,'' he said between puffs. "It's fairly

24

straightforward. The Vatican's opened up part of its secret archives to the public. They've got a couple hundred or so documents on display, stuff like Henry VIII's annulment petition. Can't remember which wife he was trying to dump then. Anyway, it should be pretty interesting. You're to meet a Father Chapman over there a little before ten.'' He picked up some clippings from the desk. "Here's something from *L'Osservatore Romano* on the exhibit. I guess that's all, unless you have some questions.''

''Don't think so,'' said Durant, pleased at getting a free hand in the story, even if it was only a feature.

Sibille squinted at his watch just as the door opened and a squat, bearlike man with a full beard ambled through. A stubby, unlit cheroot hung perilously in a corner of his cherubic grin.

"Ah, Francois!" said Sibille, waving him over. "Francois Rivette, I'd like you to meet our newest addition, Craig Durant.''

Rivette stuck out a hand. He had thick fingers that felt almost calloused at the tips, but there was a touch of gentleness in his grip.

"Bienvenu, mon ami," said Rivette. "Or perhaps I should say *benvenuto,* in keeping with our locale. You're new to Rome? You'll love it here, especially the signorinas, the food, the wine. . . .''

"Francois has only been here a month, but he already knows the place like a native,'' Sibille explained. "He's been free-lancing as a cameraman for years— Vietnam, the Middle East, and a few occasional stints covering the neighborly disputes in Africa. You find Rome quite a change, eh, Francois?''

"A magnificent city, second only to my native Mar-

25

seille, which I may never see again because of the death wish these people have when they get behind the wheel." He turned to Durant. "Driving here isn't for the faint of heart, but you needn't fear today because the invincible Francois will be in command." Rivette bowed slightly, then motioned Durant to follow him toward the door.

"By the way," said Sibille, "I'd like some nice close-ups in your piece, if it's not too much trouble, but see if you get me something besides an endless parade of old papers."

Rivette jabbed at the air with his cheroot. "You are twice blessed, my dear Michel. First, because God in His wisdom has given you the benefit of my talents, and second, because He's made me so forgiving of people who can't tell a mechanic from a true *artiste.*" He blew Sibille a kiss, winked at Durant, and disappeared down the hallway.

He led the way to a battered Fiat coupe that looked like a relic of at least two wars. Beneath its camouflage of rust, the remaining paint had faded to a pale blue, except for the left front fender, which had a spotless coat of bright metallic red. There were dents all along the side of the car and a large gouge behind the right door.

"Unique, don't you think?" asked Rivette. "No thief with any honor would give it a second look, and the dents warn the world that I'm a formidable opponent." He gave the reluctant passenger door a bang just in front of the handle, then smoothly pulled it open and, with a broad smile, beckoned his guest to be seated.

Durant cringed but got in anyway. He was surprised

to hear the engine light up immediately with a strong rumble, and the tachometer twitched violently upscale as Rivette blipped the throttle. He turned to Durant with a wink. "Of course, what lies beneath the skin is not so easy to see, *n'est-ce pas?*"

He gestured toward a small gauge set into a bracket below the dash panel. It was labeled "turbo," and it rose and fell with the pitch of the engine. The speedometer was of a different make than the other instruments and looked newer. Its calibrations read to two hundred forty kph, which Durant nervously converted to something around one hundred fifty miles per hour.

Rivette patted the steering wheel as he spoke. "She may look tired, but like a good woman, she's always willing. Her former owner was in the . . . ah . . . import-export business in Nice until his health forced a sudden retirement. I bought it from his widow when the Customs Police were through." His fingers traced the stitching where a deep slash in the upholstery had been sewn shut.

Suddenly, he gunned the engine and the car shot into the traffic. Durant choked back a startled gasp as they wheeled across the oncoming lanes into an impossibly small break between two northbound cars. "See?" laughed Rivette. "Invincible!"

Durant's seat was jammed all the way forward in its tracks, so he sat with his arms locked around his knees. There were shoulder belts in the car, and when they seemed to settle into the traffic flow, he took advantage of the lull to lock his snugly into place.

Rivette caught a glimpse of Durant latching the buckle, rolled his eyes heavenward, and shook his head.

He turned to face his passenger. "What do you think of Rome?"

Before Durant could answer, the Fiat lurched violently as Rivette swerved to avoid a car door that opened in front of them.

"*Imbecile!*" Rivette shouted, ignoring his brakes and shaking his fist at the transgressor as they roared by. Durant recoiled from the intensity of Rivette's explosion inside the closed car. His heart was pounding, and he wondered if his last memory were going to be of a rusting Fiat with a bearded madman at the wheel.

"You were going to say something?" asked Rivette, the near collision already gone from his mind.

"I—I've only been in Rome since yesterday. I was hoping you'd help me get my bearings."

"Ah! What I could show you about this glorious place! I have a belief, deep in my bones, that when God created Rome, He was smiling."

Durant chuckled. "What about Paris? I've always heard that that was the center of the Earth for romantics."

"By the time God got there, I think He was drunk." Rivette shrugged. "Paris? A painted bawd. But Rome? Rome is an elegant, cultured madame, with the grace of three thousand years of experience. We owe much to this collection of hills on the Tiber." He braked hard for a stoplight.

"Let me begin with some history." He swept a hand across the intersection. "This is Via del Corso, one of the busiest streets in Rome."

"So I see," said Durant as he tried to loosen the bite the shoulder belt had given him from the abrupt deceleration.

28

Rivette warmed to his subject as the light changed and they drove on. "Corso takes its name from the fact that horse races were run on this street for nearly four centuries. It was only two hundred years ago that they were finally banned."

Rivette dodged a creeping horse-drawn carriage, then cut sharply back to his lane as the road narrowed, hemmed in by a ravine of grimy marble. "By the way, where did Sibille put you up?"

"The Albergo Nazionale. It certainly is interesting, but—"

Rivette laughed and dismissed the hotel with a wave. "For reasons known but to himself and God, Mike loves that place. I think it's too expensive, and personally, I've never been fond of living in a museum. I'll speak to the *concierge* where I live. It's a *pensione* not far from the Teatro del Opera." He turned with sudden hope in his eyes. "Say, you don't happen to like opera, do you?"

Durant shook his head. "To tell you the truth. I haven't thought much about it since I took music appreciation in college."

"A shame. Still, it's not surprising," he added with a sigh. "I've never met a reporter yet with any class."

Durant put a hand to his mouth and coughed to hide a smile.

They sped between domed twin churches and onto a broad square. "Piazza del Popolo," said Rivette. "Once, if you journeyed to Rome from the northern provinces, this was your entrance to the city. Now, just one more traffic circle." He pointed to the center of the square, where a tall obelisk stood, shrouded in green scaffolding. *"Roma redditus.* They're always restoring something here, so you'd better get used to it."

They made a quick turn out of the *piazza,* and the cupola of St. Peter's loomed ahead. Rivette squeezed in between four dingy tour buses as traffic funneled across the Tiber, wrinkling his nose in distaste at the fumes seeping into the car.

The exhaust made Durant's eyes burn and he fought the urge to sneeze. "I'm afraid to ask, but is all this traffic headed for the Vatican?"

"Indeed," Rivette nodded. "This is Viale Vaticano and there is the museum."

Inside, Rivette stacked his equipment in a corner of the foyer while Durant waded through the mob of tourists around the souvenir counter. They stood three deep to peer through the finger-smudged glass cases and buy postcards, books, and tiny replicas of ancient statues, all going for much more lire than they would anywhere else in Rome simply because they were being sold within a stone's throw of the Papal Residence. Durant found a blue-uniformed attendant and, nearly shouting to be heard, told him they'd come to see Father Chapman. The man left to convey the message.

A few minutes later, a tall bespectacled priest with a thick crop of white hair came out of a corridor. "I'm John Chapman," he said, shaking hands with Durant and Rivette. He had a distinct Oxford accent. "Delighted you could come." He pushed his glasses back up on the bridge of his nose and glanced at the gear by Rivette's feet. "Would you like some assistance?"

"Merci, Father," Rivette replied as he hefted the

camera and videotape recorder off the floor. "But I'm used to hauling it around."

The priest nodded and walked back toward the corridor. Durant started after him but felt a restraining hand on his sleeve. He turned to see Rivette smiling and pointing an imperious finger at his lighting case. Durant picked up the heavy box and they followed Chapman to a service elevator. The door closed off the noise and the car lurched gently upward.

They stepped out under a canopy of color. Frescoes swept up the walls and across the vaulted ceiling. With Chapman in the lead, they walked through a series of long galleries under a panorama of saints, angels, and miracles. It was a dazzling display, and Durant began to lag behind as he became absorbed in the painted scenes.

"This is the Apostolic Library," he heard Chapman tell Rivette.

"I don't see any bookshelves," said Rivette, his irreverence untempered by his surroundings.

A slow one-way tide of tourists drifted through the rooms. The more studious bent over glass cases to examine old manuscripts and books. Others, like Durant, were simply overwhelmed. He fell further and further behind as he tried to take in everything at once.

The priest stopped and watched Durant with an amused smile. Durant was staring at the ceiling as he walked, and he brought his eyes back down just in time to avoid a collision. "Oh! I'm sorry, Father," he said, his cheeks coloring.

"Quite all right. I take it you've not been here before?"

"You're right. I just arrived in Rome."

"Well, I find that refreshing. I don't have a lot to do with the tourists, you know, and I'm afraid that I've gotten so accustomed to the treasures in this place that half the time I don't even see them. If you'd like, I'd be happy to give you a guided tour some time. It'd give me a chance to take a good look at everything again."

They passed a large, ornately carved door. "That's where we need to go," said Chapman, "but I don't have a key. We'll go through the reading room next door."

As they went through the entrance, Chapman looked at Rivette over his glasses, which had slipped back down. "I think you'll find that we do have a few bookshelves in this library after all," he said.

They were in another gallery like the ones they had come through, except that here shelves filled with books stretched from floor to ceiling. A few men worked in silence where they sat, scattered about long tables in the room. Chapman gestured at the shelves. "This is a small part of the seventy thousand early manuscripts, books, and codices we have here," he whispered. Rivette's eyebrows arched upward in appreciation.

Chapman opened the next door with a key. "We keep this room locked, except when the exhibit is open from ten till noon," he explained as they stepped through. "I must tell you, I'll be glad when this year is over and the archives close up again so we can get back to normal."

The ever-present frescoes changed in this room. Now, they were of popes, sternly guarding the cases and shelves that climbed halfway up the wall.

Rivette set down the videotape recorder and began to adjust his camera.

"If we could," Chapman asked, "is it possible not to use any bright light in here? We're concerned that some of this material could be damaged by that kind of exposure."

Durant looked to Rivette, who glanced up at the ceiling light fixtures, then peered back into his camera. *"Bon.* It'll do."

Relieved, the priest asked, "Where do you want me to begin?"

"It would help if you could fill me in about some of the more interesting pieces before we do the interview," said Durant. "Meanwhile, if it's all right, Francois will start shooting the room and the display."

"Certainly. I've obtained permission for you to film them."

Rivette winced at the priest's ignorance of the difference between newsfilm and videotape, but moved off without comment to begin shooting.

Chapman stepped over to a glass counter that enclosed a large yellowish document dotted with red wax seals. "Visitors seem to find this one interesting," he began. "This document was a key weapon in an historic battle of wills. On this parchment, Henry VIII petitioned Pope Clement VII for annulment of his marriage to Catherine of Aragon so he could marry Anne Boleyn. Those seals are the endorsements of seventy-five bishops who warned the pope what would happen if Henry didn't get his way, which, of course, he didn't. If he had, European history might have been quite different."

Durant took sketchy notes as Rivette focused for a close-up.

The priest was beginning to enjoy the lecture. He adjusted his glasses and peered down through the top of another case. "This is the oldest document in the exhibit, an eighth-century compilation of regulations for the preparation and maintenance of ecclesiastical documents."

"There's nothing earlier?" asked Durant. "I thought recorded church history ran back much further."

"It probably did at one time, but Holy Mother Church hasn't always been the most stable of institutions. Emperor Diocletian destroyed whatever very early collections there were back in the year 313, and Rome was sacked three times after that before these regulations were written. It wasn't until the seventeenth century that someone got around to centralizing the scattered collections in one location, and that process took nearly two hundred years to complete. Incidentally, when Pope Paul V ordered these archives created, he banned anyone from reading the documents. Aside from peeks by a few church scholars, this is the first look the modern world has had at most of what's on exhibit."

With Durant in tow, Chapman walked around the room, pointing out other documents on display. Rivette followed but worked as if he were alone, laying out each shot painstakingly before he committed it to the finality of his videotape.

Chapman walked over to the shelves and gently caressed the leather binding on a large volume. "There are millions of documents in these archives. We've been cataloguing them for three hundred years, but . . ." His voice trailed off into a shrug.

"Craig, where would you like the interview shot?" asked Rivette, reaching down to change the videocassette in his recorder.

Chapman's expression turned grim as Durant lined him up with a bookshelf in the background. "Father, just relax and we'll get through this with no trouble," said Durant. "We'll just talk about what you've already told me."

Rivette gave the equipment a final check, focused on the men, and rolled the tape. Halfway through the first answer, the priest's words were stifled by a fit of nervous coughing and he had to stop to clear his throat.

Durant smiled. "Forget about my bearded friend, Father. Just talk to me." He repeated the question and Chapman relaxed, the electronic invasion all but forgotten as he trod the familiar ground of ecclesiastical history.

When they'd covered all the major points of Chapman's briefing, Durant asked, "Father, I really thought you'd have some Biblical texts on display. Are there any gospels in the archives from the time of Christ?"

"Unfortunately, no. The earliest Christian texts anyone's found so far are from the second century. We don't know of any writings which date contemporaneously with the time of Jesus. There weren't many literate people around then, you know, even among the early Christians. A text from that time would be a staggering find."

With the interview over, Rivette disconnected his equipment while Durant scrawled a few concluding notes. A door behind them slammed, and a short elderly man in a rumpled suit came tottering in their direction. He gazed toward the floor, unaware that anyone else was in the room.

"Dr. Muller," called Chapman loudly, "there's someone I'd like you to meet."

Startled, the old man looked up. He ran a hand across his forehead to push back a shock of white hair that threatened to overwhelm his wire-framed glasses.

"Dr. Muller," the priest began, "this is Mr. Durant, a reporter—"

"Reporter!" cried Muller. His face lit up and he pumped Durant's hand vigorously. "Yes! I've been expecting you. Please, please wait right there. I'll be right back! We can go to my office. I'm so glad you've come. Just wait right here!"

The old man headed out the way he'd entered, but stopped to give a reassuring wave. "I'll be right back. I'm so glad you've come!" He disappeared through the door.

"What was that all about?" asked Durant.

"I'm afraid I can't say," said the priest with a shake of his head. "I've known Andrew Muller for twenty years, but I don't think I've ever seen him quite so flustered. He's one of the thirty experts who work on the archives. Andrew is a little up in years and inclined to be somewhat odd at times, but the man has an exceptional talent for ancient languages. We worked together at Oxford years ago before coming here."

"What do you think he wants?"

"I haven't the vaguest idea."

Rivette locked the lighting case and came over. *"C'est tout.* Ready when you are, Craig."

"Francois, hang on a minute. I want to find out what this is about."

Rivette shook his head. "Let me save you the trouble. That man is obviously going to waste your time and mine."

"Maybe not. I'd just like to know what's got him so worked up about talking to a reporter. If you don't want to wait, I'll meet you back at the bureau. I'm going to see what he wants."

Rivette's eyebrows met in a perplexed furrow. "I'd be surprised if he knows what day it is. Besides, he's obviously mistaken you for someone else. A waste of time, I tell you."

"Could be," said Durant, "but he's got me curious."

"Well, good luck, then," said Rivette with a shrug as he turned to the priest. "Father, how do I get out of here?"

"I'll show you out," said Chapman. "May I carry something for you?"

"Since my friend has other plans, *merci.*" He smiled and handed the priest a small case.

Durant thanked Chapman for the interview, and Rivette and the priest started back toward the main reading room. They'd almost reached the door when Muller burst through it with his eyes locked on Durant, oblivious to the other two men.

"Right this way," said Muller as he gently pushed Durant along. "Just follow me."

Muller unlocked another heavy door and allowed Durant to pass through, then followed and locked it behind them. They were in a narrow, dimly lit corridor. Durant guessed it was one of the back passages that honeycombed the Vatican, a relic of the days when a quick disappearance was sometimes required, but still useful today to avoid visitor traffic in the museum.

Muller put a hand on Durant's shoulder and held up his other arm like a torch as they began to walk down the corridor.

"Please, this way," he said with a feverish glint in his eyes. "I'm so glad you've come."

Chapter Three

Muller's office was a small room overlooking the museum's Belvedere Courtyard. There had been a time when its occupants might have watched the papal entourage come and go from the Borgia Apartments across the way. But that was long ago; more recent pontiffs had chosen to live in rooms that faced St. Peter's Square, and blinds were kept drawn across the Borgia windows now to shield the frescoes inside from the decaying effects of sunlight.

The office had been overrun by the trappings of a scholar. Bookcases crowded the marble floor; still more books and papers were piled on every available flat surface. There was barely enough room for a small wooden desk, a swivel chair behind it, and two straight-backed chairs in front. Muller cleared a stack of books from one of the chairs and motioned his visitor to sit.

Durant was immediately struck by the warm, stuffy atmosphere. The room smelled of aging paper, like an old library.

"Would you like something to drink before we begin?" Muller asked. "Tea, perhaps?" He fiddled with an electrical outlet in a corner as he spoke.

"No, thank you, sir." Almost immediately, Durant became aware that it was getting much warmer. In the corner where Muller had been, the coils of a small space heater glowed bright orange.

The old man eased into the swivel chair and followed Durant's glance. "Oh, don't worry about that. It's never plugged in unless I'm here. I find this palace terribly drafty. Parts of it are over five hundred years old, you know."

"Palace?"

"Yes. That's what it is, after all, the end product of a long line of men who believed themselves to be Christ's personal representatives on Earth." Muller's voice took on an edge of distaste. "They all lived here in regal splendor, and each one added to this complex for the greater glory of God and himself."

Durant shifted uneasily, trying to escape the feeling that Rivette had been right about the utility of this meeting. "Dr. Muller, why did you want to talk to me?"

The old man adjusted his glasses and peered happily across the desk. "I must say, I'm delighted that you were able to come. It seems a bit unusual, I'm sure, but you'll find it worth your time." He leaned forward conspiratorially. "Two weeks ago, the Israeli government secretly requested the evaluation of a new archaeological find in the Khirbat Qumran area. It's to be done by Dr. Johann Buchmeunster."

"Who's he?"

"Johann Buchmeunster is one of the world's foremost experts in Middle Eastern paleography," said Muller, suddenly irritated. "He was instrumental in deciphering a very important group of manuscripts found in the same region back in the late 1940's.''

Durant looked blank.

''The Dead Sea Scrolls, my boy!''

''Yes . . . well, I'm afraid that I don't know much about that,'' Durant confessed.

''So I see.'' Muller frowned quizzically for a moment, then continued. ''The site of this new find is a cave about eight miles south of modern Jericho. The major items of interest are several earthen jars, some of which contain what appear to be ancient manuscripts wrapped in linen.'' The old man's face took on a youthful vigor, and his hands seemed to have lives of their own. Durant began to take notes.

''This method of storage and the location of the cave suggests that this site may be part of the library of the Essenes, who first became known to us when the Dead Sea Scrolls were translated.'' He paused, gauging the effect of his pronouncement.

Durant hesitated, afraid that too many basic questions might cut short the interview.''Who were the Essenes?''

Muller stared across the desk for several seconds before he answered. ''They were a Jewish sect, like the Pharisees and the Sadducees. You do recall *them?*''

''Er . . . of course.'' Durant looked down at his notebook to avoid the old scholar's eyes.

''The Essenes segregated themselves in a desert community that was flourishing at the time of Christ, not far from where this cave was discovered. This latest find involves three manuscripts. Two are badly damaged, with only small fragments left. Buchmeunster will be translating the one which appears to be most complete. It's had some degree of deterioration from worms and moisture over the years, but it seems to be largely intact."

"Why do that here in Rome? Wouldn't the Israelis have experts who could handle this?"

"I've asked myself the same questions," Muller admitted. "The Israelis consider such antiquities to be national treasures, and they rarely allow any of them to be sent abroad. My feeling is that they've already had their own people do an evaluation, and that they want a second opinion before the translated text is made public."

"Why didn't Dr. Buchmeunster go there?"

"He's not been in the best of health, and his doctors have advised him not to travel. So, the Israeli government asked that the letter be housed in the Vatican Archives, and that Buchmeunster work on it here."

"Letter?" asked Durant.

"Excuse me?" said Muller, tilting his head to one side.

"You said *letter*. Is that what it is?"

"Oh, I'm sorry. I meant *manuscript*," the archivist said quickly, a hint of apprehension in his reply. "Did I say *letter?*"

The small room had become an oven, and Durant could feel his shirt clinging to his back. He was tempted to escape into the cool hallway but forced himself to stay for a few more questions. "You mentioned that these manuscripts were in a cave. How were they found?"

Muller's eyes grew bright. "In much the same way as the Dead Sea Scrolls were discovered. The cave had been closed off by a rockfall centuries ago, and it re-

42

mained untouched until a recent earthquake broke the seal. Two Bedouin boys stumbled across it. The entrance fell in on one of them, and a rescue party made the actual discovery.''

"What happened to the boy?''

The scholar's face turned pensive. "Oh . . . he was killed. An unfortunate tragedy.''

A knock at the door punctuated Muller's reply. "Come in,'' he called out.

An auburn-haired woman in her mid-twenties walked in and extended her hand as Muller rose with a smile.

"Signorina, what can I do for you?''

"I'm Antonia Marsiglia. One of the museum staff gave me directions to your office.''

Muller's smile remained, but he gave no response.

"We had an appointment for this morning,'' the young woman continued. "I'm a reporter for *La Scoperta.*''

"Oh, my.'' Muller slid back into his chair and cradled his forehead in his hands. "Oh, my.''

The woman looked at Durant, who gave her a sheepish grin, then back to Muller. "I can come back later,'' she said.

"No, no, no,'' said Muller. "I'm afraid I've made a terrible mistake, signorina. Please forgive me.''

"Signorina Marsiglia, perhaps I can be of some help,'' said Durant. "If it's all right with you, Dr. Muller?''

The old man nodded.

"I'm Craig Durant, and I work for Global News Service, an American TV network. I was in the archives this morning, doing a story on the exhibit, when

43

Dr. Muller came along and apparently thought I was the reporter who had the appointment with him."

"I don't suppose you bothered to tell him about that mistake, did you?" she hissed, her dark almond eyes narrowing. "Dr. Muller," she exclaimed, "you told my editor that this was going to be our exclusive! How could you give it to this—this American!" She leaned across the desk, scolding him like an insubordinate child. "Have you any idea what you've done?"

"I know, I know. I'm so sorry." Muller turned his palms upward and shrugged. "For some reason, I just didn't expect a woman."

Her olive skin flushed crimson. "You could at least have remembered that you were giving this story to an Italian newspaper, not to American television!"

"I think we're getting upset over nothing," said Durant calmly.

"Over nothing?" Antonia slammed her purse down on Muller's desk, turned her back, and stared at the ceiling.

"What I mean is that I don't think my editors in New York are going to be very interested in this story, at least not immediately. I'd be willing to wait a few days until you get it into print."

She searched Durant's face. "You'd be willing to do that?"

"Sure. I need some time to work it up anyway, because it doesn't offer much in the way of pictures. Of course, I need a favor in return."

The woman's eyes narrowed again. "Aha!"

Durant gave her a disarming wave. "No catch. I'd just like you to have lunch with me."

44

"Of course," Antonia said with a half smile. "Just let me get my interview done first."

When she'd finished with Muller, they picked their way through a herd of waiting buses outside the museum and walked to Girolamo's, a small *trattoria* a few blocks away on Via Famagosta. Twenty or so tables were crowded into the dining area, and scores of straw-bound Chianti bottles hung from oaken beams overhead. They joined a small group of waiting patrons, mostly men in business suits.

"Ah, Toni!" said a man with a thin grey moustache. He pressed her hand to his lips.

"Bellissima!"

"Ciao, Armando." She continued in rapid Italian, "How is life at *Il Messaggero?"*

"Ah, *cara mia, 'e un disastro,"* he replied with a shrug. "You could make it much better, but my wife wouldn't be happy if you did, no doubt. I don't suppose you came here for lunch just because you knew I'd be here, eh?"

Antonia laughed gently and shook her head. "No, I just caught this fellow in the act of stealing my exclusive, and I think he's trying to atone for it by taking me to lunch. I'm not that easy to please, you know."

The man winked at Durant. "Watch this one, signore. She writes with a soul of fire, but she has a heart of ice."

Antonia switched to English. "Craig, this is Armando Colletti, who works for my main competition. He says—"

"Si, capisco," said Durant, cutting her off. *"Buon giorno,* signore. I'll remember your advice."

45

Antonia stared at Durant and blushed. "Oh, I had no idea you spoke Italian! You should have told me."

Durant held up a hand in a gesture of surrender. "As I recall, our first conversation didn't give me much of a chance. Anyway, don't worry about it. Anyone can make an innocent mistake."

They were shown to a table in the back corner, slipping past a waiter with a towel-draped arm who was singing *La Donna 'e Mobile* for the benefit of a middle-aged woman and her companion, a much younger man with slicked-back hair.

Durant held Antonia's chair while she sat down. "Look," he said, "I think you have the wrong idea about why I asked you to lunch. I did it because I wanted to find out more about you, not because I felt guilty about talking with Muller. That really was an accident."

Antonia's eyes softened. "I'm beginning to think you mean that. Well, okay." She held out her hand. "Let's try this again. To start with, please call me Toni. Antonia's the name my editor makes me use professionally. He thinks it gets more respect. Italian men seem to have trouble dealing with women who aren't mothers, nuns, or mistresses."

Durant clasped her hand in his and was surprised by its warmth. "My pleasure. And I'm really sorry about the confusion this morning."

The singing waiter arrived, still humming his aria. He winked at Toni and nodded to Durant as he placed their menus on the table. Durant opened his and was about to ask for a moment to look it over, but Toni spoke first.

"Che raccomanda?"

46

The waiter smiled, took a deep breath, and revised Mozart's libretto to fit the special of the day:

> *"Fettucine Girolamo,*
> *si, 'e fantastico,*
> *con antipasto,*
> *de—liz—i—o—so!"*

"Bravo!" Toni applauded. "We'll take it, and a bottle of frascati."

The waiter bowed with another smile and left.

Durant shook his head and wondered what Rivette would have thought of the waiter's performance. "Do you always order like that?"

Confusion flickered across her face, then her brown eyes fixed him with a curious stare. "Oh, you mean skipping the menu? Usually. Most Romans do. But I thought you'd have known that, as fluently as you speak Italian. You've been here quite a while, I bet."

"No. In fact, I just got here a couple of days ago. I grew up speaking it, though. My grandmother was from over here . . . Padua, I think."

"A very old town. If you're going to be from the provinces, that's better than most." She pulled a slim gold lighter and a pack of Gitanes from her purse, and tamped the tobacco end of one cigarette lightly.

"You've been there?" he asked.

"I've been through it. My parents had the idea that if they ran me through enough museums and galleries, some veneer of civilization would eventually soak in."

Durant held the lighter while Toni drew deeply on the cigarette, then exhaled.

"Actually," she continued, "that gave me a pretty

47

good background for this job. I spent time at the Sorbonne, Vienna, and Cairo University."

"Cairo? Isn't that a little off the beaten path of the culture tour?"

"I decided it would be interesting to learn a little about the Middle East. I really don't know very much about anything in particular, but I can ask questions in six languages. When I finally ran out of schools, journalism seemed a natural choice. Besides, it's almost like not having a job. I just write about what everyone else does."

Durant laughed. Like so many other reporters he knew, Toni was a victim of the thrill of vicarious living.

"That's one of the things that drew me into this business," he said. "I started part-time at a TV station when I was going to school in New Orleans, a great news town by the way. When I graduated, I found a job reporting and doing some documentary work in San Antonio. I really enjoyed that until Uncle Sam decided I should be out saving Vietnam for democracy."

Toni's mouth tightened into a grim line. "You were part of *that?* I'd have thought someone schooled in the proud traditions of your American press would have recognized that imperialistic adventuring for what it was. I'd have taken to the streets in your place!"

Durant bristled. "Look, I'm just a journalist, not a political philosopher. I don't take personal action on what I think about the things that are wrong with this world. I just try to point them out to everyone else so they can make intelligent decisions about how things are run."

Toni pressed her attack. "That's a convenient ar-

48

gument, Craig. That's the *old* view of the role of the press. I think a journalist ought to act on his convictions and be right there at the barricades with everyone else!"

The arrival of their lunch forced a pause in their debate. Toni picked thoughtfully at her pasta for a moment, then smiled. "That was very rude of me. I hardly know you, and here I am sounding like the Red Brigade. I'm sorry." She raised her wine glass. "To friendship, I hope."

Durant clinked his glass against hers. "So do I. Actually, I didn't have much to do with fighting that war. Someone got the idea that I'd be a perfect guide for the network crews in our area, so I spent most of my time shuttling them around. When my hitch was up, the CBS folks needed an extra hand in Saigon, so I went to work for them."

"You were a war correspondent?" Toni's voice carried a note of awe. "For CBS? What are you doing here working for . . . what was the name?"

"Global News Service. I thought the CBS job was pretty good until I found out that I wasn't a *real* network correspondent. Officially, I was a 'salaried stringer,' an independent. I worked my ass off, but they never would transfer me to a stateside bureau. Finally, I quit and took a job in Dallas. From there, I went to New York, and here I am."

The subtleties of the stringer/correspondent distinction were lost on Toni. "Have you ever had a big exclusive?" she asked.

"No, can't say that I have. How about you?"

"I've been in on a couple of good stories. We caught a deputy in the Foreign Ministry last year in a heroin

49

operation out of Naples. He turned prosecution witness, so no prison, but at least he's not in the government any more. He was advocating a plan to sell Italian arms to Israel."

"Heroin, huh? Sounds like a nice piece of work. How'd you get onto that?"

Toni shrugged. "It's not that hard when you know the right people. I had some very helpful contacts who'd been gathering information on him, but they couldn't get anyone at the Ministry of Justice to listen. They were quite happy to let me have it."

"That kind of setup worries me. The tip is invaluable, but I always wonder if I'm being used to do a hatchet job on somebody."

Toni waved his concern aside. "There are consequences every time you uncover a scandal, but that's something the deputy should have considered before he got involved in the heroin trade. The story was accurate, and that's what counts, isn't it?"

Durant sipped the frascati, letting it play on his tongue while he pondered Toni's insensitivity toward the targets of her work. He knew the rules competition placed on a journalist: Speed and accuracy are the keys to survival; tell critics the public has a right to know. But there'd been times when he'd sat in empty newsrooms late at night and searched for some sort of balance in the system. He wondered how deep inside Toni's humanity had been driven by ambition.

She read his face and sighed. "I think I just did it again. I don't mean to sound so callous. It's just that I want to be really good at this. I want to be the top reporter in Europe. When that happens, people will pay attention to what I write, and then maybe I can get some things changed." She looked at her watch. "And if we don't leave right now, I'll have to change employers."

They walked back to the Vatican in silence. When their conversation resumed, it had none of the philosophical stress of their lunch. Durant found himself interested in seeing more of Toni, in spite of their professional views. First impressions could be wrong, he reminded himself, and he resolved not to make any more snap judgments about her.

Soon, the museum lay just ahead, with St. Peter's rising in the background. They were crossing Viale Vaticano when Durant saw a white-haired man leave the museum and set off briskly for the street corner, his face hidden by the tilt of his head. As the man neared the corner, a small van parked up the block started its engine and squealed out of its space, hurtling toward him. He reached the curb and stepped into the street.

"Hey! Look out!" screamed Durant.

The man jerked up in sudden awareness. He half leaped, half fell backward, landing hard on the curbstone as the van swerved toward him and missed, its driver waving an angry fist.

They ran to help the man, who lay stunned in the street, his glasses beside him on the pavement. It was Muller. Durant strained to read the license number on the van, but it disappeared around the corner into the traffic.

"Oh—h—h." Muller shook his head slowly and tried to raise himself on his elbows. "My glasses, where—?"

"Here they are." Toni handed them over.

51

"Ah, good. Not even scratched." The archivist put them on and sat up, but Toni gently pushed him back when he tried to stand.

"I think you need a doctor. Let us get—"

"No, that won't be necessary." Muller smiled. "I'm just a little shaken. If you'd be so kind?"

Toni and Durant helped the old man to his feet.

"Dr. Muller," Toni protested, "you really ought to be checked!"

"I'm just fine, signorina." He winced as he bent to brush off his trousers. "I don't think there's anything broken. I'll be a little bruised tomorrow, but the truck didn't touch me."

Durant wavered between anger and dismay. "I think we ought to call the police and report a hit and run. Maybe they—"

"No! No!" Muller cut him short, visibly agitated. "It was only some careless fool. He didn't pay enough attention, that's all. Please, I'm fine. Let's leave it at that."

"But, Dr. Muller, that van deliberately tried to—"

"Thank you so much for your concern." Muller gave Toni's hand a pat as he took it from under his arm. "I must get home for lunch now. *Arivederci.*" He smiled weakly and walked away.

Chapter Four

Morning was already half gone when Durant managed to get himself fully awake. He'd intended to spend the day getting a feel for the city, but he gave in to a bad habit of shutting off the alarm for a few minutes of extra sleep.

He dressed quickly and bought a copy of *La Scoperta*'s early edition at a newsstand across the street. He ordered coffee and a doughnut at a small *tavola calda* next door and scanned the paper.

Apparently, Toni's story hadn't impressed her editors as the major exclusive she thought it should be. It was on page three, about four inches of a single column. There was no speculation about the manuscript, just a report of how it was found and the fact that Buchmeunster was doing the evaluation.

Reading the story brought back the excitement in Dr. Muller's eyes. Durant decided to skip the sightseeing and pay Muller another visit.

At the museum, Durant's best efforts to explain that he didn't want a tour were met with incomprehension from the guards. After several attempts, both in English and Italian, he succumbed and bought an admission ticket. Their understanding instantly improved, and they gave him directions to Muller's office.

The door was closed and he knocked, hoping the trip hadn't been a waste.

"Come in," came Muller's voice from inside.

The old scholar was bent over a table in a corner of the room, absorbed in a large leather-bound book. He had his back to the door, and Durant stood waiting for what seemed to be several minutes before he turned around.

"Oh! Ah . . . Mr. Durant." They shook hands and Muller beckoned him to sit. "I'm afraid I tend to get wrapped up in things sometimes. I'd forgotten for a moment that anyone was here." He settled behind his desk. "Well, what brings you back so soon? I thought that after the row you and that young lady had in this office yesterday, you'd decided not to do anything about Dr. Buchmeunster's manuscript until her story got published. You're not here to break that promise?"

Durant laughed. "No, sir. Her story was in the paper this morning. I've come to see you about something else."

Muller brightened. "This morning? Have you seen it? Do you have a copy, by chance?"

"I'm sorry. I didn't bring it with me."

"Ah. Well, perhaps I'll find one later. What was it you wanted?"

"Actually, I'm interested in the Dead Sea Scrolls. I need some background for my story on the manuscripts, and I was wondering if you could tell me where to find it."

"You've come to the right place, if you've a little time." He busied himself in the corner, disconnecting the electric heater and plugging in a small hot plate with a yellow enameled kettle on it. "Would you care for some tea? Coffee?"

"Coffee, thanks." Durant prepared himself for instant, an experience he'd never been able to enjoy, despite having swilled enough of it, in newsrooms over the years, to fill Lake Erie.

Muller set jars of sugar and coffee on a corner of his desk. "I've been studying that particular discovery— the Qumran scrolls—for more than thirty years, although I never actually worked on the deciphering of them originally. If this new find is in any way related to them, it ought to be a genuine treasure." He leaned back and began the story, his eyes faraway.

"The saga of the Dead Sea Scrolls has all the mystery and intrigue of a cinema thriller. All one would need to add for today's audience would be some romance and, of course, a little sex." The scholar chuckled as he drew Durant into the tale.

"Imagine, Bedouin shepherd boys stumble across a cave while tending their flocks. The cave is filled with earthen jars containing manuscripts, but they've no idea of the value of what they've found. The scrolls, mostly in small fragments, are taken to Bethlehem and sold to dealers in antiquities." Muller leaned forward and arched his eyebrows. "Mind you, these priceless documents were kept in such things as shoeboxes and cigarette cartons!"

He handed Durant a cup of hot water and continued, the excitement building in his voice. "Once archaeologists knew what was on the market and its probable value, they took great risks. They met in dirty back rooms to try to buy fragments, often dealing with men whose usual line of merchandise was stolen jewels."

For the next forty minutes, Muller delivered a nonstop history of the Dead Sea find, giving Durant little opportunity to edge in questions. For the Bedouins, Muller explained, it was a classic lesson in the law of supply and demand. Because of the constant threat of Arab-Israeli fighting, manuscript fragments would often change hands in secret meetings at night. Buyer and seller would hurry away, thankful to escape once more from a sniper's bullet.

He stopped abruptly and seemed to have no intention of continuing. Durant waited a few seconds and asked, "Well, did they finally get all of the manuscripts?"

The archivist beamed. "Now that I have you interested, I think it's time for you to do some reading." He got up and hunted through the shelves behind his desk. "The original finds, starting in 1947, included eleven caves with more than five hundred manuscripts. Ah! Here it is!" He dusted off a thick volume and handed it across the desk.

"Dr. Muller, I—"

"Oh, don't worry about it. Return the book whenever you can." Muller blocked further protest with a shake of his head and forged on. "You know, there was a good deal of controversy about the early publication of these scrolls. Perhaps that's why the Israelis want an independent evaluation this time."

"Why? What was the problem?"

"It seems some inexperienced researchers grasped at a reference in those texts to someone called the 'Teacher of Righteousness.' To them, that suggested a clear connection to Jesus of Nazareth, possibly spoke of Jesus himself. This speculation was widely reported in popular magazines and newspapers. Some accounts even claimed the Dead Sea Scrolls had shaken Christianity.''

"What did you think?"

Muller looked pensively into a corner of the ceiling before he spoke. "Well, as a scholar, my only interest is in historical accuracy. Many well-known experts in the field, including Dr. Buchmeunster, devoted years to the study of those manuscripts, and none of them reached the extravagant conclusion that those two men, Jesus and the Teacher, were one and the same. Of course, that never received much exposure in the press, and the damage already done couldn't be corrected.''

Durant felt irritation welling up. This was an argument he never liked to hear, although he had to admit that it was often true. On a typical news day, the fact that a fire had been put out was not as likely to get reported as the story that a new one had started. He decided to change course. "Tell me, Doctor, how're you feeling? You took a pretty nasty fall when that van tried to hit you yesterday.''

Muller paled and there was a trace of fear in his eyes, a look that reminded Durant of a small animal with its paw caught in a steel trap. "It was . . . only an accident. That's all. I'm feeling ju—''

A knock at the door cut him short. It opened and Father Chapman entered, followed by a short strawberry blonde not long past twenty.

"Hello, Andrew. Sorry to intrude.'' Chapman nodded at Durant. "Didn't realize you had a guest.''

"Quite all right, John.'' His composure regained,

Muller shook the priest's hand and turned to the woman. "It's delightful to see you again, Rita. You've completed your studies?"

"Yes, thank you. Father's got me on here at the museum until my graduate program starts next summer." She gave Chapman's arm an affectionate squeeze.

"Excellent. A degree from the Sorbonne is a considerable achievement."

"Mr. Durant," said Chapman, "may I present my daughter Rita? This is Craig Durant, a reporter for American television."

The girl smiled with a warmth that lit up her blue-green eyes. Durant shook her offered hand, feeling a little silly over the confusion he knew was plain on his face.

Chapman laughed. "I should tell you that sometimes people do find our relationship a bit peculiar, Mr. Durant. Rita really is my daughter in more than a pastoral sense. I didn't become a priest until middle age, well after my wife died. Now, of course, it's our private joke when she tells people who don't know us that she's my child."

"I certainly fell for it." Durant smiled good-naturedly and checked his watch. "Well, I don't want to be a pest, and I've got to get going. Very nice to meet you, Rita, and nice to see you again, Father." He shook Muller's hand and picked up the book. "Thanks for the time and the information, Doctor. I wonder if you'd do a background interview for me tomorrow, just on the Dead Sea Scrolls?"

Muller grinned. "A pleasure, my boy. Come by about ten. Oh, and keep the book as long as you like."

Durant left the office and found the elevator, but he had to step back while a tour group came trooping down the corridor. He thumbed through the book while he waited. It was *The Ancient Library of Qumran* by F. Cross Jr., published thirteen years after the discovery of the scrolls. There was a bookmark in the middle, and he took it out while he read from the page where it had been. Someone had underlined a passage:

There is no reason to believe that the ancient discoveries in that lonely desert are at an end.

How right that author was, thought Durant as he pressed the button to summon the elevator. He turned the bookmark over as he put it back in place. It was an old photograph, discolored with age.

There were two men in it, standing in front of a Gothic church. One looked like a much younger version of Andrew Muller; the other seemed about the same age. Both wore the soutanes of Catholic seminarians.

Rivette suppressed a shiver as he stepped out of the mid-afternoon sun into the deep shade alongside the Teatro del Opera. He burrowed deeper into his light jacket and tightened his grip on the bottle of wine he carried, then checked to be sure the wedge of cheese was still in the jacket pocket.

Brooding Wagner drifted faintly through the stage door. He rapped loudly and leaned back to wait, letting his mind coast with the music.

The door creaked open, spilling a crescendo into the

street as one eye and a crop of frizzy hair peered out. *"Allora?"* asked a voice as the rest of the head emerged.

"Francois!" The face lit up, and the door flew open wide to reveal a burly man in a red plaid shirt. *"Mio amico!* It's good to see you!" He looked back inside, then turned eagerly to Rivette. "Hurry! You're just in time for Lohengrin's entrance." He grabbed Rivette's arm and pulled him inside.

"My favorite scene," said Rivette, almost stumbling on the step.

They locked arms around each other's necks as they walked. Rivette tapped his friend's chest with the bottle and raised his eyebrows expectantly. "Do you have them?"

Sorrow flooded the man's face as he shook his head. Rivette's eyebrows fell back into place. Then, with an impish grin, the stagehand reached into his shirt pocket and produced a pair of green tickets. The two men roared with glee.

"Shhhh!" echoed across the backstage. "This is a dress rehearsal!"

They moved into a corner and whispered.

"Frederico, you're a genius!" Rivette turned the tickets slowly in his hand, admiring them like rare jewels. "I'm not going to ask how you got these. Do you realize there are people who would kill to get into this performance?"

"Niente. Only a small favor for a friend." He clapped Rivette on the shoulder and gestured toward the stage. "You'd better hurry."

Rivette smiled and bounded up a small spiral staircase in the corner, then hurried across a catwalk to the theater's lighting loft.

The old wooden platform creaked under his weight. He settled down between two spotlights, sitting with his legs dangling over the side and his forehead resting against the handrail.

From Rivette's perch, the singers were Teutonic chess pieces moving across an unmarked board. He nodded approvingly as Elsa finished her plea for a hero to defend her honor. The trumpets sounded and the herald called out for Elsa's champion. Rivette unwrapped the cheese and looked anxiously offstage. The herald called again and two stagehands bent to pull at a thick rope. The music swelled and the swan came slowly into view, carrying Lohengrin. Rivette uncorked the wine and washed down a mouthful of cheese. His whole body swayed with the music.

The loft groaned again, unnoticed by Rivette. His arms flailed the air, the bottle a glass baton as he urged the orchestra onward and mouthed Lohengrin's promise to do battle. A thin man with sparse white hair and a threadbare sweater eased along the platform, clutching a black beret with one hand and the railing with the other. When he reached Rivette, he looked over the edge. His face went pale and he jerked his eyes back to ceiling level. He grabbed the railing with both hands and sat down.

"Providing your own refreshments nowadays, Francois?" He smiled contemptuously.

Rivette kept his eyes on the stage. He swallowed another bite of cheese and gulped more wine before speaking. "It's what comes of working for those Americans. They have no appreciation for the needs of the soul."

61

"Certamente." The man tapped Rivette's paunch. "I see you've been making sure yours doesn't suffer."

Rivette belched gently and faced his visitor. *"Mére de Dieu,* but you turn up at the worst of times!" His arm swept over the action below. "Lohengrin is about to battle Frederick."

The thin man shook his head. "No matter when I come, it's always the wrong time. For you, every scene is the best."

Rivette offered his bottle to the visitor, who declined, so he took another swallow and went back to singing with the orchestra. The man cleared his throat and tried to pick up the conversation, but the music surged and swords clattered from the battle on the stage. He raised his voice and tried again.

"You're in the news business, my friend. Here's a tip for you. We've heard Abdul Sayeb is in Italy."

Rivette tensed but kept his eyes on the singers. What's that supposed to mean to me?"

"Sayeb is probably the most dangerous man alive. He's a zealot with a remarkable talent for assimilating himself into the culture, wherever he happens to be. His sentiments appear to be Palestinian, but his loyalties? . . . Only God knows."

"Why here? And where is he?"

"If I knew, would I be suggesting that you run this down?"

"What's his description?"

"None."

Rivette turned slowly in the thin man's direction until their eyes met. He let a look of disbelief play on his face.

"Francois, nobody's ever gotten a good look at him,

at least not anyone who's been able to give us the information. You hear that he's here or there, then he's gone without leaving a trace . . . or any witnesses."

Rivette exploded. "How do you expect—?"

"Shhhh!" The man raised a finger to his mouth and looked anxiously at the stage for any sign that they'd been overheard.

"How do you expect me to find a man you can't even describe?" Rivette's voice was a hoarse whisper. "He's certainly not going to sign up for a papal audience with his real name!"

The white-haired man braced himself on Rivette's shoulder and the handrail and stood up. "We don't care what name he uses. Just find him."

Rivette clenched the neck of the bottle tightly, his fingers blanching as anger forced the blood from them.

The visitor turned up both palms in supplication. "Just do the best you can for us, Rivette. I only ask for miracles every other month. See you next Thursday. Oh, and by the way, could we find somewhere else to meet?" He looked over the side of the loft again, shook his head, and left.

Chapter Five

A full moon was rising as the taxi sped by the Teatro di Marcello, shrouding the decay of its ancient walls in a silver sheen. The driver coasted downhill, swerving around a crowded tour bus, then turned sharply onto Ponte Fabricio. The bridge had been built before the time of Christ, and while new empires came and old ones went, its one-lane roadway served them all as a link to Isola Tiberina, the island in the Tiber.

Toni found her palms sweating when the taxi rolled to a stop. She paid the driver and resisted an impulse to hurry as she laughed her way past two admirers. She dismissed them with a half smile and strolled into the foyer of Sora Lella, leaving their whistles to fade into the hiss of the river rushing by below.

The dinner invitation had been a spur-of-the-moment call that immediately set her on edge. Toni knew that men often made plans for dinner with hopes of dessert in bed, but Durant's voice had carried no hints of anything beyond a warm smile over a friendly meal. Yet her defenses were up. She took a deep breath and let the waiter lead her under a canopy of hanging paper lanterns.

Durant sat, nursing a drink by a window that over-looked the river. He smiled when he saw her approach.

"Sorry I'm late, Craig," said Toni as he settled her into a chair. "I was about to leave when my editor decided I should rewrite the top of my story for to-morrow's edition."

"That's all right; happens to everyone. Would you like a drink?"

Toni nodded and turned to the waiter, but Durant spoke first. "Please, allow me. *Vogliamo Verdicchio dei Castelli di Jesi, 1979, per favore.*" The waiter bowed and left.

"That's very good," Toni laughed. "I'm im-pressed."

"I've been doing some reading. Can't always drink this, you know," said Durant, taking another sip of his Scotch. He let the warmth of the drink slide him a little deeper into the chair, then gave Toni another apprais-ing look.

He wondered if she expected some ploy aimed at spending the night together. That was still almost re-flex with him, and he felt the old, familiar moves com-ing to the ready. Most of the television women he'd known didn't want anything else, just intensely physi-cal, quicksilver affairs; they feared any commitment beyond the one that drove them like lemmings toward progressively larger jobs. Toni's behavior didn't seem to fit the mold. It was neither the "let's-make-it-I'm-a-star" of the young and confident, nor the "please-won't-you-love-me" of someone who'd been on the circuit too long. Puzzled, he forced the usual games aside.

"Craig, I can't understand it. I really thought the

exclusive I did on the Qumran manuscript would get better exposure.'' Tony wrung her hands. ''This story could have major impact if the document is genuine, you know? My editor just doesn't seem to grasp that.''

Durant reached out and placed her hands gently under his, back on the table. ''Whoa! If you're going to get to the top of this business, you're going to have to put up with an occasional fool who thinks your stuff is garbage. The trick is to wait him out. Sooner or later, either the fool gets promoted to management, or you get a better job.''

Toni gave him a squeeze. ''Nicely put. You may have just explained Italy's main problems. We must have a government full of former editors. But what do I do about this story? It needs to be told.''

''Don't give up on it. As one famous Irish-American once said, 'Tomorrow is another day.' ''

She frowned. ''What Irish-American said that?''

''Another woman who'd just had a man tell her he didn't give a damn.'' Durant gave the freshly uncorked wine an approving taste and waited while Toni's glass was filled, then raised his own. ''Now, if you please, let's talk about you and me and why we're here.''

''*Salute,*'' said Toni, returning the toast. ''I'll give my editor another chance to recognize the story of the decade.'' Her smile was back.

Durant ordered dinner for them both, this time without looking at the menu, then settled back as Toni told him more about the politics of working in the Roman press corps. He watched her hands underscore her words, counterpoint in a symphony of enthusiasm. Toni was open and unpretentious, although she carried her body in a way that told him she was well aware of

66

her sensuality. And, despite her obvious journalistic aggression, Durant found that he didn't view her as a competitor.

Even with Stephanie, it had never been quite that way. She'd been as deft as he was at turning up the big stories in New York, maybe better. But they'd overcome their newsroom rivalry, the two of them, for the promise of something more permanent than a-minute-thirty worth of video fame at six P.M.

Stephanie. A memory he'd locked away, out of reach on a back shelf but always there, like a dull ache from an old fracture.

The waiter arrived with their food and the news that Craig was wanted on the telephone. He excused himself and took the call in the bar. It was Sibille.

"Craig, you have a new assignment tomorrow. Come in early and take Rivette to cover the metro strike, catch all the stranded commuters."

Annoyance rose in Durant's throat at the bureau chief's change in plans, but he kept it to himself. "Thanks, but I have something on for the A.M. already, a story I came across when you sent me over to the Vatican to talk about old books."

"Oh, yeah." Sibille made no effort to keep the irritation out of his voice. "The scroll thing. I saw that in the daybook. Well, you won't be doing that tomorrow. I got a call a while ago from that priest you interviewed—Chapman? The guy you're supposed to talk to—Muller, is it? He's in the hospital."

Disbelief shot through Durant like a shiver. "What happened? How is he?"

"Don't know. Chapman said they don't think he's going to make it. I think he's over at Salvator Mundi."

Durant felt a sensation of wariness take root in his mind, something beyond curiosity but short of suspicion, as he hung up. He was still trying to put his finger on it when he got back to the table.

Toni immediately read his distress. "Craig, is there something wrong?"

"It's Dr. Muller. He's been taken to the hospital. He—"

"What!" Her face went taut. "When? Is he—?"

"He's still alive, but the doctors don't know about his chances."

"We should get over to the hospital and see how he's doing." Toni shook her head. "I knew we should have made him see a doctor after that fall."

"I don't think that had anything to do with it. I saw him yesterday and he was fine. I'll call over there and ask about him after we eat."

"Craig, I really think we should go to the hospital now," she insisted. "I'd feel terrible if anything—"

Durant looked at the half-eaten meal on Toni's plate, then back at the rapidly cooling veal parmigiana on his own, and sighed with resignation. "All right, we'll go if you really want to. After we eat."

John Chapman had the disquieting sensation that he and everyone else in the waiting room had been frozen in time, suspended while The Fates rolled the dice on Andrew Muller. The only hint that told him otherwise was the wall clock, which marked the end of the third hour of their vigil. Kathryn Muller, a grim-faced woman in her eighties, sat silently, her eyes betraying a mind that was somewhere else. This must be what

68

hell is like, Chapman thought, at least for her. Outliving a husband, then having to face the prospect of losing her only child. He wondered if the old woman was praying. Or was she thinking of the boy-child she'd borne, trying to borrow life from the memory to replace what was ebbing from the twilight man in the next room? She clutched a worn Kleenex, but each time her tired eyes would fill with tears, she'd force them back. Chapman had been fighting his own emotions, trying to keep the lump in his throat from gaining the upper hand. He wanted to tell the old woman to go ahead and cry, but her stoic face kept him at arm's length.

Rita seemed better able to cope. In the hour since her arrival, he'd watched her stay busy trying to make Mrs. Muller comfortable, finding her a soft chair from the doctor's lounge down the hall and getting her some juice from the cafeteria. She'd been the only one to draw any reaction—a brief smile of thanks.

Chapman's concentration was broken by the rustle of heavy fabric and the disciplined snap of heels in the hallway. A short grey-haired nun entered the room, carrying a mein of authority as crisp as the conservative white habit she wore. She peered back at him through small oval-lensed glasses and walked over to sit by Mrs. Muller.

"Excuse me, signora," said the nun, giving the old woman's hands a gentle pat. "I wanted to let you know that your son is conscious. He asked for a priest. There happens to be one in the building—an American—who should be here shortly."

Mrs. Muller's composure broke. She fell into the nun's arms, sobbing. "Thank God! You don't know how long I have wanted this. For years, he's refused even to speak with me about his faith, and now . . . Thank God!''

"Pardon me, Sister." Chapman rose from his chair. "I'm a very close friend of Dr. Muller's. A familiar face might be a great deal of help to him. If he wants to talk with a priest, I'd like to—''

"No, Father," said the nun, shaking her head. "I'm sure his doctors will let you see him shortly, but he specifically asked for someone other than you to hear his confession. I'm sorry.''

Chapman sat back down, running a hand through his hair in bewilderment. He was, Chapman admitted to himself, a bit hurt despite his understanding that Muller could find it harder to share his sins with a friend than with a complete stranger.

A tall, dark-haired priest stepped off the elevator a few moments later. He had a young face, Chapman noticed, and an athletic body that he carried with gentle confidence. He spoke quietly with Mrs. Muller, and she seemed to fill with renewed hope. Then he smiled and walked down the hall to the intensive care ward.

Chapman was still seated, absently cleaning his glasses, when Durant and Toni arrived. He didn't hear their greeting until Durant touched him lightly on the shoulder. Chapman put the glasses back on, stood, and extended a hand.

"Ah, Mr. Durant. It's nice to see you again. I called your office about the interview with Andrew tomorrow, but I didn't expect you to come here.''

"Well, actually, we thought we might have some information that could help. By the way, let me introduce Toni Marsiglia of *La Scoperta*. Father John Chapman.''

Chapman smiled tiredly and took her hand. ''Yes, I believe I've read your stories from time to time. A pleasure.'' The smile faded. ''But what could you tell me that would help?''

''A couple of days ago,'' said Durant, ''we saw Dr. Muller almost get run down by a van. He fell trying to get out of the way, and it looked like he took a pretty bad crack on the head.''

''We tried to get him to go to a doctor,'' Toni put in, ''but he wouldn't listen.''

''Sounds like him.'' Chapman shook his head.

''We thought the doctors ought to know,'' said Durant.

''Thank you. That was very thoughtful.'' Chapman spoke reassuringly, trying to put them at ease. ''I'll pass it along, but I don't think it had anything to do with Andrew's condition. He's had a very serious coronary. Let me introduce you to his mother. This has been a terrible shock for her, so please don't mention the fall.''

Durant motioned Toni to follow as they walked across the room.

''Kathryn Muller, may I present Craig Durant and . . .'' Chapman's voice trailed off as he gestured toward Toni.

''Toni Marsiglia,'' she added quickly.

''Of course.'' He turned back to Mrs. Muller. ''Kathryn, they heard about Andrew's attack and came to see how he was.''

''That's very kind of you,'' said the old woman, taking Toni's hand.

"How is Dr. Muller doing?" Toni asked.

"Not good, I am afraid. A priest is with him now." Her voice trembled, but her eyes remained dry. Her control had returned.

The young priest came back into the room. His face was drawn, and he leaned heavily against the door frame as he spoke.

"The doctor says you may go in now, but don't stay too long. He's very weak." His message delivered, he stood mute and offered no aid as Chapman helped Mrs. Muller out of the waiting room.

Durant watched the young priest sag against the wall, as though he needed its support to keep from collapsing in a heap. His eyes were closed and his face churned with anguish. His lips moved in silence.

"Excuse me, Father," Durant finally asked. "Are you all right?"

"Oh . . . I'm sorry," the younger man said, suddenly aware. "I didn't hear you."

"Are you feeling okay? You don't look well."

"Oh, I'm fine," he answered weakly. "Would you excuse me? I have to make a call."

The priest moved with resolution. At the nurses' station he asked for a telephone directory, flipping through it until he found a section that he read more slowly, running his finger down the page. He underlined a number and dialed, leaving the book open for reference. When the call was answered, his voice rose almost immediately to near frenzy. It carried clearly to where Durant was sitting.

"I must speak to him! No, it's for his ears alone, not yours! He's where? Have him call Father Steve Richardson! St. Susannah's parish! This is very urgent, do you understand?'' He slammed the telephone back into its cradle and sat alone in a corner, fists pressed against his forehead.

Chapman and the doctor brought Mrs. Muller back into the waiting room, each supporting an arm. They eased her onto the couch, and the doctor turned to face the others. His voice was gentle but matter-of-fact. ''Dr. Muller has just died.''

Rita sat on the couch and cradled the old woman's hands in her own. Mrs. Muller sat motionless. The others watched in self-conscious silence, embarrassed at intruding on her grief, all wanting to speak comfort but finding none to give. That was the young priest's job, thought Durant, but Richardson was staring at the doctor, his face suddenly bloodless.

''Might there be someone who could have Mrs. Muller spend the night?'' asked the doctor. ''I think it would be best for her not to be alone.''

''She can stay with us,'' said Rita. ''We've been planning on it.''

''*Bene.* I'll prescribe a sedative in case she needs it for sleep. And, Father Richardson, could you? . . .'' The doctor stopped in mid sentence as his eyes searched in vain for the priest. He frowned, but continued as if there were nothing amiss. ''Father Chapman will help with the arrangements.''

Chapman and Rita helped Mrs. Muller to her feet, leading her slowly down the hall. Toni followed, but Durant hung back for a glance at the telephone directory Richardson had left on the counter.

It was still open to the page he'd used. The underlined number belonged to the Sacred Congregation for the Doctrine of Faith. That was a name Durant knew more from reading history than from his own backsliding Catholicism; it spoke of inquisition and sniffing out heresies. The priest had called the Vatican's Holy Office.

Chapter Six

For Steve Richardson, the only thought was escape. He walked quickly away from the intensive care unit, oblivious to the stares drawn by his stricken face. He began to run, slaloming through the corridor traffic. An exit sign beckoned ahead. He drove through the door and pounded down the fire stairs.

Richardson closed his mind to everything but the jolt of his foot hitting the next step. For six flights he ran, trying to shake the feeling that he was spiraling into a dark pit. When he reached the bottom, he fell against the outside door, letting it press against his forehead. He closed his eyes and waited while the coolness of the night seeped through the glass and brought back a feeling of equilibrium. When the mist of panic had lifted, he burst through the door and ran again. A damp wind hit him in the face as he lengthened his stride. It was two blocks to where he'd parked. He was grateful for the extra distance now and the feeling of release it gave him.

Richardson was panting heavily by the time he reached his car. He leaned against it, arms outstretched, and watched his breath paint a pulsing cloud on the car's window. Automatically, he found the keys, opened the door, and slipped behind the Alfa Romeo's wheel.

It was an old roadster, one of the few luxuries Richardson could not deny himself, a graduation gift from his family. When persuaded, it ran well, but its reasons for doing so often seemed more spiritual than mechanical. He turned the key and willed it to start. The engine caught with a throaty roar.

Richardson looked for an opening and booted the car into the traffic. He sped past the park and Villa Sciarra, and its ancient wall took up the Alfa's song as he worked through the gears.

The priest drove almost on reflex, losing himself in the car's exuberant response. He crossed back over the Tiber, flowing silver in the moonlight, and turned north along its bank, heading for the center of the city. As he drove, Richardson began to think clearly again, as if the emotions which threatened to overwhelm him earlier belonged to a different man.

Luck was rarely on his side and certainly hadn't been tonight. It was luck that had put him in the hospital. It was luck that had put him at Muller's bedside to hear his confession. It was luck that had sent the cardinal in charge of the Holy Office to a retreat beyond reach of the telephone. Had the cardinal been at his residence, perhaps he and Muller could have talked. But Muller had died before that meeting could be arranged. Luck again.

Richardson knew that some of his colleagues would be shocked at his inability to see Divine Purpose behind his situation. There'd been a time when he could see Purpose in every cloud, every river, and the old men who sat in the parks. Then, he'd begun to doubt. He was sent to Rome to nurture his faith in the roots of the Church. After two years as a priest in the shadow of St. Peter's, he no longer doubted God's existence. From time to time, though, Richardson had the impression that He got a little too busy with the overall plan and had a tendency to let the details slide. It fell to mortals to worry about the fine points, such as Muller's confession, and there wasn't anything to be done about it. Muller's unburdening would have to remain secret. He was still priest enough to believe that.

Traffic stopped by the Palazzo Quirinale and waited while a motorcade left the Presidential Residence. Richardson watched the limousines slip away, their blackness silhouetted against the building. He followed the procession past the Defense Ministry, then turned off at Piazza Barberini for St. Susannah's and home. The moon was disappearing behind the edge of a fresh overcast, moving up fast from Ostia. Rain tomorrow, he thought.

The rectory was dark, except for a pale glow from the den. Waves of cheering from a huge crowd drifted down the hallway toward him. They gave way to a choral hymn as he neared the room.

Monsignor Jacob Otis, Richardson's superior at St. Susannah's, snored gently on a recliner in front of the television. There was a late news summary on, with a scene from St. Peter's.

"Ah, Jake," Richardson sighed. He shook his head and retrieved the old man's reading glasses from the floor.

"*Viva! Viva il Papa! Viva!*" The cheers came again, building to a constant roar as the pope appeared at his

77

apartment window. Richardson sat, drawn by the image on the screen and the announcer's words.

"Il Papa Luca primo, one of the most beloved pontiffs of the modern church. The pope of the *pampas,* as his people have come to call him. A firm advocate of human rights, he has, from his first years as a parish priest, been at odds with those governments who did not respect the poor, the hungry. And now, as the first Latin American pontiff, Lucas I continues to speak out for the uplifting of man."

The pope waved at the throng below, flashing a smile that set off the high cheekbones of his Incan ancestry. His hair, startlingly black for a man in his mid-sixties, was close-cropped under his white skullcap. A balding cardinal, about the same age but considerably heavier, stood in the background.

"But there is concern in Vatican circles, concern that the pontiff's vocal criticism prompts more anger than change. Even those who staunchly support the Holy Father's approach to world affairs are said to be worried over his personal safety. *Cardinale* Giacomo Frescobaldi, shown here with the pontiff at an audience last Wednesday, reportedly has warned of likely retaliation. Frescobaldi, who heads the Congregation for the Doctrine of Faith, is said to have urged Lucas I to increase security for public appearances or to avoid them altogether."

Richardson shuddered and switched off the set. Muller's face boiled up in his mind, twisted with anguish.

"Steve." The old priest yawned and sat up. "I was beginning to worry." He gave Richardson a questioning smile.

"I'm sorry, Jake. I had to hear a final confession tonight, and I'm afraid I just forgot to call. It upset me a little, and I sort of lost track of the time on my way home."

"Someone we knew?" The monsignor stood, anxiety rising in his voice. "One of our American community?"

"No, just someone passing through. I happened to be in the hospital when he asked for a priest."

Otis nodded. "Good you were there, anyway. These things are never easy, are they? I think most people save it all up until they know they're going." He started for the hallway. "Oh, Steve, by the way, would you mind taking any night calls? I have the early mass in the morning."

"Sure, Jake, no problem. Good night."

Exhausted, Richardson fell into bed and was quickly in a fitful sleep. He dreamed of feeling Muller's grip on his arm and seeing the haunted glint in his eyes. Muller's face was contorted and his mouth worked as he tried to speak. The hold tightened on Richardson's arm, crushing muscle and bone, making him share the agony in Muller's soul. The old man pulled Richardson closer, but still the words would not come. He opened his mouth again, wide, and screamed the loud, piercing ring of a telephone.

Richardson jolted upright in bed and opened his eyes

79

to a blinding flash. The ring came again, followed by a rolling clap of thunder. He turned on the light and found the telephone. The lighting flashed again as he picked it up.

"Chi parla?" said Richardson, trying to control the shaking in his voice and his hands from the adrenaline rush of his awakening. He cringed at the next explosion of thunder.

"Father Richardson, please." The woman was a native English speaker, and she was nervous. "Steven Richardson? Is he there, please?"

"Speaking." Richardson shook the sleep from his mind and tried to place the voice. He didn't recognize it as one of St. Susannah's regular parishioners, but the church served countless other Americans each year who were just passing through Rome. The woman had a flat midwestern accent and sounded near tears. "May I help you?"

"Yes! Thank God you're there! My father's been hurt and he needs a priest. Could you come?"

Richardson looked out the window. The rain was falling in sheets. "Well, I'll certainly help if I can. Where are you?"

"I'm at the clinic in Rocca di Papa. My father was hiking when he fell, and they brought him here."

The alarm clock caught Richardson's eye and he made a mental note of the time: two-thirty A.M. It was not a night to drive into the Alban hills, and it would take considerable time getting there. "If it's an emergency, I think you'd better talk to the village priest. He'll come, I'm sure, and he's a lot closer to you than I am."

The girl's control broke with a sob. "No. Dad

wouldn't talk to anyone else. He—he asked specifically for you."

Richardson was beginning to resign himself to a long night. He braced for another cascade of sound as lightning lit up the *piazza* below. It came sharply and rumbled off toward the hills to the south. He wondered if it was raining where the girl was. She'd be too upset to notice. "Please, get hold of yourself. I'm sure we can get you some help."

The girl managed to calm herself to the point where she was only weeping. "I'm sorry. It's just that I'm so scared. He's all I have, you know."

"I understand. Who is your father? Do I know him?"

"No, I don't think you've met, but he's very impressed with you. He doesn't live in Rome, but he's attended several of your masses. My father is Samuel Gaines."

Another pulse of adrenaline shocked Richardson even more awake. Samuel Gaines! The man whose historical novels had made the early Christian era come alive for him as a young seminarian. The man who'd made a fortune from his books and donated most of it to establish centers for interfaith study. Samuel Gaines, now needing the comfort of a priest. "Please see what you can do to get the village pastor, just in case you need him. I'm leaving right now, but it may take quite a while to get to you in this weather."

"Oh, thank you, Father! Bless you! I'll tell Dad you're coming. It'll be a great relief."

Richardson scrawled a short note for Monsignor Otis about the call, dressed quickly, and left.

He was soaked by the time he reached the Alfa where

he'd left it on the *piazza,* but it started without protest, and he was pleased to see that its canvas top had kept the interior reasonably dry.

The city's storm drains were hard put to keep up with the downpour. Water had risen in the streets by the Baths of Diocletian, lending its ancient walls a moat. Richardson detoured and drove on slowly, trying to avoid the deeper-looking puddles. The ignition wires would be soaked by any good splash under the car, and he couldn't risk a stall. He passed the Termini station, and the torrent streaming down the Alfa's windows dissolved the outlines of several late-night workers who'd taken shelter in its entrance. Wax men, all of us, thought the priest, melting away a little more each day, never really knowing when there'd be nothing left.

He pushed on toward the southeastern edge of the city and was soon on the road to Frascati and, from there, to Rocca di Papa. He was alone as he started the winding climb into the Alban hills. The rain stopped, and Richardson began to relax. He wound the roadster's engine up, but kept his speed down because of the wet pavement. From a sweeping turn, he could see the storm still raging over Rome, the boiling clouds almost incandescent from the ceaseless lightning discharge inside. It was a sight that left him in awe, and he found his eyes drawn to the storm, trying to lock its image away in his mind.

Suddenly, the car was broadside, hydroplaning through standing water.

"Jesus!" Richardson cranked the wheel frantically, fighting for control. The car spun completely, then lurched as it hit drier pavement. He stopped the car and braced his forehead against the steering wheel until his arms and legs stopped shaking.

"My God!" he said, still breathing heavily as he put the car back in gear. "My God!"

It had been over an hour since the call from Rocca di Papa. He wondered if the village priest had been summoned for Samuel Gaines. Probably not, he thought, as he accelerated up the road. Soon, his headlights caught vague outlines of vineyards flanking the road, and then he was into Frascati.

The town lay sleeping, its *piazzas* emptied by the late hour and washed clean by the rain. The streets were deserted except for one set of headlights Richardson saw come out of a side street in the center of town. The smell of damp earth seeped into the car as he drove past the gardens of Villa Aldobrandini, whose terraces had provided a commanding view of Rome for nearly four centuries. Then the lights of Frascati were gone and Richardson was heading uphill to Rocca di Papa. The clouds had closed in again and he couldn't see anything ahead but the surface of the narrow road itself. He shivered involuntarily at the knowledge that there wasn't much on either side of it except a sharp drop. There was a brief flash in the rearview mirror, headlights well behind him. Some other fool driving at this hour, he thought, and relaxed a little, glad for the company on the last leg of the trip. Balancing the need for haste against his instinct for survival, Richardson wound the Alfa's engine a little harder to pick up speed, then shifted to a higher gear and focused his concentration on the road.

A few seconds later, Richardson was blinded by a stab of brilliant white light close behind. He slammed the rearview mirror out of line to kill the reflection and leaned forward, trying to see what was ahead. The light flashed to a lower beam and back up again, then there was a rattling blast from an air horn.

"Damn crazy bastard!" Richardson exploded. He rolled down his window and waved at the car behind to pass.

The horn blew again, followed by a jolt from behind. "What the hell?!" Richardson checked his outside mirror for a look at the other vehicle. It was a large black Mercedes sedan, equipped with powerful quartz driving lamps. It bumped him again, this time hard enough to crumple the Alfa's bumper. The blow distilled his annoyance into fear.

He downshifted violently, floored the engine, and pulled quickly away from the Mercedes. He opened the distance between the two vehicles rapidly at first, taking the twisting turns on the inside as he continued to accelerate up the hill. *Come on, baby!* The turns were his ally, the only place where the Alfa might best its pursuer. He could never outrun the Mercedes, with its V-8, on the straightaway. Richardson concentrated on remembering each curve ahead, seeing it in his mind's eye and setting up the turn.

But the black sedan began to close the gap almost immediately. *Damn!* Richardson sickened with the realization that the other driver knew the road far batter than he ever could, and that his chances of reaching the sanctuary of the hilltop village were nonexistent and getting worse. *Hail Mary, full of Grace* . . .

The Mercedes kept gaining: forty-meters . . . now thirty . . . now fifteen. *Holy Mary, Mother of God* . . .

The road flattened abruptly. Richardson moved to

the middle, blocking any attempt to cut him off. The Mercedes weaved, probing as it surged toward him. *Pray for us sinners, now and at the hour of our death* . . .

A glint on the roadway! He swerved right to miss the pool.

The Mercedes was gone. Richardson looked back and saw it sideways in the road, still in a slide from hitting the puddle. He willed more speed from the Alfa, even though it had no more to give. The lights of Rocca di Papa were closer. With luck, he could be there before his pursuer could catch him.

He glanced back to see if the Mercedes had turned around.

The wheel spun uselessly in Richardson's hands. More water! The Alfa began to skid toward the edge of a curve, still barrelling forward. Its front wheels left the road and the car hurtled off into blackness.

Richardson screamed.

In the glare of the headlights, a line of trees raced up the slope to meet him.

Chapter Seven

The guard replaced the telephone and turned to Durant. *"Gràzie,* signore. You may go in." He touched the bill of his cap in deference and opened the massive door.

Durant's footsteps echoed on marble as he walked into the entrance hall of the *Palazzo Sant' Uffizio.* The stone faces of cardinals watched impassively from their niches in the wall, guardians of the Faith, even in death.

A short, powerfully built man in a trim business suit sat reading a newspaper at the far end of the hall. He rose with a smile as Durant approached, but the slight bulge under his left arm warned that even high officials of the Church were not immune to secular violence.

"Ah, Signore Durant?" He ran a pen halfway down his list of afternoon appointments, checked his watch, and wrote in the time. "Sign next to your name, *per favore."*

Durant handed back the pen and glanced at the newspaper. It was open to a photo of a burned car being pulled up onto a mountain road with a caption that read: "Missing Priest Dead?" He didn't bother to study the picture; he'd already seen it and the short story that went with it.

That story had already prompted another appointment earlier in the day. He'd been to see Monsignor Jacob Otis at St. Susannah's almost immediately after reading of Steve Richardson's disappearance.

The old priest's eyes had been sunken with fear and fatigue. The *carabinieri* had come to see him about five A.M., just as he was getting ready for early mass.

"They told me they'd found his car, burned and smashed off the road above Frascati. I didn't even know Steve was gone until they came. Then, I found this." He reached into his pocket and handed Durant a crumpled note. "I thought perhaps Steve might have been taken to the clinic at Rocca di Papa by some passerby, so I called there. They'd never heard of him. They'd never heard of Samuel Gaines, either." His voice trembled as he shook his head. "Oh, God! My Steve! What could have happened?"

For Durant, the question now was not only what had happened, but why. He would begin his search for the answer with the man Richardson had tried to reach from the hospital, the head of the Vatican's Holy Office.

"This way, signore." The security man led Durant down another corridor to a large salon that was lined with golden draperies. As he walked into the room, Durant realized that the draperies had actually been painted onto the walls; there were more traditional frescoes further up. Two carved marble floor lamps threw their light at the ceiling, putting its sculpted octagonal patterns into sharp relief.

Behind an ornate desk sat a rotund man in a black

soutane. A red skullcap covered much of what late middle age had left of his white hair. He was absorbed in a thick volume that lay open on the desk. When Durant's escort coughed politely, the man took off his half-lensed glasses and looked up.

"Scusi, Eminenza." The escort bowed slightly and left the room.

Durant tensed against the reaction bred into him by a boyhood spent in the parochial schools of New Orleans. Priests were to be obeyed, young Craig had been told, and a bishop was to be respected. But a cardinal was a Prince of Holy Mother Church and was to be honored accordingly. He'd shelved that long ago with the rest of the lore of his youth, and except for his father's funeral and the wedding of a cousin, he hadn't been to mass in ten years. His interviews with church officials never crossed over from courtesy to subservience; it made him feel objectivity was preserved. None of them, however, had been one of the pope's elect.

The cardinal came around his desk with a reserved professional smile. He had the puffy jowls and purplish nose of a man who enjoyed eating, drinking, and moving as slowly as possible, but he surveyed his visitors with alert brown eyes that gave Durant the impression he'd been inventoried, catalogued, and filed away before the man even spoke.

"You are Signore Craig Durant? I am Giacomo *Cardinale* Frescobaldi." He extended a hand that bore a large ruby ring.

Durant's eyes were drawn to the ring, badge of Frescobaldi's office, to be kissed as a traditional sign of obedience.

"My pleasure, Your Eminence." He shook the

hand, hating his guilt and the scowling nuns of his memory who made him feel it.

The cardinal chuckled. "I never know these days what people will do when they meet me. Sometimes I'm tempted to put my hands in my pockets. Please." He gestured toward three leather chairs clustered around the fireplace. Several photographs sat framed on the mantel: Frescobaldi on a microphone-filled podium, Frescobaldi on the set of a television talk show, Frescobaldi shaking hands with the American president. Durant waited until the prelate had eased himself into the middle chair, then sat.

"Now, signore. I am always honored to have a visit from the foreign press, but your calls this morning for an immediate appointment was a bit unusual, eh? Such an urgent request usually comes only when the Throne of St. Peter is suddenly vacant, which, *Deo gratias,* it is not." The cardinal folded his hands across his abdomen and squeezed his gold pectoral cross between his thumbs. "So, why did you want to see me?"

"Well, Eminence, I wanted to talk with you about the disappearance of a priest from St. Susannah's parish."

Frescobaldi nodded somberly. "Tragic. I heard about it this morning. I don't—"

A side door opened, and a young priest with sandy hair stepped in, clutching a notebook under his arm. He carried an air of confident busyness, despite a barely noticeable limp. There had been someone like that in Durant's high school class: lame since birth, academic wizard, a constant volunteer for every dull extracurricular chore. Extremely ingratiating, equally manipulative. Nobody had really liked him, but he'd made sure everybody of importance needed him.

The cardinal's face brightened. "Ah, there you are. Come and join us." As the priest headed for the empty chair, Frescobaldi introduced Durant and explained, "I hope you don't mind, signore. This is my secretary, Carlo Guglielmo, without whom I would be lost. I am the Holy Father's official watchdog for matters of faith, but Carlo does all the work. He may be able to help you if I can't."

Durant nodded and continued. "I take it, Your Eminence, that you know about Father Richardson's car being found?"

"Yes, but as I was about to say a moment ago, I don't know anything but what was in the newspapers. Carlo has, of course, been in touch with the police, but we have no details. Some sort of accident, they say?"

"Did you know Father Richardson, Eminence?"

The prelate opened his hands and shrugged. "No more than I would know any of the several thousand other priests who lived in this city. Why do you ask?"

"I thought maybe you'd met him. That could explain why he tried to call you last night."

Frescobaldi shook his head. "Excuse me, that's not possible. I was out most of the evening, but I had no messages. I would have known."

"Forgive me, Eminence, but he did try to reach you. I was sitting within earshot when he placed the call, and I know he talked to someone at this residence. When he left, I checked the telephone directory he'd used. He'd underlined your number."

Frescobaldi gave his secretary a quizzical look. "Carlo, is this true?"

90

Guglielmo's eyes met the cardinal's with no hesitation. "A man did call while you were gone, *Eminenza*, said he would speak only with you. When I told him you weren't here, he became upset. He refused to give me his name. When I asked if I could take a message, he hung up, and he didn't call back."

"It may have been a coincidence"—the cardinal leaned back with a deep sigh—" or it could have been Richardson. But why?"

"Eminence, that's the first unanswered question," said Durant. "The second is why he was called out in the middle of the night to a mountain town to tend to a man nobody there had even heard of."

"Then you don't think Richardson simply lost control and wandered away from the wreckage in a daze?" Frescobaldi's face was deeply troubled.

"I'm a very careful journalist, Your Eminence, and I don't like being pushed into quick conclusions. But I'd be surprised if this was accidental."

Guglielmo cleared his throat. "Signore, the investigators haven't talked about anything other than an unfortunate mishap. There's been no mention of any conspiracy."

"I wouldn't know, Father. I haven't talked to them yet. There are a couple of other things, Your Eminence. Shortly before he tried to call you, Father Richardson had stopped in to see a patient at Salvator Mundi named Dr. Andrew Muller, who died a few minutes later. And there's this." Durant reached into his jacket pocket and pulled out the photograph from Muller's archaeological text, then handed it to Frescobaldi. "That's Muller on the left, I think. I'd like to know who the other man is."

The cardinal squinted at the photo and asked Guglielmo to retrieve his glasses from the desk. When he'd put them on, Frescobaldi studied the picture intently for a moment, then shook his head. "It won't be easy to find out, signore. This was taken in the 1930's, from the look of these boys. Many church records were destroyed during the war. But Carlo will see what can be done." He handed the photograph to Guglielmo. "I am always pleased to help you gentlemen of the press, if I can." Frescobaldi's practiced smile—the same face he wore in the fireplace photos—glowed anew.

"Thank you, Your Eminence," said Durant.

Guglielmo turned the photo back and forth, examining it closely. "Interesting, signore. Might I ask where you got this?"

"I found it, Father. I met Dr. Muller last week at the Vatican, and he loaned me a book. That was in it."

The young priest smiled with the same polished expression as his cardinal. "A piece of history. Intriguing, to wonder what life was like for those men."

"Some of us still remember, Carlo." Frescobaldi's tone was chiding but good-natured. "You know, signore, I would ordinarily suggest that you might check back with the seminary yourself. In this case, however, I think that could be a problem for you."

"I'll be glad to try. Do you recognize the church?"

"Yes. It has quite a history, actually. It's the Castle Church, where Martin Luther nailed his ninety-five theses to the door. It's in Wittenberg. That is now part of East Germany."

Chapter Eight

Toni slowed for the turn through Porta Pinciana, letting the Maserati snarl as she coasted through the weathered stone gate. She reveled in the sound and the sun-warmed smell of the car's leather seats. With a quick nudge of the accelerator, she moved easily into the traffic along the huge park of the Villa Borghese. The road ran on to the northeast, and Toni picked up speed as she passed the zoo and left the park behind.

The landscape soon turned to hillsides dotted with old stone cottages among the vineyards. The Maserati flew along the winding pavement, flashing past slower vehicles with a flick of the wheel. Toni turned on the radio loud to be heard over the engine. It was solid rock, a pulsing tale of fast living with no attachments. She threw back her head and sang.

At the bottom of a hill lay a large iron gateway to a narrow road up into the trees. Toni slowed to look it over, then shook her head and started to push the car back up to speed. Around the next turn, she braked hard to avoid a battered yellow Volkswagen beetle on the shoulder. Its rear hood was open and a large farm truck was parked next to it. A man in overalls stood gesturing as he spoke to someone who was bent over the car's engine, as if in prayer. He smiled broadly when Toni approached and blew a kiss as he waved her on.

A long climb brought her within view of a village nestled in a long valley, with farms stretching out on either side. Toni eased into a lower gear and started down, looking anxiously for signs of a gate. She reached the outskirts of the village without finding any, so she turned around and started back. There was a stucco roof, half hidden in a stand of tall pines up on a hillside. She drove slowly along, then turned onto an unmarked gravel road heading up the hill. It wound among the trees until it came to a large stone villa. Toni stopped the car short of the broad circular driveway and sat looking at the building, with its massive portico.

She pulled a Leica from the glove box and focused on the villa. Before Toni could press the shutter, there was a sound like a rifle shot from the woods back down the hill. Instinctively, she ducked and twisted the rearview mirror for a look behind her. There was another loud report, and the yellow Volkswagen she'd seen earlier came up the narrow road, backfiring again as it climbed. Muttering under her breath, Toni pulled the Maserati up onto the villa's driveway.

The dilapidated car rumbled up in a cloud of blue smoke. When it sputtered into silence, a cadaverous young man got out and ran frantically over to tap on her window. Reluctantly, she rolled it down.

"Do you have the time?" he asked nervously.

Toni checked her watch. "Ten-thirty."

The young man's face lit up with relief. *"Benissimo!*

I have an appointment with *Dottore* Buchmeunster for a job interview, and my professor warned me to be prompt.''

Toni smiled broadly and opened the Maserati's low-slung door. She swung her legs out, then reached back over to the passenger side, making sure that her skirt slid halfway up her thighs. She pretended to hunt for her purse for a moment, then gracefully pivoted around. ''How nice. What kind of job is it?''

The man twiddled his tie, his senses dead to everything but the sight of her legs.

Toni put her hands on her knees and leaned forward to catch his gaze. ''What kind of job is it?'' she asked as warmly as she could.

''What? Oh!'' His face went red and he took a step backward, as if more distance would help restore his composure. *''Mi dispiace,* signorina. I . . . ah . . .''

Toni pulled herself out of the car and offered her hand. ''I should introduce myself. I'm Bettina Tedesco.''

The young man flinched slightly, then clasped her hand in a sweaty grip and nodded briskly. ''Pietro Listi. I'm to interview for the position of secretary.''

Toni clouded her face with concern and sympathy. ''Oh, I'm afraid you're too late. I was hired for that job yesterday. There was no call to cancel your appointment?''

Listi's smile melted into a blank look of confusion. ''No. But I was told only this morning that the job was still open. You can't be—''

''Someone should have called you.'' Toni shook her head sadly.

Listi spread his arms in dismay. ''That can't be true!

I'm so well qualified. You wouldn't have been hired in my place!"

Toni fixed his eyes with a sympathetic gaze. "I'm reporting for work right now."

Listi sighed deeply and walked back toward his Volkswagen, shaking his head. "I must be on my way, then. There must have been some mistake. I'm so well qualified, and—and my professor says *Dottore* Buchmeunster hates women!"

"Arivederci, signore!" Toni prayed that the young man's car would start. It did, and she waved until Listi, still shaking his head, disappeared down the driveway.

A pair of stone lions guarded the villa's wide marble steps. Toni hurried confidently up and rang the bell. A few seconds later, a short thin man in butler's livery opened the door. He had a bulbous nose that was nearly as shiny as his bald head.

"Buon giorno," she began. "I have a ten o'clock appointment with *Dottore* Buchmeunster. A job interview."

The butler stood silently without any indication that he understood. Toni tried again. *"Guten Morgen. Ich—"*

"Italian will suffice, signorina," said the butler. "However, I fear you are mistaken. We are expecting a man."

"No, there's no mistake. When I see him I'll explain. Tell him I'm here, *per favore.*"

"As you wish." The butler's eyebrows arched until they wrinkled his scalp. "Come in. You may wait inside while I tell *Il Dottore* you are here, but I doubt he'll even see you." He held the door open for her, then pulled it shut and headed across the room, expecting Toni to follow.

She stood transfixed, her eyes caught by the grand staircase as it swept from the black and white tile floor to the three large crystal chandeliers overhead. A sixteenth-century nobleman hung full length on the opposite wall, frozen in lace and pomp. A pregnant young woman posed in another oil alongside, wearing a knowing smile. The portraits brought Toni's gaze back down to the impatient stare of the butler.

"Whenever you're ready, signorina?"

He led her to the drawing room, where floor-to-ceiling windows on one wall poured light onto the dark paneling that made up the other three.

"You may wait here." He directed her toward a brocaded Louis XVI armchair. "Whom shall I say is calling?"

"Pietro Listi."

The wrinkles appeared on the butler's bald scalp again as he looked at Toni for a moment, but he made no comment. He crossed to the far side of the room and knocked softly on a heavy oaken door.

"Come in!" boomed a voice from the next room.

The butler quickly opened the door just enough to slip his narrow frame through, then pulled it shut quietly, leaving Toni alone. She turned slowly, surveying the room. A large blue and gold Oriental rug glowed in the morning sunlight, covering much of the glossy hardwood floor. A tapestry hung above the marble fireplace, sprawling a medieval battlefield across the entire wall. Overhead, a frescoed red and gold web shrouded the ceiling except in the center, where four angels held a painted Earth aloft with golden cord.

The door across the room opened with a speed that made Toni jump. The butler reappeared and announced, *"Il Dottore* will see you now."

"Gràzie," said Toni, suddenly feeling tiny and frail.

She was shown into a room that was smaller and much darker. It was walled on three sides with floor-to-ceiling bookshelves. A huge curved mahogany desk stood in the center on another Oriental rug.

"Come in, come in!" The speaker stood with his back to the room, silhouetted against sheer drapes that had been drawn across a large window at the other end. He was looking out the small part that remained open. "Sit down, *bitte,"* he said, without turning around.

Toni sat on the edge of a chair directly in front of the desk.

"Signore Listi. I distinctly recall requesting a male secretary. Either you are a master of disguise, or your parents indulged a cruel sense of humor when they chose your name." There was no trace of humor in Buchmeunster's words.

Toni smiled at the silhouette. "Good morning, Dr. Buchmeunster. My name is Bettina Tedesco. Pietro Listi has taken another job, but he told me about this appointment with you, and he thought I might be acceptable."

"Did he, indeed!" said Buchmeunster acidly, continuing to peer out the window. His hands were clasped behind his back, and he began to rock back and forth from heel to toe. There was a long pause before he asked, "Do you need this position?"

Toni squirmed on the edge of her chair. "Yes, sir. I'm a university student in Rome, and I need the money." She prayed that Bettina Tedesco still existed in the student records. It had been two years since Toni had bribed a clerk to create that identity for her research on a story about campus radicals.

The pace of Buchmeunster's rocking increased. Toni's eyes darted about the room as she sat with her hands in her lap, feeling a bit like a convent schoolgirl waiting for the Mother Superior to speak. The desk in front of her was as cold and businesslike as its owner. Two lamps were mirrored in its high gloss, and the few items on it—a spotless blotter, a letter opener, and a telephone—had been carefully arranged. Only a large bunch of decorative grapes and a silver tray with six crystal goblets and a decanter seemed out of place.

"What are you studying, signorina?"

"Languages and ancient cultures. I hope to become an archaeologist."

At this, Buchmeunster ceased to rock, but he didn't turn to face her.

"What languages have you?" The sarcastic edge was gone from his speech.

"Italian, French, German, English, and Arabic."

"Arabic?" Buchmeunster's tone portrayed genuine curiosity. "Wherever did you learn that?"

"My father was in the oil business. We lived in the Middle East for twenty years, on and off, before he retired." Still, Buchmeunster kept his back to Toni. She began to grow angry.

"And where do your parents live now?"

Toni didn't answer. She rose, took one of the goblets from the tray, and stepped off the rug. Then she opened her hand, letting the goblet shatter on the hardwood

99

floor. She gazed at the shards, startled by the destruction.

Buchmeunster turned slowly and stared at Toni. Then, hands still clasped behind his back, he moved across the room until he stood within reach of her.

Toni jerked her head up. Buchmeunster's face was expressionless, but his grey eyes conveyed furious disbelief. "I—I'll pay for the glass," she said, making no effort to hide the fear in her voice.

"That may take some time. That was a 1725 English wineglass. If it interests you, it was decorated with diamond engraving and Jacobite slogans. You have destroyed a museum piece."

"I'm sorry. I had no idea." The apology came hard, and she wondered if it sounded as unconvincing as she felt.

"I should hope you did not. You are quite sure of yourself, are you not, young woman?"

"Yes, I know. My father says that's my greatest fault."

"Sit down!" He waved her back to the chair and awkwardly settled himself behind the desk. "The Scriptures say you should honor and obey your father, but it does not require you to take as gospel everything he says. Of course, in your case, I think he may well be correct."

Toni smiled but dropped it quickly when Buchmeunster did not return it. He began to stroke his salt-and-pepper beard. "You did not like the manner in which I conducted your interview?"

"No, sir. I thought the least you could do was look at me."

"That is why you broke the crystal?"

Toni looked down nervously at her lap. "Yes."

"You were right. I was very rude, and I ask you to forgive me. But I must say, I would have thought your parents could have taught you more self-control." Buchmeunster knitted his fingers into an arch. "Now, then. I do need a part-time secretary. Someone for two hours or so in the evenings."

Toni sat back in the chair and tried to forget the burning knot in her stomach.

Buchmeunster swiveled his chair around, got up, and walked toward the window. "You are honest, signorina?"

"Honest?"

"Yes, trustworthy," said Buchmeunster as he opened the drapes to reveal the villa's entrance drive. "You can be trusted not to divulge what you see and hear in this room?"

"Certainly, sir."

"And if you are so honest, Signorina Tedesco, why did you tell Pietro Listi that you already had been hired for this position?" He gestured toward the driveway. "Is that not what you told him out there?" He turned to confront her, a slight smile playing on the corners of his mouth.

"Yes, that's what I told him." Toni met his gaze squarely.

"Why?"

"Because I wanted to work for you, sir. You have an outstanding reputation in the field of paleography and I thought I could learn a great deal. I'm sorry. I'll go now." Tears welled up, and she tried to force them back, hoping to make a respectable exit. "Please excuse me," she said as she jumped up. "I'll send you the money for the glass."

"You will sit!" Buchmeunster shook his head irritably. "Why must women carry on so! Actually, the glass was only a copy."

Toni sat.

Buchmeunster walked back to his desk and sank into his chair with a sigh. "Herr Meckendorff, my secretary for many years, became ill and had to return to Austria."

"Austria?"

"Yes," said Buchmeunster, nodding. "That is where I live most of the year. My family established a winery at Gumpoldskirchen in 1756." He laid a hand gently on the decanter in front of him. "This is one of our finest vintages . . . 1975."

"I see."

"Yes . . . well, since Herr Meckendorff left, I have had to keep up with things myself. I am doing some research at the Vatican in the mornings, and I work here in the afternoons." He pointed toward an electric typewriter on a corner table. "I have become an adequate typist, although I really abhor that machine."

He turned back to the decanter and lifted it reverently. "You know, the coming of a good year is an enigma to me. All my life, I have been learning to read the signs—the right grapes, the right weather, the right soil. Sometimes, the signs are perfect but the wine is a disappointment. But every once in a while, when you expect mediocrity, you open a cask and pour out magnificence. It is puzzling, you agree?"

Toni nodded.

Buchmeunster pointed a finger across the desk at her.

"You are also enigmatic, signorina. You say you are a student and need money, yet you drive an expensive automobile. You apply for employment, yet you enter my house under a false name and you destroy an antique goblet to get my attention." He nodded pensively. "I am fond of puzzles." Suddenly, his eyebrows gathered in a frown. "You do type?"

"Oh, yes," said Toni brightly.

"Good! It is settled, then." Buchmeunster smiled. "Monday you will start."

Lucas I smiled and stepped out from behind his desk. "Ah, Eminence. It's good of you to come."

Frescobaldi returned the smile and crossed the papal study. "It is always a pleasure to be invited, Holy Father."

They shook hands and joined in a brief embrace. "It's good to have friends who don't bow and scrape, Giacomo, if only in my apartments. Somehow, I used to have more of them."

"Traditions die hard, Holiness. They are still there, but you are no longer just their brother Lupe."

The pope's laugh was tinged with sadness. "True. Odd how the color of a cassock can change your whole life, isn't it? Come, sit with me." The lilt of his native *pampas* was in his speech. In public and in private, he avoided the plural pronouns carried by his office, preferring to sound more like a single man of Christ than a head of state.

They settled into velvet-cushioned chairs near the window. Late afternoon sun warmed them both. There was a decanter with two glasses on a small table next to the pope. "You'll join me, I hope? *Concha y Toro* from a friend in my village."

"Of course, Holiness. *Gràzie.*"

Lucas I handed a glass to the cardinal and poured one for himself. "Now, to what shall we drink?"

"As always, Holy Father. To Christ, to His faith."

The pope nodded. "And, I would add, to the men who keep it safe."

Frescobaldi gave a slight bow of his head. "Your confidence is greatly appreciated."

They touched glasses and drank.

"Giacomo, it is as prelate of the Congregation for the Doctrine of Faith that I wanted you to visit today." He set his wine back on the table. "You and I have known each other for a very long time."

"Indeed, Holiness. It has been my privilege." Frescobaldi studied the pontiff's face, searching for some hint of what he wanted but finding none.

"Since I first arrived, fresh from San Luis with my new red hat, in fact. I was so accustomed to dealing with generals and presidents-for-life that bending the curia to my wishes seemed a simple matter."

"I remember, yes." Frescobaldi allowed himself a smile at the memory. "You amazed us all with your persistence."

Lucas I shook his head and chuckled. "In my country, there were so many needs but so little time. So, I would always hurry and never rest, but it seemed everyone here would rest and never hurry."

"No doubt. It is our national character. But"—he shrugged—"Italia endures, and so does the church in her keeping."

"So it does. How did you first put it?" The pope

looked off into a corner, combing back through the years. "Ah, yes. 'Lupe, you've only been at this for a short time. They've had nineteen centuries to convince themselves—' "

" '—that everyone else is wrong,' " the cardinal echoed. They laughed together.

"You were right, Giacomo. I was a bit overzealous."

"Only a little, Holiness. Frankly, I admired that in you. I still do. Even if we've had our differences." He drained his glass.

"But they've never been on matters of faith, have they, Eminence? On that, we've always agreed." The pontiff rose and walked to his desk. It was a simple table wrought of teak, bare except for a Bible, a blotter, and an angular Christ, His agony frozen on an ebony cross. The desk was so much like its owner, Frescobaldi thought; purposeful, without pretense, unyielding.

The pope turned, slightly stooped from the effects of an interrogator's beating long ago in the spring of his priesthood. "We don't differ now, do we? You haven't changed and espoused the views of those mad Dutchmen?" It sounded almost like a joke, but there was no smile behind the words.

"No, Holiness. I remain the champion of my pope and my church." Where *was* this going? Frescobaldi wondered.

"It was because of your faith that, when I was chosen three years ago, I made you head of the Holy Office." He began to pace behind the desk, a pose from his days of teaching seminarians. "I wanted someone there who was my brother in matters of doctrine, not a sophist who would let us drift to the edge of schism.

I trust you, Giacomo. You are my confessor, my advisor, my friend."

Frescobaldi left his chair to stand by the pope. "I am all of those things, Holiness, and thankful to our Lord Christ for the honor. You must know that by now."

"Then why, Giacomo, do I feel your disapproval?" He gave the cardinal a piercing stare. "You were furious with the liberationists. 'They should build a new shrine,' you said, 'to our Lady of the Warm Gun.' You would have burned them if I'd let you."

"They should all be excommunicated." Frescobaldi's mouth curled into a sneer. "Preaching the Gospels as a text for revolution."

"We cannot risk driving them out! We need them if the Church is to remain any moral force at all in those places, and that is essential."

"I concur." Frescobaldi struggled to keep his voice even against the pope's rising anger. "With no priests, there *is* no Church, but their views must be changed."

"Then why, when I toured Latin America, trying to draw them back into the fold, do I return to hear from those curial fools that you don't think I should have made the trip? That I said too much?"

"It is not your message I disagree with, Holiness. It is where and how you deliver it." Frescobaldi shook his head. "First, the Warsaw Pact, then the Libyans, the I.R.A., and now your own priests, heretics though they be. Before long, there won't be anyone left who wouldn't be happier with you dead."

"Except the people, those who value Christ's justice and his truth." The pope's tone softened, and he placed a hand on the cardinal's shoulder. "Giacomo, you have

106

always been the diplomat, the negotiator, while I have been the inflexible authoritarian. I need your support in this. Without it, our weaker brothers will lose heart, and the oppressors will do what they wish. We cannot let that happen."

Frescobaldi sighed wearily. "They'll kill you, Lupe, no matter what I think or what all the bishops in this world think. If you must speak out, then I will stand by your side. But for the sake of us all, have some care for your safety. Hold smaller audiences, put on more guards. And stop your pilgrimages to every dark corner of the world you can find."

"No, Giacomo. That might save my person, but it would imperil my soul." He picked up the black crucifix. "This was once a shapeless piece of jungle wood. The man who crafted this knew that a Christian must use his talents to be a living symbol of God's truth. Can I, as the Vicar of Christ, do less?"

Chapter Nine

Rivette slowed his pace and stretched slightly to raise his nose higher into the morning air, breathing in the freshness of the pastries cooling inside the small *panetteria*. He let his senses float with the aroma and followed it through the door. He bought three *crostate*, nibbling on one as he moved back onto the street. The others he would save for *La Nonna*. The old woman fancied them, he recalled, and that might be of help.

There was a loud knot of people on the corner ahead. He stepped around their growing argument, a dispute over a Vespa with a flat tire, and found the address. It was one of those ageless Roman buildings that could hide a villa or a collection of cold water tenements behind its crumbling three-story facade. From the top floor, a wrinkled woman with her hair in a black scarf lowered a basket and called to a street vendor for oranges.

The apartment was upstairs, just off the second landing. The sound of an ancient Enrico Caruso recording drifted toward him. It stopped abruptly when he knocked. After a second knock, then a third, footsteps creaked toward the door, but it didn't open.

"Che vuole?" asked a young woman.

Rivette tried to put a smile in his Italian that would carry through the closed door. "A friend. I've come to see *La Nonna.*"

"Impossible. She is not receiving any guests. She is—"

"Ah, but I'm a special friend, seeking news of another. Tell her that, *per favore;* she'll see me."

"I don't know what you're talking about. *La Signora* is indisposed. Go away before you disturb her!"

"Such a beautiful voice." Rivette let a note of regret creep into his words. "My day will be lost if I can't meet the lovely creature who owns it. If I can't see *La Nonna,* at least give me the pleasure of gazing on your face. My heart—"

"Please! Go away! Now!"

Rivette sighed loudly. "If you insist, but kindly tell *La Nonna* that I brought two *crostate* for her. There was a third, but I'm afraid I ate it."

The girl's frustration turned to annoyance. "For the last time, lea—"

"Idiota!" A stronger, older female voice cut off the protests inside. "Let him in!"

The door was opened by a girl of around twenty, who was trying to watch him and gauge her mistress's reaction at the same time. She was pretty, but her smile was taut with anxiety. *"Avanti,* signore," she said, gesturing Rivette into the room.

La Nonna sat by the window, a slight figure dressed in black, almost lost in her massive wooden chair. Her face was mottled with age, but her piercing eyes were clear, and they quickly appraised her visitor.

"Allora," said the old woman. "So you are a friend. My friends bring gifts. What have you brought?"

Rivette moved closer, holding out his wrapped pastries. "For you, *Nonna.*"

The old woman took the package and opened it, then nodded and set it on a small table next to her. *"Bene.* Sit. We will have some refreshment and talk." She pointed toward another chair and spoke to the girl.

"Maria, our guest would like something to drink. Bring us *cappuccino.*"

"Scusi, signora, but we've run out. I was going to get—"

"Then go and get it now, child, and don't keep us waiting!"

The girl grabbed a small purse and left quickly with a deep nod that was almost a bow.

"Foolish child," said the old woman with a shake of her head. "But she has ears that stay open and a mouth that stays shut." She turned and locked Rivette in her gaze. "So you come to me once again. What do you want this time, eh?"

"To pay my respects. Friendship."

The old woman picked up one of the *crostate* and bit off a piece. "You are always so thoughtful to bring such things, even though the third one seems to get eaten every time. You are a very long time in coming to see me, *Fratellino.* You have been back in Rome for nearly two months."

Rivette winced at the nickname. "You are the only one who calls me that, *Nonna.*"

Her frail shoulders rose in a shrug. "So did my son. He gave you that name, and it fits. You need someone to watch over you now and then. You need help now, don't you, Francois?''

"*Si*, I do. You always know.''

"You were Paolo's comrade in arms. He married young, you know.'' Her voice carried an edge of bitterness. "But his wife . . . That whore! He was so angry when he found out. He would have killed her if she hadn't run off with one of her lovers. You met him not long after that, when he left Rome.'' The old woman smiled. "He loved you like a brother.''

"I failed him, *Nonna.*''

"No, *Fratellino*. He was near death when you carried him out of the desert to the monastery.'' Her eyes took on a faraway look and she fingered the gold cross that hung on a thin chain around her neck. "Because of you, Paolo died in a house of God, his confession heard and his sins forgiven, instead of alone in the wilderness. That is a debt I can never repay. That is why I will always know when you need help. *Allora,* tell me. What do you want?''

"I seek a man, an extremely dangerous man. He is called Abdul Sayeb.''

The old woman shook her head gently. "The world is full of dangerous men, Francois. What is so special about this one that you have to find him?''

"He is a terrorist, *Nonna,* a killer of the worse kind. He takes life not for honor or family or even for money. He is a fanatic, a weapon in the hands of the extremist group whose philosophy he's attracted to at the moment. He's like a ghost, a presence sensed but never seen, leaving chaos and death when he vanishes as quickly as he came.''

"This man is not like the *Brigatisti*, with their communiqués, always telling the world how shooting the kneecaps of some businessman is a blow for social justice. We could find one of those fools in a moment. What you ask may take time.''

''There isn't any. We think Sayeb is in Italy now, probably here in Rome, but we have no idea what he plans. He must be found—and quickly.''

''Time may be your ally, *Fratellino,* if he waits a while before striking. Such a man cannot exist for very long in a vacuum. He must have shelter from others, and the strain of his life may make him careless. One or the other will betray him eventually.''

Rivette clenched his hands together, molding them into an uneasy ball. ''You may be right, *Nonna.* But I can't wait around for him to appear. We don't know how long—''

''Nonna! Nonna!'' Maria burst through the door, sobbing. Her face flushed and tear-stained, she ran across the room and sank to her knees in front of them.

The old woman shook her roughly, trying to force her back to composure. ''Maria! *Che cosa?* Tell me! What's happened?!''

The girl wept brokenly, fighting to gain control. ''Isa—Isabella! She's dead!''

''What! How? What are you saying?''

The sound of a polite cough drew their attention to the open door, where a well-dressed man with greying hair stood waiting just outside. *''Permesso?''* he asked, showing a small identification case as he entered. ''I am Barzini of *Pubblica Sicurezza.* May I ask, do any of you know the young lady who has the corner apartment on the third floor?''

La Nonna's face turned impassive, a shield drawn up

112

between herself and the detective. "No, *Ispettore*. She only came in last week. I've never even spoken to her."

Barzini gazed thoughtfully at the old woman for a moment, then at Maria, who was still weeping. "Perhaps the Signorina—"

"She knows nothing, signore. Absolutely nothing."

The detective turned to Rivette, who simply shook his head.

"And I don't suppose," said Barzini, "that any of you would recall seeing or hearing anything peculiar lately? You see, someone seems to have killed her."

He was met with silence.

"Dunque . . . dunque . . . dunque . . ." Barzini sighed, stroking his chin. Then he brightened and clapped his hands together. *"Allora.* Memory is a strange thing. Perhaps something will come to you later, and you'll let me know, eh? I'm a curious man, so I'll keep checking back in case you remember." He smiled and started back toward the door, but stopped suddenly. "There is . . . one other thing."

Barzini pulled a plastic evidence bag from his jacket pocket and held it up to display the small yellowish fruit inside. "Have you seen anything like this before?" He turned the bag slowly as he spoke, revealing some red smears on the fruit's skin and one area that seemed to have had a bite taken out of it.

"What is it?" asked Rivette.

"I hoped one of you would know, signore, or that you could tell me if anyone in this neighborhood grows them?"

The old woman sniffed. "Nobody around here would have anything to do with such a thing. It looks evil."

Barzini nodded. "True, signora. Yet it makes for

such an interesting crime. A girl is killed, there is no sign of forced entry, no weapon found at the scene, no witnesses. Just a body mutilated in ways decency won't permit me to describe, and a strange, bloody fruit. The work, I think, of a very persuasive but extremely vicious mind. Interesting, indeed.''

Chapter Ten

The heavyset old woman, clad in black, coughed as she swept a rag across the top of the writing desk. She rearranged the notepad and pencils, which were already in perfect order, and paused to pick up a small framed photograph. "Stefano," she sniffed, dabbing at her reddened eyes with the dust rag. *"Caro bambino."* She shook her head and put the photo back where it had been. *"Diavola!"* She spat in disgust and left the room, crossing herself as she went.

"Caterina!" called a voice from downstairs.

"Si, Monsignore." The woman hurried down to the first floor and arrived out of breath.

Monsignor Otis was slipping into his coat. "Caterina, I'm going over to San Silvestro's for the afternoon. Maybe hearing confessions there will be better than waiting here for news about Steve."

Caterina nodded and dabbed her eyes again.

The priest reached into the closet for his red-tasseled *biretta.* "If anyone calls, just tell them I'll be back later, except the police, of course. Tell them where I've gone, but don't tell anyone else, okay?"

"Si, Monsignore."

"Ah, good. *Ciao.*" Otis smiled wanly and headed out the door.

Caterina started for the kitchen, but stopped and sank to her knees as she passed the small shrine in a recess off the hallway. She clasped her hands tightly in supplication and pressed them against her forehead as she prayed. *"Sacra Madre,* Mother of God and of us all, hear me. As you loved your Son, I have grown to love Stefano as my own. Since he came, my life has been full again. Watch over him and bring him back again safely. And send a sign that he is in your care. For me, *Madre,* and for the *Monsignore.*" She made the sign of the cross, then braced her bulk against the wall and stood, hearing her knees crack loudly as she rose.

The front door knocker echoed in the hallway, and she shuffled tiredly to answer it.

"Buon giorno, signora," said the visitor. "I'm Craig Durant. Is Monsignor Otis in?"

"No, signore."

"I was here yesterday, and I hoped to be able to talk with him again. When do you expect him back?"

"He didn't tell me. By dinner, *certamente,* but before then?" She shrugged.

Durant rubbed his hands together and shoved them into the pockets of his overcoat. "Pardon me, signora, but do you suppose I could come inside for a moment? It's getting chilly out here."

Caterina's eyes narrowed as she surveyed the stranger. "The *Monsignore* will return later. If you will leave a message, I will ask him to call."

"Signora, what I have to discuss with Monsignor Otis is very important." He pulled his notebook from a jacket pocket and scribbled his telephone number, then tore out the page and handed it to her. "It concerns Father Richardson."

The old woman drew in her breath sharply as she took the paper from Durant. "It is such a cold day, signore. Perhaps you would like some *cappuccino* to warm you up?"

"*Gràzie tanto,* signora. I'd like that." He grinned and stepped in.

She led the way to the kitchen, smiling to herself as she passed the hallway shrine. She seated him and set out a plate of *cornetti*. "Just baked this morning, signore," said Caterina as she moved quickly. Her fatigue was gone now, and she hummed as she brewed the coffee.

Durant bit into one of the sweet rolls. It was still warm inside. He let the taste flood his mouth while he pondered the old woman's sudden change in heart. When the *cappuccino* came, Caterina anxiously sat down and joined him.

"Signore, you have news of *Padre* Richardson?"

Durant set the cup down and spoke as gently as he could. "Signora, I—"

"Caterina, *prego,* call me Caterina."

"Caterina, I haven't heard anything but what I read in the newspapers. I'm looking for him myself."

The anticipation left her face.

"I'm a reporter . . . *cronista.*"

Caterina folded her arms and scowled. "What do you want of him?"

Durant spread his hands in what he hoped would be read as a gesture of sincerity. "I'm from American television, and I've been looking into his disappearance."

117

A tear escaped, spoiling her studied reserve. Others quickly followed, and she hastily patted her apron pockets for a handkerchief. Finding none, she pressed a table napkin into service but said nothing.

Durant felt his opening and pushed in, shoving aside his guilt at playing on the old woman's emotions. "I met Father Richardson the night he disappeared. He'd been to visit a man who'd had a serious heart attack—a last confession, I guess. The man died a few minutes after Richardson came out, and it seemed to upset him terribly. Do you know why?"

Caterina sobbed brokenly. "He—he is such a gentle boy. Even though he is a priest of Christ, death always upsets him, not because of those who died, but . . . he so deeply feels the sorrow of those left behind. Sometimes—sometimes I—"

"That must have been it." Durant sensed her reluctance to trust him. "He seemed to be very sensitive."

"He would come in sometimes from a funeral, and he would cry. The first time I saw it, he was embarrassed. But later, he would talk to me, and I would tell him, 'It will be all right, *bambino.*' Then he would smile and give me a hug." She nodded sadly. "When my husband died ten years ago, I had no children, nobody, so I came to work for the *Monsignore.* Then Stefano came. God sent him to me as the son I never had. I pray God brings him back to me again, signore. He must."

"You may be able to help find him, Caterina. Have the police talked with you?"

"Those fools?" the woman hissed. "I hope God has more in mind than them."

Durant leaned closer. "I've been running my own

118

investigation, and I think it's going to be important to talk to anyone Father Richardson might try to contact if he were in trouble. Is there anyone you can think of? Anyone?''

Caterina frowned. "He could always come to me."

"No. If it's the kind of trouble I think it is, he couldn't come near you or Monsignor Otis. There's got to be somebody else."

The old woman sat silently for a few moments, then shook her head. "There is someone—may God forgive me for my thoughts about her—he might have talked to." Her words came slowly, as though they burned as she spoke them. "Last year, Stefano met an American woman. She is . . . how do you say? . . . divorced. Her name is Sandy Newcombe. They began to see each other often, and he—"

She stopped to pick up another napkin as the tears began to flow again. "He told me that he loves her and that he might leave the priesthood to marry her. But this is not easy for him, because he also is very much in love with God and His Church."

In Piazza Navona, a woman smoothed her heavy sweater and positioned herself in front of the Fountain of the Moor, sidestepping to follow her husband's stage direction. She had once been stunning, but now, like the buildings around her, she was reluctantly content to hold the line at attractive respectability.

They had the *piazza* to themselves, except for the pigeons and a flower vendor who lazily shaded his eyes with a broad-brimmed hat. The husband stepped backward into the street to frame the scene. Just as he raised the camera, a taxi slammed on its brakes to avoid hitting him.

"*Cretino!*" yelled the driver, punctuating his assessment with a shaking fist. When the photographer moved out of the road, the driver pulled up and gave him a malevolent glare while the passenger got out.

Durant tipped the driver and walked on into the *piazza*. Halfway down its length, he turned into a fading orange building, checked its directory, and took the cage elevator to the third floor. Two doors down the hall, he knocked.

The door eased open hesitantly an inch, the length of the play in the chain lock. "*Sì?*" inquired a well-modulated female voice. "*Che vuole?*"

"I'm Craig Durant, Mrs. Newcombe."

"Do I know you? I don't think we've met."

"No, I don't think you would. I'm an American television reporter."

The door closed quickly, not quite a slam, but an obvious dismissal. Durant knocked again. "Please, Mrs. Newcombe. I'd really like to talk to you."

"About what? I don't have anything to do with Italian politics, labor unions, or designer dresses, and it's obvious that I'm not the pope. That's about the list of possible topics, isn't it? Unless you think I'm the Red Brigade."

Durant waited a moment before speaking. "I've come about someone I believe is a friend of yours, someone I need to find."

"I have very few friends, Mr. Durant, and I know where to find them myself. Anything else?"

"I want to talk to you about Steve Richardson."

The door cracked open again, slowly. There was a

120

sigh from behind the chain. "Should that mean any-thing to me?"

"I've been to the rectory. I've spoken with Caterina. I know it does."

The chain slid off and the door opened further. A woman nearing thirty stood inside. Durant felt his memories stir, all the pain and all the pleasure. Her hair was a deep blond, a cascade ending just above her shoulders, and she watched him with clear emerald eyes. Except for her finer nose and two inches she lacked in height, Sandy Newcombe could have been Stephanie. She gave him a look of exasperation. "All right. What's this about?"

Before Durant could answer, a small child yelled from the back of the apartment. "Mommy! Mommy!"

"I'll be right there, Justin." The woman turned back to Durant. "I'm sorry. We really have nothing to discuss. I have a little boy who has a high fever and the flu, and I don't have time for this."

"I won't take long, Mrs. Newcombe. It's just that I—"

"Mommy!", the child cried again, sounding near tears.

"I'm coming, sweetheart!" She gave Durant a look that was half resentment, half plea to be left alone. "Now look, Mr. . . . ah . . . what was your name again?"

"Durant, Craig Durant."

"Mr. Durant, this really is impossible. I can't talk to—"

"Mrs. Newcombe, Father Richardson has disap-peared. He may be dead."

Her face went white as her self-assurance crumbled. "Look, I haven't seen hi—"

A tiny boy grabbed her legs and stared at the tall stranger.

"Oh, hell! Come in. I'll be with you as soon as I can get him settled."

She was back in a few minutes without her son. "I put him in bed with some books and a teddy bear. He'll keep busy 'til he dozes off." Her hands were shaking as she reached into her purse for her lighter and a cigarette. Durant lit it for her, and she leaned back in the chair, inhaling deeply. "I heard about Steve yesterday morning. Mr. Durant, what—what could have happened?"

"Nobody knows. His car was found wrecked and burned near Frascati. It looked like he'd run off the road."

She turned away to hide the tears while she blinked them back. Her voice quavered. "And . . . Steve? They couldn't find him. Where is he?"

"The police have been searching, but there's not a trace. I was told Father Richardson had been seeing you. I thought he might have been in touch."

Sandy Newcombe shook her head vigorously. "I don't know where you got your information, Mr. Durant, but whoever told you about my relationship with Steve should have told you that it's over. It's been over for nearly two months, and I haven't seen him since it ended. He hasn't come here."

Durant nodded slowly. "I guessed that. But I thought I might try anyway. I'd like to find him myself."

"Why? He . . . we haven't done anything wrong.

Our relationship was accidental, and it was innocent. What—''

Durant held up a hand. "Please. I'm not trying to intrude in your life or his. I saw Father Richardson at Salvator Mundi Hospital before he disappeared."

Sandy's face went taut.

"Mrs. Newcombe, I saw him make a telephone call, then become extremely upset and leave. I want to know more about that call and about the patient he visited before he placed it."

"But his car." The tears came again. "It was wrecked and burned!"

"True. But his body hasn't been found. I think he's alive, but in great danger. And if you've been in touch with him, you may be, too.

She turned away and hid her face in her hands. Durant reached out and gently pulled the hands away, forcing her to look back at him.

"Tell me. If Steve Richardson were alive, would he come to you?"

Sandy stood and walked to the window. She was silent for a moment, then turned to face him. Her words were coldly even. "Look, I haven't seen Steve Richardson in months. I don't expect to see him. That's what I told the priest who came around this morning." She sighed heavily. "I wish to God I knew he was all right."

"Do you want to see him again?"

Her control wavered. "Mr. Durant, I think you'd better go."

Chapter Eleven

Toni blew out the match and checked the reflection of her dining table against the Roman skyline in her window. It looked straight up Via Conciliazione, and the candles lent the distant dome of St. Peter's a crown of fire. She gave own image an approving glance, then lowered the lights and turned on the stereo to heighten the effect. Vivaldi flooded the room. She hunted around the dial, found nothing better, and went back to RAI and its "Four Seasons." Not exactly what she had in mind, but it would do.

The lid of a boiling pot began clattering its own concerto, and Toni hurried to turn down the gas on her ancient stove. It was a tiny kitchen with no ventilation, and when she opened the other pots to check their progress, the bouquet of her cooking rolled through the apartment like a fragrant cloud. She stirred a saucepan absently, letting her mind dwell on expectations for the evening ahead. A knock came from the front door and she went to answer it, pausing just long enough to give the scene one more look.

"Haven't started without me, I hope?" Durant held

out a slim paper bag. "I brought something along. I know you told me not to, but—"

Toni pulled a graceful ruddy bottle from the bag and smiled. "Ah, Barolo! One of my favorites! But you didn't need to bring this! Some Chianti would have been fine."

Durant shut the door and shrugged. "The man at the shop told me this wine is just for special occasions. Dinner with you seemed like an appropriate event."

"You're foolish, but sweet." Toni gave his arm a squeeze as she led him to the dining table and handed him a corkscrew. "I'm nearly through, so why don't you open the wine and pour us both a glass?"

"Fine." His eyes followed the contours of Toni's slacks as she headed for the kitchen. She was a tall, well-shaped woman who moved with grace, sure of her effect on men. There'd been something of that in Stephanie, he recalled, although her nuances were beginning to blur in his memory. With a sigh, he opened the bottle's foil top, carefully twisted in the corkscrew, and gave it a firm tug. The cork stuck firmly in place. "How's the manuscript story going? I haven't seen anything on it recently."

"Well, it's a little slow at the moment. Since Muller's death, I haven't really been able to come up with anything new."

"Me, either." Durant tugged again. Still the cork didn't budge. "I was thinking that we may have to wait for the study to be completed, and then, who knows if it'll ever get released." He scissored the bottle between his thighs and grabbed the corkscrew resolutely with both hands.

"Oh, I don't think so," said Toni. "There's always

125

some way to find out what's going on if you want to work at it hard enough."

Another hard pull brought out two thirds of the cork. Durant held the bottle up against the candlelight and saw the rest floating like a crust inside. "Nice going, sophisticate," he muttered.

Toni emerged from the kitchen bearing a hot casserole, and she set it in the middle of the table. "That'll need to cool off a while. Lasagna ought to go well with that Baro—" She turned to see Durant looking back and forth from the upheld bottle to the broken cork in his hand, and Toni burst out laughing.

"Well, it just stuck a little," he said sheepishly, "and I gave it a good tug. Got any more wine?"

"Don't worry. *Mama* Toni can fix it." She went back to the kitchen and returned a moment later with a small tea strainer. "Purists may sneer, but they don't have to use that corkscrew. Here." She held the bottle over the strainer and poured them each a glass.

"Nice trick."

"Every Italian student learns that one. I used to save a lot of money on cheap *vino,* but I learned that the wineries save a lot of money on cheap corks. Shall we sit while dinner cools a little?"

Durant followed her over to the couch, where she kicked off her shoes and tucked her feet beneath her. There was a travel poster on the opposite wall, a beach scene, empty except for a girl sunning her back with her bikini top undone. He sat next to Toni, unconsciously draping an arm near her shoulder. Her perfume drifted through his mind, a warm haze flirting with his senses.

"Craig, something has to turn up on the manuscripts. The fact that Buchmeunster's evaluating them certainly isn't secret anymore. Hasn't Chapman told you anything?''

"Nope. In fact, I haven't seen him since the night Muller died.''

"They can't keep the lid on forever. Someone around there knows how the study is going.''

Durant took a pensive sip. "Maybe. But you know the people around the Vatican better than I do. Anyone who can keep Henry VIII's annulment papers locked away from public eyes for four hundred years isn't going to be talking about something that's not even finished. I haven't heard a thing since the day you and I met.''

"No new clues?''

Durant shook his head.

"Craig, I need to be entirely honest with you. I'm working on a new angle.''

"Oh? I have to say I'd have been very surprised if you hadn't been.''

Toni bit her lip and looked into her glass. Durant felt an inward shiver; that was the move Stephanie always made when she felt vulnerable. "I've been debating whether to tell you. I haven't told anyone, not even my editor.''

"Must be something really big if I'm at the top of the list," said Durant with a chuckle. "You dug up your own scrolls now?''

"Be serious, Craig. I've taken another job.''

Durant stared at Toni, meeting her eyes with his. The smile faded from his face, replaced by a look of frank astonishment. "Things must be worse than I thought at your paper.''

"No, it's not like that at all. I just had this idea for getting more information on what's going on with the study."

"And what's leaving the paper got to do with that?"

"I didn't leave it. I took another job in my off-hours. I'm working part time as a secretary."

"In the Vatican?"

"No. I'm working for Dr. Buchmeunster at his villa. Typing correspondence, that sort of thing."

Durant whistled low in appreciation. "Well, that certainly is getting it right from the horse's mouth."

Toni looked perplexed. "Pardon?"

"Oh, sorry. I meant that certainly would be a good place to find out what's really going on. Have you interviewed him? Does he know you're a reporter?"

"No, at least I don't think so. He doesn't act as if he knows." She stood abruptly. "Why don't we go ahead and eat? I'm sure it's cooled enough."

Durant followed Toni to the dining table and sat down opposite her. "Look, are you sure that's the right thing to do? Posing undercover to get a crooked bureaucrat is one thing; infiltrating a scholarly investigation by the Vatican is quite another. Don't you think you ought to tell Buchmeunster who you really are?"

"Of course not. The truth is the truth. We have a right to know that truth, and any tricks I have to play to get it aren't going to change the facts. They're just a faster way of finding out." She handed him a plate heaped high. "I hope you like the lasagna."

Durant pushed some food onto his fork but didn't lift it to his mouth. "Don't you think he has the right to know the truth about you?"

"No! Do you think for one moment that Buchmeunster would say anything about his evaluation if I told him I'm a reporter? I doubt it!'' She slashed viciously across her lasagna, reducing it to mangled strips. ''That makes him an enemy of the truth, and I believe that a journalist can use any means necessary to deal with such a person. He waives any right to find out who I am.''

Durant shrugged and reached for the wine bottle, uncomfortable with her logic but seeing its inevitable conclusion. ''I think I'll have some more Barolo.''

''Pour me some more, too, please.''

With the glasses refilled, Toni took a long sip and began to laugh. ''You know, this *is* a silly discussion. I haven't found out a thing yet except that he owns a winery in Austria.''

''You're kidding. How'd you learn that?''

''That's all I do, business correspondence for the winery. I come in to work in the evenings, he hands me a stack of letters to answer with his handwritten replies. Some writing! No wonder he's good at deciphering ancient languages. Then, he either sits at his desk and reads or goes off somewhere in the house until I'm done. I have yet to see one scrap of information about the manuscripts.''

Durant chuckled again, more at his own concern over Toni's zeal than at her frustration. He relaxed over the meal as she recounted her first meeting with Buchmeunster and her fear before he told her the glass she'd broken in the interview was only a copy. She'd worked hard to perform for Buchmeunster after that, although she'd usually arrive at his villa dead tired from her daytime job. She'd even done some reading on wine production. If she showed enough interest in his business, Buchmeunster might begin to trust her enough to involve her in the evaluation. Of course, she couldn't even hint that she knew about his manuscript work or he'd get suspicious. So for now, she wrote long letters, most of them in German and French, about grapes and the cost of wooden casks. Her eyes shone as she spoke, and she had a way of pursing her lips slightly when there was a point she wanted to ponder. They were soft-looking, and she kept them moist.

Between bites of the second course, *zuppa di verdura*, Toni explained that there were some interesting things about the job. Buchmeunster himself, for one, and his butler, Vittorio, who seemed to vacillate between Gothic brooding and Roman indifference.

"Vittorio hasn't told me yet, Craig, but I'll bet he knows quite a bit about what his master does. I'm going to get something big on this story eventually, you know. Maybe Buchmeunster himself will tell me, or he'll let something slip."

She took both of his hands in hers. They were warm and soft, and she leaned forward just enough to give him a good view of her breasts through the deep V-neck of her blouse. He resisted the urge to take a deep, appreciative breath.

"You know, Craig, you and I could really accomplish a great deal if we worked this story together. I'll share what I get with you, and you can share what you get with me. I'll work Buchmeunster, you work the Vatican and the Israeli government and whomever else you can think of. It'd be a great combination!"

So that's it, thought Durant. Things are a little slow, so until something turns up, get someone else to feed you something to keep the editors happy. And what happens if she does get lucky? Another embargo until she gets her story into print? He smiled and squeezed her hands. "We can talk about that, but I don't want to do it tonight."

"Ah! I'm sorry. I've let my enthusiasm run away again." She stood and led him toward the couch. "We can talk about anything you like. Anything."

Durant felt himself stiffen with anticipation. He looked thoughtfully at the couch and at her, then shook his head. "I don't think we'd better, Toni."

She flinched as if his rejection had been a physical blow. "Well, I . . . ah . . . I thought we'd—"

"It isn't you. It's me. You're beautiful, warm, and I'd love to stay. But if I sit down with you on that couch, I don't think I'm going to want to leave. And I want more from our relationship than that kind of casual encounter. Do you understand?"

Toni smiled again, put her arms around him, and squeezed. "Has anyone told you, Signore Durant, that you're a wonderful romantic? I have another idea. Let's go down to Via Veneto and find a table. We'll watch everyone else watch us."

Chapter Twelve

Late autumn moonlight filtered through the trees, bathing the driveway in a bluish glow as Toni gunned her Maserati up the hill to Buchmeunster's villa. It rolled to a stop and she switched off the ignition, letting the engine choke into silence. She sighed deeply and shook her head at the stone lions by the entrance. You look like I feel, she thought, cold, hard, and waiting to tear someone to pieces. After more than a month, she was beginning to wonder if working for Buchmeunster had been such a good idea after all. She hadn't seen anything but correspondence concerning the family wineries; not once had Buchmeunster even mentioned his work on the manuscript. Her editor was getting impatient with the lackluster, routine pieces she'd been doing every day and so was she. The story would have to break soon, she thought, or it would break her.

When she reached the top of the marble steps, the door flew open before she could knock. Vittorio beckoned her inside, his face flushed and anxious. *"Gràzie a Dio!* You've come. I was afraid tonight you might not."

"I haven't missed work yet. What's wrong?"

Vittorio wrung his hands. "It's *Il Dottore*. He's in a terrible mood, signorina. It started with a letter that came this morning. I don't know—"

"Vittorio!" Buchmeunster's bellow came from the study. "That was Signorina Tedesco's car. Show her in immediately!"

The old butler cringed and dropped his voice to a whisper. "He didn't even want his usual after-dinner brandy. He's not supposed to drink, you know, but he always takes a little something." He glanced over his shoulder toward the study door.

"Vittorio!"

"Si, Dottore!" He turned back to Toni. "You'd better go in."

Buchmeunster paced the floor behind his huge desk, muttering to himself. His hair was unkempt and there were crumbs in his salt-and-pepper beard. He gave Toni a scowl. "Take a letter, signorina!"

Toni nodded and headed for her usual working place—a small desk with a typewriter.

"No! No!" Buchmeunster rushed ahead of her. "Sit over"—he flung his arms in several directions—"over there!"

Toni sat in a corner and watched him shuffle books and papers in a frenzy. He kept his back to her, trying to prevent her from seeing the desktop, but she caught a glimpse of his trembling hands.

She cleared her throat hesitantly. "Excuse me, *Dottore*. Could I have my pad and pencil?"

"What?" Buchmeunster looked at her uncertainly.

"My pad and pencil. I'll need them if you're going to dictate."

133

"Oh! Of course." He began to search the desk frantically and knocked over a stack of books. He grunted but didn't stop to pick them up.

Toni cleared her throat again. "Try the top right-hand drawer."

The old man nearly pulled the drawer out of its tracks. He scurried over and gave her the pad, then went back to the typing desk. Toni felt the beginnings of a laugh, but she hid it with a cough.

"This letter is to be sent to my nephew, Wolfgang. I will give you his address later." He continued to gather the paper debris, still blocking her view. *"Meine Liebste Neffe,"* he began, then stopped and stared at the window across the study. "No, this letter, I think, should be written in French. Wolfgang has no talent for languages, so he would have to work very hard at reading it. On second thought, he would undoubtedly persuade his wife to translate it for him, and I do not need to burden her any further. Let's leave it in German."

Buchmeunster regained his composure as he dictated. After all of his agitation, Toni was surprised to see that it was a routine business letter. There was even a compliment, passed on from a local innkeeper who was pleased with the winery's service in restocking its casks.

As the letter progressed, Buchmeunster reorganized the papers in front of him, thumbing through them and making neat piles. He retrieved the fallen books, stacked them, and eased himself into his chair.

"Now, that comes to the end of our business, Wolfgang." He rubbed his eyes and breathed deeply. "New paragraph. You have betrayed me and your entire family, Wolfgang. You have brought disgrace not only upon yourself, but upon our good name as well."

Buchmeunster stopped abruptly. He rose and walked back to the typing desk, where he rummaged through several drawers in growing irritation. Finally, he found a new ribbon cartridge. He pulled the old one out of the typewriter and shoved the new one in its place. That done, he raised a finger in the air and resumed the letter.

"Your father—my brother—kept women all over Europe. He spent vast sums of money to keep his hedonistic life a secret from your mother and from all the other people who made our vineyards great. Never— not even in his most bacchanalian moments—would he let a hint of scandal reach Gumpoldskirchen. But you have flaunted your sexual preference in public, so that now I even hear about your lovers in Rome in a letter from a tongue-wagging innkeeper."

Toni raced to keep up with the man's angry words. His voice rose to a near shout, and he brandished the discarded cartridge like a club.

"Unless you cease this behavior immediately, I shall take steps to have you removed from any management responsibilities. I shall also disinherit you and make certain everyone else in this family does the same!" He slammed the cartridge down on the desk.

Toni jumped. There was a long silence before she asked, "Is that all?"

"Is that not enough?!" Buchmeunster gathered the stacks of papers and books into one large bundle and tucked it under his arm, with the cartridge on top. "I want that to go out in the morning mail. You may leave when you have typed it." He crossed the room and fished a set of keys from a pocket. "I trust that I have your strictest confidence in this matter, signorina. I should not like to have my family's indiscretions provide grist for the *klatsch* mill at the university."

"Of course, sir."

"Good."

Toni threaded a page into the typewriter but watched Buchmeunster out of the corner of her eye. He reached into the bookshelves and moved several volumes to expose a wall-mounted lock. He inserted a key, and an eight-foot span of the shelving began to swing out into the room. Toni started to type furiously, hoping Buchmeunster might offer some explanation, but he paid her no further attention. When the shelves had swung out to a sixty-degree angle, she could see there was another room behind them. He slipped through the opening, leaving the keys dangling in the lock.

Toni had to stop three times for errors. She forced herself to slow down, both for accuracy and because it let her pay more attention to what Buchmeunster was doing. She couldn't tell from her chair, and she resisted the urge to stop typing and walk over for a peek into the other room. She tried to listen through the noise of her typing for the sound of any activity.

"Dottore! Dottore!" Vittorio's frantic voice shattered her concentration. The servant banged on the study door. "I must talk with you!"

There was no reaction from Buchmeunster. Vittorio raised his voice higher and hammered the door again. Toni pulled it open and narrowly missed getting the old man's fist in her face as he started another barrage.

"Dio santo!" he wailed. "Where is *Il Dottore?"*

Toni pointed toward the open bookshelves and started to explain, but Buchmeunster emerged before she could speak.

"Vittorio! You have a good reason for this, I hope?" He stood imperiously by the wall entrance, waiting for his answer.

"Forgive me, *Dottore.* I know you didn't want to be disturbed, but"—he wrung his hands and looked at Toni as though she might be able to say the words for him—"there is a broken pipe on the third floor. It's flooding, and I don't know how to turn off the water!"

"Gott in Himmel!" Buchmeunster stormed out of the study with Vittorio in his wake.

Toni closed the door behind them and leaned against it, feeling the adrenaline pound through her. She dashed back to the typewriter, ejected the new ribbon, and rushed with it into the hidden room.

A desk was built into one wall, and it held a fluorescent work lamp that was the only illumination for the room. Steel file cabinets lined two other walls, and in the dim light she could see the elliptical faces of lock cylinders set into each one.

She crossed to the first cabinet and tried the lock, but it had been pushed in to latch it shut. She tried the next. It was locked. She moved along the row, gaining speed as she dragged her fingers across the locks to check them. The next five were latched. She was driven by the feeling that Buchmeunster's manuscript work was somewhere in the files, but she was consumed by the fear that he'd return at any moment. *Hurry* . . . She was almost running. Twelve more cabinets, all locked.

Toni tripped! Pain ripped through her leg, forcing tears to her eyes and smothering her with nausea. Her ankle! She rubbed it with one hand and cradled her head in her arm. It took several deep breaths to clear the haze from her mind.

The image of Buchmeunster finding her in this room grew more vivid. If he caught her, she'd probably be arrested. *Back into the study, now!* She tried to stand, but her shoe straps cut into the ankle, already swelling black and blue. She unbuckled the shoes and dangled them on her arm like oversized charms as she tried to put some weight on the injured foot. It didn't seem broken, at least; that was something. She bit her lip and grabbed the handle of a file drawer to pull herself up. Pain washed over her again, and she slapped her hands on top of the cabinet to keep from falling. Her fingers brushed the lock.

It was open!

Toni jerked away as if she'd stepped on a cobra. Gingerly, she tugged the top drawer open. There, in front, lay another cartridge for the typewriter. She took it out and looked for the one she'd brought in. Where was it?

Damn! It had fallen on the floor when she tripped. Agonizingly, she lowered herself into a squat, fighting back another wave of nausea. She reached for the cartridge, but it was too far away. She stretched and tried again. Still short of the mark.

Desperate, she took one of her shoes and swatted at the cartridge. On her second swing, she connected. It

138

came skittering toward her, and she picked it up. She inched back up to a standing position, put that cartridge in the drawer where the other had been, and closed it, leaving it unlocked.

Toni hopped along the wall and out into the study, clutching the cartridge she'd taken from the cabinet. She shoved it and the shoes into her purse.

When she got back to the typewriter, her ankle had become a large purple mass. She forced herself to ignore its throbbing and switched the machine back on, but it didn't have a ribbon. Frantic, she hunted through the desk until she found another. She crammed it into the machine.

Ten minutes later, she was three quarters of the way through the letter. Buchmeunster hadn't come back. His keys still dangled in the lock across the room.

How much longer? Five more minutes would do.

She searched the drawers again: typing paper in the top left, paper clips and staples in the center, the right empty. Further back in that one, under a couple of old dividers, she found a cold, hard ball. It was a dirty lump of typewriter cleaner. Toni squeezed the clay in her palm, but it barely gave. She worked it until her fingers turned red, then white from the effort. Finally, it softened.

The room whirled when Toni stood, but after another deep breath, it stopped. With a quick glance at the study door, she made her way painfully to the bookshelf.

Buchmeunster's key wouldn't budge. She would have to turn it, let the bookshelves close again, then remove it. Her eyes darted back to the door. She gave the key a twist and pulled it out as the entrance began to whine shut.

The sound of distant voices came to her, getting closer. Quickly, she pressed the key hard into the clay, first one side, then the other. The voices grew louder. She slipped the clay into her pocket and put the key in the lock. The bookshelves reversed direction.

They were inches from being fully spread when Buchmeunster opened the study door. Toni gasped, but before he could see the moving wall, he turned back to his servant. "Vittorio, you will please be certain that you wake me an hour early tomorrow."

The wall reached the end of its travel. Toni relaxed until she realized that she was standing next to the lock. She took two steps sideways as Buchmeunster entered the room.

He gave her a puzzled stare. "Signorina Tedesco, is there something wrong? You have finished the letter?"

"Not quite. I was looking for a German dictionary. Some of the words you used tonight aren't in my vocabulary. I'm sorry." She shrugged. "I thought I saw one over here the other day."

"I moved it. Here you are." He handed her the book and disappeared behind the shelves.

Toni rested against the wall and closed her eyes to summon strength, telling herself that it was almost over. She hopped from chair to chair back to the typewriter and sat down to finish the letter.

Buchmeunster reappeared a few minutes later, just as Toni had finished addressing the envelope. She picked up her purse and hobbled to his desk, where he stood preoccupied with the rest of the day's mail. "I hope the damage upstairs wasn't severe, *Dottore.*"

"Not so good, I am afraid. There was some irreparable damage to the rugs and some pieces. But the interesting items escaped." He stopped, seeing her bare feet for the first time. "What has happened to your shoes? And why are you hopping about?"

Toni smiled weakly. "Oh, I twisted my ankle earlier today. Perhaps I should have called in sick, but coming here means such a great deal to me. I'll see you tomorrow."

Buchmeunster nodded. *"Auf Weidersehen."*

Toni's street was deserted by the time she got there. Her ankle was a black and purple mass, and that was her accelerator foot. There'd been a couple of false starts at Buchmeunster's villa until she managed to get the Maserati rolling fast enough down the long driveway to stick it into third gear. From there, she could maintain road speed without having to use both feet to shift. Fortunately, the only traffic light she'd caught was near Piazzale Flaminio. There hadn't been anyone in sight, so she'd lurched on through it.

Parking was another matter. The closest comfortable-looking space was a block up from her apartment, on the *piazza*. She'd never be able to walk that far. There had to be something nearer.

Just across from her building, there was a narrow spot she might get into with some luck. She pointed the rear of the car in that general direction and gave the accelerator a gentle tap.

Pain exploded through her leg, twisting into her thigh. The Maserati bounced off the curb.

Toni closed her eyes, willing herself not to vomit. She shifted and played the clutch, letting the high idle pull her out into the street.

Another shift. She took a deep breath and nudged the gas again, feeling her ankle sear from the pressure on the pedal. She hit the car in front and stalled the Maserati's engine.

It restarted grudgingly and she made another attempt. She bounced off the car to the rear this time, setting off another wave of agony in her foot.

She was at an angle, halfway in the street, but there was no way she'd do any better tonight. Given the usual efficiency of the *Vigili,* the car wouldn't be hauled away before noon, anyway.

Toni grabbed her handbag, glad for the reassuring bulk of the ribbon cartridge inside. She reached across the seat for her shoes, but the pain held her back. She gave up and slid gingerly out of the car, trying to keep most of the weight on her good foot.

"Hey, *cara!*"

She whirled toward the voice.

He was rough-looking and perhaps twenty-four or twenty-five. "Give me the keys!" He gave her exposed thighs a long look and came toward her.

She checked her building across the street. No escape there; the lobby was dark, almost certainly locked.

He was nearly at the car. "Come on, the keys! You take me for a ride, eh?" He moved closer and reached for her purse.

Toni tried to sink back into the Maserati, but he jerked open the door.

"You know, I have a better idea." The stench of his breath turned her stomach. "We'll go up to your apartment. We'll have a little party."

"You son of a bitch!" She came at him, wielding the Gucci bag like a mace. It connected with his head, and he reeled back a step.

"No party, eh? Then how about a kiss?" He grabbed for the purse, but Toni wouldn't give it up. The catch gave way, dumping her notebook and Buchmeunster's ribbon cartridge noisily onto the pavement.

His eyes were drawn to the sound for no more than a heartbeat.

He turned back to see Toni's automatic leveled at his face.

"I'll give you a kiss, you bastard!"

"Please . . ." His arms fell to his sides and he retreated slowly. "Please, I didn't mean—"

"Run! Run, you bastard!" She gestured up the street with the muzzle. "One . . . Two . . . Three . . . Four . . . I'm shooting when I reach ten. Five . . . Six . . ."

The thug spun and ran into the darkness. His footsteps died away as she finished the count.

Toni collapsed against the car and sank to the ground as the pain in her ankle returned.

She put the cartridge and the notebook back in her purse and hobbled across to her building.

In her apartment, Toni paused for a quick inventory in the mirror. There were deep circles around her eyes, her makeup was streaked, and her long auburn hair was everywhere. She shook her head and sighed.

Toni poured herself a half glass of scotch and collapsed onto the couch. Yesterday's newspaper was still there, open to her story, which had been buried on page three without her by-line. "No more second-rate scandals for me!" She tossed it aside and laughed, still shaky from her encounter on the street. "From now on, every front page in Europe!"

She gave the cartridge a close look, turning it slowly in her hands. It seemed to be a solid block, except where the ribbon film passed in and out. She twisted it, but the cartridge wouldn't give.

There was a dimple in one corner, and Toni dug at it with a nail file. The file barely scratched the plastic before it bent in half.

"*Damn!*" She pitched the file into a corner and limped into the kitchen. There had to be something better. Finally, she found a flat-bladed screwdriver. Back at the couch, she jammed it into a groove on the cartridge and whacked it with her hand. The blade wedged the crack open a bit, but the cartridge was still in one piece.

Toni laid a heavy book on top of the cartridge for ballast, stuck the screwdriver against the plastic seam, and hammered it with her fist. The cartridge shattered, and the ribbon wound off onto the floor.

"Thank God," Toni muttered as she rolled it back up. The carbon film turned her fingers black.

The ribbon had an endless series of transparent impressions where the typewriter had struck. She began to transcribe them into a notebook, setting them out in groups of five—five groups across the page.

After three quarters of an hour, there were six pages filled with jumble, and she went back through them, trying to some clear place to begin.

2JUNE .SCRO LLWEL LPRES SERVED

The date was simple. She blocked off the words next to it one by one.

2 June. Scroll well preserved.

She'd been right! These were Buchmeunster's notes on the manuscript!

Toni scanned through the pages. How much had he managed to translate? There were endless dates and more of Buchmeunster's comments on the condition of the scroll.

THEWS CHRON NICLE SOFTH
RISEN JESUS THATT ELLOF THECH
IEFPR IESTS WHOSA IDTEL LPEOP
LEHIS DISCI PLESC AMEBY NIGHT
ANDST OLEHI MAWAY WHILE WEWER
EASLE EP.

Toni underscored the name so boldly that the point of her pencil snapped. She picked up another and sorted the letters until words emerged. It was a quotation from Matthew's account of the Gospel:

Tell people his disciples came by night and stole him away while we were asleep.

Toni skimmed on through the pages until she came to the end. There was a current date, apparently for Buchmeunster's latest entry. She broke it out easily.

145

Were the chief priests right? Could two men have rolled the stone away? How could they have managed to fool his friends?

Toni's hands shook. "My God!" she whispered. She took the pencil and started to work backward from Buchmeunster's questions.

There was another name: Nicodemus.

It was three-thirty A.M. by Durant's alarm clock when the telephone jarred him awake.

"Craig? It's me, Toni."

"What?" Durant yawned, trying to shake the feeling that this was a very strange but dull dream.

"Wake up, Craig! I'm onto something important."

"I was doing something important before you called."

"You have to wake up and listen to me!"

"What? Why are you doing this to me?"

"Listen. I finally have some information from Buchmeunster. I've got a copy of one of his memos. It's about the manuscript, I'm sure of it."

"How'd you get it?" Durant sat up in bed, his misgivings about Toni's methods suddenly rekindled. "Did he give it to you?"

"Never mind that. He's been working steadily on it. The scroll seems to be in excellent condition."

"That's nice." He looked longingly at his pillow. "Any indication of what he's doing with it?"

"No, not really. There are some notes on Nicodemus. I looked him up. He's the Pharisee who secretly visited Christ. Buchmeunster's apparently been wondering if it was ideologically possible for Nicodemus to have joined the Essene sect.''

''Yeah, Muller told me about them. They wrote the Dead Sea Scrolls.'' He yawned again and felt the urge to roll over and let Toni talk until her voice faded into his dreams. ''Toni, this is all very interesting, but I'm not much on history lessons at this time of the morning. Does Buchmeunster have any idea what the manuscript is about?''

''Well, ah . . . no.'' Toni paused, and Durant nearly hung up. ''It's really a pretty vague memo, Craig. There's not even a hint.''

Chapter Thirteen

Lightning flashed to the east of the city, casting an eerie silhouette of the old tower of Santa Maria in Trastevere. A fitful breeze warned of the coming storm. The young woman impulsively pulled a scarf from around her neck and tied it over her blond hair as the first scattered drops hit the pavement. She hurried past the old church, hoping to hail a taxi before the rain drove the late diners from the outdoor tables at Ristorante Sabatini across the *piazza*.

As the rain began to fall harder, the woman gave up trying to force her aching feet to walk quickly in high heels. She paused to snatch off the shoes, then ran for the taxi stand around the corner. The taillights of the last cab disappeared into the downpour as she got there. She slumped against a peeling wall, breathless and defeated.

"*Perdono,* signorina," said a deep voice close by. Startled to find that she wasn't alone, the woman turned to see a tall, greying man step out of the darkened recess of a nearby doorway. He shielded his light sports jacket with a large umbrella.

"Please don't be alarmed," he said with a gentle

smile. "I thought perhaps you might like to share my refuge for a moment until it lets up a little."

"*Gràzie,* signore." She wiped a strand of dripping hair out of her face and mustered a grateful smile of her own. "I was trying to get a taxi, but I'm afraid I got here too late." She shivered as the dampness worked its way in.

The man moved his umbrella so it protected them both. "I was trying to do that myself, but . . . no luck." He handed the umbrella to the girl, then draped his jacket over her shoulders. "Forgive my taking the liberty, but you seem to have a chill. Why don't you let me get you a cab, and you can stay back out of the rain while I do that?"

She hesitated, unsure of his motives, but the reassurance in his smile convinced her. He led her to the shelter of the doorway, then stepped back out into the rain and loudly hailed a yellow Fiat as it splashed by. He opened the door and came back to escort her with the umbrella. "Your coach, signorina."

The girl moved quickly to the car and nodded her thanks. "You're welcome to share the ride, signore. It may be a while before another comes along."

The man looked around at the street, now completely empty, and glanced at his watch. "I'd really appreciate that. *Gràzie.*"

They drove slowly through the Trastevere district, its usual Saturday night clamor now drowned by the storm. The man patted his chest absently for a moment, then turned apologetically. "*Scusi.* I'm afraid you have my cigarettes. Would you? The inside left pocket." She pulled a slim silver case from his jacket. He lit cigarettes for them both and exhaled a tired

149

cloud. "Is it always like this in Rome? It seems to rain every time I come here."

She pulled the coat closer around her shoulders and shook her head at the rivulets forming on the taxi window. "Lately, it seems that way, signore. But at least I've never gotten caught in it on the way home from work before. Are you visiting or here on business?"

"A little of both, actually. I have interests south of here, but I prefer to stay in Rome when I come to check on them. Sometimes I stay for a few weeks, if I can. I travel frequently, though, so it's not easy to find the time anymore."

The girl's face brightened. "What do you do?"

"International business relations, acquisitions, mergers, that sort of thing. Sounds interesting, but it's rather dull, except for the places I visit. I don't have a family, so the travelling isn't a problem. And you?"

"I manage a *bottega*. We sell purses made in Yugoslavia to Frenchmen and Japanese who think they're buying Italian."

"Ah, so you're international, too." He laughed with a warmth that crinkled the deep lines around his vivid blue eyes. "But does it always keep you out this late? It's already Sunday."

"We stay open Saturdays to catch the tourists when they come to take in the wild nightlife in Trastevere. I live alone, so . . ." Her voice trailed off into a shrug.

"You must enjoy your job. How else could you be so lovely after working all day and half the night?"

Now it was her turn to laugh as she wiped back another lock of drenched hair. "I go to mass on Saturday mornings. It gives me strength to run through the rain."

He chuckled. "You know, here we are talking about my life and yours, and I haven't even found out who you are. I am Julio Cagliari."

She took his outstretched hand. *"Piacere,* Signore Cagliari. Francesca Tuminello."

"Prego, call me Julio."

The cab rolled to a stop outside a fading apartment building on Via Monterone. Cagliari sheltered Francesca to the entryway with his umbrella, then reached to help her shed his jacket.

"Please wait." She stopped his hand with hers and pressed it to her shoulder. "You've been so kind, getting me this cab, coming so far out of your way. I thought perhaps . . ." She smiled uncertainly. "Would you like a drink or maybe some *cappuccino* to drive out the damp before you go?"

"I'd be honored, but not if it's going to cause any trouble for you. You certainly don't have to—"

Francesca cut him off with a squeeze of her hand. "I'd like you to come up."

She had a small apartment, four floors up. Francesca poured two brandies, settled Cagliari onto the couch, and went to change. His eyes strayed while he waited, coming to rest on a photo of a younger Francesca in a wedding gown, posing with a darkly handsome groom. Cagliari moved until he could see into the other room and watch the girl's wet clothing come over the screen. She emerged a few moments later in a blue dressing gown, her hair pulled up tightly in a bun. She blushed when she saw where Cagliari was sitting, then came over to him.

"I want you to understand, Julio. I'm not the sort of woman who does this." She looked nervously down at her brandy. "I don't bring strange men up here. It's just that you—"

Cagliari put a finger to her lips. He pulled the girl to him and held her. "Someone has hurt you, and that hurt has not yet gone away, has it?"

Francesca drew back, startled, tears welling up. *"Mio Dio!* How could you know what I feel?" She turned away, weeping and shaking her head. "I'm making such a mess of this. I'm so sorry. Please go."

Cagliari cradled the girl's chin in his hand and pulled her gently around to face him. "Forgive me. I didn't mean to upset you, *cara.* But it took no imagination to see what you've been through." He nodded toward the wedding portrait. "It's in your eyes, even in how you live. You loved a young man and married him. At first, it was ecstasy, but then, as young men so often do, he found other pursuits, yes? For a while, you forgave, you tolerated, anything to keep him. But he was gone more and more until you couldn't ignore it any longer. Finally, memories and hope weren't enough, and you sought comfort from someone else. Your husband couldn't accept that, so he divorced you. Since then, you've tried to fill his place with others, but they've all been shallow men, empty of any real love. You still grieve over losing him, don't you?"

"Yes," said Francesca softly, losing her doubts in the blue depths of Cagliari's eyes. "You understand so much, as though you've known me for years. But you must think me terrible to grasp at you like this, someone I've hardly even met. I don't even know why I did it. I—"

Cagliari took her face in both hands. *"Capisco.* You are lonely. So am I."

152

Their kiss was deep and eager. Francesca pressed against him, her desire rising quickly after long restraint. Cagliari loosened the sash of her gown and caressed her breasts softly as he brushed his lips gently on her neck. Francesca fumbled at the buttons of Cagliari's shirt as they kissed again. Then, with her gown fully open, she moved against his bared chest. He stroked her hardening nipples, then laid her back gently on the couch and explored her flesh with his mouth, tracing a path to the white barrier below her navel. Cagliari reached inside the silk and softly massaged its secret prize. Francesca began to moan, an almost animallike sound that increased as he tugged her panties off and let his lips continue their odyssey.

"Julio," she whispered, demanding. "Now."

"Yes," Cagliari breathed. "Now." He reached for his jacket pocket and pulled out a small brown envelope. He emptied it into his hand and held the contents up for her to see. "First, *cara*, for me. It will be good, I promise."

The girl's eyes widened as she stared first at the small yellow fruit, then at Cagliari's face. The smile was still there, but the understanding was gone from his gaze, replaced by something much colder. She moaned again, arching her back as she reached for him. "No . . . Just take me. Please."

Cagliari thrust the fruit in front of her mouth, almost touching her lips. "You must eat this first. I insist. It will take only an instant, then I will love you as that man never did."

Fear crossed Francesca's face, shoving desire aside. "No! What do you want? Why are you doing this?" She tried to push him away and get off the couch, but he held her down. She heard the metallic click of a knife sliding open, then felt its chill against her throat.

"Listen, *puttana!*" Cagliari hissed. "You will take a bite or I will slash your throat here and now, and you will die most painfully. *Capisci?*"

The girl nodded slowly as tears began to roll down her cheeks. She opened her mouth and gingerly placed her teeth around a tiny area of the fruit's skin.

"A big bite, *puttana.*" He pressed the knife point, drawing a small drop of blood from the skin of the girl's neck.

Francesca opened her mouth wider, taking half of the fruit in her mouth.

"Chew it!" The blade pressed harder.

She sobbed and did so.

Cagliari's eyes were frozen with hate. "Now swallow," he said softly.

Francesca gulped twice, then began to thrash on the couch and grabbed at her chest and throat. In seconds, she was still, her eyes blankly peering upward.

Cagliari held the knife up to the light and wiped it clean. Then he pulled the dead girl's legs apart and bent with the blade over her body.

Chapter Fourteen

The video recorder strap bit into Rivette's shoulder as he huffed down the sidewalk toward the entrance to Rome's zoo, the Giardino Zoologico. The parking area had been full, so he'd left the Fiat by the Galleria Borghese at the southern end of the park. It was warm for mid-December, and when Rivette came to the gate, he set the recorder down to mop his forehead with a bright red kerchief and check with his watch. Nearly three. He'd be on time.

He pushed through a ring of onlookers around a small corral, trying to avoid bashing into any of the children who stood around the fence. There was a post that would brace his shots, but a tiny red-braided girl sitting next to it started to cry when he looked her way. Her mother, also a redhead and about twenty years older, tried to comfort the child, but the cries only grew louder. She sighed helplessly and rocked the girl back and forth.

Rivette set down his equipment and slapped a hand across his face, hiding it all. Startled, the child stopped. Slowly, he uncovered one eye and wiggled a bushy brow. She began to giggle. He drew the hand down and pulled his face into a rubbery scowl. More giggles. The hand went back up, then off again, and he flashed her a broad grin. The little girl laughed, and her mother returned Rivette's smile.

He switched on his camera and rolled the videotape. A small boy in a long robe and a cotton beard came into the corral, leading a burro. There was a young girl on its back, clothed in flowing white. A boys choir off to one side began to sing as the couple made their way around the fence. They stopped just short of the one complete circuit, where a priest and two acolytes stood waiting.

The priest spoke about the donkey that carried Mary to Bethlehem. Then, he sprinkled holy water on the burro and everyone else within reach. He spread his arms in benediction, and the burro lost its patience and urinated on his shoes, to the joy of the watching children.

When the ceremony was over, Rivette walked back across the grounds and ducked into the shade of the herpetarium for a moment's rest. A large constrictor hung from a tree branch inside its glass cage, testing the air with its tongue and eyeing Rivette as he peered in. He shuddered and walked on until he came to a snake that was throwing scoops of sand up over its back. He watched, fascinated, as it slowly buried itself.

"Cerastes Cornutus," said a voice behind him. "One of the deadliest of the vipers. If you watch, you'll see him disappear completely. But he's there, waiting to kill when he hungers again."

A thin-faced man in a black beret—the man who'd disturbed his eavesdropping on Lohengrin—came up to the cage. His lips were set in a tight line, and his grey eyes made no effort to hide their dislike. "I haven't seen you at the opera lately, Francois. You really should come more often."

"I've been busy."

"So we've heard. But you must keep in touch, you know. It makes life so much more difficult if I have to call your office to find out where you are."

Rivette gave him an apprehensive glare.

The thin man held up a hand. "Don't worry, discreet as always. But that's how we found you here." He watched the snake, which had buried itself completely except for its eyes. "Do you know what the Bedouins call this snake, Francois? *Il mut il dellaan*—the shadowy death. An appropriate name for so treacherous a creature, eh? Coincidentally, our sources tell us that's the same name certain groups in the Mideast have given Abdul Sayeb." He turned back to Rivette. "Have you found him?"

Rivette breathed deeply, trying to control the combination of distaste for his interrogator and his frustration at the question. "No. But I have been working very hard at it. There's not a trace."

"We know he is here in Rome." The thin man fixed him with a hard stare. "There's a great deal of concern about Sayeb's possible mission here. He must be found soon, and you'll have to do it."

"But you've never even given me a description!" Rivette felt his anger rising.

"If the Holy See becomes unexpectedly vacant again, do you want to be the one to explain how you let it happen? Find him! Now! Before someone steps on the snake." He rapped sharply on the cage, and the buried viper rocketed out of its hiding place and struck at the glass.

The Volvo sedan wheeled smoothly through the early evening traffic, coasting past the twin churches of Santa Maria del Popolo and through the stone portal ahead onto Via Flaminia.

"Oh boy, Grampin!" Justin Newcombe bounced on Sandy's lap, forcing her to tighten her arms around him. "A circus!"

"Yep. With lions, tigers, and maybe a few unicorns." Phil Duffy shot a wink at his daughter, who rolled her eyes toward the roof. They'd been planning this for a month, and Duffy's tales had fed his grandson's excitement until Sandy was near the breaking point.

"Dad, really."

"Oh, come on, Sandy! Just because you've never seen one. You just didn't go to the right circuses."

"I don't thi—"

Duffy swerved sharply as an aging Peugot wagon cut sharply into the lane, blasting its horn. Panic flashed across his face but faded when the wagon accelerated and changed lanes again, honking at its next victim. He cinched the shoulder harness a little tighter against his paunch. "Drunken idiots!"

"What's wrong, Mommy?" Justin looked anxiously at Sandy. She took a deep breath, trying to force the shakes out of her voice before she spoke. "Nothing, sweetheart. Just another crazy driver."

Duffy laughed. "Did you see the way I dodged 'em, Justin? Learned that from when I was a cowboy.

Wasn't much older than you, come to think of it. Handling this car is just like my horse. No sweat, boy."

Justin smiled. "No sweat, Grampin!" He started to bounce on his mother's lap again.

"Dad, I really wonder if this is a good idea. You know, going out alone like this."

Duffy ran a hand through his thick white hair. "Aw, you worry too much, just like your mother. For once, I'd like to be Justin's grandpa and nothing else, just for tonight. You can't wear the striped trousers all the time, you know? I checked it out. We'll be perfectly safe."

Sandy nodded and smiled, although she wasn't entirely convinced. Still, this was the happiest Duffy had been since her mother's death eight months earlier. She sighed with resignation and shifted Justin on her lap.

"Say, listen, Justin." Duffy touched his bulbous nose and leaned toward the boy. "Did I ever tell you how I got this?"

Justin shrieked with glee.

"Why, I was in a circus once. Ran away with my friend Sweeney to find our fortunes."

"Were you a clown, Grampin?"

"Wanted to be, that's for sure. But you have to break into that, you know. Sweeney and me, we traveled around the country with that circus putting up the Big Top. They used to have tents, you know, big, huge things, big as the Coliseum your mama took you to see.

The boy's eyes grew wide. Sandy turned her face toward the window to stifle a laugh.

"Why, they'd spread that canvas out like a giant

pancake. We'd drive stakes all around it with hammers the size of baseball bats. Then I'd jump on my elephant and make her pull a long rope to raise it up."

Justin's mouth fell open. *"Your* elephant?"

Duffy nodded. "You bet. She'd rear up on her hind legs and make terrible noises and try to throw me off, but she never could. I'd make her pull that tent until it was like a great big umbrella. You could put St. Peter's in it." Duffy slowed and turned off at the exit for the Olympic Stadium.

"What was her name, Grampin?"

"Whose name?"

"The elephant."

"Oh, yes. The elephant. Why . . . ah . . . Mabel."

"Mabel," Justin repeated. "That's a funny name for an elephant."

Duffy nodded, glad he was being waved into a parking place.

Sandy took her father's arm and let Justin walk slightly ahead. "I heard a little different story from Grandpa Duffy. Wasn't that when you and Sweeney ran away and wound up having to clean out the lions' cages? Grandpa said you came home reeking and didn't mention running away again for at least six months." She gave him a squeeze.

Duffy laughed gently. "I'm saving that for when Justin's old enough to appreciate the deep philosophy behind it."

Their seats were high up in the second level. The boy scrambled up the steep incline, leaving his mother and grandfather behind as they puffed along. Once they reached the seats, Duffy took care to point out all the aerial equipment and nets that had been rigged for the

160

performance. Justin's attention was riveted, but after a few minutes, he began to squirm in his seat.

"Justin, honey, do you need to go to the bathroom before the circus starts?" Sandy asked.

"No, Mommy." The boy's grimace telegraphed a different, more urgent message.

She took him by the arm. "Come on. We'll be right back." Halfway down the steps, the boy shook loose from her grasp, wanting to walk without holding his mother's hand. When they reached the bottom, he slipped away. She caught a glimpse of him, an elf dodging through the onrush of giants, as he disappeared toward a concession stand.

"Justin! Come back here!" she yelled, not caring who heard her irritation. "I'm not putting up with this! Justin!!" She walked in the direction the boy had taken, sweeping her vision below the beltline of the crush around her. Any second now, up there past the next group, she would find him, laughing at his mother. "Justin!!"

No sign of him. He was hiding. "Okay, Justin! I've had it." Anger was coming on and she fought it, not wanting to ruin the evening. "Come back here!"

She listened, hoping to hear his small voice carrying over the clamor from the concession stand.

Nothing.

There were steps ahead, and Sandy mounted them for a better view. She searched the crowd, but Justin was nowhere to be seen. Anxiety caught hold and spread like a flash fire inside her.

The band began to play. She found the restrooms and called out.

"Justin! Justin! Come out of there. The show's about to start. Grampin will be worried!"

There was no sound from inside.

"I mean it. I'm going to be very angry with you if you don't come out right now!"

Spectators were rushing to their seats and she pushed through them, desperately seeking any sign of the boy. "Justin! "JUSS—TINN!!"

A fanfare blasted overhead, but there was only silence from the restrooms.

Sandy's anxiety fused into panic. She whirled to run for help.

A hand smelling of greasepaint clamped over her mouth from behind and dragged her violently into a dark alcove. She struggled to break free, but her assailant shoved her against the concrete wall and pinned her with his own weight. The crowd cheered as a bouncy circus march floated down from the stands, heightening Sandy's disbelief at what was happening.

In the half-light, a painted clown face hovered in front of her. The reek of onions on his breath made her gag.

The clown's voice rasped with malice. "If I remove my hand, you will not scream." He tightened the grip on her mouth for emphasis. "Say nothing. Just nod."

She did, tears blurring her vision as she tried not to think of what was going to happen.

He slipped the hand down slowly and looked her over, up and down, for what seemed to be an eternity. She prayed that he would fade away like a bad dream. When he didn't, she prayed that he'd get on with whatever he had in mind and be done with it.

The man's face and neck had been greased white.

The red mouth, outlined in black, mocked her terror with a frozen grin. A baseball cap hid the top of his oversized orange eyes.

"We have Justin," he finally said.

Sandy gasped. His hand flashed, slapping her hard across the mouth. Pain shot through her body as her head slammed against the concrete wall.

"Damn you!" the clown hissed. "I told you to keep quiet. Not a word! *Capite?*"

She wept openly, just short of sobbing, as she nodded slowly. She bit her lip and tried to force back the scream that welled up inside. Her boy's life might depend on that.

"That's much better. Now, listen carefully if you ever want to see your son alive again."

Chapter Fifteen

Toni hefted a large zucchini and glanced at the grey-haired woman who tended the stall. The vendor's chubby face lit up when she felt a sale in the wind. *"Delizioso,* signorina." She nodded with an urgency that made her wattles shake. "From Sardinia just this morning. Sweet as honey."

Toni turned the squash slowly in her hand and let the firm set of her mouth do the bargaining. The vegetable woman sensed the tide turning against her and changed her approach. She tapped the sign in the squash bin and leaned toward Toni as she spoke in a lower voice. "This price is a mistake. I told my son to fix it, but—" She shrugged. "I'll give you two for that price."

"Bene!" Tone smiled as she put the zucchini into her string shopping bag and picked another. She handed the vendor a crumpled bill and took Durant's arm, and they wandered on through the farmers' market. Durant was intrigued by the rainbow of produce spread out in cases and baskets, but he was relieved when Toni decided not to browse through the fish counters. They'd managed to stay upwind of them so far.

Durant reached for her bag. "Here, let me carry that."

"You don't have to bother. I'm used to shopping like this."

"Please, I insist. Besides, it'll give me a place to carry my *panettone.*" He held up a small box of the holiday bread.

Toni's laugh had warmth, like the carols chiming from a church in the distance. "Okay. But only because of the *panettone.*"

As they walked on through the throng of late-afternoon shoppers, Durant found that his feelings for Toni were more than physical attraction and curiosity. She was a friend, she was a sympathetic colleague, and she was also becoming someone he wanted to be with every day, even if only for a few minutes. Toni filled a need Durant hadn't known he could still feel.

The only other person who'd ever touched him that way was Stephanie. When she'd left his life, that part of him, that vulnerability, had closed up and shriveled like a jagged scar. They'd been building, so he'd thought, toward a life together, until he'd mentioned marriage. It hurt down to his soul when Stephanie had skipped out without a trace, finally choosing her television career instead. Durant wasn't sure he wanted to risk that kind of pain again.

"So, Toni. How are things with your manuscript story?"

She shook her head slowly. "Not too well. I talked with my editor about what I'd found out. I told him that Nicodemus's name had turned up, and that the scroll may have been written by Nicodemus himself. That certainly would sell quite a few papers in this

165

town. He's intrigued, but he doesn't think I have enough to go to press."

"Can't say I disagree, although that's certainly a story I wouldn't mind breaking myself. A man who knew Christ certainly might tell us a lot we don't know. But it does sound like a lot of speculation at this point."

"It's *not* speculation! I've seen Buchmeunster's memo! Why else would he ask for all that information?"

"Why don't you ask him?"

Toni shot Durant a scathing look. "For someone I let carry my shopping bag, you're not very nice."

"Peace. Only joking."

"I went to a great deal of trouble to get that memo. That kind of thing isn't just left lying around, you know. I think it'll turn out to be the key to the story."

Durant stopped and pulled her around to face him. "Toni. Where *did* you get that memo?"

"You know better than that. Do I ask you for your sources?"

"No. Did your source ask for protection?"

Toni pulled away. "Well . . ."

"Did you *have* a source for this memo? Did someone leak it to you?"

"Look, I don't have to tell you this." Her face reddened.

Durant grabbed her hand and pulled her close again. "Listen, Toni. I care deeply about what happens to you. I'm no authority on Italian law, but it seems to me that there's a fundamental difference between investigative reporting and theft. For God's sake, what have you been doing?"

Her denial was sharp. "Nothing that anyone else

who's so close to cracking this story wouldn't do. And I'm not in any trouble, so stop worrying!''

Durant let go of her and sighed. ''Okay. I'm sorry, but I am worried, and you can't keep me from doing that. Just be careful.''

Toni smiled and stroked his cheek. ''Yes, I can see that you are. You're a sweet man, Craig Durant.''

They walked on again until they came to a stall filled with porcelain miniatures. Durant found a small reproduction of Michaelangelo's ''David'' and bought it. ''For my mother,'' he told Toni. ''Too bad she won't get it in time for Christmas. Guess it'll be for her birthday. Have you shopped for your parents yet?''

Toni's face clouded. ''I'm not sending gifts this year.'' There was a note of bitterness in her voice. She looked at her watch anxiously. ''Oh, Craig, it's later than I thought. I've got to get back to the office. Call me tomorrow, okay?'' She gave him a peck on the cheek and squeezed his hand, then headed off into the crowd.

Durant watched her go, then realized he still had her shopping bag. He called after her, but she was gone. With a shake of his head, Durant handed his figurine back to the vendor to be wrapped, wondering all the while if he'd ever know what hurt Toni kept inside, in the secret self she guarded from the world's prying.

Mike Sibille tapped his pipe idly on the desk and nodded at the voice on the other end of his telephone. ''Yes, Inspector Barzini. I understand your need for discretion. But we're interested in following your investigation. You've had a number of women being murdered here, and the killer's methods do seem bizarre, even for Rome, don't you think? Isn't there something you could tell me? What about the little yellow fruit you keep finding next to the bodies? Please, don't ask me 'what fruit.' We know all about that, at least." He closed his eyes and shook his head as the detective apologetically put him off. Orders were to keep things under wraps, and orders were orders. "Fucking Nazi," Sibille muttered. "What? I said *gràzie,* Inspector. But the minute you can tell me anything, I want to know, okay? *Bene. Ciao.*"

He hung up the telephone and glanced at the wall, where a plastic bulletin board carried a grease-pencil roster of the afternoon's assignments. There was to be an appearance by the Saudi Oil Minister in an hour and a half at the Quirinale. New York wanted that for the late satellite feed.

Durant walked into the bureau, munching the remains of a salami sandwich. "Still no dice, *kemosabe?*"

"Of course not. You got any idea on how to undo twenty-three hundred years of bureaucratic tradition? No wonder Rome fell. It's amazing anybody got around to reporting that it *had* fallen."

Durant pointed the end of his sandwich at Sibille to stress his point. "You, sir, have the warped perspective of the American journalist. The idea is not to care that it fell. Life goes on."

"So it does." He paused to light his pipe. "You have an assignment at five. Saudi bigwig meets Italian bigwig. Where's Francois?"

Durant swallowed. "Not my day to watch him. Isn't he due in?"

"He's probably laying in a stock of more *panettone.*"

168

Sibille pointed to a growing pile of small boxes on Rivette's editing bench in the corner. "Damned things are everywhere. They don't bake them; they must breed them."

"It's tasty. And it is the season."

"Yeah. You know, I've never seen Francois eat that stuff. Do you think he does? If he doesn't, it'd be the first thing he's turned down."

"Maybe he's using them for barter."

"Not unless he could trade them for something else to eat." Sibille took a thoughtful puff on his pipe and walked over toward Rivette's bench. "He doesn't seem to chase women, apparently drinks only in moderation. But he's drawn to the table like a magnet. In fact" —he picked up a box of *panettone*—"we ought to put one of these in the window to see if it prompts him to check in . . . a little bait."

"You worry too much. He'll be here in time." Durant wiped his mouth free of the sandwich, wadded up the napkin, and fired it at a wastebasket by Sibille's desk. It barely missed the bureau chief's head as he crossed the room.

"Hey! Would you look at this?" Sibille's attention was riveted on the street below.

Durant joined him at the window. A heavy black Cadillac sedan sat parked, with two men in nondescript suits standing near it who looked nervously back and forth up the street. A white-haired man, shorter than the others and carrying a middle-age bulge, got out of the car.

Sibille leaned closer. "I'll be damned! That's Phil Duffy! He's the chairman of Agatech."

"So? How do you know him?"

169

"Christ, everyone in Rome knows him. His outfit is one of the biggest NATO electronics suppliers. He's also one of the CIA's back-channel conduits for what's really going on in the Warsaw Pact. Remember what I told you about the bar at the Albergo Nazionale? There's a corner table where he holds court just about every night. The Russian attachés all come and sit near it, straining to pick up the good stuff. Hell, sometimes they even sit with him!" They watched the white-haired man speak briefly to the pair of bodyguards, then stride into the entrance of the bureau's building.

"He's coming here! Goddamn!" Sibille rushed to his desk and hurriedly stacked the day's newspapers and teletype stories into orderly piles. He finished just as a knock came at the door.

Durant opened it. "May I come in?" asked Duffy.

"Certainly, sir." Durant stepped aside and offered his hand. "I'm Craig Durant."

The man smiled wearily. "Phil Duffy. My pleasure, Mr. Durant."

Sibille shook hands with Duffy and guided him toward the only chair that had its vinyl upholstery still intact. "Please excuse the accommodations, sir. What can we do for you?"

Duffy sighed heavily and stared at the floor for a moment. When he looked back up, Durant could see that he had the sunken eyes and deeply lined face of a man very near the limits of exhaustion. "Actually, I've come to see Mr. Durant. Alone, if I may."

Sibille gave Durant a curious look. "That's fine, Mr. Duffy. I have some things to do in the wire room, if you'll excuse me."

When Sibille had closed the door, Duffy sat wringing

170

his hands for a moment, then spoke. "Mr. Durant, what I'm about to ask you may require a certain amount of faith on your part. First, I'm going to ask you not to report the fact that I'm making this request, or my reasons for it."

Durant shook his head. "That's not the sort of agreement I like to make."

Duffy nodded and held up a hand. "I know, I know. And I want to tell you that I don't like asking for it, either. But I think you'll agree, if you hear me out, that there are greater considerations at stake here than what your viewers know about. And I think the whole story—a bigger one—may be reportable later. For now, though, this has got to be off the record."

"How about 'not for attribution'?"

"I'm not much on the jargon you boys use, but if that means you can tell the story and blame it on some unnamed official, no. This has to be between you and me."

"Okay. But I'm going to want the story later."

Duffy shifted position and locked his tired eyes on Durant's. "I know that you've been looking into the disappearance of a priest named Steve Richardson. And I know that you've been to see a young woman named Sandy Newcombe about it."

Durant was startled. "I haven't told anyone outside this bureau about that. How did you know?"

"She's my daughter. Newcombe is her ex-husband's name. Justin is my grandson."

"All right. What's your concern with Richardson?"

Duffy looked down again and cradled his face in his hands, as though he were trying to summon the strength to continue. "Justin—Justin has been kidnapped."

"What!"

"Kidnapped from the circus two days ago." He shook his head slowly in grief. "I shouldn't have taken them there. Went without security, trying just to be the kid's grandpa, you know?" Tears came to his eyes, and he paused to blink them back.

Durant's mind raced as he tried to file as many details of the conversation as possible, storing them away to be jotted down after Duffy left. "Have you been to the police? Has there been a ransom demand?"

"We can't go to the police. The people who took Justin . . . they don't want money. They want us to find Richardson. I've come to ask your help in doing that."

"Look, that may be impossible. The guy's been missing for over a month, there's no trace of him at all. He's probably dead."

Duffy gave Durant an icy stare. "I can't believe that, and I won't. He *has* to be alive, and I'm asking you to find him."

Durant walked over to the window and watched the bodyguards as they kept an eye on the limousine. "I'd like to help, but I'm not a detective. I have no official standing to do anything, and I can't force anyone to answer my questions. You've come to the wrong man."

"You're a reporter. You can ask around in places where I can't even go, I'd draw too much attention." Duffy fought the quavering in his voice. "I don't have any idea why these people want to trade Justin for that priest. I don't even know who they are, but that doesn't

172

matter. We have to find Richardson, and you're our only hope." He put a hand to his eyes and bent over in the chair, weeping quietly. "You've got to help us. They're going to bring Justin to St. Susannah's on Christmas Eve, and if Richardson doesn't show up for midnight mass, they're going to kill my grandson!"

Chapter Sixteen

Lunch took Rivette to a hole-in-the-wall *trattoria* just north of the Termini station, a gathering place for the neighborhood but generally avoided by tourists. It was tucked in between a vegetable stand and a low-rent *locanda* that furnished rooms to travelers who were between trains.

He headed for an empty table, but his attention was drawn to two women sitting nearby. One was Maria, who'd come running hysterically into *La Nonna*'s apartment with news of murder. The girl next to her was weeping, and Maria offered her a handkerchief. There was a curiously familiar object on the table in front of them, but Rivette couldn't quite make it out. He ordered a carafe of *vino rosso* with three glasses, then invited himself to their table.

"*Mi scusi*, signorina," he said to Maria as he set down the carafe. "May I join you? I'm Francois Rivette. We met at *La Nonna*'s."

Marie gave him a look of suspicion but nodded recognition. *Si*, I remember. It was the day Isabella was killed."

Rivette smiled understandingly as he poured the

wine. "A difficult time for you. She was a good friend?"

"Yes." Her tone was guarded. "Why do you ask? You didn't know her."

"True, I didn't." He shrugged. "If you'd rather not talk about her, I apologize. I just thought you might like a sympathetic ear. Living with *La Nonna* can't be an easy thing to do."

Maria's face flooded with apprehension.

"Oh, don't worry, signorina." Rivette laughed gently. "I'm only an acquaintance of hers. I don't tell tales. She's as difficult a crone as there could be."

Maria relaxed. "You're right about that, signore. She's been after me about Isabella. I cried for days after they found her. *La Nonna* told me life was for the living and to let the dead fade into memory."

"And for you, it's not easy to let go of old friends, eh?"

"*Sì*. I've known—I knew Isabella for as long as I can remember. She and I grew up in the same building, played together, shared our secrets. She was like a sister. She . . ." Maria's voice trailed off as her eyes misted over.

"*Che peccato*. I'm so sorry. Do the police have any idea who did it?"

Maria shook her head slowly. "No, not a thing. And now Teresa has lost her cousin." She nodded to her companion, who was crying as she turned a small object over and over nervously in her hands. "They found her last night in her room. Dead, the same as Isabella."

"She was"—the other girl spoke brokenly between

175

sobs—"so young. And so *bella*. There was no reason for her to die like this!"

"*Si*, tragic." Rivette strained to see what was hidden in her hands. "To die young with life spread out before you is a great waste."

The grieving woman spun angrily toward him. "Needless! Senseless! Cristina had just started a job . . . *concierge* at a *pensione* near the Piazza della Repubblica. We were supposed to meet when her shift ended at midnight, but she never came." Teresa pressed her hands against her forehead, giving Rivette a better glimpse of what she held. It was small and yellow, a shade he'd seen somewhere before.

"I waited for an hour, then I went to the *pensione,* but she'd left on time. So I went to where she lived, but the police were there." Her hands came down. "They wouldn't even let me in to see her. I stood in the hall and waited until they took her away. Why did it happen? Why?" Her voice shook with rage, and she turned her palms upward in a plea for insight.

In the center of one of them was a small yellow fruit, identical to the one Barzini had found with Isabella's body except this one hadn't been eaten; it was completely intact. Rivette snatched it from her hand. "Where did you get this?"

She grabbed angrily for the fruit, but Rivette pulled it back beyond her grasp. "What are you doing?" she demanded. "That's mine! Give it back!"

"I'm sorry, but I'd like to look at it for a moment longer. And I'd like you to tell me where you got it."

"What business is that of yours? I want it back!"

Rivette waved a calming hand. "*Per favore*, I don't mean to be rude, and I certainly don't want to intrude on your grief. But I must know where you got this. It may have something to do with your cousin's death."

The girl hesitated, her anger unsure. "I—"

"Please, signorina, I know this is difficult. I'm not with the police, but I am interested in finding out where this came from. It may lead to the killer."

"I—I found it," Teresa said, still not certain of Rivette's intentions. "It was while the *investigatori* were keeping me away from Cristina's room. She lived on the fourth floor, and there was a coin-operated elevator that would take you up for fifty lire. It was so different from any fruit I've ever seen. I guess that's why I picked it up. It was in the elevator, right under the coin box."

Rivette shuddered as he walked down a broad stairway into the humid twilight beneath the Polyclinic Hospital. The steps led him into a yellow-tiled corridor of storerooms and cubbyhole offices, a netherworld of medical bureaucracy. Its ventilation system seemed older than the building itself, leaving the air with the taint of acetone, hot rubber, and stale urine.

A new odor appeared as he turned a corner—formalin, with a strong hint of something even less pleasant lurking underneath its pungency. It grew sharper as he came to the end of the corridor and a windowless doorway under a sign that read *"Medico Legale."* Rivette tucked his unlighted cheroot into a pocket, took a deep breath, and entered.

He found himself in a large room that had once been antiseptic white, but years of assault by preservatives and disinfectants had given it a cast that was almost a pale grey. Stainless steel refrigeration doors ran along the tile of two walls in a double row, and a line of porcelain dissection tables filled the floor. A white-coated man sat, bent over one of them, his back toward the entrance. A small cart was drawn up by his side, and Rivette could hear the gentle clink of metal on metal as the man picked up a surgical instrument, maneuvered it in front of him, then exchanged it for another on the cart. Satisfied, the man straightened as far as his hunchback would allow and spoke into a microphone that dangled from a gooseneck overhead.

Rivette moved closer until he was near enough to be heard, but he kept his distance from whatever was on the table. *"Mi scusi,* I'm looking for *Dottore* Manetti.''

The man swiveled his stool slowly around. His sparse hair was trying to escape in white electrified tufts. He pushed a pair of thick spectacles up under his thatched brows and peered at the intruder. ''What for?''

''Information.'' Rivette concentrated on avoiding a glance at the table.

''Manetti is not an encyclopedia. You'd need to be more specific, and you'd need to tell him who you are. . . . *If* you were to be asking him, that is.'' His voice was burned-out, more wheeze than speech.

''Please, where is the doctor? When does he return?''

The man scratched his chin, revealing a sleeve stained with gore and dirt. ''One question at a time. Manetti does not know everything. Who are you and what is it you would like to ask him?''

''Francois Rivette. I'm interested in the murder of several women. How they died.'' He tried to keep impatience out of his words.

"Ah! Death . . ." The man's eyes brightened as he smiled. "Now, that is something about which Manetti knows a great deal, indeed. But you wouldn't be able to ask him about it."

"Why not?" Rivette was seized with the urge to stretch the man out and dissect him on one of his tables.

"Because he wouldn't be allowed to tell you." He pointed to a sign over the door. "In case you can't read it from here, it says that investigative reports can't be released without authorization."

Rivette pulled out a fifty-thousand lire bill and held it at eye level.

"Signore, I am shocked!" The man leaned forward to examine the money. "Do you think Manetti's integrity would fall so cheaply? No!"

Rivette added a one-hundred-thousand lire note to the first.

The response came more slowly this time. "No! Manetti would not be bought." He shook his head vigorously. "You'd just have to come back when you've gotten the proper forms."

"Madre," Rivette muttered. He dug deep in a pocket and produced another one-hundred-thousand lire bill, which he flexed between his hands to test its crispness. He rubbed all three notes together between his thumb and forefinger as he held them out.

The man stared at the money, transfixed. "I can see that you are obviously a man of good intentions. Manetti has never been one to let formalities stand in the way of legitimate inquiry." He grabbed the bills and tucked them into a shirt pocket. "Now, in whose untimely end are you interested?"

"I only have first names. Cristina and Isabella. They would have been in their late teens, early twenties. Cristina dead in the past week, Isabella a month or so ago. There may have been some mutilation of the bodies."

"Cristina . . . Isabella . . ." His mouth crinkled and his eyebrows knit busily, then he nodded. "Manetti remembers. *Si*, two beautiful women, interestingly dispatched. Not like this signore here."

Rivette forced his eyes to follow as Manetti turned back toward the table. A human hand was pinned down with the stump of an arm attached. The fingernails had been partially pulled loose.

"Simple gunshot to the head," Manetti pronounced. "Then, a hacksaw to spread him around. Not a very imaginative job, really. I have most of the rest of him put away. His fingernail scrapings may tell us where he'd been and what he was up to." Manetti shrugged with his eyes. "That's what I like about this field of medicine. It's far more intriguing to discover after the fact how people died than to diagnose it in advance and make them comfortable until they go."

Rivette cleared his throat and swallowed, trying to purge the sudden taste of bile. "Cristina and Isabella?"

"Ah! Of course." Manetti walked over to a file cabinet and pulled out several folders, then laid them out on an empty table. "Look here. Your two, and four more who seem to have met their ends in essentially the same way. All but one had some sort of fruity pulp in her stomach, freshly eaten because it had not been digested. Each one was found at least partly nude, from the waist down, and each one had been mutilated in exactly the same fashion as the others."

"But how were they killed, *Dottore?*"

"That is the most interesting part. Suffocation, all of them. For Cristina, that was by simple strangulation. But for the rest, no significant marks at all around the neck, no obstruction of the airway. A puzzle, *si?* So, I took another look at the pulp from the stomachs. I can't identify the fruit, but it was saturated with succinyline chloride."

Manetti beamed at his discovery, but his smile waned when he saw Rivette's perplexed look.

"Don't you see? That's what did it! It's used in anesthesia to paralyze the striated muscles, stop the breathing. In large doses like this, it's certain death."

"But what about the other girl, Cristina? Why strangulation?"

"My conclusion is that in each case, the killer persuaded—or forced—his victims to eat the fruit. Two of them have scratch marks at the base of the neck, so it was likely at knife point for them. Your Cristina probably wouldn't give in, or the murderer forgot the fruit. So, he just killed her with his hands."

Rivette nodded slowly. "But what about the nudity? The motive? Rape?"

Manetti shook his head. "No, nothing that simple. There was no sign of sexual contact at all, at least not recent enough to have coincided with the time of death."

"Then why? Random murder?"

"No, not random. I suspect these killings had a common motive, but I haven't a clue just yet. It lies in the mutilation, I think." He shuffled through one of the folders until he found a large color photograph of the genital area of one of the dead women. "In each

181

case, the tip of the clitoris had been neatly removed, not just sliced up or slashed, but excised with surgical precision. Too perfect a match from woman to woman to be mere coincidence. I think they were all done by the same hand.''

''But why? Who would do that?''

Manetti shrugged. ''Obviously, this is the work of a psychopath, but one with an unusual background.'' He tapped the photo. ''I saw a good deal of this kind of thing a long time ago, when I served with a United Nations peacekeeping force. I used to see quite a lot of Moslem women, particularly in rural areas, who had infections from this or worse. It's known as the Sunna circumcision in some parts of the world. The old men used to claim that it was done because a woman's sexual urges needed curbing. I'd say that whoever did this spent considerable time in the Middle East.''

Chapter Seventeen

The path wound deeper and deeper into the forest, where the shade was so thick that midday was never more than perpetual dusk. The traveler kept this eyes toward the ground, not wanting to lose the trail. A long time had passed since he'd begun the journey, but he couldn't remember exactly when that had been. It had been easy at first, but the path had grown faint, and now the underbrush clutched at him and tore his monk's robe. He considered looking for an easy detour, but fear of not being able to find the way back onto the trail kept him from leaving it.

Suddenly, the path opened into a clearing, and the traveler had to stop for a moment to let his eyes readjust to the brilliant sunlight. A pond glittered in the clearing's center. A breeze gently rippled across it, driving a flotilla of leaves that had settled onto the water.

He could see two figures across the pond at the water's edge, a woman and child. They waved, but the glare kept him from seeing them clearly. He squeezed his eyes shut, trying to compensate for the brightness.

When he opened them again, dark clouds were rolling in. He now saw that the pond was a lake, and what he'd thought was the other shore was actually a small island. The wind was rising sharply, kicking the lake into a froth that threatened to inundate the island. The two figures on it shouted as they waved.

"Steve! Steve! Help us! Come to us!" The wind moaned over their voices, giving them the reedy sound of someone more dead than alive, but the traveler knew them instantly.

"Sandy! Justin! Hold on! I'm coming!" He grabbed at his robe and gathered it about his waist. He began to run, kicking to break away from the brush, but it clung to him and grabbed at his legs. He tripped and fell, and as he regained his feet, the traveler heard the voices again. They had risen to terror-filled screams.

"Please! Steve! You're our only hope! Save us! Come to us! There isn't much time!"

He fell into the brush again. When he regained his feet, the island was gone.

"No!" The traveler yelled. "No! No! No—o—o—o—o!!"

Steve Richardson bolted upright in the cot, with his lips stretched tightly in a scream. In the darkness he was disoriented, a feeling of limbo that heightened his terror. Trembling, he whirled until his eyes found the last glowing embers in the fireplace. He sat on the edge of the cot until the shaking stopped, then threw another log on the coals. He shoved some straw in around the wood and coaxed it into flame with a wheezy bellows. That done, he wrapped himself in a blanket and walked around the inside of the ancient

184

stone cottage, trying to keep warm until the fire took hold.

Dawn was starting to tint the Tuscany hills. Richardson watched as the daylight grew, giving life to a pale layer of frosts that had come during the night. In the weeks since his arrival, most of the trees had shed their leaves and they stood naked now against the lightening horizon. The nights had grown colder, and when Richardson ventured outside, the air warned that one morning soon he would gaze out this window and watch the dawn break on a cover of snow.

Richardson turned from the sunrise and went back to the fireplace. He put a kettle on to boil and set about his morning routine, trying to get his blood circulating.

He splashed his face with water from the wash basin. The shock of its chill made him gasp and set his heart pounding. Moisture ran off his full beard, and he wished for the thousandth time that he could find a razor in the cottage.

He shed his blanket and spread it out to protect himself from the cold of the stone floor. Quickly, he began to jump, spreading his arms and legs, touching down, and jumping up to bring them back together. After a minute of this, he was breathing heavily, but he no longer felt the temperature.

Then came the push-ups. Facedown on the blanket, he counted out sixty good ones and grunted to force four more. He rolled over and stretched through sixty-four sit-ups. For the last five, Richardson had to rock his body and jerk painfully for the needed leverage.

185

He'd followed this regimen every morning since he'd first sought shelter here, adding one push-up and one sit-up to his usual twenty for each day spent at the cottage. He told himself that this was an excellent opportunity to improve his physical condition, but in his darkest moments of self-knowledge, he knew that his pain was one more act of penance for the suffering he'd caused those who loved him.

With his exercises done, Richardson pulled on slacks and an old woolen sweater and took the now-boiling kettle off the fire. He made a quick cup of instant coffee and surveyed the cupboard to see what there was for breakfast.

When he'd first arrived, the larder had been full. The cottage belonged to an American artist he'd befriended. It was the artist's habit to come to the Tuscany hills in the summer but to spend his winters in warmer climes, where the tourists would buy his paintings. When the owner was gone, the cottage was open to anyone with a key, as long as the visitor agreed to abide by the rules of the house, which were posted on a sign above the cupboard:

My house is your house. Jesus taught us to share what we have, and you are welcome to eat as much as you need. However, since I've never learned His trick with the fish and the loaves, please replace what you've taken before you leave.

Richardson read the sign and shook his head as he looked at the nearly empty cupboard. He wouldn't be

186

refilling it this time around. He hoped the next wanderer didn't arrive hungry.

He pulled out a tin of dried beef, some salt crackers, and the remaining half of a chocolate bar he'd eaten for lunch the previous day. He arranged his meal on the rough table and bowed his head.

As he prayed, he recalled the fear in which he'd come to this place, a terror born of the events of the night he'd been summoned to Rocco di Papa.

Miraculously, he'd survived the crash. He'd been thrown clear and had landed, unhurt except for some scratches, in some brush out of sight of the roadway. Stunned, he'd lain there while he listened to his pursuers survey the wreckage from above.

"He's finished," said one man, his Italian heavy with a Neapolitan accent. "Let's destroy the car and get out of here."

"Not yet," said the other, whose accent Richardson couldn't place. "We must be certain he is dead. Go and look in the car."

"Ridiculous! It's too hard to get down there. We can look from here." There was a loud bang and the landscape lit up as a flare arced into the sky. "You see? Look at that car! Nobody could survive that! And just to be sure—" The flare gun barked again, and Richardson saw his car explode in a ball of flame.

"Imbecile! Do you want the whole *carabinieri* down on us? We still have to be certain. Get down there and check the car!"

Richardson heard the Neapolitan swear as he stumbled down the slope. He saw the man silhouetted against the burning car and watched him peer into the flames. "He's not here! There's no body!"

A string of curses erupted from the man on the road. "Then we must find him! The priest must not escape alive!" Another flare lit the scene and the man on the road scrambled down to search.

With the roar of the burning car to mask his movements, Richardson burrowed into the underbrush and took refuge in a small depression that had filled with rainwater. He lay flat in it for what seemed like hours, with the water reaching almost to his nose. He listened as the two men beat through the brush.

"What do we do now?" asked the Neapolitan.

"Tell the others where he lives, who he sees. I want him found!"

When his pursurers left, Richardson waited until daylight, then hitchhiked away from Rome, heading north. Terrified of what might happen if he returned to St. Susannah's, he'd fled to the only safety that came to mind, this stone cottage.

From the start of his exile of fear, Richardson had continued to pray as a priest. As first, it had been mainly thanksgiving for his deliverance. Later, he tried to pray for understanding, but the terror of his narrow escape haunted him, shutting off attempts at anything but ritual.

The fear was gone now, replaced by despair. Nearly out of food and still with no solution, Richardson wept and laid open his soul to its Maker.

"Dear Jesus, I've tried to understand what you want of me. In my vanity, I've hurt others deeply, for which I'm truly sorry and repentant. You burdened me with an old man's last confession, a secret which I can share

188

only with you. Then, someone I don't even know tried to kill me. If I go back to Rome, they'll almost certainly succeed. I'm afraid, Lord, afraid of dying and afraid that I'll fail you.

"For these past weeks, I've tried to hear your voice within me, sought to live my life as you would in my place. Yet, I still don't know what you want me to do. I haven't much strength left to wage this fight. Lord, please help me find the way."

When he'd finished the meager breakfast, Richardson left the scraps on a plate in the corner for the mice who shared the cottage with him, then donned a heavy jacket and went outside to chop more wood. It was mind-numbing work, and he lost himself in its rhythm. He kept it up for a couple of hours, turning out a fair-sized pile of logs. The job left him tired, and when he came back into the cabin, he brewed another cup of coffee and sat in the rocker by the fireplace. Before long, he dozed off.

The dream came again, but this time the woods were burning behind him, and he had to run along the path to stay ahead of the flames. When he reached the pond, the trees on the other side were already ablaze. The island in the center was his only safety. Sandy and Justin were there, calling out to him.

"Steve! Steve! You must come to us!"

He jumped into the water and started swimming for the island.

Richardson was awakened by a crash. Startled, he found the cup in shards by his feet.

He stood and tried to wipe the vision of the island from his mind, but it wouldn't fade. He would have no more peace here. It was time for him to leave and put his life in order. Time for decisions. He had to see Sandy.

He cleaned up the broken cup, banked the fire, and set out for Siena.

The ancient walled city was not far away, and soon he was within sight of the *Torre di Mangia,* the commanding fourteenth-century guardian of Siena's skyline. There was a telephone office near the Piazza del Campo. The attendant took the number and directed him to an empty booth.

He listened as the telephone rang.

"Chi parla?" asked the voice of Monsignor Otis.

"We have a collect call from George Otis. Do you accept?"

"George Otis? . . ." The old priest sounded puzzled. "But my brother's been d—"

Richardson coughed loudly into the mouthpiece. *"Scusi,"* he said immediately.

Otis drew in his breath sharply. "Yes, operator! I'll accept."

Richardson waited until the operator left the line before speaking. "Are you alone, Jacob?"

"Yes, I—Steve, it *is* you! Mother of God, where have you been?" Otis's voice cracked with relief. "We thought you were dead. Oh, how I've prayed you weren't!"

The old man's words cut Richardson like a lash of guilt. "Jake, I've been hiding."

"Hiding? From whom?"

"From myself, I think. I'm sorry, I can't give you any details right now. But I'll be there soon."

"Thank God, my boy. Is there anything I can do now?"

"Yes. Pray for me, Jake. For me and everyone I touched."

When Otis hung up, Richardson placed another call, in his own name.

This time, the request for the answering party to accept charges was met with silence. *"Per favore,"* the operator said, irritated. "Do you want the call or not?"

The woman at the other end was struggling to regain her composure. "Oh, yes, operator! Yes!"

"Sandy! It's me, Steve!"

"Oh, God! You don't know how long I've been praying that you'd call."

Richardson fought back tears of his own. "Sandy, is anything wrong?"

She let a sob escape, then forced a thin thread of control into her voice. "Yes. Justin's been kidnapped."

In a state of shock, he listened as Sandy told him how the boy had been taken, and the anguish that followed as she and her father had tried to find the child and locate Richardson. He covered his mouth with a hand so that no sound of his pain would reach her. How could they do this, he thought, to an innocent child he loved like his own flesh?

Sandy finished. There was no more crying, only a desolate sigh.

He swallowed, trying to relieve the tightness in his throat. "What do they want?"

Calmly, she told of the demand that Richardson appear at St. Susannah's to say midnight mass on Christmas Eve. If he did, Justin would be returned to his mother. In the end, her restraint gave way. "Steve,

I'm scared!" she sobbed. "Why did they do this? What do they want with you?"

"Sandy, we're not going to worry about me right now. We're going to get Justin back safe and sound, and that's all that matters."

"I know, but—"

"No buts, Sandy. I'll see you and Justin at midnight mass, and I want a smile. Okay?"

He could hear her expression change at the other end. "Okay," she whispered.

He replaced the phone and stood in the booth, letting the tears come freely.

One hundred miles to the south, a man stubbed out his cigarette as the voice-actuated recorder in front of him whirred to a stop. He slipped off his earphones and leaned back, watching his companion at the window. *Bizzarro,* that one, who stood bracing the high-powered binoculars. He knew without asking that they were trained on the Papal apartments and the security below in St. Peter's Square, as they had been every Sunday when the Holy Father recited the Angelus from his study. There was a fluttering of distant applause, and the binoculars came down. The watcher noted the time and left the window. He had a restless, menacing way about him, the carriage of a serpent considering its next meal. "Well?" he asked.

The man at the recorder nodded. "There was a call. For her."

"And?"

The eavesdropper's cigarettes were under the earphones. He lit one up without answering, a small defiance to show that he, at least, was not intimidated by the Presence across the room.

The other man came slowly toward him; the intense blue eyes smoldered with malevolence. "Perhaps I haven't made myself clear." He took the cigarette, broke, it, and tossed it to the floor. "I ask questions only once. Then, you answer."

"Viene," the listener said quickly. "He's coming."

Chapter Eighteen

The videotape shuttled at high speed, then Rivette slowed the action to a crawl, nudging the joystick to move the picture frame by frame in search of the perfect editing point. Satisfied at last, he slapped the red button on the editor console and leaned back to watch the machine go through its dance of recueing, rolling forward, and rearranging the magnetic images on the master cassette. Rivette chewed happily on his cheroot while he watched the timer count off ten seconds, then punched another button to cue the finished story back to the beginning.

"Another masterpiece!" he called to Durant. "Are you ready to feed it back to New York?"

"Yeah, just a minute." Durant ripped a sheet of multi-carbon paper out of the old manual typewriter and laid it on his desk. "Just let me get the lead down so they'll have it all." He punched a stop watch and read the copy out loud for time.

"Italian police are still searching tonight for the killer of Luciana Canova, whose murder is the latest in a series of brutal slayings that have rocked that country's capital. Canova, whose work with the poor of Rome made her a national figure, had become controversial in recent years for her open liaison with the Italian Minister of Finance. Despite protests from family and possible political repercussions, he was among the large crowd of mourners at Canova's funeral today in Rome.''

Rivette stabbed at the air with his cheroot. ''Passable, but it needs something, *n'est-ce pas?* How about adding that the minister's wife sent her regrets. She was out buying a new dress to mark the occasion.''

Durant tossed the script in Rivette's direction and cradled his forehead in his hands. ''You can't blame me for writing style today, friend, not after you showed me every dive in Trastevere until three A.M. You have caused me to do serious damage to myself.''

Rivette chuckled playfully and rubbed his head with both hands, aping Durant's headache. ''Your problem isn't where we go, but what you do when you get there. Moderation, *mon ami*, is what you need to practice.''

Durant rummaged through the desk, hoping for an aspirin bottle. ''Moderation? That's close. I couldn't even keep up with you.''

''You didn't complain last time. You lack seasoning, that's the problem. Now, tonight, we can tr—''

The telephone cut him short. Sibille, sitting across the room, dropped the latest edition of *L'Osservatore Romano* onto the pile of decaying newsprint by his desk and grabbed the receiver on the second ring.

''Chi parla?'' Sibille growled, then softened the edge in his voice. ''Ah, *buon giorno,* Inspector. Yes, he's here.'' Sibille covered the telephone with his hand. ''It's Barzini. You got anything on this Ca-

nova killing? He ought to be good for something we can use."

Durant shrugged noncommittally and took the telephone from Sibille. "I appreciate your returning my call, Inspector. How are you?"

"Bene, signore. I assume this inquiry is—*come si dice*—for the record?"

"That's why I called, yes. We'd like to know what's going on with the Canova murder. Can you tell me anything?"

Barzini's voice took on a tone that reminded Durant of thousands of other official statements he'd heard: automatic, glib, and evasive. "The investigation continues in that matter. A number of arrests have been made."

"Serious arrests?" Durant asked, feeling his way through the man's deliberate vagueness in the hope of stumbling across some buried nugget of genuine information.

Barzini chuckled. "Signore Durant, this is a serious case. Any arrests made are serious. Do you think I'd want to admit to the Minister of Justice that we're doing anything less?"

Durant elaborately cleared his throat to signify his understanding of the man's predicament. "I see, Inspector. Any details, identities?"

"For publication, no. But off the record, we swept up the usual *degenerati* who'll be out on the streets again within forty-eight hours." Barzini spoke softly now. "Signore, this is a real puzzle. Seven very brutal murders and no suspect at all. And you can't believe how the pressure is on. The Justice Minister is a good friend of the Finance Minister, you know."

"Well, I'll be grateful for whatever you can tell us . . . about this or any other significant developments."

The man at the other end of the line paused. "Ah, *si*. I fear the news on that isn't good. We have found no trace of your priest."

Durant felt a shudder of disappointment. "You're sure? What about the town near where the car was found, Rocco di Papa? Someone must have seen something?"

The investigator's sigh carried a message of tired resignation. "Nothing. If they did, they're not saying so. They think it's Mafia business, or worse, *brigatisti*."

"Who searched the area? There were no clues at all?"

"The *carabinieri* combed the scene and asked around the nearby farms, but with no success. One of their commanders is an old colleague of mine, and he's been keeping me posted on their efforts. Their search has spread over most of Central Italy."

"Is that a usual procedure, calling out that kind of manhunt?"

"This doesn't seem to be a usual case. A missing priest, a car full of bullet holes. And, interestingly, the *commendatore* told me there've been numerous inquiries from the Congregation for the Doctrine of Faith at the Vatican."

"The Holy Office?" An image came to Durant's mind: Cardinal Frescobaldi's secretary insisting there'd been no call from Richardson the night Muller died. "Was any reason given?"

"No. Some sort of heresy nonsense, I suppose."

"Possibly. Well, thanks for the help, Inspector."

"*Prego. Arivederci.*"

Durant met Sibille's expectant face with a shrug. "Barzini says they've swept up a few suspects, nothing definite."

"That's it?" asked the bureau chief, tapping his pipe on a nearby wastebasket. "Where's my lead in that?"

"Try something original like, 'The investigation continues tonight.' New York'll go for it. Sounds like home to me."

Sibille shot him an irritated glance. "Well, push Barzini some more on it, will you please? That sonofabitch knows more than he's telling. In fact, why don't you and Rivette get in a car and go make the rounds to see what else you can dig up on it. This gal was well-known, and the heat's really got to be on because she's the seventh one to die like this. And besides, it's almost Christmas. They can't be letting her killer walk the streets. Something has to turn up."

Rivette grinned and slapped the script and videotape for the Canova story up against Sibille's abdomen. "Enjoy your chat with New York. Satellite's up in ten minutes." He picked up his jacket and headed for the door.

Durant, conditioned by now to the marginally controlled insanity of Rivette's driving, slumped deeper in the seat of the Fiat and tried to will his hangover away as they wove through the traffic along the Via Veneto.

Rivette careened around a bus that stopped too quickly, then turned to his passenger. "Well, where do we go now? Back to the *questura* to bend another detective's ear about Canova's murder?"

"Later. There's something else I need to do first."

"Too early for lunch. Too late for breakfast. Didn't you go before we left?"

Durant rolled his eyes. "Boy, are you on a roll to-day. No, there's somebody I need to see. Drive up toward Piazza Navona."

Rivette raised a puzzled eyebrow and swung around the next corner.

Durant had hoped to go out alone, but Sibille had taken care of that with this assignment. He needed to let Sandy know that he wasn't having any success finding Richardson, but the telephone was out of the question; hers was likely bugged. Immediate personal contact was the only way, and that meant having to fill Rivette in on the kidnapping.

"Francois, do you remember the story on that priest who's been missing?"

"The one whose car they found burned? *Oui.*"

"I've been looking for him myself."

Rivette pursed his lips. "Not an easy task at this late date, *n'est-ce pas?* It's been four or five weeks since he disappeared. Why do you want him? A good story, I hope?"

"That's part of it. It's still in the confidential stage and we have a source to protect, but it's quite a tale." Briefly, he laid out the entire puzzle to Rivette, from the night he and Toni first saw Richardson outside Muller's hospital room to the kidnapping of Justin and the demand to exchange the boy for the priest.

The photographer rubbed his beard pensively. "And you think Richardson may hold the answers to all of this?"

"It's possible. And he's the only key to freedom for

that little boy. Phil Duffy was convinced, that's for sure."

Rivette nodded. "So, who are we going to see?"

"Justin's mother. She lives back off the *piazza*. Pull over here."

They slowed to a crawl as they approached the Fountain of the Moors, but Rivette made no move to park. He shaded his eyes and peered up the *piazza* past the fountain. "Craig, which building is hers?"

"Fifth one up on the left. Why?"

Rivette pointed at a panel truck directly across from Sandy's apartment house. "*Telefono*. But it's the wrong color, and I don't see any cable reels on it." He stopped the car and watched as a repairman left the truck and walked over to a tourist cafe nearby, where he sat down at a table with a redheaded woman and another man.

Durant leaned toward Rivette's window for a look. "So? Maybe they have new trucks. If you're not going to park, I'll just—"

Rivette slammed the car into gear and scooted back into the traffic as a tourist by the fountain focused a camera in their direction.

"What the hell are you doing?" asked Durant.

"You aren't the only one interested in that house. She's under surveillance. And if I spotted three that quickly, there have to be more I didn't see."

"What surveillance? One truck the wrong color? And what spooked you about the guy across the street?"

"Telephone repairmen don't generally lunch with tourists, and the man by the fountain had a very long telephoto lens. He didn't need it for the scenery."

Durant sat quietly as they drove on, stunned by his

own naivete. After more than a decade as a professional observer, it still hadn't occurred to him to look for the obvious. If Rivette hadn't picked up the surveillance, that lapse could have cost Justin Newcombe his life. "What do I do now? I still need to get in touch with her."

"L'amour is the answer."

Durant gave his driver a classic double-take.

Rivette smiled broadly. "In *Roma,* nobody asks any questions when a pretty woman gets flowers."

"What am I supposed to do? Just walk right past those guys with a bunch of daisies in my hand?"

"Of course not. We'll have someone else do that, only it won't be daisies. After all, they're from a secret admirer. You're going to send a dozen long-stemmed roses. If they see that, they'll know it's *amore* without a doubt."

Livorgno's was a posh flower and dress shop on Via Condotti. A well-coiffed matron behind the counter made a quick appraisal of Rivette's scruffy appearance and Durant's look of confusion. She wrinkled her nose in distaste and inquired icily if she could be of help.

Rivette elbowed Durant toward the counter, but the reporter could think of nothing except how silly he felt.

"Mi scusi, signora," said Rivette with an incandescent smile. "Forgive my friend. His mind is troubled by a very touchy matter."

The saleslady frowned skeptically. Rivette pressed the attack.

"He's the nephew of the Swedish *ambasciatore;* you can see his Nordic lineage by the hair and the eyes."

The matron gave Durant's face a second, more careful going-over.

"He's only been in the city for a few weeks," Rivette continued. "However, he's become quite smitten with the daughter of a high cabinet minister. He wants to make a tasteful statement of his feelings for her, something eloquent but discreet."

The woman's face softened a bit. "But why doesn't he approach her directly and tell her himself?"

Rivette nodded. "That would be best, but he doesn't speak our language very well. And there is another small impediment—"

The matron's eyebrows rose questioningly.

"—her husband."

Now it was the saleslady's turn to nod knowingly. Rivette continued, building the lie.

"As fortune would have it, he's in France for the next week or so. As you can see, this calls for the utmost discretion. My friend will send a dozen red roses, long-stemmed.

"*Certamente,* signore. I'll place the order right away." She excused herself with a slight bow of the head.

Rivette handed Durant a pen and two small cards. "Now, Craig, the address. And don't forget to send a love note. We'll seal it in an envelope and send it along with the flowers."

Durant scrawled a line, then another, but they made no sense. He tried again, but no luck. Three more cards lay crumpled on the counter before he finished a verse that he liked:

> I seek your love, but find it not,
> While others guard your heart.

I send this token of my faith,
While love remains apart.
C.

It was dark when the ATAC bus dropped Richardson at Piazza San Bernardo. St. Susannah's was a short walk across the square, and he was grateful that the night would cloak his shabbiness.

The church was empty except for two or three people toward the front pew, who gave the ragged intruder a brief glance, then retreated to the solace of their rosaries. For a moment, joy rose in Richardson's heart at being back before the Altar of God, and he forgot the terror of the past weeks. He lost himself in the colors— red, green, and gold—that bounced off the marble walls. He breathed deeply to catch the evergreen in the air.

There was a crèche in place, complete but for the vacant spot between Joseph and Mary. Tonight, a child would lay the figure of an infant in that place to herald the coming of the Christ. It had been set up to the left of the communion rail, by the Chapel of Genesius, patron saint of actors. Genesius could certainly help with tonight's performance, Richardson thought.

He knelt at the rail and buried his face in his hands, praying from the depths of his pain.

"Oh, dear, all-powerful infant. You were born into a treacherous world, yet your Father protected you. Tonight, a small boy's life is threatened. In your name, sweet Jesus, I ask the Father to keep Justin safe from all harm.''

As he finished, the side door opened and a row of ceiling lights flicked on. He kept his head down and listened as footsteps moved down the aisle. When he heard the priest enter the confessional, Richardson crossed himself and slowly rose to his feet.

He'd thought about this moment over and over. This time, confession would be more than a listing of sins, real and supposed. He would need to reach out to his confessor for reassurance. But it was the love, Richardson knew, that he craved most of all.

He brushed back his unkempt hair and went into the booth, sitting where there would be no barrier to separate him from the priest. He kept his head down as he spoke.

"Bless me, Father, for I have sinned. It has been more than four weeks since my last confession. These are my sins.'' He held his forehead with his hands, shielding his bearded face from view.

"Father, in the past month I have been angry with God innumerable times. I felt he gave me an unbearable burden and then deserted me. Sometimes, I think I hated Him.'' He paused, and his shoulders began to shake. "I am a priest, but I have been denied that way of life.''

Richardson jumped as he felt the confessor's hand on his shoulder. He looked up at Monsignor Otis, whose face was lit by a gentle smile.

"Welcome home, Steve.''

The tension of the weeks of fear poured out, and Richardson wept. "Oh, Jake, I'm so afraid! I've felt so alone since I left! So alone!'' He began to sob, not realizing that he was now cradled in the old man's arms.

"You've felt alone, Steve, but God's always been there."

"But I couldn't feel Him! I'm empty! No feeling! God knew I wasn't strong enough for this!''

"Sometimes, God empties our very being, only to fill it again to overflowing.'' Otis pressed his cheek against the top of the young man's head and rocked him gently, trying to reach into him with comfort. "It's been done for a reason, I'm sure.''

Richardson jerked away from the old priest's grasp and pulled back into his chair, his eyes blazing with a mixture of anger and sorrow. "A reason? What reason could there be for playing with a small child's life?'' His voice was a ragged whisper. "How could God allow that to happen?'' Otis said nothing, waiting for the young priest's private devil to consume itself.

"Four weeks ago, I heard a dying man's last confession, a confession I wish I'd never been born to hear." He paused and stared off into a corner with an expression that told Otis he was really looking within. "Another priest could have dealt with this much better. Why did I have to be the one?''

The monsignor sat silently, watching his friend go through the agony of sifting his feelings. He listened as Richardson recounted everything that had happened since he left Muller's hospital room, leaving out only the man's name and his confessed sins.

When Richardson finished, his anger was spent,

drained away by the telling. He turned to Otis with pleading eyes. "You'll help me tonight, won't you?"

This time the embrace was for the confessor, who drew the young priest to him gently, like a mother caressing a son on his way to war. "Yes, Steve. And may God give us both the strength to get through this night."

Chapter Nineteen

The Fiat backfired loudly as Rivette let the engine coast in gear and turned off Via XX Settembre. Cars were filling up Piazza San Bernardo rapidly, but he rejected Durant's suggestion that they take one of the few remaining spaces. After a thoughtful chew on his cheroot and a long look around, he pulled the coupe into an alleyway marked by a sign that displayed a car silhouette with a line drawn across it.

"Francois, you can't leave the car here. They'll tow you away."

Rivette gestured back over his shoulder with a thumb. "If I leave it out there, we'll be stuck until New Year's. The Faithful will park us in." He set the emergency brake and reached for his equipment on the back seat. "Besides, there won't be any police around here. The ones who aren't at mass themselves are home eating *panettone*. Why don't you go on inside? I'll be along as soon as I get rigged up."

"Okay. You know what kind of footage I want?"

"Of course. Christmas in Rome, *beaucoup* pretty pictures, just like everything else we've done tonight."

The Frenchman gave him a mock salute. "Trust me. Dynamite stuff, *Capitaine.*"

Durant dipped his fingers in the chill of the Holy Water and slowly touched them to his forehead, stomach, and shoulders. The gesture still came automatically, although it felt alien after his long absence from active Catholicism. An image flashed through his memory: frowning Sister Cecilia, her ruler at the ready to correct any first graders who tried to slip into the school mass without making the sign of the cross.

His footsteps echoed in the nearly deserted nave of St. Susannah's, where worshipers would stand shoulder to shoulder within an hour. There were only a few parishioners there now, kneeling as they sought relief from their private troubles. A small group of young men and women arrived, college-aged by Durant's guess, chatting loudly as they entered. Their voices fell to a whisper at an angry glance from one of the early arrivals, and they scurried off behind a door in the chancel.

Altar boys were lighting candles toward the front of the church, throwing a warm glow on the evergreen boughs that had been tied with large red bows across the marble communion rail. Durant's eye was drawn to a woman who knelt near the crèche, her body so rigid it was almost in spasm. Just behind her, a heavyset white-haired man slumped forward in prayer. He lifted his face toward the cross above the altar as Durant approached. It was Phil Duffy.

Certain now that the woman was Sandy, Durant genuflected and knelt three feet from her. Her eyes were locked on the empty manger. He clasped his hands, bowed his head, and whispered.

"Sandy."

Her shoulders jerked as he broke her concentration.

"Sandy, don't look this way. It's Craig Durant. Are you all right?"

Sandy's hand came to her mouth, muffling her reply to anyone but Durant. "I'm all cried out. Just numb."

"I want to help you, but I couldn't find Steve."

"I know. I got the flowers. Thank you." Her voice began to quiver. "Steve's coming. He called. But Justin—" She sniffed back the tears. "I haven't heard anything since the night they took him. I—I—" Sandy's head dropped, and she hid her face in her prayer-clenched fists. After a moment, she crossed herself, stood, and unsteadily made her way back toward the first pew. Durant and Duffy both reached to help her, and Sandy's father nodded his thanks without a sign of recognition.

Durant turned back to the empty manger. He hadn't prayed in years, but now he desperately wanted to ask God to reunite Justin with his mother. He searched his heart, but there was nothing. Finally, he began to stumble through an "Our Father." Even that came haltingly, but at least it gave voice to his soul.

> Oh, come all ye faithful,
> Joyful and triumphant,
> Oh come ye, Oh come ye
> to Bethlehem.

The first carol of the night floated out from the side chapel that served as a choir loft. The same young group that had arrived so noisily now sang, fully robed, to herald the humble birth of an infant nearly two thousand years ago.

The moon was absent this Christmas Eve, leaving the countryside around Dr. Buchmeunster's villa cloaked in impenetrable black velvet. Toni groped along the path to the rear of the mansion, guided only by the faint flicker of a gas lamp set high in the wall above the servants' entrance. Stray embers sailed out from the chimney, along with a pall of smoke that drifted down in the stillness and burned her eyes.

A scratchy rendition of *Madama Butterfly* floated toward her as she rounded the corner of the building, where two windows spilled a cheery glow into the yard.

Her knock was answered by Vittorio, who flung the door wide.

"Signorina Bettina! Avanti, avanti!" He grabbed her by the arm and ushered her inside. It was a comfortable-looking room, lighted mainly by an ancient floor lamp and a fire that warmed a hearth at one end. The old butler smiled as he took Toni's coat and guided her to a settee near the fireplace.

"I expected you sooner, signorina." His tone hinted at the need for an explanation and his eyebrows rose expectantly, setting up wrinkles across his forehead and onto his bald scalp.

"Well, I—" Toni shrugged as she accepted a glass of wine that he pushed into her hand.

Vittorio was silent for a moment, then raised his glass. "It's not important. You're here now. *Salute.*"

"Salute." Toni took a sip and examined the delicate

fluting in the glass. "This is certainly beautiful, I've never seen anything quite like it."

Vittorio smiled. "*Sì*, it is. Lucia and I bought these in Venice on our wedding trip." He turned for a moment toward the fireplace with a distant look in his eyes. Toni followed his gaze and saw a picture of a much younger Vittorio above the mantel, arm in arm with a beautiful girl who held a bridal bouquet. The old butler spoke again, his voice wistful. "Lucia loved these glasses. She would only bring them out on special days or for honored guests. That *presèpio* was also Lucia's." He gestured toward a manger scene that had been spread out on the mantelpiece, with the figures of the Madonna and child, Joseph and the wise men carefully arranged. "Every Christmas Eve I set it up as she did, then I polish these glasses and drink to her memory. Sometimes it's almost as if she is still with me."

Toni felt like an intruder. "You must have loved her very much."

"I still do." Vittorio turned from the fireplace and walked over to shut off the phonograph, which was methodically clicking in the center groove of the record. Then he smiled broadly and clapped his hands. "Come, come! We must eat!"

Toni joined him at the table, which was covered with dishes. Vittorio refilled their glasses and passed her a platter of *panettone*. "So, tell me. Why are you spending Christmas Eve with an old man and his memories instead of with your family? Or your *innamorato?*"

"My father's traveling in America on business, and Mother went with him. I'm hoping they'll be back in time for us to celebrate *Befana* together. But my boy-

211

friend is flying in early tomorrow, so I'll be with him for Christmas.''

Vittorio beamed. "Ah, *amore*."

"There is one small problem. Alberto gave me a pair of diamond earrings for my birthday, and I think I lost one last night in *Il Dottore's* study. I'd like to find it before he comes in tomorrow."

Vittorio raised his glass. "Well, it's wonderful to have a visitor. Let's celebrate awhile, then I'll help you look for it."

Joy to the World!
The Lord is come,
Let earth receive her King.

Durant strained to sing the entrance hymn, but his vocal cords, unaccustomed to anything but the even cadences of the spoken word, wouldn't take the key. After a few cracking bars, he gave up and left the singing to the choir. In the pew in front of him, Sandy and her father stood silently, their eyes fixed on the altar. Her knuckles were white where she gripped the end of the pew. Duffy braced her with an arm around her waist.

The procession flowed toward the front of the church, led by two acolytes bearing tall candles. Another young man followed, holding aloft the Bible. Behind them came a very small boy who solemnly carried a porcelain infant on a pillow. Smiles followed him up the aisle and around the front pew to the crèche, where he carefully laid the doll in the empty manger.

Sandy and Duffy turned to watch. Durant felt his

throat tighten when Duffy looked back at his daughter with tears on his cheeks.

Two priests, robed in gold, came up the center aisle. It was several seconds before Durant recognized Father Richardson. He was thinner, his blond hair was shaggy, and there were deep lines around his reddened eyes, but the agitation Durant had seen that night at the hospital was gone.

A gentle smile came to the young priest's face when he reached Sandy's pew. He stopped and took her hand, and letting the rest of the procession pass him by.

"Thank you," said Sandy in a voice just above a whisper.

"You promised me a smile, remember?" Richardson put his hand to her cheek and brushed away a tear. Her lips trembled and a smile appeared.

"God will be with us tonight, Sandy. I'm sure of it." He gave Duffy's arm a squeeze, and the old man slowly nodded. Then Richardson turned and walked to the altar.

> "In the name of the Father,
> and of the son,
> and of the Holy spirit."

Monsignor Otis raised his arm high and made the sign of the cross over the congregation, which chorused its response.

> "Amen."

> "The Grace and Peace of God our

Father and the Lord Jesus Christ be
with you."

"And also with you."

Vittorio's eyes fluttered shut and his jaw went slack
with an easy sigh. A half-full glass of wine dangled
precariously from his hand where it was draped over
the end of the sofa.

Toni continued to chat happily. "I really enjoyed
Florence when I was there. The Duomo Museum was
fascinating." She leaned over and gently pried the glass
from his grasp. As it came loose, the old butler stirred
with a suddenness that caught her breath. He slid quietly over on his side, like a doomed ship rolling over,
and snuggled comfortably into a souvenir pillow em-
broidered with a picture of the Eiffel Tower. He began
to snore loudly.

There were two doors out of the room. One, Toni
knew, led back outside. She slipped her purse over her
shoulder and stole quietly through the other. As soon
as it closed behind her, she felt a damp chill that seemed
to envelop her. She pulled a small flashlight from her
purse and tried to get her bearings.

The light revealed a threadbare carpet leading down
a long, narrow hallway. There were doors all along it,
probably servants' quarters or storerooms, she thought.
She followed the hall through several turns, fighting the
uneasy feeling that the hall was a maze in which she'd
taken a dead-end turn. Finally, her light caught a reflection of white ahead. The hall ended at a pair of
French doors, and she took a quick look through the

214

curtains. It was the entrance into the main part of the house. The grand hall was on the other side, its chandelier glinting in her flashlight's reflection.

It was locked.

"Merda!" Toni slammed her fist against the door. The lock refused to budge. Furious, she flashed her light around the end of the hall. There was another door.

It opened.

Her flashlight bounced off white tile and stainless steel. She made a quick survey of the room, glimpsing pots and pans, strings of garlic, and wire mesh baskets of onions, all hanging from the ceiling. With a quick glance over her shoulder, Toni stepped into the kitchen. There was a swinging door on the other side, the most likely way into the rest of the villa.

She went through it, and the floor changed from wood to marble. She tried to walk softly across it, but each click of her heels on the stone echoed in her ears like a cannon shot. The noise died away when she reached the center of the room, where a long table sat flanked by chairs on a huge Oriental rug. She stopped to listen for any sound of discovery.

Silence.

The dining room led into the grand hall, with its sweeping staircase. Toni breathed a sigh of relief as she crossed it and reached the drawing room. The entrance to Buchmeunster's study was on the opposite side. The door was closed.

She put her ear to the wood, but all she heard was her own anxious breathing. Satisfied that anyone inside the room would have to make some noise, she tried the knob. It wouldn't turn. She rattled it angrily, but the door remained locked.

"Damn!" she whispered. With a sigh of resignation, she dropped to her knees and dumped the contents of her purse on the floor. In the dimming glow of her flashlight, she fumbled through the pile and pulled out a plastic credit card, which she worked against the latch. After a few moments, the card slid home and the latch snapped back. She bent to gather the debris of her purse.

Then, through the darkness, a door slammed just off the second-floor landing. It swept over her like a thunderclap. Whoever had done it was starting down the stairs in her direction.

> "For Zion's sake I will not keep
> silent,
> and for Jerusalem's sake I will
> not rest,
> until her vindication goes forth
> as brightness,
> and her salvation as a burning
> torch."

Father Richardson's voice was just short of an exuberant shout as he told anew the ancient prophecy of Isaiah. Durant watched him during the First Reading. Richardson's eyes were lit with fire, an illusion caused by the nearby candles. Still, he was a man quite different from the priest Durant had seen the night Muller died. His face was etched with fatigue, but it betrayed no anxiety or tension, only joy at the promise of the coming Messiah.

In the back of the church, Rivette braced himself against a pillar and framed a tight shot of the choir as they began to sing the responsorial psalm. He zoomed back smoothly to include the jammed pews. Then, a close-up of the two priests. It was a long telephoto, not one of his favorite techniques, but he didn't want to leave his vantage point just yet. He took a deep breath to steady the shot. Both priests were looking in the choir's general direction; that would edit well. As they turned toward the congregation, Richardson seemed to be searching the faces of the worshipers who stood packed behind the rear pews. Rivette took the camera from his shoulder and looked uneasily around.

It was Monsignor Otis who took the lectern for the Second Reading. Richardson wore a slight smile as he listened, never letting his eyes stray toward Sandy.

> "Alleluia, Alleluia, Alleluia.
> Good News and great Joy to all
> the world.
> Today is born our Savior, Christ
> the Lord."

While the church filled with song, Father Richardson knelt in front of the monsignor for his blessing. At the lectern, he looked down at the page before him for a moment, then he took the microphone from its stand and walked down the marble steps toward the congregation.

"Before I read tonight's Gospel, I'd like to invite all the children to come to the crèche and listen to the word of God up here with me." He held out an inviting arm as the first few escaped from the pews and ran up the aisles. "Watch these kids as they come. They give themselves freely if you let them. That's how God wants us to be, like little children." A small girl with long blond hair arrived first and locked the priest's leg in a bear hug, touching off a flurry of laughs from the congregation. Richardson chuckled and patted her head. "Some of us run, some of us are shy. Some of us need a helping hand to get here. But no matter how we come, God wants us with him tonight and every night."

He arranged the knot of children in a semicircle in front of the crèche so that each one could see. Then he sat on the steps among them and spoke, drawing them into his story.

"In those days, Caesar Augustus sent out a decree. . . ."

Sandy buried her face on the front of the pew, and her body shook silently. Justin hadn't come to the crèche.

Toni switched off her light and crouched in the darkness, listening as the footsteps reached the bottom of the stairs and moved shakily toward the study. She pulled the door shut and looked frantically for an escape route. There was only one exit, and it led back toward the approaching footsteps. She would have to think of something else.

A flashlight beam swept raggedly across the entrance of the drawing room, giving her a quick glimpse of the opposite wall. There was a shallow alcove, perhaps once used to display a statue. Toni kicked her purse and its debris off to one side and flattened herself into the alcove, wishing for complete invisibility.

The oncoming light found the study door. Its glare kept Toni from seeing who held it. The beam moved forward erratically, accompanied by grunts and raspy breathing. The intruder bumped into a chair, and the flashlight clattered to the floor. *"Scheiss!"* The voice slurred off into mumbling as he bent to retrieve the light. Its glow caught the speaker's face.

Every nerve in Toni's body screamed as she bit her lip to keep silent. Buchmeunster!!

His hair was tangled and damply matted on his forehead, and his eyes were pink with fatigue and alcohol. He tottered unevenly toward the study door, stopping so near that she fought back a wave of nausea from his rancid breath. She froze, not even blinking, and hoped that he wouldn't turn in her direction.

Buchmeunster swayed as he pulled a set of keys from his pocket. He fumbled to hold them in the flashlight's beam, which also illuminated Toni's spilled purse on the floor. He separated out one key and stabbed at the doorknob until it found the lock, then he reached for the knob and crashed heavily into the door. The impact threw it open and sent him sprawling against the door frame. He caught himself, took a deep breath, and lumbered into the study, trailed by a jingling from the floor.

The purse! Buchmeunster's foot was hooked in the strap, dragging it behind him like a sea anchor. The scraping of the keys on the marble shrieked in Toni's head like a falling bomb. She shut her eyes and waited.

The noise stopped as Buchmeunster collided with a

large wing-backed chair in the darkness. He went hand over hand around it, shedding the purse strap as he moved. He leaned against the chair, swaying gently as he took aim for the light switch on the wall and pushed off toward it.

Toni eased out far enough to steal a glance into the room, throwing herself back against the wall as light spilled from the doorway. After a moment to let her nerves recover, she chanced a peek inside.

A clinking sound floated back from where Buchmeunster bent over the desk with his back to the door. He raised a cut glass goblet to the light, sloshing its amber contents onto the floor with an unsteady hand.

"Ach, my old friend. So much you say to my palate, yet no secrets you tell. Why are you so different from the year before? Why is not the year after the same as you?" He paused for a sip, brushed his tongue across his lips, then tilted his head back and drained the glass. A rivulet of wine trickled down his beard. He wiped it away with the back of his hand and set the goblet down. "For every cipher, there must be a key. I will know them all in time. Even yours, my friend."

Toni inched into the room on her hands and knees, hoping Buchmeunster wouldn't turn around and see her trying to retrieve the purse. As he lifted the decanter, she reached around the chair, hooking the keys and pulling them gently until she could close her hand around them to guarantee their silence. When she had them, she tried for the purse. Her fingers brushed the strap but came away empty.

Buchmeunster whirled and swept the bookcase wall with his still-shining flashlight. He focused on a row of books near eye level and wobbled across the room toward them.

Toni scuttled frantically to keep the chair between her and Buchmeunster's line of sight. The study door, only a few feet away, now seemed on the horizon.

He reached the shelves, set his glass down on an empty space, and began to thumb the bindings. A hail of unwanted volumes thudded to the floor as he searched. Halfway through the second shelf, he stopped and hefted a green book. He leaned against the shelves as he leafed through it, loudly calling a roll of the authors inside.

"Shelley . . . Tennyson . . . Keats . . . Byron . . ."

Toni glanced anxiously toward the door, then back at Buchmeunster. He was absorbed in the bookshelf. She chanced a break for the door and scooted toward it on her knees.

"The Vision of Judgment!" His arm fell to his side with the book, but a finger caught his place.

Toni sprawled in the hallway and hurled herself into the alcove as Buchmeunster turned around. He struggled for balance and shuffled toward the wing-backed chair. He braced himself against its back and opened the book to address his audience.

"Your attention, please!" His words slurred as he swept his gaze from right to left and called for silence in the great assembly hall of his mind. "I've come here tonight to enlighten you on a subject we all must face." He paused to step over to his desk and pour another glass.

"Death." He took a sip and staggered back to his podium.

"The Vision of Judgment by Lord Byron!"

"Saint Peter sat by the Celestial Gate.
His keys were rusty, and the lock was dull."

Toni crouched in the shadows by the door frame, breathing deeply to stave off panic. Buchmeunster rambled on.

"So little trouble had been given of late,
Not that the place by any means was full."

Toni flattened herself against the door and reached into the light for her wallet, then her compact. She drew them to her chest and stared at her purse. It was not more than three feet from where Buchmeunster stood.

He paused to gulp half the glass, then resumed in a quieter voice. The chair now seemed more prop than podium as he swayed against it.

"The guardian seraphs had . . . on high,
Finding their charges past . . . care below."

Toni took off her shoes and crawled toward the purse. If she could retrieve it, she'd just tell Vittorio she'd left her earring somewhere else and leave Buchmeunster to his oratory.

There was silence.

Toni's eyes shot upward, expecting to find Buchmeunster glaring at her. She breathed a silent prayer of thanks when she saw him inching around to the front of the chair. He deflated into it with a huge sigh. She froze and waited until his head tilted forward and his breathing turned deep and regular, then she picked up the purse and crept back to the doorway. She swept all her spilled possessions back into the purse, snapped it shut, and stood to leave.

Buchmeunster let out a gentle snore. Toni bit her lip and looked again. His eyes were closed and his chin was resting on his chest. His breath gurgled like a soggy bellows.

Toni took a key from an inside pocket of her purse. She stepped over to the bookshelf and found the lock. With another quick glance at the sleeping man, she inserted the key and gave it a twist. The shelves began to move with a whine that made her teeth grind, but it didn't bother Buchmeunster at all.

"Signorina Bettina! Signorina Bettina!" Vittorio hailed her, echoing from the great hall.

Toni turned the key again and the shelf reversed its motion. The motor cut off just as the old servant appeared in the doorway.

"I think our employer has had a lonely Christmas Eve," said Toni sympathetically. She replaced some books on the shelf to hide the lock.

Vittorio came across the room and stared unhappily down at Buchmeunster. "This happens every Christmas. He always says he's going out, but this is how I find him. Did you speak with him?"

"No. He was like this when I found him." She carefully piled a stack of books on the floor.

"He's so lonely. At least I have my memories." He shook Buchmeunster's shoulder gently, but the man didn't stir.

"Can I help you get him to bed?"

"Just help me get him awake enough to stand on his own two feet."

They struggled to lift the sleeping man out of the chair, and Vittorio managed to get a shoulder under one of his arms. Buchmeunster stirred and peered at him through a heavy-lidded eye.

"Mein Freund," he mumbled with a half smile. He flailed at the air with his free hand and tried to pick up the speech where he'd left off, but stopped in mid sentence when he saw Toni.

"Vittorio! Who is this in my house?"

The old butler looked in her direction and held a finger to his lips. "Don't worry, *Dottore*. This is my niece, Angelina, who's just come to spend part of her Christmas with me. You've met her . . . three years ago."

"Ah . . . yes." Satisfied, Buchmeunster let himself be led from the room. Vittorio stopped by the door.

"Signorina, why don't you look for your earring now. I don't think you should mention this visit when you come back to work next week." He turned and steered Buchmeunster out of the study. Snatches of slurred poetry floated back after them.

When they were gone, Toni closed the door and quickly shoved volumes aside until she found the lock. She turned the key and stood back as the motor hummed and the wall began to open. When it was wide enough, she switched off the motor and slipped into Buchmeunster's secret room.

She flipped on the light and the small copying machine, then crossed the room to the file cabinets. First, a careful count to locate the one where she'd found the ribbon cartridge. Then, she took a thin pick from her pocket and set to work. It was a solid cabinet, but the lock gave up quickly.

With her pulse racing, she thumbed through the top drawer. There were two cartridges now. Buchmeunster was making progress.

Behind the ribbons were several folders. She pulled them up one by one to read the labels. When she came to one marked "Nicodemus Codex," she slipped it out of the drawer and fed the pages to the copier.

The machine clanked through its job, terrifying her that Buchmeunster would hear it and come storming back in, stone sober and furious. When it was done, she carefully reassembled the originals in order, placed the file back in the drawer, and relocked the cabinet. She gave the room one more quick glance before turning out the light and closing the bookshelf door. Nothing was out of place.

> "Take this, all of you, and eat it.
> This is my body which will be
> given up for you."

Monsignor Otis held the large communion Host high, drawing every eye to the altar as he chanted the age-old consecration.

Off to one side of the church, Rivette knelt and rolled his tape, pleased with a two-shot of Richardson standing next to Otis and chanting as the old priest raised the chalice.

> "Take this, all of you, and drink
> from it.

> This is the cup of my blood, the
> blood of the new and everlasting
> covenant. . . ."

Durant stood with the congregation and joined their response without conscious effort. The words floated up from his memory, unclouded despite years of disuse. He tried to focus on their meaning, but his thoughts kept racing ahead to communion. What if Justin didn't come forward? The boy could be dead. Richardson might well be, too, before the mass ended.

If the young priest shared Durant's tension, he didn't show it. His face was relaxed and confident as he and Otis left the altar.

> "O Come, O Come, Emmanuel,
> and ransom captive Israel,
> that lives in earthly exile here,
> until the Son of God appear."

The parishioners began to file into the aisles as the choir began the first communion hymn. Rivette moved toward the front and framed a wide shot of the church as they lined up. With a crowd like this, he thought, they'd be a long time getting through.

Richardson came down to the center aisle, just in front of where Sandy knelt. With Duffy's help, she rose to her feet. Richardson held the Host in front of her and smiled.

"The body of Christ."

Sandy's eyes welled up as he placed the wafer in her hand. "May He be with us all tonight," she whispered.

"He always is. I know that now."

Durant watched as Sandy knelt in the pew. She turned sideways, scanning the faces in the line as they shuffled in her direction. Suddenly, her eyes grew large and she tensed, gripping the back of the pew for support. Durant touched her hand for reassurance but kept himself from turning around for a look.

Rivette panned close-ups of the communion line. Hands clasped before them, they crept forward with a warm expectation on their faces. But there was one dark man whose eyes glowed with hate. Rivette tilted the lens down, following his arm. There, with a restraining hand tightly closed on his shoulder, was a little boy, anxiously searching the pews.

"Mommy!" Justin yelled.

Sandy smiled at him, tears pouring down her cheeks, but sat frozen with fear. The dark man pushed Justin forward before he could reach for his mother.

Rivette followed the pair to the front of the church with his camera. Richardson read the man's face, then traced the sign of the cross on Justin's forehead and turned back to his captor. "You're forgiven, we all are. That's the meaning of all—"

An explosion rocked the church as Richardson jerked backward and sprawled on the marble with his chest torn open. The dark man fired twice more at the priest with his .44 Magnum, a weapon designed to kill by devastation. Then he fired the pistol into the air and trilled his tongue in the blood-curdling yell of a desert tribesman. Screaming broke out in the congregation.

"The Homeland is ours!" He put the gun to his own head and pulled the trigger a final time.

Panic flashed through the church. The parishioners

227

coalesced into a single throbbing mass of terror, running for the doors.

"Mommy!" Justin screamed, spattered gore dripping from his face. "MOMMY!!"

Durant leaped for the boy. "Duffy! Get Sandy! We've got to get out of here!"

Duffy threw his arms around Sandy, who was staring in shock at Richardson. He lifted her to her feet and dragged her from the pew.

Durant ran through the chancel door with Duffy and Sandy close behind. During his years as an altar boy, he'd often slipped out the back door of his parish church after mass to avoid a tongue-lashing for being late. He was in luck. Saint Susannah's had an exit behind the altar. They were through it in a matter of seconds and out into the safety of the night.

Monsignor Otis cradled Richardson's head in his hands. The young man's breath was shallow and there was a gurgle when he tried to speak.

"Oh God, Jake . . . Oh God, I'm cold."

"It's all right, Steve. I'm here with you." His eyes brimmed over and he turned his head to hide the tears.

"Justin . . . Jake, the boy. Did he? . . ."

"He's safe, Steve. And Sandy, too."

"Loved them both . . . so wrong . . ."

Otis shook his head slowly and wept as he watched the young priest's life ebb from his eyes. "You saved Justin, Steve. You came back because of your love. There's nothing wrong with that."

Richardson smiled, then sighed and was gone.

Otis drew a cross on Richardson's forehead and closed his eyes. "He comes to You, Lord. May you forgive him . . . and me."

Rivette squeezed through the crowd, trying to work his way back toward the altar. He nearly tripped over a tall white-haired man who stood near the side door.

"*Scusi!* I'm clumsy with this equipment."

The man turned and stared at Rivette and his camera, sweeping him up and down with intense blue eyes that seemed much younger than his leathery face.

"*Permesso!*" tried Rivette again. "*Pardonnez-moi!* I'm sorry. Let me pass!"

The man said nothing, but he dipped his fingers in the Holy Water, crossed himself, and slipped out into the darkness.

Chapter Twenty

The Volvo's speedometer climbed sharply as Durant sped downhill toward the glitter of Piazza Barberini. Its stores had closed, but there was a steady flow of cars across it, revelers who preferred to welcome Christmas in the chic cafes on nearby Via Veneto. Ahead, an elderly Citroen meandered from one westbound lane to the other. A cluster of cars trailed it, honking and flashing high beams. The Volvo closed the distance quickly. Durant spotted a break in the traffic, downshifted, and shot past in the opposite lane. A late-running bus lumbered out of nowhere directly into his path. He braked hard and skidded into a side street as the lights of the bus flashed by.

When the car came to a stop, Durant breathed deeply until his heart rate receded toward normal. He put the Volvo back in gear and accelerated down the narrow pavement. The rearview mirror was clear of any pursuit. Thankful, he made two quick turns and headed north.

Justin sobbed in the back, his face buried against his mother. Duffy sat with one arm braced against the front seat and the other around Sandy.

Durant slowed by the Spanish Steps for the worshipers who spilled down from *Trinità del Monte,* then pushed the car back to speed and took another look. "I don't see anyone chasing us, at least not openly. Everybody okay?"

"Just shaken up. We'll be fine." Duffy took out a handkerchief and tried to wipe the blood off his grandson's face, but the boy pulled away and tightened his grip on Sandy.

She caressed her son's head. "It's all right, Justin. You're with Mommy now. I'm not going to let go of you." She absently watched the lights blur past. "Last year was the first time he really knew what Christmas was all about. He was so excited. What do I tell him now?"

They whirled past the obelisk in the center of Piazza del Popolo and followed the flow around the circle. "Why don't we double back and go to my place?" said Duffy. "We'll be safe there."

"We won't get there if they know your car," Durant warned. "I don't think this was an isolated terrorist. Someone set him up, and they may be looking for us. It'd be better to go to a hotel and call someone to take you back." He drove onto Ponte Margherita and checked the mirror again as they joined the thinning traffic across the Tiber.

Duffy nodded. "Yeah, I forgot. This isn't my armored limo. How about the Rafael? It's easy to get to and out of the way."

"Fine. You keep me on course, and we'll ditch the car there for now."

They traveled south along the river, cutting back across as Castel San Angelo loomed up on the right.

Durant broke the silence reluctantly. "Mr. Duffy, I think you'd better tell the police about all of this tomorrow."

Sandy spoke, her words empty of any feeling. "Yes, the police . . . the police."

Duffy pulled her closer. "Sandy, we did everything we could. Steve knew that."

"Steve." She brushed the tears from her cheeks. "Daddy, did you know I love Steve? I do. There's nothing wrong with that. He loved me, too. He told me so." She took her father's hand. "I just wanted Justin to know a man like you, Daddy—kind and gentle and giving. Steve was all that . . . and much more."

Now it was Duffy's turn to weep. Exhausted, he let it come.

"We never made love, never." Sandy's voice cracked. "It was so hard for us because we loved each other very much. But tonight, Steve gave me the baby we could never have. He gave me Justin."

There was the smell of roast turkey and smoldering wood in Toni's apartment when Durant stepped in. A dying fire struggled in the fireplace and cast its flicker on a dinner set for two by the hearth. He gave the champagne bucket a gentle nudge. The bottle sloshed gently against the metal. Its ice bath had been gone for hours.

Toni was asleep on the couch, nestled in a cocoon of quilts and throw pillows. Not wanting to wake her, he slipped out of his bloodstained jacket and sat quietly on the floor. A wisp of hair lay across her cheek. He pulled it back gently and was relieved that she didn't stir. He studied her half-hidden face and ached for the peace she seemed to enjoy. Would he ever be able to sleep again?

Her eyes opened and she gave him a sleepy grin. "How long have you been here?" She stretched and wrapped her arms around his neck, drawing him to her.

"I don't really know." He stroked her forehead, then ran his finger down the side of her face and traced the outline of her lips.

"I had a late supper planned," she said.

"So I see. It was a very romantic idea. Sorry I spoiled it."

"You said you'd be back by one." She craned her neck but gave up trying to see the wall clock in the semidarkness. "What time is it?"

"After three." He took her hands from around his neck and softly kissed her fingers.

Toni laughed gently. "You certainly know how to get my mind off the subject." Her smile faded as she saw the deep lines of strain on Durant's face. "Craig, are you all right?"

"Don't ask me that right now." His tone was urgent, almost a plea.

Slowly, Durant brought his mouth close and kissed her. He brushed his lips lightly across her face, afraid that his long-restrained passion would bruise her. Her breath deepened and she reached for him. Then, he stopped and took her hands in his once again.

"Toni, I love you."

She tried to speak, but he covered her lips with his. This time his caress engulfed them both. When they pulled away, his voice was a whisper.

"I know that now. I love you and I want to make you happy. I need to know if you're sure, too."

Without hesitation, she sat up and kissed him, her lips parted. Her arms slid around his waist and pulled him against her. He kissed Toni's neck and laid her back on the couch, where he studied her with the quilt pulled away.

A sheer beige gown clung to her, outlining each contour of her body. It rose midway up her thighs and only half veiled the dark triangle above. Her erect nipples rose against the thin fabric, inviting his touch. He pulled the straps from her shoulders, then stroked and kissed the soft warmth of her breasts.

"Toni," he whispered," you're beautiful."

Rivette sliced off a thick piece of *panettone* with a pocket knife and chewed it while he waited for the monitors on his videotape editor to come to life. The recorder had been rolling when the gunman fired, but it had been jostled quite a bit in the bedlam that followed. It wouldn't play back at the church, and he wasn't sure he'd gotten anything. The desk man in New York was very interested, though, so he'd have to put together whatever video there was for the early satellite feed.

When the screens began to glow, there was a clear picture of the inside of St. Susannah's. *"Sacre Mère,"* he said through a full mouth. "At least there's a good beginning."

He put the Christmas bread aside and began to shuttle through the tape, scribbling notes as he went. Nice wide shots from the back of the church to start with, good close-ups of the priests at the altar. He put the machine in fast forward and let it run a couple of minutes ahead. When the picture came back, he was staring at the communion line as it moved forward. He cued past that, found the gunman and Justin, and followed them up the aisle. Just before they reached the priest, Rivette put the tape back into normal play and turned up the audio. The choir filled the room as Father Richardson bent to bless the little boy, then spoke to the killer. Rivette strained but couldn't hear his words under the singing. The shots silenced the caroling in mid-phrase. Then the screaming began.

"Damn!" Rivette put a cheroot in his mouth and began to chew on it furiously. *"Damn!"* He ran the scene again, this time in slow motion, and watched Richardson's face just before the man pulled the gun. The priest was completely calm as he began to speak, and his expression didn't change until the first bullet ripped through his chest. Rivette closed his eyes and turned away from the monitor. *"Pourquoi?* What's going on here?"

He nudged the joystick and rolled the tape back to the start of the communion line, looking for a point to pick up the action. Suddenly, he locked the tape into stillframe.

There on the screen, just off the aisle, sat the old man he'd collided with at the side door after the shooting. Rivette adjusted the monitor contrast and stared at the image, stroking his beard.

"Have we met before, *père ami?* Why do I think I've seen you somewhere else?" He tapped the screen with the cheroot while he pondered the old man's face, then shot upright in the chair. "Because I have!"

Rivette scrambled across the room and ran his hand along the shelf of tape cassettes until he came to one marked "Canova/funeral." He slammed the tape into the editor's second deck, then raced it forward until he came to the crowd outside the church. He moved it carefully, shot by shot, until he came to a close-up, then froze the picture on the extra monitor. It was a middle-aged businessman, conservatively dressed, with touches of grey in his hair, a moustache, and dark eyes.

Rivette sat down and looked slowly back and forth from one image to the other. "The age isn't the same, the hair isn't. But your nose, your ears, and your eyes? *Vieux homme,* I am beginning to think you aren't as old as you look."

Chapter Twenty-one

Toni yawned and reached across the bed. "Craig?"

There was no reply, only the bells of a Christmas Day mass in the distance.

Startled, she brushed the hair from her eyes and sat up to look around. The jumbled pile of Durant's clothing was gone from the floor. "Craig?" Silence again. With a sigh, Toni let the sheet fall away from her nakedness, its coyness no longer needed. She cupped her breasts and recalled Durant's eager caresses. The memory of his urgency set her pulse racing. They had sought each other hungrily, with no restraint, until release came roaring at them both like the Milan-to-Rome Express.

She stretched and left the bed for the living room, pausing to study herself in the full-length mirror. She was certainly tired of the games men played to try to get her into bed, but she was never unthankful that Nature had given her the equipment to attract them. Maybe Durant could change that for her. No more games.

There was fresh coffee on the stove. Toni poured a

cup and sat down at the table. A carnation lay on her placemat with a note next to it:

I couldn't find a rose, so this will have to do.
Thank you for everything.
Deadline calls, but I'll see you later.
Merry Christmas.
Love, Craig.

She sipped her coffee and smiled at the flower. "You're a little wilted, but sincere." Probably left over from someone's Christmas Eve party, she thought. Still, it was a nice, caring thing to do. So like him.

It was obvious to Toni that Craig was in love with her. He'd even turned back her one attempt to seduce him until he was sure that he was. And he was sweet, and *molto bello*. Even that scene in the market over how she'd gotten the information about Buchmeunster's manuscript was because he was worried about her. He really cared.

"But, *caro mio*, do I love you?" She studied the flower, twirling it slowly in her fingers. "That's not why you're here, Antonia. There's important work to be done, and you'd be wise not to forget it. You're going to be at the top very shortly. All you've ever wanted to be."

She set the flower aside and pulled a copy of Buchmeunster's report from a kitchen cabinet, then sat down and began to leaf through it. How would things go if she shared the translation with Craig, let them both break it at the same time? It would certainly get a good deal more coverage than if she did the story alone in *La Scoperta*. That would be the way to guarantee worldwide exposure in record time. Good for the story, good for her, good for Durant.

"But, signore"—she picked up the flower again—"you didn't bother to tell me what was so important that you had to rush out on Christmas morning without even a kiss. What are *you* working on that you aren't sharing with me?"

She put the flower, blossom-down, into the dregs of her coffee. "Not this time, Craig. You can have it right after my exclusive hits the street."

Durant closed his eyes and let the soft hiss of the satellite audio lull him to a state just above sleep. The only thing that kept him from going completely under was the abrasive ring of the telephone at the other end of the circuit. He'd need to be coherent when someone got around to answering.

"News, Ramirez." The man in New York sounded far off and wide awake, even though it was two A.M. there.

"Juan, this is Durant. Who's on the desk?"

"I am at the moment, *honcho*." There was a crunching sound and Ramirez's mouth was full when he spoke again. "Excuse me. Christmas lunch." He paused to swallow. "Hey, I saw some of that stuff Rivette got from the church, we got it for voiceovers. Great footage! Got to lead the morning show. Did this guy really get smoked right there by the altar?"

"Yes, he did." Durant felt a sudden disgust for himself, Ramirez, and journalists in general. Ramirez had reduced the world to simple terms: no people, no feel-

239

ings, just pictures and as much on-screen action as he could get.

"Priest gets blown away by terrorist crazy! Dynamite shit!" The man in New York whooped. "Wish I could've been there to see it. What a story! Merry fucking Christmas, Father!" Ramirez rolled the last phrase slowly around on his tongue, stretching it out with relish. Durant pictured him, feet propped on the desk and smiling, now that his newsday was saved from an endless parade of carolers and Christmas dinners at transient shelters across America. The producer would be happy, so Ramirez would be happy.

Durant wanted to scream, but he kept his words even. "Who's putting the show together?"

"Aleta. Let me get her on." Ramirez muffled his yell with a hand over the phone. "Hey, Davis! It's the Roman cavalry coming to save your ass!"

The producer was cool when she came on the line. "Really, Juan. Why don't you go clear the wire machines?"

"Already did."

"Then go play in the traffic."

Ramirez hung up without another word.

"One gets weary of Juan's ebullience at this time of the morning. How are you doing this Christmas Day, Craig?" Aleta's tone warmed as she spoke. Durant recalled meeting her during his familiarization tour with Global in New York. Tall, black, and scholarly, she ruled her newsroom with a smile and an iron hand.

"I've been better, Aleta, but thanks anyway."

"So I hear. I've seen the video from Rivette. Tragic, but certainly impressive. What can you give us?"

"What've you got in mind?"

Aleta mused for a moment. "I was thinking, perhaps, of a villa on the Adriatic, but if you can't arrange that, I'd settle for something on the order of a minute-thirty. I'd go one-forty-five or even two if you had something to carry it besides the actual shooting."

Durant thought quickly. He wanted to firm up the connection between Justin's kidnapping, Richardson's death, and the priest's behavior after the deathbed visit with Muller. If the story broke piecemeal, the information he needed might disappear. There was a lot more to it than just a kidnap-murder involving an American industrialist's grandson. Italy's news services weren't onto any details yet; at least it wasn't on the news wires. Nor were they aware that Durant had helped Duffy and his family flee the church. He hoped to be out of Rome when they got wind of that.

"I think we can do a comfortable one-thirty, Aleta. We have some pretty good background stuff and some speculation we can pull from the papers here, sort of a recap. Some're saying it was some kind of Islamic terrorist cell. A couple of others think it's probably Red Brigade work."

"You were there. What do you think it was? How about a first-person piece?" The producer's voice was friendly, but it carried a strong message that she expected her suggestion to be followed.

Durant cringed. Withholding a source was one thing; not telling the producer about some hard information, as well as his own role in the story, was quite another.

"I don't think a first-person is a good idea. He looked dark—Middle Eastern to me—but he could've been Armenian for all I know. This is an Italian terror

241

attack. They've had a lot of it, and I think it'd be better to report how they see it instead of what I think."

Aleta sighed. "I sense the philosophy of another purist who doesn't like to be part of the story. No reporter involvement, is that it?"

"No, not this time." Durant forced a chuckle for her benefit. "I just think the piece would be better my way."

"Okay. One-thirty plus another ten seconds for a lead." She paused, and Durant could hear her typing at a video terminal, where the tentative newscast lineup was being laid out. "We'll call it 'dead priest.' Nice enough?"

"Super."

"We'll have the bird back up in another hour or so, if you can be ready to feed then. Call me back with the script. *Ciao.*"

Durant hung up and swept the pile of newspapers in front of him to one side.

"Word from New York, *patron?*" Rivette slid onto the corner of Durant's desk and jabbed in the direction of the telephone with his cheroot.

"Yeah. They want a package, minute-and-a-half. The footage all right?"

Rivette nodded. "As always. Did you expect anything less?" We have the shooting itself, the crowd during the mass, and lots of madness afterward. I want to talk to you about that, by the way. While I was getting the tape after the shooting, I bumped into someone by the doorway. He loo—"

"Let me cobble up something for Aleta. I'll cut a voice track and we can get the thing edited and back

242

to New York." He threaded a sheet of multi-part paper into his typewriter.

Rivette slipped around the side of the desk to Durant's line of sight. *Bien.* As I was saying, this man looked just li—"

"Great. New York says your footage was great." He rubbed his chin and began to type furiously.

Rivette retreated to his editing desk, where he sat and watched Durant pound out the story, pausing for a moment now and then to read parts of it for length. Ten minutes later, Durant ripped out the last page, gave a copy to Rivette, and went off to the sound booth to put his script on tape.

From the script times and his notes, Rivette had the video scenes edited in sequence and ready when Durant returned. The reporter watched while Rivette added on the narration for the finished product.

"Very nice, Francois. How you made sense out of the bedlam after the shooting, I don't know."

"*Merci,* Craig." Rivette smiled. "Now, there's something else I'd like to show you, and I think you'll find it interesting." He put the tapes of the shooting aside, loaded two more cassettes into the machines, and watched the digital counters flash until the editor found the timing points he'd punched in. "*Voilà!*" Still-framed images appeared on the monitors: the old man from St. Susannah's and the middle-aged businessman from the Canova funeral. "Look at them, Craig! Look at *him!*"

Durant stared at one picture, then the other. "Him? What do you mean, *him?*"

Rivette tugged anxiously at his cheroot. "Don't you see it?"

"There's some remote similarity, I guess, but their ages, their eyes, I don't—"

"*Merde!*" Rivette slammed a fist onto his worktable. "Can't you see? Forget the nose. Look at his ears! Look at the eyes! It's the same man!"

Durant jumped, startled by Rivette's impatience. "Well, the faces are a little alike. . . ."

"A *little?*"

"But there's so much age difference, the weathering of the skin, the bags under the eyes. It's got to be coincidence, that's all."

Rivette stood and spread his arms oratorically. "Look, you didn't see this guy close up. I blocked his way accidentally by the door when everybody was trying to get out. You should have seen the way his eyes cut right through me when he saw the camera. This is no ordinary man. He's the same man I saw at the Canova funeral. I swear it!"

Durant shook his head. "I'm sorry, Francois. I just don't think so. Excuse me." He turned and went back to his desk.

There was some unopened mail from the day before. Durant thumbed through the pile, stopping when he came to an envelope with a return address for the Congregation for the Doctrine of Faith. Inside was a note and the photo he'd found in Andrew Muller's archaeology book. The note read:

Signore Durant:
After some inquiry, we have managed to identify the man who appears in this photograph with Andrew Muller. He is Father Ernst Schwemmer,

who is still active as a priest. He is stationed at the Cathedral of San Lorenzo in Lugano.

Yours in Christ,

Giacomo *Cardinale* Frescobaldi

Durant pulled a map from his desk and squinted while he searched. He found Lugano in the Lake District, just over the Swiss border. A day by train, he thought. Quicker if he flew. He thumbed through his address book, then picked up the telephone and dialed.

"Chi parla?"

"Father Chapman, this is Craig Durant. I'm sorry to disturb you at home."

"Quite all right, Mr. Durant, although I'm not used to receiving calls this early on Christmas morning."

"I know. I apologize for the hour. I have something urgent to discuss, and if you don't mind, I'd like to come visit you."

"Well, tomorrow afternoon I'll be in my office for a while. That would be fine."

"I need to come today. Now, if possible."

"Now?" Chapman seemed completely dismayed. "Whatever for?"

"Have you seen the papers?" No, he wouldn't have it. Happened after deadline. "Have you listened to the radio?"

"No. Why?"

"Then you don't know?"

"Know what?" Chapman was becoming irritated. "This *is* Christmas, Mr. Durant. I have guests coming and I'm not in the mood to play games!"

Durant took a deep breath and let it out slowly. "Father Steve Richardson was killed last night. Shot to death while saying midnight mass at St. Susannah's.''

There was stunned silence before the priest spoke. "My God! But I thought he'd disappeared, been missing for weeks!''

"He was, but he came back, Father. That's why I need to see you in person. Today.''

"I still don't see—" Chapman's voice carried a mixture of shock and confusion. "I don't understand. That poor man. He looked so distressed the night Andrew died.''

"That's exactly why I want to talk to you. I think there's a connection between Richardson's death and Andrew Muller.''

"That's ridiculous! You can't possibly think—''

"Father, it's too difficult to explain over the phone. I have to see you. Now.''

Chapman said nothing for a moment, then sighed. "Very well. Come as soon as you can.''

Durant hung up and headed for the door, but Rivette caught his arm and gestured again at the monitors.

"Craig, on my mother's grave, those men are one and the same. My instincts tell me. Sibille wants a lead on the maniac who's been killing women. I think this could be the man. There's a reason for his presence at the Canova funeral and at this terrible event at St. Susannah's. He's a part of it all, somehow.''

"Look, Francois"—Durant gave in to impatience—"I'm sorry, but I don't think they're the same man. I'm just not convinced. Now, excuse me, I've got to go.'' He brushed past and left the office.

" 'I'm just not convinced?' '' Rivette yelled toward the closing door. " 'I'm just not convinced!' Since when should I have to convince a journalist of anything? What happened to reportorial initiative?'' He bit the end off a new cheroot and grumbled as he spat it into his wastebasket. "Take pretty pictures, *monsieur* photographer, but don't tell me you can develop a story on your own.'' Rivette turned back to the video faces. "Well, *I'm* convinced, and I'm going to do something about it.''

He stuck the funeral tape and a small black and white monitor in a canvas bag, then picked up his portable videotape recorder. Then he headed out the door, his cheroot going full tilt.

Chapter Twenty-two

For once, most Romans seemed to be off the streets instead of in their cars. Durant easily found Chapman's address and a place nearby to park his middle-aged Opel. It was amid a row of blocklike residences off Viale Guilio Caesare, an attempt by Mussolini's architects to repeat in concrete what the builders of Imperial Rome had done with marble. Durant rapped the knocker and waited.

"Merry Christmas, Mr. Durant." Rita Chapman smiled in the doorway. "It's nice to see you again."

"Merry Christmas to you, Ms. Chapman." Her hand was soft and warm as he shook it. "I'm really sorry to barge in like this."

"Please, don't worry about that. It's really quite all right. And please call me Rita. Provided, of course, that you'll let me call you Craig?"

"Sure. That would be . . . fine." Durant was distracted by two small faces who peered curiously up at him from around Rita's dress. They were mirror images with blond curls, identical except for the chocolate moustache one of them wore.

Rita seemed puzzled but laughed when she followed

his gaze. "Oh! Girls, this is Mr. Durant. Craig, these are Kathleen and Kelly. They belong to my brother Paul. They're visiting for the holidays." She pointed the twins down a hallway. "I'm sure Maria has more cookies, if you ask nicely. Off with you, now!" The girls giggled and ran off noisily.

Rita led Durant to the library, where Chapman was tending the fireplace. Shock was still etched on his face.

"Father, I'm really very sorry to come like this, but—"

"Please, don't apologize. I'm afraid I don't understand any of this." He sat tiredly in an overstuffed leather chair and motioned Durant to another. "Rita, would you get us some coffee, please?"

"Of course, Father."

Chapman watched her go. "I saw no reason for her to hear any of this, at least not yet. Now, tell me what's going on. I thought Richardson was still missing, had been unaccounted for for quite some time."

Durant nodded. "He was, but he turned up at St. Susannah's last night and said mass. I don't think anyone knew where he'd been. Nobody seems to have any idea."

"And someone killed him during the mass?"

"Yes, during communion. A man came up in line, and when he reached the front, he pulled out a gun and started shooting."

Chapman's eyes betrayed a struggle with disbelief. "He just shot Richardson? Nothing else?"

"Well, the guy did scream something about a place called 'The Homeland.' Then he killed himself."

"Does that mean anything to you?"

"Not particularly. He was obviously some kind of

249

extremist, but I really can't think of a motive. The only clue I have is that Richardson disappeared the night he saw Dr. Muller at the hospital."

"I hadn't been aware of that. Didn't make the time connection, I guess." Chapman watched the fire for a while before speaking again. "You know, confessions can be a difficult burden, especially final confessions. That boy looked exhausted when he came out of Andrew's room."

"Father, as I told you on the phone, I think there may be a link between Richardson's murder and whatever happened when he and Muller were alone."

Chapman shook his head. "I can't believe that. The confession is sacrosanct. Even nonbelievers in this country know that."

"So is the mass, Father. That didn't stop Richardson's killer."

"True. But why?"

Now it was Durant's turn to stare at the flames. He weighed his obligations toward Duffy against the possibility that Chapman, once convinced, might provide more information.

"Look, Father. There's quite a bit about this that hasn't been reported. I don't think it's common knowledge, and if it got out right now, I think it'd ruin any chance I have of getting to the bottom of this. So, I'll have to ask you not to repeat any of this."

The priest nodded. "Of course."

"Steve Richardson was seeing an American divorcée here in Rome. She has a young son. After Richardson vanished, someone kidnapped the boy and agreed to return him only if Richardson came to St. Susannah's to say midnight mass on Christmas Eve. The killer marched the boy up in the communion line and let him go right when they got to the front, just before the shooting started.''

Chapman took off his glasses and ran both hands through his hair. When he looked up again, he seemed much older. ''Then one has to conclude that whoever wanted Richardson knew he was still alive. And that points to them as the likely cause of Richardson's accident when he disappeared. They tried to get him on the road and knew they'd failed.''

''You knew Andrew Muller well, didn't you? Did he have any Islamic connections?''

''Anybody in his line of work gets to know quite a few people in the Middle East, from the local *muhktar* to the royal princes. He and I were on a great many digs together over the years, but I can't think of anyone who'd have wanted to harm Andrew, let alone kill a priest who'd talked with him before he died.''

''Did he ever mention anything about being in a Catholic seminary when he was young?''

Chapman was plainly startled. ''Old Andrew? Not likely. The man was a confirmed atheist. He and I would debate God by the hour.''

''I'd like you to have a look at this.'' Durant pulled out the photograph he'd found in Muller's book. ''See the man on the right?''

Chapman took the photo and looked at it closely. ''That could be Andrew. There's certainly a resemblance.'' He cupped the picture in his hand, weighing its message, and passed it back. ''I must say I'm more than surprised. Stunned is more the word. Andrew, a seminarian.''

''I've found out who the other man is—a priest

named Ernst Schwemmer. He's at a church in Lugano. I'm going to pay him a visit."

"I should be very careful if I were you. If all this is tied together, whoever got Richardson is not going to be happy with you poking around. I'd certainly keep it quiet."

There was a knock, and Rita entered. "Excuse me, Father. I thought you'd like to know that Mrs. Muller is here."

"Of course. Please show her in." Chapman turned back to Durant. "By coincidence, I've invited Andrew's mother to spend Christmas Day with us. She has no one left, you know."

"Well, I'd better be going. I appreciate your seeing me."

"Not at all. I'd like you to stay to dinner, if you've the time."

"Thanks, but I've already made some promises about that. I really have to go."

They rose as Kathryn Muller came into the room. She was bent with age and fatigue, but Durant could see from the softness in her face that she had once been extraordinarily beautiful.

"Kathryn, it's good to see you." Chapman gave her a hug and a peck on the cheek. "I'm glad you could come."

"It's good of you to invite me, John." She had a kind smile and a Germanic lilt to her speech.

"Kathryn, this is Craig Durant. He's just popped by to wish us a happy holiday." He shook Durant's hand warmly. "You're sure you won't stay?"

"Sorry, I can't."

"I understand. Watch out for yourself. Can't be too careful these days, you know. Rita will show you out."

"Thanks."

Rita led him to the door, frowning as they walked. "You know, Mr. Durant—"

He chuckled. "You said you'd call me Craig."

"Craig, I've been worried about Father. He's been overworking himself lately. Did he seem all right to you?"

Durant shrugged. "He seems tired, but other than that, I didn't notice anything. And I'm afraid I didn't give him the cheeriest news for a Christmas morning."

"Yes, he told me about your call. I can't believe anyone would do something like that, especially in a church. That poor priest." She shook her head. "Thank God nobody else was hurt."

"At least there's that. Well, thank you, Rita."

"You're welcome." Rita waved as he walked out to the street. "And Merry Christmas, Craig."

"Yeah. Merry Christmas." He got into the Opel and tossed Muller's photo on the dashboard. Muller, an atheist? He hoped Father Schwemmer had a good memory for old acquaintances.

Christmas dinner passed at a leisurely pace for the Chapman household. John Chapman sat at the head of the table, trying to preside in a festive spirit, but in odd moments, the faces of Andrew Muller and Father Richardson would come to mind, one by one, and merge into a single, distorted image. Could there really be a connection?

"Father. Father, it's time for dessert."

The priest looked up to see Rita staring anxiously across the table. "Oh, I'm sorry, Rita. Too much on my mind these days." He laughed nervously.

"I know," said his daughter. "Why don't you go sit down with Mrs. Muller? The girls and I will get dessert ready."

"A good idea. Come along, Kathryn."

Back in the library, Chapman eased Mrs. Muller into one of the chairs by the fire and walked over to a small cabinet. "Sherry?"

"It's a bit early for me, John."

"This is a holiday, Kathryn. I recommend it." He poured two glasses and sat down next to her. "You're looking well."

"John, you are some priest. You can't even tell a convincing lie." She laughed gently. "Still, that is nice of you to say. It has been very hard since Andrew died, you know."

"I should think so."

"You know, I always expected that my husband would die before I did. That was the way in my village. So many old women, so few old men. But most of those women, they were grandmothers by the time their husbands were gone. I was so young, not even thirty, when Hans was taken from me." She gazed at her glass, lost in its color. "After that, Andrew became my whole world. I know that was not good for either of us. How many times did I tell him that he was my little man? As he grew older, he seemed so serious and calm, but he was in turmoil beneath, so undecided about life. I sheltered him too much."

Chapman reached out and touched her arm. "Kathryn, every parent has those worries. I knew Andrew for thirty years. You didn't—"

"Please, John." She smiled weakly and patted his hand. "I have been thinking about this since Andrew died, and it needs to be said. You are the only friend of his I know well enough to say it to."

Chapman said nothing, letting the old woman choose her own course.

"When Andrew became a scholar, I was so proud. But still, he seemed at war with himself. Such anger he had, sometimes at the world, sometimes at little nonsense things. But never at me. Always to his mother, he would show a smile." Mrs. Muller sighed deeply as her pain poured forth. "It was because of me that Andrew never married, you know. He would tell me, 'Mama, I will always be here for you.' And now he is gone. I never even thought of life without him. It has been very difficult for me these past weeks."

The priest nodded wordlessly, not wanting to interrupt her unburdening.

"And this morning, I heard the news that the priest who saw Andrew at the hospital was murdered while he said mass." She shook her head slowly. "So young. So cruel an act."

"Yes, Mr. Durant told me about it. I was shocked by the news."

Mrs. Muller smiled again. "Please excuse me. I did not come here for this. But I did want to ask you to do a favor for me."

"Certainly."

"I'm eighty-six now, John. At my age, you think about how fragile life is." She reached into her purse and handed Chapman a small letter-sized envelope. "I would like you to keep this and to open it only if something should happen to me. There are some loose ends that would need tending to. I'd like you to take care of them."

Chapman turned the envelope in his hands, wondering what it held. "Kathryn, I'll be happy to do that for you. But don't you think you'd better consult a solicitor? Italian laws on this sort of thing may be rather odd, you know. And you certainly needn't worry about this now. After all, it's Christmas."

"John, I want you to do this for me. You have always been a man with good judgment. You will know how to handle this." She closed his hands around the envelope, then stood. "And now, I think I will go help your daughter with those beautiful little girls."

When she was gone, Chapman sat looking at the envelope, running it between his fingers absently. He felt something flat and hard in one corner and explored it more closely. A key? With a shrug, he walked over to his desk and closed the envelope in a drawer.

Mass had just ended at St. Balbina's church when Rivette arrived. He parked across the street by the ruins of the Baths of Caracalla and walked back, watching the small crowd of parishioners in front of the church drift slowly away. He left his equipment under a cypress tree in the courtyard and slipped into the edge of the group to wait until he and the priest were the only ones left.

"Buon Natale, Padre!" Rivette beamed as he shook the priest's hand. "A great day, don't you think?"

The old man seemed startled by Rivette's rush of

goodwill, but he recovered quickly. *"Certamente,* my son! A wonderful day, by the grace of Our Lord *Gesu."*

"And a lovely mass, *Padre.* Well said, indeed!" He continued to pump the priest's hand furiously.

"Do you think so? I hoped it would be. So many come to The Lord only for Christmas and Easter. I try to draw them back into the fold when I can reach them." His greying brows rose above a large Roman nose. "But I'm afraid I get too *ardente."*

"Not so." Rivette shook his head and put one hand on the old man's shoulder. "You hit the mark today, *Padre.* A perfect balance between fervor and dignity."

"Ah! *Bene!"* The priest grinned broadly and patted his ample belly with both hands in pleased relief. *"Gràzie,* that's nice to hear. We don't get much in the way of appreciation these days, you know. Just, 'Father, my husband does this' or 'Father, my daughter does that.' They come to my well to drink, but they never tell me how the water is."

Rivette gave him an understanding nod. "It can be a thankless role."

"True. But that's how our Lord *Gesu* found it, I suppose." He peered curiously at his visitor. "You know, it's odd, but I don't recall seeing you at my church before. I'm sure I would remember you."

"I'm not from this parish, *Padre.* My name is Francois Rivette. But I've been here before. I came to the funeral of Luciana Canova."

"I am Father Cusimano." He sighed heavily and shook his head. "Signorina Canova. How tragic."

"And brutal. And senseless."

Cusimano's lips were set in a firm line, his cheer now completely gone. "She was such a good person.

257

So full of compassion for the people. And no one can find her killer. The police are helpless."

"*Padre,* this murderer may still be hiding among us. He may even be watching us hunt for him."

Cusimano's eyes grew large at Rivette's suggestion. "*Madre!* Do you really think that's possible?"

"Yes, quite possible. And we may all have clues that we've never thought about." He guided the priest by the arm as they strode over to the tree to retrieve the video equipment. "Even you may know something important, *Padre.* I'd like you to look at a picture for me."

"You are from the police?" The old man looked genuinely worried.

"No." Rivette smiled to relieve the priest's tension. "I have nothing to do with them. But I do want to find this killer, and you may be able to help me. May we go into the rectory?"

Inside, Father Cusimano watched in growing confusion as Rivette set up his monitor on a small table and hooked it to the recorder. Rivette pushed some buttons, and the screen came to life with the black-and-white close-up of the man from the funeral.

"Now, Padre, I want you to look closely at this man. Have you seen him before?"

Cusimano wrung his hands anxiously and studied the screen for nearly a minute before speaking. "He—he is not from my parish. I would know. Where did you get this picture?"

"Signorina Canova's funeral."

The priest relaxed. "Ah, then I might have reason not to recognize him. She had many friends who came from all over the city to pay their respects. Still . . ." His brow worked again as he took a closer look.

"Yes, *Padre?* You do know him?" Rivette leaned forward, as if his physical effort could prompt the old man's memory.

Cusimano leaned back in the chair and sighed with a shake of his head. "Forgive me, signore. I thought for a moment that he looked familiar, but I don't remember him. Yet, I think I should."

Rivette sank back with a sigh of his own, feeling his glimmer of hope fade away. "I know. It's hard to recall these things sometimes. But please think about him some more."

The old man spread his palms in a gesture of supplication. "Life has not been easy in this parish lately. People come, people go. And I'm not a young man anymore, you know, although I'm not ready to retire by any means. But so much has happened. It's so hard to keep it all straight."

"Comprendo, Padre." Rivette began to resign himself to a wasted trip.

"To make matters worse, signore, one of my priests has been on sick leave, and there have only been two of us left to cover all of the masses." Cusimano shrugged apologetically. "But my old seminary classmate, *Cardinale* Frescobaldi, has been loaning us priests from his staff to help on Saturdays. Sometimes they take the whole schedule, and we have a holiday." The old priest chuckled. "That way, we don't have to hear confessions."

Rivette laughed indulgently and wondered how he could make a graceful exit.

Father Cusimano's expression suddenly turned wistful. "You know, Luciana Canova was a devout woman. She always came to confession, every Satur-

259

day. In fact . . ." He turned back to the image on the screen and stared hard.

Rivette shot forward, willing the priest's memory to respond. "Yes? Is he familiar to you now?"

"No." Cusimano sighed again. "One of *Il Cardinale*'s priests was on duty alone here the Saturday before Signorina Canova was killed. I thought for a moment that your man looked like that priest, *un poco*. But . . ."

"How are they the same, *Padre?*" Rivette's voice was taut with insistence. "What do you remember?"

"Well, he was much younger, this priest. But his face, around the eyes. That is much the same, if you allow for aging."

"This priest's eyes, do you remember the color?"

Cusimano nodded, glad at last to redeem himself with a positive response. "Oh, *si*. He had eyes that were most peculiar. That is why I can remember them. I have a good memory for people, you know. That is why I am head of this parish. I know all of my flock from the first time I meet them. I'll remember you next time you come, you'll see. Ask anyone here, they'll tell y—"

Rivette took the old man's arm in both hands and squeezed. "Please, *Padre!* The eyes! What color?"

Cusimano turned, startled by the demand in Rivette's voice. "I've never seen anything like them. They were a piercing blue. To look at them was to see the sky."

260

Chapter Twenty-three

It took most of the next day for Durant to sell Sibille on a trip to Lugano. At first, the bureau chief was irate that Durant had been sitting on the details of Richardson's murder, but he calmed down when the complexity of the entire story was laid out for him. Durant left out any speculation on what Buchmeunster's manuscript might turn out to be, since the only information he had on that was secondhand from Toni, and he was increasingly skeptical about how she'd gotten it.

In the end, Sibille agreed to let Durant make the trip, but if it turned up nothing, the story as they knew it would have to be reported. It wouldn't be much longer before some other news outlet in Rome stumbled across enough leads to put it together.

There was a late Alitalia flight to Milan. He made it with minutes to spare, spent the night at the Hotel Augustus, then walked to the rail station and caught the *diretto* in the morning.

The train took him just across Italy's northern border to Lugano, nestled against a lake by the same name at the edge of the Alps. As the train pulled in, Durant was surprised to see green lawns with no snow, an image that clashed with his Christmas card notion of Switzerland in late December.

He left the station and crossed the street to catch the funicular to Lugano's Old Town. It was a short ride down, and he spent most of it adjusting to another surprise—palm trees set against the mountains.

The funicular ended its run in Piazza Ciocarro, and Durant had to backtrack up the hill to reach Cathedral San Lorenzo. His heavy wool jacket turned uncomfortably warm, so he took it off and slung it over his shoulder.

The church was an imposing Renaissance structure that brooded above Lugano's waterfront, giving the impression that while it was glad to see the town prosper as a resort, it didn't entirely approve of all the hotels and shops that came with success.

There was no answer to his knock at the rectory, so he walked around to the terrace. Several tourists stood there taking pictures of the panorama below. There was also a thin, balding priest sitting in the sun. He was absorbed in reading a slim black volume.

Durant cleared his throat and tried to concentrate on the phrase-book German he'd memorized on the train. *"Guten Morgen, Vater. Wo ist Vater* Ernst Schwemmer?"

The priest turned from his book with a look of curiosity before he replied in English. "You've found him. Did you come all the way from America just to see me?"

Durant was startled by Schwemmer's directness. "Well, I . . . no . . . but I did come here to see you. How did you? . . ."

Schwemmer tapped his book. *"Summa Theologica.* 'The priest is a man of power and authority,' says

Thomas Aquinas, at any rate. After the two-millionth confession, you begin to understand him." Schwemmer smiled indulgently. "You're not from the Continent, or you'd know we speak Italian in this canton. The British would not have bothered with any language but their own. Canadians rarely come here, so you must be an American." He beckoned Durant to the empty chair next to him. "You'll forgive me if I don't stand. Rheumatism, you know. The sun's good for it. Now, what can an old curate do for you?"

"My name's Craig Durant, Father. "I'm a reporter based in Rome, and I've come about someone I think you used to know."

"I've met a great many people over the years, Mr. Durant. I hope it's someone I can remember."

"Dr. Andrew Muller."

The priest turned toward the lake and rubbed his chin pensively. "Andrew Muller."

Durant handed Schwemmer the photograph from Muller's book. "It's been quite a while, but I wonder if you recognize this."

The priest glanced at the picture and stood as he handed it back. "Shall we take a walk, Mr. Durant? Helps the rheumatism, you know."

They strolled off the terrace and back down toward the center of the Old Town.

"Mr. Durant, you should see Lugano at the peak of the season. Sailboats on the lake, shops jammed with tourists, and the casinos going full tilt. Sometimes it seems as if half of Europe comes here to play. But it's a very quiet town for a priest, actually. Aside from mass and sightseers at the cathedral, I don't get many visitors. Now, suddenly, I've had two people come to inquire about a man I haven't thought of in forty years. Odd, don't you agree?"

He led the way into a small *taverna* at the foot of the hill. It was nearly empty, and they took a table by a back window that overlooked the lake.

Schwemmer waved to the barkeep. *"Due feldschlosschen, per favore.* Are you familiar with our Swiss beer, Mr. Durant?"

"No, I haven't tried it."

"Well, I find it curative." The two steins arrived and Schwemmer took a long drink. "Now, as I was saying, a priest came to see me about Andrew . . . let me see, about three weeks ago, it was. His name was Bergamo. He'd a terrible scar across one cheek."

Durant tensed. "Did he tell you why he was interested in Dr. Muller?"

"Not really. Only that he was from some obscure Vatican department and that poor Andrew had died."

"What did he want to know?"

The priest shrugged. "His background, what I knew of him when we were in seminary together."

Durant felt his heart skip a beat. He took a sip of beer to keep from appearing anxious. "When was that?"

"Oh, years ago. I went to school with Andrew when we were boys in Seehausen. He was a brilliant student, a bit different from the rest of us, but he had a fiery mind. Excelled when we went on to seminary. Andrew tutored me for many a Latin exam. I had a pretty hard time of it after he left."

"He didn't graduate?"

"No." Schwemmer gave Durant a hard, appraising look. "Did you know Andrew, Mr. Durant?"

"Not really. I'd met with him a couple of times before he died."

"Then why have you come all this way from Rome to ask me about him? Are you going to write a memorial of some sort? He was quite a scholar, I understand."

"No. I have personal reasons for wanting to know."

"They must be very compelling for you to be stirring the dust of forty-odd years. There are very few people left whose memory of that time is clear. Mine isn't always what it should be."

Durant swished the beer around in his mug as he weighed Schwemmer's words. "Father, a priest was murdered in Rome while saying mass on Christmas Eve."

"I read about that. A terrible thing. But what would Andrew have to do with that? He died back in November."

"That priest heard Dr. Muller's deathbed confession. He was one of the last people to see Muller alive."

Schwemmer smiled skeptically. "Mr. Durant, I must have heard ten thousand last confessions in my lifetime. I'm still healthy."

"The night Muller died, that same priest disappeared. The police found his car in the mountains south of Rome, smashed and burned. He was missing for nearly a month, until someone lured him back to his church on Christmas Eve."

The old priest's smile faded into a look of reluctant belief. "Lured? What do you mean?"

"Whoever was looking for this priest found out that he was very close to a young woman and her son. The

265

little boy was kidnapped and used as bait. He was released in the church just before the priest was killed.''

"Mein Gott!" said Schwemmer, his voice little more than a hoarse whisper. He stared at the lake, where an excursion boat was preparing to cast off. "Such a horrible deed.''

Durant pressed his advantage. "Dr. Muller was an expert in ancient Middle Eastern languages. Did he have any interest in that area when you knew him?''

"Oh, yes." The old priest nodded, his eyes faraway as they probed his memories. "Andrew read voraciously about other religions, at least as much as the rector would let him. He was always comparing them to our own, picking up little similarities here and there, particularly with Islam. He probably knew the Koran better than most Arabs. It doesn't surprise me that he turned out to be an archaeologist.''

"Tell me, Father. Why did Muller leave the seminary? Doubts?''

"Everyone who tries to contemplate God and His universe has those from time to time. It's just His Way of keeping us from becoming too smug, I suppose. No, there was nothing wrong with Andrew's faith.'' Schwemmer paused for another mouthful of beer, which he swirled around thoughtfully.

"Priests have always been a rather peculiar lot, Mr. Durant. Guardians of the soul against the frailties of the human will, but damned if they start acting too much like human beings themselves. Seminary life back then was practically medieval in its discipline. It was the opinion of the authorities that Andrew simply didn't fit the mold. And that, in the eyes of the Hounds of God, was the ultimate sin.''

266

"But what was it that made him not fit?"

Schwemmer crossed his arms. "We are talking about events of nearly half a century ago. How can that possibly matter?"

"Look, at least one man is dead already because of something that involved Andrew Muller. If I knew why, maybe I could prevent anyone else from being killed, but I don't. You may hold the key."

The old priest looked silently out the window. The excursion boat was pulling slowly away from the quay. "Is his mother still alive?"

"Yes."

"A remarkable woman. Must be well up into her eighties by now, I should think." Schwemmer turned back to Durant, his face somber. "There's no reason to destroy her son's reputation. That's all she has left, you know. So I tell you this only for background, not for publication. Agreed?"

Durant nodded.

"In the spring of our final year, Andrew and another student went off to Berlin on holiday. They were to be gone only a few days, but it was nearly two weeks before Andrew returned alone. The police located the other fellow a few weeks later, living on Unter den Linden with a rather notorious female impersonator. Of course, he was summarily dismissed by the rector. As for Andrew . . . well, guilt by association was a moving force in Germany back then, and seminaries were no different." He leaned across the table toward Durant. "Mind you, Andrew never seemed at all abnormal to me, and there never was anything concrete found against him. But rumors about him began to

267

spread. Pressure mounted for his expulsion, and finally, the rector had Andrew purged."

"With no evidence, no hearing?"

Schwemmer smiled grimly. "You Americans are so naive about the niceties of justice. No, he was simply put out of the fold a few months before graduation. I remember when he left. They told him right after vespers, wanted him out that night so there wouldn't be a lot of talk among the other fellows about seeing him leave. I watched him pack. He was furious. Near the top of his class and being treated like a felon with no proof whatsoever. He swore revenge on Holy Mother Church and left in a blind rage. That was the last I saw or heard of him." The priest sighed, relieved by his disclosure.

"Did anyone take him seriously?"

"Oh, I never told anyone else, not even that fellow from Rome. You're the first to know. I didn't think anything would ever come of it, and as time went by, I think I was proved right."

Durant paid for the beer, and they walked together toward the funicular stop in the *piazza*. Schwemmer decided to ride along. They climbed aboard the nearly empty car and sat by the door.

"You know, Mr. Durant, I have great difficulty believing that Andrew could have anything to do with the violence you've described. Even when we were very young, when the other children would bully him because of his brilliance, he wouldn't strike them back. He wasn't capable of it."

"Seems to me he'd want to get even somehow. Didn't he ever try?"

Schwemmer gestured toward the backdrop of villas

and mountains, sliding slowly by as the car climbed toward the rail station. "Have you noticed that Switzerland is a very ordered country? Everything neat, in its place, and air so crystal clear that you can see for two hundred kilometers if you're high enough. Andrew's mind was like that. The most sophisticated abstractions were effortless for him. In debate, he would find the flaw in any argument and chip away until it crumbled. He was the intellectual better of practically everyone, and he drove himself to prove it to them all. That was his weapon."

"It doesn't sound like he had many friends."

"Oh, no one likes to be shown his own stupidity, and Andrew was quite good at that. But he valued what friendships he had, and he tried hard not to make enemies. He—"

The car lurched heavily. Near the top of the run, it hung motionless while inertia was spent, then began to roll backward on the rails, slowly at first. The motorman pulled on the emergency brake, but it did nothing. He tugged harder on the lever, then pumped it frantically, but the car's deliberate acceleration continued. The door whooshed open, and through it, the shrieking of the wheels rose in an earsplitting crescendo.

Schwemmer turned to Durant, whose hands were frozen to the grab rail with white fear. There was no fear on the old priest's face, only a tranquil smile. He chopped down hard on Durant's wrists to break the grip, throwing his own body against the reporter and hurtling him out the door into the green blur.

Durant hit the grassy slope and rolled in an explosion of pain. When he stopped, the sky faded into bright flashes, then blackness. He shook it clear and gingerly tried to pull himself up. Pain lanced through one shoulder and he fell. Dislocated, he thought. He managed to raise himself to a sitting position with the other arm and looked around. Over the waterfront, there was a growing cloud of smoke. He followed it to its source, the remains of the funicular and an oil truck burning on the *piazza*.

The smoke was clearly visible from the excursion boat on the lake, where a well-dressed white-haired burgher sat by the rail, peering at it through binoculars. The steward didn't wish to disturb him, but his job required that all passengers be attended to. He cleared his throat and presented his tray.

"Perdono, signore."

The tourist didn't respond but kept his binoculars trained on the fire just above the harbor.

The steward tried again. *"Entschuldigen Sie, mein Herr.* Would you care for something to drink?"

The passenger lowered his field glasses and turned to the steward. *"Ja,"* said the tourist, his cold blue eyes impassive as he took a small glass of *kirschwasser* from the tray. *"Bitte."*

Chapter Twenty-four

John Chapman rubbed his eyes, put his glasses back on, and went back to the start of the page. It was a curious text, a copy of an early Greek translation of Cyril of Jerusalem's *Catechetical Lectures*. Its syntax made Chapman wonder what the translator's native tongue had been.

His housekeeper's gentle knock broke his concentration. *"Mi scusi, Padre."*

"Yes, Maria. What is it?"

The library door opened and a short, thin woman in black entered, wringing her hands. *"Telefono, Padre.* They asked specifically for you, although I told them you were not to be interrupted. I—"

Chapman held up both hands in a gesture of peace and reassurance. "Please, Maria. It's all right. I'll take the call." He slipped past her and headed for the telephone near the entryway, regretting his decision not to install an extension in the library. The housekeeper trailed after him, more than a little curious as to what was important enough to disturb her employer so early on the last day of the year. Chapman gave her an impatient look, and she retired toward the kitchen, muttering something he couldn't quite make out.

"John Chapman. *Chi parla?*"

"Forgive me, Father, for this intrusion. I am Inspector Barzini, *Publica Sicurezza*. May I ask, are you acquainted with one Kathryn Muller?"

A chill of foreboding rose like a wave on Chapman's scalp and washed down his spine. "Yes, I know her well. Why?"

The detective was professionally sympathetic. "I'm afraid there has been an unfortunate mishap at her residence. A fire of unknown origin, not very large but quite smoky."

"Where is she? Is she injured?"

"I'm sorry, Father. She was apparently asleep when the smoke caught her. She was found still in bed. The investigators found a note in her personal effects. It said that you should be informed if there was any emergency. My condolences, Father."

Chapman suddenly felt very old. His head pounded and a tide of dizziness swept over him, forcing him to grab the table for support. The blood pressure medication. He'd forgotten it at breakfast. Chapman took several deep breaths, trying to shake the feeling that he was about to collapse.

"Father?"

The detective's voice brought the priest's attention back to the telephone. He felt the room stop spinning, and the sensation passed. "Yes?"

"Perhaps you know whether Kathryn Muller had any relatives? There are formalities to be observed, you know."

"No, I don't think so. She had a son, but he died several weeks ago."

"Oh. In that case, perhaps I may impose? I'm sorry,

Father, but someone must identify her remains and make the arrangements. Could you?"

"Of course."

"*Gràzie*, Father. Just come to the *questura* and ask at the desk. The sergeant will tell you where to go."

"Fine. I'll be there shortly, Inspector. *Arivederci.*"

"*Arivederci*, Father."

Chapman replaced the telephone and started for the hall closet to get his coat. Memories of thirty years of knowing Kathryn Muller flooded his mind.

Christmas Day. The envelope!

He did a quick about-face and went to his desk in the library. With shaking hands, he pulled out the envelope and tore it open.

There was a small key inside, wrapped in a handwritten note. He sank into his chair and read it.

Dear John,

I was hoping that I could ask you to return this letter unopened someday, but since you're now reading it, I must assume that I'm dead.

I trust your judgment, John. I know that I can rely upon you to protect Andrew's reputation if at all possible. I will be forever in your debt.

In this envelope, I've enclosed a key to a safety deposit box at the *Banco di Santo Spirito*. The contents of that box I now give into your keeping.

Yours in deepest friendship,

Kathryn Muller

The cab wove slowly through a wet morning rush hour, heightening Chapman's anxiety over Kathryn Muller's bequest. After what seemed like hours in one long traffic jam, the driver let him out just down the block from the marble fortress of *Banco di Santo Spirito*. Chapman almost sprinted to the entrance.

A portly guard in an *opéra-bouffe* uniform stood inside, watching the rain. Chapman pulled on the door handles with no effect. The guard simply smiled at the dripping-wet priest who was trying to gain entrance.

Chapman knocked politely, but the guard only nodded. Chapman had a sudden impulse to kick in the glass, but he knocked again and pointed to the lock. "*Apra, per favore!*" He yelled in the hope that someone else inside would hear, preferably someone with more authority than the guard. More sense, at least.

The guard gave him a blank shrug and pointed to the large clock in the foyer. It read 8:28 A.M., two minutes before official opening time. It began to pour, and Chapman seethed as he pressed further under the recessed entryway to avoid as much of it as he could.

At precisely eight-thirty the guard pulled a set of keys from his pocket and opened the door. Chapman's wet shoes nearly dumped him on the slick marble as he strode grimly to the information counter. A young woman sat with her back to him, talking animatedly on the telephone and filing her nails.

"No, Rodolfo! I am not going out with you again unless you take me to dinner tonight. No, I don't care about your wife! *Cretina!* No, you won't get even a kiss from me if you don't! *Che? Bastardo!*" She slammed down the telephone and concentrated on her manicure.

Chapman cleared his throat but drew no reaction. He lost what patience he had left and slapped his hand loudly on the countertop.

The girl jumped and spun around with an angry look on her face. It melted into indifference when she saw the soaked priest in front of her. "*Si?*"

"Excuse me, signorina. Where do I find the safety deposit box department?"

The girl pointed out a desk at the end of the row of teller cages. "Over there, *Padre*." She smiled briefly and went back to her nails.

Chapman went to the desk, where a greying man in an equally grey suit rose to greet him as he approached. Chapman could feel his fists clench and his mouth setting into a tight line. He inhaled deeply and willed himself to relax.

"Now, *Padre*, I am Pietro Macelli. How may we be of service?"

"I'm John Chapman, and I'm here for a friend, Kathryn Muller. She's asked me to check some items in her safety deposit box." He paused to let Macelli make the next move, wondering how far he'd have to go before he ran out of truth and had to start weaving some facts from scratch.

The bank man furrowed his brow. "Well, now. That might pose a problem. It's not your box, after all. We would require some authority."

Chapman smiled politely. "Oh, there's no problem, signore. I've known Mrs. Muller for years. She's asked me to do this as a favor because she's out of the country and wants some papers from that box sent to her. I'm following her explicit instructions."

"Still, we'd need some documentation. You never know. Sometimes people come and tell me they have permission to open a box, and it turns out later that the person who supposedly gave it was dead. We'd need a court order unless you have some written authority from the box holder."

"I see." Chapman fought the urge to run out of the bank. He forced an annoyed glare and scratched his chin, drawing Macelli's attention to the clerical collar. The reaction was immediate.

"Oh! *Padre*, I don't mean to imply . . . That is, I don't think you . . ." He spread his hands in a broad gesture of helplessness. "I'm sure you understand."

The priest felt his entrenched distaste for deception begin to stir. He shoved it back into a corner of his mind. There couldn't be any more attempts at this later. News of Mrs. Muller's death would reach the bank shortly, and that would mean having to go through the courts for access to the box . . . a delay of months, perhaps years. He would have to bluff.

"Some time ago, Kathryn had me sign some sort of papers for this, but I don't know if she ever sent it back in to the bank."

Macelli brightened. "That would solve the problem. I'll have a look." He pulled a set of wire-framed glasses from his jacket, put them on, and began to thumb through a large card file box next to his desk. "Ah! *Eccolo!*" He nodded approvingly and held the card for Chapman to examine. "You see? Proof of authority. Now, we'll see about opening the box. Why didn't you say so?"

"Actually, I had forgotten." The priest stared at the card, more than a little surprised to see his own name on a signature line, although the script certainly wasn't his.

"*Si*, according to this, the card was sent back to us two weeks ago. Now, if I could have some identification?"

Chapman handed over his driver's license, which Macelli compared with the man sitting across the desk, then returned.

"*Bene!* Let's go and sign you in, then. I'm sorry about the delay, *Padre*, but we can't be too careful nowadays, what with the *brigatisti* and all."

Dizziness hit Chapman as he stood, buckling his knees and dropping him against the desk. Macelli gasped and caught the priest before he could fall any further, lowering him gently back into the chair.

"You're very pale. Should we call you a physician?"

"No." Chapman was disappointed by the lack of conviction in his voice. It came out as a reedy whisper. He tried again and managed a more normal tone. "I'll be fine."

Macelli scurried off and returned a moment later with a short dark-haired man in an expensive suit that was far too tight for his girth. There was a red carnation in his lapel. Macelli kept a deferential distance as the new man took command, shooing off the knot of people who'd gathered around the desk, sending a secretary for water, and instructing Macelli to locate some smelling salts.

"Forgive me, *Padre*, but you do look ill. We should call you an ambulance immediately."

"No, I'll be all right. Just need a moment, that's

all." Chapman struggled to regain his balance. "I'm a little weak. Had the flu."

The bank officer smiled solicitously. "Are you certain?"

Chapman nodded and pulled himself to a standing position. "I'm really very sorry about this. I appreciate your kindness, but I wonder if we could just go and open the box? I'm quite all right now."

"Of course." The dark-suited man snapped his fingers in Macelli's direction, who stood waiting with the smelling salts several feet away. "Escort *Il Padre* to the vault and give him whatever he needs. You are to assist him until he leaves."

Chapman silently cursed the bank officer's obsequious nature and wondered how to get rid of Macelli. He didn't want anyone else around when the box was opened.

Chapman focused all his will on looking normal as Macelli led him to the elevator. When they reached the vault, he leaned heavily against a wall, hoping that its cold strength might prop up what little was left of his own.

"Ah, number 97! This is the one you want." Macelli tapped a box in a chest-high row and turned around. He gasped at the priest's appearance. Chapman's face was nearly grey and it glistened with sweat.

"*Padre*, are you well? Are you certain you don't want us to get you medical attention?"

Chapman mustered a weak smile. "No. I'll be quite all right. *Gràzie*."

Macelli peered at him uncertainly. "*Allora*, perhaps you'd just let me remove the box for you."

"No, that won't be necessary. I can do it, believe me."

"Well, if you'll just sign—" Macelli patted the pockets of his suit. "I've forgotten the signature card. Perhaps you could just sign the register while I get it?"

"Certainly." Chapman waited until he was alone, then eased along the wall to the small table where the register lay open, trying not to acknowledge the sensation that his right side was growing numb. He tried to pick up the pen, but it kept slipping from his grasp. Finally, he grabbed the pen with his left hand, transferred it to his right and, working with both, managed to close his fingers around it.

His entire body shook from the effort it took to move the pen across the page. When he reached the edge, he dropped the pen and it clattered to the floor. Chapman stared in growing horror at what he'd written, an illegible scrawl that wandered from one line to another.

Macelli returned and stared to compare the card to Chapman's entry in the register. After a moment, he looked up. "Forgive me, *Padre*, but perhaps you could come back another time. I don't think—"

"No!" Chapman was startled by the resolve in his voice. "I must get into that box today. My dizzy spell has affected my writing, that's all. Now, if you will follow your superior's instructions to assist me, kindly unlock the box." He held out Mrs. Muller's key in his good hand.

With a shrug, Macelli took that key and one of his own, and inserted them in the lock. He tugged on the box to loosen it and gave Chapman a coolly officious smile. "Is there anything else you'd like? Do you wish me to stay?"

"No. You've been very kind and I appreciate it very much. *Gràzie*."

"*Bene*. If you need me for anything, please let the guard outside know." Macelli gave a slight bow and left the vault, exhaling loudly with relief as he went.

Chapman worked his way around to the box, pulled it open with his left hand, and lifted the lid until he could see inside it. It held only one item—a bulging manila envelope. It was too tightly wedged to lift out with one hand. He tried to dig it out with both, but another wave of dizziness washed through him, sucking away his strength. The only feeling left in his right arm was a dull numbness that confirmed it was still there, and he couldn't lift it any higher than his waist.

Chapman braced his body against the wall and pried hard with his good hand. The envelope came free. He lifted it and squinted at the large block printing on the front:

PROPERTY OF FATHER JOHN CHAPMAN

Chapman eased the envelope over the edge. It snagged on a corner and tore when he tried to free it. A red hardbound notebook fell out. He slid down against the rows of boxes until he was sitting on the floor, then waited for his vision to clear. It improved, but there was still a slight blur in his right eye. He drove back panic with a deep breath and opened the book to the front page. It was filled with Andrew Muller's tight script. Chapman squinted and began to read.

He was near the end of Muller's narrative when the sound of a clearing throat broke his concentration. Macelli frowned at him from the vault entrance. "Forgive me, *Padre*, but it's been nearly an hour. I thought perhaps . . ." He tried to help the priest off the floor.

"Please, I can do this myself." Chapman pulled himself up along the wall, praying that his left arm wouldn't give way. "If you want to help, get me a large envelope and a pen."

Macelli nodded vigorously and left. Chapman used his remaining strength to slip the notebook back into its envelope. When Macelli came back, he put that inside the large bank envelope and sealed it, then laboriously printed an address across the front.

"Now, signore, I need to have this taken immediately by bank courier. It's extremely important that it be delivered quickly, and I don't want the courier stopping anywhere else along the way."

The bank's man looked pained at the request. Chapman cut him off before he could protest. "Is this something you can do for me? Or do I need to ask your superior?" He let his body sag against the wall. "You know, I'm starting to feel dizzy again. I may need that doctor and ambulance after all. Unless, of course, you can get me a taxi straight away and dispatch the courier without any further delay." He closed his eyes and clutched at his chest for effect.

Macelli paled and took the envelope. "Of course, *Padre. Certamente.*"

The clouds were breaking up by the time Rivette joined the flow of pedestrian traffic through the St.

Anne gate into Vatican City. He walked the narrow streets until he came to the papal gardens, where the sun was beginning to pull the dampness off the ground, wrapping the fountains and trees in a low haze. The noise of the Roman streets began to fade as he walked deeper into the gardens, and Rivette found himself drawn into their serenity as he strolled among the manicured greenery.

A shrill scream rushing toward him set the photographer bristling with alarm. He wheeled toward the sound, and a blow glanced off his legs. A high-pitched laugh followed, whirling around him from a source he couldn't spot. He snapped into a defensive crouch, but all he saw were two dark-haired boys, no more than ten, shrieking their delight as they disappeared up the path and into the shrubbery.

Rivette closed his eyes and forced himself to relax. When his breathing had returned to normal, he got his bearings and resumed his walk, heading for the walled tower of San Giovanni. Near the tower, he left the main path and turned toward a greenhouse in the middle of a large rose garden.

A rich tenor voice floated out as he approached, making him smile with anticipation. *Rigoletto*, one of his favorites. Inside, he found a squat, bearded monk who sang as he worked over a tray of orchids. The monk paused to try for a high C but cracked it. With a shake of his head, he wiped his hands on the heavy cotton apron he wore and resumed the aria, taking the note an octave lower. Rivette listened, the cheroot in his mouth keeping time like a baton as the monk sang, until he could resist no longer. He pulled out the cheroot, cleared his throat, and joined the aria in full voice.

Startled, the monk turned but continued to sing, and they flew to the end of it together.

"*Bravissimo!*" Rivette applauded.

The monk smiled broadly and bowed toward Rivette. "To you as well." He wiped his hand again and held it out. "I'm Brother Sebastiani. Who might you be?"

"Francois Rivette." He shook the hand. "I was nearby and heard you singing."

"*Si*, I do a good bit of that. I don't get much company here, although most of what you see in the way of flowers in the Holy Father's gardens are my work. So, I entertain all my children." His arm swept the hundreds of plants as he spoke.

"They're beautiful. So many varieties."

Sebastiani nodded. "We have plants from all over the world here. Some we have to keep in the greenhouse because the climate's not right. It's quite a collection, at least to horticulturists. Would you like a tour?"

"Certainly. But first, *Fratello*, I wonder if you might be able to help me. There's a plant I found that I just can't identify." Rivette pulled a plastic bag from his pocket, with the small yellow fruit Teresa had picked up in the elevator. "Have you ever seen one of these before?"

The old monk took the bag and turned it as he held it up to the light. "Interesting. You found this, you say?"

"Actually, I didn't find it, a friend gave it to me. Do you know what it is?" He stuck the cheroot back in his mouth and began to chew it expectantly.

"Oh, *si*. You friend has exotic tastes. This is *solahum*

sodomeum, the Apple of Sodom. You'll see it occasionally in a greenhouse. I keep a few myself. Here, let me show you." He led Rivette to a corner where four of the small shrubs were growing in large pots.

"Do these grow wild?"

"Oh, that would be extremely unusual in this country. They're native to the shores of the Dead Sea. I only have them because of their religious significance."

Rivette gave Sebastiani a quizzical look, hoping for a clue as to why a brutal killer would leave the fruit at the scene of each crime.

The monk pulled one of the shrubs closer. "These are considered to be a symbol of sin in the Middle East. Back in the Crusades, travelers brought back stories of a beautiful fruit they found growing where the ancient cities of Sodom and Gomorrah were supposed to have stood. It was very tempting, but if you reached out to take one, the fruit turned to smoke and ash in your hands."

"But they seem solid enough to me."

"Oh, what the Crusaders saw was probably just insect damage and dry rot. The ones we have don't do that. These are part of the nightshade family. They're just ordinary plants with a peculiar history."

"Are they poisonous?"

"Oh, I don't think a bite or two would do much. They're not much worse than a lot of houseplants. In fact, one fellow came by here a few months ago and wanted to keep one in his room. He told me he'd spent years in the Middle East and wanted something to remind him of it."

Rivette felt his pulse quickening. A profile of the killer began to appear in his mind: possibly born Arab or Israeli, a religious zealot with some bizarre notion of sin that he sought to purge by murdering women . . . *If* this was the same man he'd seen at Richardson's murder and at the Canova funeral. "This man, *Fratello*. Do you remember what he looked like?"

The monk stroked his beard for a moment. "He was a priest. Can't quite recall his face, though. It's his eyes that stick in my mind. They were striking, the most vibrant blue I've ever seen. It was almost as if he could look at you, but right through you. Bottomless, *capisci*? Not very friendly, either. A most unusual man."

Rivette nearly bit his cheroot in two. "Can you remember anything else about him? Hair? Height?" He could no longer keep the urgency from his voice.

"No, I'm sorry. The eyes are all that come to me." Suddenly Sebastiani brightened. "But I do know his name and where he lives."

Rivette swallowed a triumphant shout.

The monk continued to speak as he led Rivette to a battered desk near the green house door. "You see, I don't usually give people my plants; it's just an indefinite loan. If they're rare in this part of Italy, I may need to get them back later for propagation. So, I keep careful records of where they go. You can't just go asking around the Vatican for this priest or that, you know." He picked up a worn ledger and thumbed through the pages, stopping to point out one entry with a ten-year-old date. "You wouldn't think someone would lie about this sort of thing, but this fellow claimed to be a monsignor with *Propaganda Fide* and turned out to be a seminarian. Since then, I've always asked for identification." He resumed flipping through the book.

"Ah, *eccolo*! Your blue-eyed priest was Lorenzo Zeffirelli. He can be reached at the *Palazzo Sant' Uffizio*, through the Holy Office."

Durant groaned as he climbed the stairs to the bureau. He'd dislocated his right shoulder in the fall from the funicular, and his arm was in a sling. As luck would have it, that was the side the handrail was on. He slipped on the steps, and a pitchfork of agony ripped through the shoulder as he bounced off the wall. By the time he reached the landing, beads of sweat stood out on his forehead.

After spending nearly a week in Lugano's hospital, he was getting the hang of being left-handed, and he wouldn't be in the sling much longer, anyway. He reached for the bureau door and reminded himself that things could have been terminally worse had it not been for Father Schwemmer.

The telephone rang as he walked in, but Sibille had it before it could ring a second time. The bureau chief listened for a moment, then held it out to Durant. "It's for you, Lefty."

Durant settled himself gingerly into a chair, trying not to hit the shoulder again. Then he took the call.

"Craig, where've you been?" Toni's voice was a mixture of irritation and curiosity. "I've been trying to reach you for days. Are you avoiding me?"

"Of course not, Toni. I've just been out on a surprise assignment, a little Christmas present from Mike." He hoped Sibille hadn't told her it was a vacation.

"Are you sure I haven't made you angry? I know I

286

was a bit cool when you came back to the apartment after lunch on Christmas Day, but after all, Craig, did you *have* to work on Christmas? That was pretty disillusioning, you know.''

"Look, you were perfectly right to be annoyed, and I'm not upset. But I did have something that couldn't wait to get done.'' Annoyed was putting it kindly in light of the scene she'd made, but he didn't really want to get back into that, and from the sound of it, neither did Toni.

"But what about the next day? Why didn't you at least call and let me know you were leaving?'' She was not convinced.

"Well, I didn't really have time. Sibille just pointed me at the door and told me to get moving. I barely made the flight. And—''

"Flight? Out of the country?''

"Toni, it never really got going. I went up to Milan to look into something, but it didn't pan out.'' Durant felt his temper heating up over Toni's insistent questions. He had to admit, though, that dropping out of sight for several days without a word was a chickenshit thing to do, especially after he'd poured out his soul in their Christmas bedroom scene.

"Craig, I have some news for you. *La Scoperta* is about to break the most significant story in two thousand years.''

Durant shot upright in his chair and felt pain tear through his shoulder from the effort. "What?!''

"I've drafted the whole story. I'm going to make a few revisions and it goes to the editor tomorrow. The whole world is going to be set on its ear by the Nicodemus Codex.''

"You have the story, all of it?"

Toni was triumphant. "Enough to know what it says, who wrote it, and that the scroll is the right age to be authentic."

"Are you sure? How reliable are your sources?"

"I've seen the translation."

Durant nearly exploded. "Well, what does it say?!"

Toni gave an exultant chuckle. "Read Sunday's edition and find out. Maybe you could buy one in Milan."

"All right. I deserve that. I'm sorry I disappeared, but it couldn't be helped, okay? Could we meet later and talk this out?"

"*Certamente, caro mio.* But not lunch. I'll come by the bureau and pick you up after work. Maybe we could have a little New Year's Eve dinner?"

"That'd be great. No work, I promise."

"Me, too."

"Toni, I love you."

"I love you, too, Craig. *Ciao.*"

"Bye."

Durant put the telephone back in its cradle and started to sort the small mound of correspondence and clippings that had accumulated on his desk. He hefted the large manila envelope on top. "Hey, Mike, are you sure this thing isn't a bomb?" It was a question only half in jest.

The bureau chief tapped his pipe on the edge of the wastebasket. "Could be, but it would have to be a well-heeled bunch of terrorists. That came by bank courier a few minutes ago."

"I hope he left a return address. Well, let's see." He braced the envelope's bulk between his knees and tore the end open with his left hand. Before he could empty it, the telephone rang again and he picked it up.

"Global News, Durant."

"Oh, Craig! I'm so glad I've found you." It was Rita, and she was struggling to keep from breaking down completely.

"What's wrong, Rita?"

"It's Father. He's in the hospital. A stroke."

"Christ! When?"

"A couple of hours ago. He was at a bank when it happened. They've got him at Salvator Mundi now."

"How is he?"

"The doctors aren't sure. They won't know for several days." Rita sniffed back her tears and took a deep breath. "I'm sorry to bother you, Craig. Father was able to talk, and he kept insisting I call you. He wouldn't let the doctors sedate him until I agreed to do it."

"Look, that's all right. I'm glad you did. Anything I can do?"

"No, thanks."

"Well, let me know if there is, okay? I'll keep in touch."

"Right. Thanks."

Durant hung up in disbelief. John Chapman, scholar and priest, did not seem like someone who would experience what the doctors so politely termed a "vascular accident." What could have happened to trigger it? He emptied the large manila envelope onto his desk and found the smaller one inside with Chapman's name on it. The hardbound notebook he pulled out of that envelope bore no identifying marks on its cover.

On the first page was a date penned in fading ink:

Feb. 6, 1939. Page after page of handwritten entries followed. He began to read:

I, Andrew Muller, begin this journal because there is no one left in whom I can confide. Anger grows like a cancer within me, and I find my thoughts turning always to revenge against Holy Mother Church. I have dedicated my life to the service of Almighty God, but evil men within His Church now block that path to me forever.

An institution, even God's church, must be judged by those who control it. If they are corrupt with error and ambition, then the church is no better. Both must be destroyed, as God wiped clean the sins of the earth with the Great Flood, so that He can build anew.

I am His instrument. I swear that I shall bring to bear all the talents God has given me to grow in knowledge and strength until one day, like our Lord Jesus, I shall drive the moneychangers and aggrandizers from the Temple. I shall not rest until I have smashed the Rock of Peter to make way for the true faith.

May Our Lord be with me.

Durant's eyes strained from the faded script, but he squinted and read on. Over the decades, in different inks and in different cities, the story continued. The last entries detailed his mistaken meeting with Durant and Toni, then his discussion of the Dead Sea Scrolls with Durant the following day. It closed with Muller's

290

question: "Has He sent me a new, more powerful tool for His work?"

"My God!" Durant's stomach burned with panic as the impact of the journal sank in. "What is this? Toni, what are you about to do?"

He picked up the telephone and frantically dialed Toni's office. She was gone for the day, out on assignment.

Chapter Twenty-five

The final night of the year arrived clear but moon-less. Durant leaned against Global's *pensione* office building, watching occasional rockets flare over the skyline and listening to the growing din of celebration. Muller's journal, tucked dōwn in a large pocket of his battered overcoat, dragged against him like a mill-stone. He pulled the coat tightly against himself to ward off a chill that he knew wasn't really in the air.

The resonance of Toni's Maserati decelerating pulled his attention back down to the street. The car coasted to a stop by the curb and he ran to it. Toni smiled as he jumped in, but the sharp glare of the dome light gave her face a hard, cold look as they kissed their greeting.

"What happened to you?" Toni asked, her eyes drawn to the sling under Durant's open coat.

"Part of my trip north. I fell."

She gave him a skeptical look.

"Really, Toni. It was accidental. I'll tell you about it later. Let's go."

Toni gunned the car and moved easily into the light

traffic. "Well, where to, signore? Dinner in Traste-vere?"

"Not right away. Could we drive around awhile?"

Toni looked puzzled and hurt. "But I thought later we'd go back to my apartment and—"

"There's nothing I'd like better." Durant put a hand on her arm and squeezed. "But I really need to talk to you first, before we do any celebrating. Okay?"

She shrugged, still mystified by his behavior. "If you say so. Anywhere in particular?"

"No. Just so we can talk. In the car will be fine."

She turned down a narrow side street, skirting a few tourists who'd come to toss coins for the sooty gods of the Trevi Fountain. Immediately a small chair crashed into the street in front of the car. Toni swerved hard. Durant's injured shoulder smacked the dash and he gasped in pain.

"Sorry, Craig. I forgot my cardinal rule about shortcuts on New Year's Eve: Stay off residential streets. Some people think throwing their household goods out the window is the only way to celebrate." She picked her way down the rest of the block, steering around the wreckage of several other pieces of furniture and a number of flowerpots. There was another loud crash just behind them as Toni wheeled onto Via del Tritone.

"Toni, I'm really sorry I didn't call you about going out of town. I know I should have."

"Forget it, *caro*. You must have had good reasons."

Durant shook his head. "No, I was just preoccu-pied. You know the story about the murder of Father Richardson?"

"I read about it, yes."

"I was there at St. Susannah's when it happened."

Toni gave Durant a look of cold surprise. "Well, well. What else haven't you told me?"

Durant shook his head. "There's a lot more. I was too upset Christmas morning to tell you about Richardson, or that there might be a connection between his death and his hearing Dr. Muller's last confession."

Toni stared at him, oblivious to the road ahead.

"Look out!" Durant screamed as he saw a large Mercedes lumber across from a side street. Toni slammed on the brakes and slid around the sedan sideways.

"Merda!" She put the Maserati back in gear and accelerated into her lane. "You've really been busy, haven't you?"

"Toni, I'm sorry. I wanted to tell you but I just couldn't. I've always guarded my developing stories carefully, and I just couldn't break the old habit."

"And I suppose now you want to work with me and get in on the scoop of the century?" She waved a fist at him, so tightly clenched that the knuckles blanched. "You know, I wanted your help months ago, but you never really gave me an answer. Now, after all I've put into this, you want me to add a few things you've come up with so you can share the credit? No!"

Durant grabbed her hand and pulled it gently down. "Toni, it's not like that. I want to work with you, but there's something you don't know that changes the story completely. That's why I wanted to talk to you before we went anywhere else."

"Look, Craig. I know that Nicodemus wrote it, I know that age tests on the scroll say it's from his time,

294

and that Buchmeunster thinks the historical references in it are correct. What else is there to know?''

"It's a fraud."

"What!!" Toni locked the brakes, stalling the engine and screeching to a halt in the middle of Via Barberini. This time, it was Durant's head that bounced against the dash.

She continued to shout, oblivious to his pain the horns honking around her. "You *are* crazy! So this is your approach, eh? If you convince me it's a fake, I won't do the story at all? You're wrong!"

Durant rubbed the knot above his forehead, checking it for blood. There was none. His own anger began to simmer, but he resolved to try again.

"Toni, I'm not playing any games with you. I'm not making this up. The Nicodemus Codex is a magnificent, carefully crafted hoax. If you'll just get us out of this traffic, I'll tell you all I know about it."

Toni nodded wordlessly and started the Maserati. They moved quickly toward the Termini station, through an underpass, then out onto Via Tiburtina. Soon, they were on the Autostrada, leaving the New Year's Eve bedlam of downtown Rome behind them as they drove east toward Pescara.

When they had settled into the sparse traffic, Toni spoke again. Her voice was forced and cold, and a hint of trembling in it told Durant she was near the edge of her control. "I want you to tell me why you're doing this. Why are you telling me, on the eve of the greatest story of my career, that I've been pursuing a fraud?"

"Toni, you've been set up. The whole world has. This thing has been planned for years, and you just happened along at the right moment."

"I don't understand! How could you possibly know that?"

"It was Muller, Toni." He patted the thick volume in his coat pocket. "He left a diary. I've read it all the way through. He laid it all out."

"That doesn't make any sense! How could he possibly have anything to do with the drafting of a manuscript that was written two thousand years ago?"

"That's the point. It wasn't."

"But the dating tests! How—" Durant squeezed her arm gently, trying to share her pain. "Look, Toni, this was a shock to me, too. It's not a pleasant story, but I think it'd be easier if I just start Muller's story from the beginning."

Toni said nothing, her mouth a grim line as she stared at the road ahead.

"Muller studied for the priesthood at one time, but he got thrown out of the seminary for reasons he didn't think were fair. He swore revenge on the Church, but he wasn't able to do anything about it for a long time. He had a talent for languages even then, and when World War II broke out, the *Abwehr* spotted him, schooled him in Arabic, and sent him to Beirut. Not much happened to him there, except that he met a young Islamic fanatic named Ahmed al-Wahhib."

Toni looked at Durant, her brow furrowed with disbelief. "The same al-Wahhib who's now the thorn in the side of every state along the Persian Gulf?"

"The same. Muller soon discovered that al-Wahhib shared his goal—the destruction of the Roman Catholic Church—although al-Wahhib thought of it as just another part of his *jihad* against the unbelievers. Muller left Lebanon after the war ended, determined to find a way to carry out his dream. He went on to study archaeology and ancient Middle Eastern languages. The Dead Sea Scrolls were discovered while he was a graduate student. That's when the idea came to him. He would forge an ancient scroll that would denounce Christianity as a fraud and would support that denunciation with facts. Of course, he'd have to invent those.''

"This is awfully hard to believe, Craig. You're talking about a man who was known as a dedicated scholar, who worked closely with the Vatican Archives for most of his professional life." She slowed the Maserati and slipped off the Autostrada at the exit for Tivoli, then accelerated again onto the open road that stretched ahead into the hills.

"Toni, he was a scholar, one of the best. It took him almost ten years to decide what the scroll ought to say and exactly how it should be said. Then, he looked up his old friend, al-Wahhib. The Arab liked the idea instantly. Al-Wahhib introduced Muller to some new friends, who found the plan fascinating. They arranged to get some authentic-looking vellum, probably from a museum, and they came up with some special ink. They took care of aging the completed scroll chemically so it would pass any dating tests. Muller was amazed at the resources these people had, but it wasn't until later that he realized the experts who were doing all this were for the KGB.''

"Oh, no! You're not going to tell me this is some kind of communist plot." Toni shook her head. "I should have known. You Americans have an obsession about that. You've never gotten over the fact that one

297

man, by himself, outwitted your security and shot your President Kennedy. This is nonsense!''

"This isn't my theory, Toni," Durant said urgently. "It's Muller's story, from his own journal. And he went on to write that the whole project slipped out of his control. There are several entries about his horror that a young scribe who'd done the actual calligraphy was murdered to ensure his silence.''

Toni continued to stare at the road ahead, guiding the car easily along the winding turns. The snarl of the Maserati's engine was rising. Durant glanced nervously at the speedometer as it slowly climbed, and he continued.

"It took a lot more patience for the next part of the plan. The scroll had to be wrapped in old linen, which had also been aged, and hidden in a cave near Qumran, where the original Dead Sea Scrolls had been found. They couldn't use an old cave, because it would have been picked clean long ago. So, they had to wait until one of the frequent earthquakes in that area opened a new one. Al-Wahhib sent out word that he'd pay handsomely for word of such a find, and eventually, one was discovered. Muller wrote that he was afraid the informant was killed to keep the location secret.'' He paused, trying to gauge Toni's reaction in the dim light from the car's instruments.

Her face was unreadable, but she was pushing the Maserati faster and faster on the winding road. After a few moments of silence, she spoke in a voice empty of any emotion. "Is there more?''

"I'm afraid there is, and this is where the story begins to get current. Muller and al-Wahhib both knew that it could take years for the plan to be carried out, possibly longer than they'd live. But that didn't matter. Al-Wahhib had a core of young zealots at his disposal, and they could carry on. Of course, Moscow's interest in the project would guarantee that, too.

"But then, I think, things began to go wrong. Muller mistook me for you, as the reporter he was supposed to leak the story to. Then he got the idea that I could be used along with you, but he didn't clear that with the people who were running the show. That's about where Muller's journal ends, but I think they decided that he couldn't be trusted and that he needed to go away. They botched the job the first time, that near-miss with the van. His heart attack saved them another attempt, but they didn't plan on Muller getting religion on his deathbed. They found out about Father Richardson hearing his last confession."

"You don't know that!" Toni snapped. "You can't be sure what was said in that room."

"Come off it, Toni! What else would a dying man talk about with a priest who's a complete stranger? What's the matter, don't you want the truth? Or don't you care anymore, as long as the copy's good enough?"

"That's not fair, Craig. Truth is my life."

"Then listen to it, dammit!" Durant took several breaths to purge his anger. "They got worried about Richardson, so they tried to get rid of him, but he survived and went into hiding. They found out he'd been involved with a young divorcée and her little boy, so they snatched the kid. They used him as bait to get Richardson back to St. Susannah's on Christmas Eve, where they took care of him. But nobody knew Muller had laid the history of this entire plan out in a permanent record." He turned to make his plea face to face. "And now I—we have the proof of one of the biggest frauds ever attempted. It's a monstrous story, Toni, the story of the decade, at least, and we have to give it as much exposure as we can. If we both—"

The glint of chromed steel in Toni's right hand stopped him cold. It was a small automatic pistol, trained on him and bobbing slightly as she flung the car along the road with her other hand.

"That's enough, Craig." She spoke softly, on the edge of a sob, and Durant could see tears begin to trickle down her cheek as she switched her glance back and forth from him to the road. "That's enough." She pushed a button and Durant heard the door locks latch home.

"Before you try anything, let me tell you that this Beretta is small caliber, but it has explosive bullets that will cut you in two, so don't move." She wiped back the tears with her gun hand. "Craig, I'm only a journalist, not a psychic. All I knew about this when I first got involved is what my source told me. 'It'll be big,' he said, 'as big as the Bible itself.' "

"This is a big story, Toni, the biggest I've ever seen. And it's the truth."

Toni shook her head. "You don't understand at all. Remember what I told you about living in Cairo? I did, in a refugee camp after my father was killed by the Israelis. My mother had to sell herself, smiling while men she hated used her body, to get me out of there. We managed to come to Rome, and she found a man who paid for my schooling and gave us a place to live. But there was a price for that, too. He was a businessman, and in return for shelter, mother had to entertain his clients, give them whatever they wanted.

300

One night, one of them got drunk in our apartment and demanded to sleep with me. I was seventeen then. Mother slapped him and refused. He killed her. I slipped out onto the fire escape and ran away."

Her voice rose as the wounds of her memory ripped open. "All my life, I've been looking for the story that would put me on top, guarantee that I'd never go back to any of that. This is it, and now you tell me it's a fraud."

The pistol wavered as she began to sob violently. Durant shifted his weight anxiously and glanced at the speedometer. It was still rising.

Toni saw him move and stiffened. The gun barrel flicked back toward his midsection. "There's nowhere for you to go, Craig. Don't make me kill you. You know, I thought you could help me give the story more exposure. But I was very wrong, and I'm going to have to do something about that. I think we're both going to go see my source and let him read the diary. Then we'll know what to do."

The Maserati hit a bump as Toni pushed the accelerator down harder, and over the engine roar, Durant heard his door rattle. He looked down and saw his seat belt buckle caught in the door. It had been too much trouble to put the belt on because of his shoulder.

The car was flashing along now, with Toni trying to keep one eye on him and the other on the road. Durant saw a sign streak by in the headlights, warning of a sharp curve ahead. They were going much too fast, and Toni realized it just as they reached the turn. She put both hands on the wheel and braked hard. The car slowed rapidly but started a sickening spin toward the edge of the road. A guardrail came rushing at her side of the car out of the darkness. Durant threw his whole weight against the door and hurtled out. The Maserati, tires still screeching, crashed through the rail. There was a muffled *crump* and an orange flash as it plowed into a stand of trees and disappeared in a ball of flame.

Durant floated in a red fog of pain that spread like a web from his shoulder. He was vaguely aware of the night sky, but the stars kept fading in and out. He heard a hollow roaring, like the engine of another car coming through a long tunnel. There was a light, and the face of a man in black with an angry scar on his cheek hovered over him.

Then there was nothing.

Chapter Twenty-six

Rita Chapman concentrated on the purplish face on the pillow. She stroked Durant's bruised hand gently as she talked, hoping she would see some change in the way his chest rose and fell beneath the hospital sheets.

"Craig, Craig, you have to wake up." Her voice was worn down from the hours of unanswered coaxing. The doctor's instructions had been clear. He was unconscious and there could be a serious head injury. Someone needed to be with Durant, stimulating him even though he didn't respond.

"Craig, it's morning. I have to know if you got the envelope my father sent you. Craig, please . . ." Her voice trailed off as she slumped forward toward the bed.

Rita jerked herself awake and wondered again what had brought her to the bedside of this man she hardly knew. She'd been with her father two floors up in Salvator Mundi most of the night. He'd been sedated to the edge of coherence, but he was still agitated. She'd told him about calling Durant, thinking that would put him at ease. Instead, Chapman had demanded that she talk to Durant again. "The envelope, make sure he has it," her father had insisted. But he'd turned aside all her inquiries about its contents, saying only, "Devil's spawn, all of them."

When the doctors had finally told Rita that her father was in no danger, she'd left his room and was on her way out of the hospital when she saw Durant being wheeled in. She'd nearly fainted from the shock of seeing his battered face, and a priest in the emergency room had helped her to a seat. Now hours later, she sat by Durant's bed and rubbed her eyes.

"It wouldn't be good for us both to snooze, would it, Mr. Durant?" Rita stood and stretched, then walked over the window and flipped the blinds open. The room brightened. "It's a beautiful New Year's Day, you know. Positively smashing." She turned, hoping his eyes would be open. They weren't.

She'd volunteered to stay because there was no one else, friend or relative, to coax Durant back to awareness. She needed something from him, too, an answer as to why her father burned to know the fate of the envelope he'd sent. Besides, Durant might need to see a familiar face if he . . . when he came around.

"Craig, we really should talk about this. It just isn't polite to make me carry the whole conversation." Rita walked to the sink and turned on the tap. It sputtered indignantly as she splashed cold water on her face. She patted it dry with a rough white towel and reached to catch a few drops that had traced icy paths down her neck. "That should help for at least fifteen minutes." She glanced in Durant's direction but saw no change. She soaked a washcloth under the tap and spread it gently across his forehead.

"Oh, God!" Frustration and fatigue washed over

Rita and she sank into her chair with tears welling from her eyes. "You have to be all right! I have to know what is so important to my father that all he can ask about is that bloody envelope! What's happening here?" She laid her head on the bed and wept, then dragged herself back to control. "No, this won't do, Rita. Simply . . . will not. You're just too tired, that's all. Maybe just a little . . . rest . . ." She eased back into the chair and closed her eyes. "Just a mo—"

Her body went limp, yet she felt aware. She sensed a presence nearby. It grew closer, coiling itself around her ever tighter, squeezing, suffocating. She fought to awaken, but she only sank deeper into blackness. A thick, sweet fragrance welled up around her, imprisoning her like a translucent fog.

Durant needs me.
Protect him.
Father needs him.

Her body was numb. Her body was cold. The fragrance closed around her, choking, smothering.

Someone's watching.
Someone else is here.
Protect Durant.

Rita willed herself to breathe, deeper, deeper, shaking off the coiled presence and the fog. She ordered her legs, her arms, to life. They sat frozen.

Move, damn you, move!

The noxious scent seeped closer, cutting off her breath.

"No!" Her voice was a scream when it came. "No!" She leaped to her feet and found herself staring straight into icy blue eyes that watched her from the foot of Durant's bed. "Who are you?"

"I'm Father Zeffirelli." The priest showed no surprise at Rita's bizarre behavior. "I came to see if Signore Durant would like his confession heard or perhaps to take communion. I understand the young lady who was riding with him was killed. I believe they were quite close."

"Oh, Christ." Rita, her heart pounding from the combined effect of the dream and being surprised by the priest, glanced at Durant. He lay still except for the shallow rising and falling of his chest. She felt her legs go rubbery and she leaned on the bed for support. "I wonder if he even knows."

"Forgive me," said Zeffirelli as he put a small black bag on the bedside table. "I didn't mean to upset you." His voice softened, but his eyes still followed her with the intensity of a coiled snake. "Is Signore Durant a relative of yours?"

"No . . . no . . . just a friend." Rita's head throbbed painfully. She massaged her temples, but it had no effect. "I'm sorry for the yelling. You startled me out of a sound sleep."

"Yes, I could tell." His gaze shifted to the patient. "How is he doing?"

Rita rolled her head from side to side and rubbed her neck. It was no help. "He jumped from a moving car. The doctors say it's a miracle he survived at all. He's got a badly sprained shoulder and some cuts and bruises, but those will heal. It's the possibility of a head injury that worries them. He hasn't stirred since they brought him in."

"I see." The priest paused as he watched her. "You look very tired, signorina. Perhaps I could stay with him for a few hours while you get some sleep."

It was a tempting offer. Rita found Zeffirelli's boyish face reassuring. Surely it would be all right to leave Craig in the care of a priest. Yet, there was something cruel in his unblinking stare that unnerved her. And her father's envelope . . . Where was it? "No, thank you very much for your concern, but I think I'll stay. I don't want to put you to any trouble."

"It would be no trouble, signorina. I have no other plans for this morning."

"Thank you again, but no."

"As you wish." Zeffirelli smiled coldly. "I'll come back later. Perhaps he'll be conscious then."

"Yes. I'm certain he will." She followed the priest to the door, trying to block the overwhelming scent of his cologne from her mind. When he was gone, she set the lock. "What a strange man."

"I didn't think I was that bad," a feeble voice said from behind her.

"Thank God, Craig! You're awake. I'll ring for the nurse."

"No, Rita. Not yet. I'm fine." He groaned as he propped himself up on one arm. "Just . . . a slight . . . headache."

"Well, at least you recognize me. But please take things slowly."

"Let's start with this. Where are we?"

"Salvator Mundi. A priest brought you in."

307

"But how? . . ." Durant's voice trailed off as weakness caught up with him. "He found you near Tivoli. He happened to be on the road behind you when it happened. You jumped just before the car went off into the trees."

"Where's Toni? I have to—"

Rita shook her head slowly, fighting a lump in her throat as she felt Durant's pain.

"But she'll be okay, Rita. I mean she—"

Rita took his hand and swallowed hard. "Craig, she didn't—"

Durant fell back onto his pillow. He stared blankly upward and tears began to well up from his eyes.

"I'm so sorry, Craig. Do you want me to call the nurse?"

"No. Just stay with me, please." He wept without saying anything for several minutes, looking at the ceiling. Finally, he sighed deeply and the tears stopped. "I remember it all now. Where are my clothes?"

"I'm afraid they're all gone. They had to be cut off of you in the emergency room. There wasn't much left, anyway, when they brought you in. They did keep your coat, but it's badly torn."

"My coat?"

"Yes, it's in the closet. But there's nothing else."

Durant was suddenly agitated. "What do you mean? There has to be! In the pocket, I had—" He sat up and threw his legs over the side of the bed, but sank back quickly, pale from the effort. "My coat," he whispered. "Bring it to me."

Rita brought the tattered overcoat to the bed. Propped on one elbow, Durant felt for the journal. His search grew more frantic. He checked inside the zip-out lining. Nothing.

"Rita, it's got to be here. I jumped with it!" His eyes were wild, his face flushed as he ran out of strength and fell back onto the bed. "Who did you say brought me in here?"

"A priest."

"Who was he? Did he mention finding a journal, a large notebook?"

"I don't know who he was. All he told me was that he'd found you. Craig, are you looking for what my father sent you?"

"Yes! And we've got to get out of here and find it!" He threw back the sheets and tried to sit up, but swooned forward from the effort.

Rita caught his shoulders and eased him back onto the bed. "You're in no shape to go anywhere. You couldn't even find the loo at the moment. We'll have to look for the journal later. Now lie still."

"Sounds like good advice to me, *mon ami*!" A wink accompanied the large grin that appeared around the door. "It's not often that a mam'selle tries to get you into bed."

"Rivette!" The sight of the swaggering cameraman, soggy cheroot hanging from his mouth like a tournament banner, made Durant smile in spite of his grief. He tried to sit up but had to settle for leaning on his left elbow.

"How did you get in here?" Rita snapped. "The door was locked!"

"There is no lock safe around Francois Rivette." He slipped a plastic credit card into his shirt pocket as he came across the room. "Besides, if I'd waited for you two to open it, I'd still be in the hall. Now, what's all the fuss about?''

Durant and Rita glanced at each other without speaking. Durant broke the silence. "Rita Chapman, this is Francois Rivette. He works with me at Global.''

Rivette glided over to Rita and kissed her hand gently. "Such an introduction hardly does me justice. But I pay no attention to this shiftless reporter. He's only jealous of my winning ways.'' He reached under the back of his jacket and produced a small bunch of red carnations, which he presented with a flourish and a bow. "Your wish is my command, mam'selle. These were intended for that malingerer, but I'd rather have them reflect your beauty.''

"Is he always like this?'' Rita wasn't sure if the bent figure in front of her planned to release her hand.

"Always. The world is his stage. Tell me, Rivette, where did you steal those carnations?''

"Steal?'' The look of an injured reputation played across the Frenchman's face. "Steal? Rivette never steals. I simply decided that these specimens were not up to the standards of the florist around the corner. Removing them was a purely aesthetic act.'' He spread his hands in a shrugged apology for the simplicity of his explanation.

Rita grinned.

"Now,'' said Rivette, "what service may I render you?''

Rita bit her lip and looked at Durant, who lay back on the bed and closed his eyes.

Rivette waited out the silence, then headed for the door. "Well, I know when I'm not needed. You know where to find me.''

"No, Francois, it's not that." Durant's voice wavered and he paused to get it back under control. "It's just that I hate to get anyone else involved in this. But I do need your help badly."

"Bon!" Rivette clapped his hands explosively and strutted like a cock back toward the bed. "That's more like it. Who do you want me to beat up? From the look of you, he must have been quite large, but I don't care how big they come." He jabbed the air.

"I wish it were that easy." Durant sucked air through his teeth to cope with the pain as he pulled himself back up on his good arm. "I'll try to make it short. Yesterday, Rita's father sent me a journal kept by Andrew Muller over the years. It proves the Nicodemus Codex is a forgery, how it was aged, what it said, everything."

Rivette raised his eyebrows nearly to his forehead and gave a long, low whistle. *"Sacre Mère!* And that old fool was behind it?"

"Yes. Toni told me she was about to come out with a major story authenticating the codex, setting out its text. She was staking her career on it, and I thought she ought to know that it was a fraud before she let that story run. She wouldn't listen to me. We were in her car in the hills near Tivoli. She pulled a gun, Francois! Accused me of trying to ruin her story! She lost control." His voice fell to a whisper. "I jumped out. She didn't." Durant turned his face toward the wall, and his shoulders shook in quiet sobs.

"I'm so sorry, Craig." Rivette shook his head slowly. "She was a beautiful girl. Tragic." He stood in sympathetic silence, pensively stroking his beard, until his friend regained composure. "Where is that journal now?"

"We don't know. It was in my coat before the wreck, but—"

"Francois, there was a priest who brought Craig into the hospital. He might know."

"Who was he?" The cheroot in Rivette's mouth rolled slowly from side to side, probing like a radar device.

"I didn't get a name. There was so much confusion when he brought Craig in, I—"

"He will have to be found, quickly. Perhaps on the accident report there's something. Do you recall what he looked like?"

"There's not much to say." Rita's lips twisted into a tight line as she concentrated. "Tall, medium build, dark hair. Oh, and a large scar running from under his right eye at an angle across his cheek. It was really ugly."

Rivette nodded. "*Bon*. That's a place to start, and I'll need that to find a nameless priest in a city of ten thousand of them. You were blessed by the Madonna, Craig, to have such a holy guardian look after your health."

Durant sniffed back tears again as he teetered on the edge of control. "It didn't help Toni, did it? Oh, God! I had no idea she would react that way. If we'd only gone somewhere to talk about it instead of me just telling her I wanted to go for a drive. She'd still—"

Rivette's pawlike hand clamped down firmly over Durant's mouth, and he shook his head sternly. "Let me tell you something. In my years of drifting along the River of Life, I've learned that one thing is always true. The current flows only downstream. What's already taken place is immutable history, and you probably couldn't have kept it from happening anyway. God controls these things, you don't. You can't blame yourself for something you couldn't foresee.''

"I just can't believe she's gone.'' Durant's tears came again. "Oh, God! I wanted to marry her. Then she accused me of trying to ruin her story! What happened.''

"Life, Craig. You can never trust it.'' Rivette smiled and gave the man in the bed a gentle tap on his good shoulder. "Now, to find your samaritan.''

"Another priest came in here a while ago,'' Rita said helpfully. "He might know the other one. Zeffirelli, his name was.''

Rivette's face turned hard. "Describe him!''

"Well, I—he—'' Rita searched for her words, flustered by the Frenchman's sudden change of mood. "He was a rather odd chap. Very solicitous of Craig's welfare, wanted to keep watch on him while I got a little sleep. He said he thought Craig might want to have his confession heard. Seemed to know a great deal about the accident and Craig's relationship with Toni. He had an eerie, almost supernatural presence. That's why I locked the door when he left.''

"*Merde, cherie!*'' Half of Rivette's cheroot fell to the floor, bitten through in his impatience. "In the name of God, what did he look like?''

"That's what was so peculiar. He was pretty well average, except for his eyes. They were like a snake, watching me as if I were his prey. They had no expression at all, and I don't think he ever blinked. They were the most vibrant shade of blue I've ever seen.''

Rivette spat out the rest of his cheroot. "We're leaving. Now! Get dressed, Craig. Zeffirelli will be back, but it will not be to save your soul."

"You think he was here to kill Craig?"

"Exactly. And perhaps you as well, if you had not been so insistent." Rivette rattled noisily around in the closet. "Where are you clothes?"

"Probably in the incinerator by now," Durant called back. "Rita says there wasn't much left after they were cut off me downstairs."

Rivette reappeared with the torn coat and dramatically peeled back the split up its side. "I must get the name of your tailor." He pitched the coat across the room, draping it over the edge of the bed.

"Muller's journal was in that coat before the wreck. We've got to find it," said Durant. "I think Toni was getting most of her information from Buchmeunster's notes somehow, which means he thinks the codex is the real thing. We've got to find the journal and get it to him."

"*D'accord*. But first, we must get you out of here before Zeffirelli returns." Rivette studied Durant for a moment, then began to unzip his own pants and step out of them.

"Francois! What the hell are you doing now?" Durant's voice was more groan than bellow.

"You take my clothes and sit in that chair facing the window." He tossed the pants on the bed. "I noticed a male nurse down the hall who seems about my size."

"You think he'll just loan you his clothes?"

The stocky photographer, now clad only in shorts, socks, shoes, and a red jade cross hanging from a thong around his neck, smiled cryptically. "Now, Rita, if

314

you'll be kind enough to help Craig assume his new identity?''

Without a word, she set about helping with the change of clothes and listened as Rivette explained his plan.

As soon as Durant was seated by the window, she left the room and started down the hall in slow, measured steps. A haggard old man crept along in front of her, trailing an IV bottle on a trolley behind his walker. She gave him a smile, but his gaze never left the floor. Ahead, a young woman in a bathrobe shuffled toward the elevator.

There was only one nurse to be found, a woman at the station in the center of the floor. Her crisp white uniform was pulled too tightly, and rolls of midriff fat rippled defiantly when she breathed. Her hair, an unnatural black with an occasional fleck of grey, was pinned back under her peaked cap in a severe bun. A perpetual scowl etched her face, and she tapped a pencil on the counter as she barked orders into her telephone. Rita stood patiently until the nurse slammed the receiver down with a mutter of disgust and turned to the front of her station.

"Si?" The nurse assumed something near a fighting stance. "What do you want?"

"Ah . . . Yes, I'm Rita Durant, Craig Durant's sister. He's in room 202."

"Si, si." The nurse ran down her clipboard impatiently.

"Craig has just regained consciousness and he's refusing to stay in bed. Is it possible to give him a sedative?"

"Bene! Dottore Fittipaldi will be glad to know he's

awake. We'll let *il Dottore* handle this when he comes on rounds. Meanwhile, just you tell your brother I said for him to stay in that bed." She punctuated her order with a stern nod, confident that her will would prevail.

"But he won't, you see. He keeps trying to walk around the room. It's going to take more than my insistence to keep him under control. Would you please see about a sedative?"

Anger played across the nurse's face, but she brushed it away with an irritated sigh. "As you wish. I'll see what's recommended on his chart and be right there."

"Thank you. But I'd prefer that you get a male nurse to do this. He's awfully strong, and he's been well trained in the martial arts. I'm afraid—"

"Nonsense!" the nurse exploded. "I can handle any patient on this floor." She drew in a breath and swelled to twice her normal size.

"I'm sure you can, but my brother is very determined. He hardly even recognized me. He thinks he can go find the woman who was in the accident with him. She was killed, you know, and he doesn't realize it."

The nurse's eyes softened. "Oh, *Madonna. Mi dispiace,* signorina. I'll see what I can do." She reached for her telephone.

"I appreciate your help." Rita smiled and strode quickly back to the room. She opened the door to find both men already frozen in place. Only a few brown curls escaped over the top of the chair to give away Durant's position. Rivette lay in bed facing away from the door, with all but a small part of the back of his head hidden. She cleared her throat.

"You chaps can relax. The nurse has to check with the doctor about the sedative."

Rivette rolled over and braced himself on one elbow. His mass of curly black chest hair contrasted sharply against the sheets. Rita chuckled in spite of her anxiety.

"And what is so amusing, mam'selle?"

"I was just picturing you in a dress."

"What?"

"You'd better hope I was convincing with my story about needing a male nurse to restrain Craig. Otherwise, you might have to leave here wearing the floor nurse's uniform. I think she's a little big."

Rivette collapsed onto the bed with a shake of his head.

Durant, eyes glazed, leaned over and massaged his temples. Rita felt his brow.

"Craig, are you all right? You shouldn't really be out of bed."

"Yeah, I'll be fine. Just not ready for a party."

"Here, give him this." Rivette tossed a pillow toward the chair.

As the pillow reached mid flight, a burly young man dressed in white entered without knocking, carrying a tray. He put it down by the bed, and his broad, pleasant smile quickly faded into a puzzled stare.

"You're not Craig Durant. I was in here earlier and I—"

Rivette came off the bed and hit the man with his full weight. The nurse's body folded like a jackknife and he fell, striking his head on the floor. He lay motionless. Rivette frowned and knelt to check the man for injury. Suddenly, the nurse ground a knee into

317

Rivette's groin. The Frenchman sailed through the air and landed with the angry attendant on top of him.

"There has been a terrible mistake, monsieur!" Rivette groaned as he spoke, wincing from the pain in his crotch. "I can explain it all."

"I'm listening." The nurse tightened his grip on Rivette's wrists, pinning him tighter. "This had better be good, or you will need that bed."

"*Oui*. The truth, of course." Rivette put on his most innocent face. "Monsieur Durant's life has been threatened. I convinced him to let me take his place in the bed for a few hours, just until the man who wants to harm him is apprehended. I expect the police will have him at any moment. In my enthusiasm, I'm afraid I mistook you for the villain. Just a simple mistake, I promise! Mam'selle Chapman will tell you I'm not lying!" He rolled his eyes toward her in a plea for corroboration.

"It's true, signore. We've all been on edge over this thing. Francois just got carried away."

The man glared at Rivette and loosened his hold. The Frenchman sat up with a sigh of relief and rubbed his wrists to get circulation going again.

"Your friend doesn't look like he needs a sedative to me," said the nurse as he turned to pick up his tray.

Rivette was on the man like a blur, forcing him to the floor and twisting both arms behind his back.

"*Bastardo!*" the nurse hissed. "You—"

Rivette cut him off with a sharp pull on both arms.

"Rita, lock the door and come over here." He smiled at the nurse apologetically. "I'm sorry we have to do this, *mon ami*, but we need your clothes. Tell me, what's in the syringe?"

318

The man twisted helplessly, rolling his body back and forth. Rivette firmly tugged his arms upward until the nurse moaned and squeezed his eyes shut.

"Think, it will come to you. What do you have in the syringe?"

"So . . . sodium . . . penta . . . thol."

"Ah, the memory is a wonderful thing, *n'est-ce pas?*" He eased some of the tension on the arms but kept the man firmly anchored on the floor. Rivette snatched the remains of Durant's coat from the bed and began tearing it into strips. The male nurse tensed, testing him, and Rivette answered with a knee into the man's kidney. "*Per favore*, don't provoke me." He wadded up one strip and lifted the man's head to cram the fabric into his mouth, then used another piece to tie the gag in place. "From the size of the dose in that syringe, I'd think you'll be snoozing in about three minutes. Rita, come and give this gentleman his medicine."

The color drained from her face. "But I don't know how to give injections!"

"Then you'll get your first lesson. Bring it here!"

"I can't do it!"

"Obviously, mam'selle, I can't do it. You must. Craig's life is in danger, and putting this man to sleep in that bed might gain us some time."

"But . . . I don't—"

"We don't have time for a nursing course, Rita! You won't hurt him if you listen to me."

The nurse rolled his eyes upward and twisted violently.

Rita picked up the syringe.

"*Bon!* Now, hold it needle end up, tap it gently to get any bubbles to the top, and ease the plunger up until the fluid comes out of the top. We want to get all the air out of it. Understand?"

Rita nodded and pushed the plunger until a clear drop rolled out of the needle.

"Now, take the syringe and stick the needle into his deltoid muscle."

She looked blankly at his arms and at the seat of his pants.

"Here! At the top of his arm! Stick it in and drain it into him."

The nurse jerked upward, nearly tossing Rivette off onto the floor. The Frenchman lashed at the back of his head, smashing the man's face into the tile. His body went limp.

Rivette sighed. "Now he'll have a headache. Hurry, Rita, before he comes around."

Rita gave the syringe a gentle push and it broke the skin. She closed her eyes and shoved the plunger down slowly, emptying it.

"*Merci à Dieu!*" Leery of any more tricks, Rivette kept the pressure on until the medication took effect, then checked the nurse's pulse and reassured his anxious watchers. "He'll be fine." He quickly undressed the sleeping man, removing pants and shirt, then put them on himself, rolling the pant cuffs up several times.

"Francois, I thought you said he was about your size!" Durant smiled, feeling some strength return.

"Stature is all a matter of mind, *mon ami*. Actually, I'm six inches taller than he is. Now, Rita, if you'll put his shoes in the closet?

They dragged the unconscious nurse to the bed and tucked him in, facing away from the door. Rivette checked his pulse again. "*Bien*. Everything is fine."

Rita looked uncertain.

Rivette gave her an exasperated shake of his head. "I promise you, he'll be perfectly well once he wakes up! If there were anything wrong, we'd call a doctor immediately!" He walked over and examined Durant's dilated pupils. "How are you doing?"

"I'm fine, I think." He didn't sound convincing.

Rivette patted Durant's hand. "*Bon.* I have two more things to do before we leave. I'll be right back."

"But you can't leave us here!" Rita protested. "Where are you—"

Rivette held up a reassuring hand for silence and slipped out the door.

Rita gripped the bedrail, hoping it would somehow drain the panic rising within her. Durant clearly couldn't be moved without help, and now she'd been left alone. If Rivette didn't come back, what would they do? She pushed the thought aside and willed her mind to shake its cloudy fatigue, concentrating on his promise to return.

The door swung open, and Rivette entered with a wheelchair. "Let's get him into this. Feeling better, Craig?"

"I guess so," Durant answered feebly.

"Hold on, only a few more moments and we'll be on our way." He sat down by the nightstand and took the jade cross from around his neck, then he began to unscrew the telephone mouthpiece.

Durant turned to watch the process. "Checking for a bug?"

"One never knows. Best to be sure." He replaced the cap, laid the receiver facing upward on its back, and dialed a number. Rita and Durant could barely hear it ring at the other end of the line. Rivette suspended the cross on its throng, allowing it to swing freely just above the mouthpiece.

When the ringing stopped, Rivette struck the jade sharply with a cigarette lighter. It rang with a sharp, high-pitched tone. He stilled it with his hand, then struck it again and silenced it. Once more, he rang the cross, this time letting the tone die away on its own. When is was finished, the bearded Frenchman put the telephone to his ear and spoke.

"*Periculum in mora.*"

He was silent for a moment, then spoke again.

"*Deo gratias.* Dominic, I need a room at the infirmary with twenty-four hour security and the full medical staff. *Oui*, as quickly as we can get there, a half hour at most. No, we don't need assistance. Just tell the guards at the Arch of the Bells that we're coming in. We don't want any unpleasant confrontations with the Holy Father's security. We'll be in a—" He turned to Rita. "What make and color is your car?"

"A Lancia, light blue."

"Light blue Lancia. *Merci. Oui. In hoc signo vinces!*" Rivette hung up the telephone and turned to meet openmouthed stares from Rita and Durant.

"Francois," Durant began. "How did you—"

"Later. I'll explain when we get where we're going. Now, we must get you out of here before Zeffirelli returns. Rita, give me your car keys. Where is it parked?"

"Zone three."

"*Merci.* You distract the floor nurse and we'll meet at the car."

Rita headed for the door, but stopped with her hand on the knob and looked back questioningly.

"Everything is going to be fine now." The Frenchman patted his shirt and frowned. "Ah!" He reached over to the pocket on Durant's shirt and grinned broadly as he pulled out a new cheroot. "Hurry, Rita!"

Rita nodded and opened the door, then froze. In the hallway, reaching for the doorknob, stood Zeffirelli.

Chapter Twenty-seven

"Hello, Father!" Rita's stomach knotted in cold terror as she stepped into the hallway and closed the door behind her. "I—I'm glad you came back. Craig will want to see you, I think, but it'll be a while yet."

Zeffirelli's voice telegraphed impatience. "Perhaps, signorina, I could just look in on him for a moment. If you'll excu—"

Rita stood resolutely between the priest and the door. "No, Father, I don't think you can do that right now. The doctors are in there giving him a thorough going-over. In fact, they asked me to leave. 'No distractions,' they said. They want to be in there alone with him until they can confirm that he has no brain injuries."

"But I only want to see—"

"Father, it'll only take a few minutes." She took his arm. "I was just going down to the cafeteria for a cup of coffee. Would you join me? I need to talk to somebody about all this. So much has happened lately."

Zeffirelli looked up and down the crowded hallway, stepping closer to the door to avoid an orderly wheeling a patient to surgery. "Very well, signorina, we'll let the physicians finish their work."

They found a two-seat table on the far side of the cafeteria. Rita concentrated on keeping the fear from her voice, wondering how long it would take Rivette and Durant to get safely out of the building. She didn't want to think about what Zeffirelli would do when he found out Durant had escaped.

"I've been under so much strain lately, Father. I can't sleep, although I'm exhausted. Do you ever feel that way?"

Zeffirelli sipped his coffee. "No."

"Well, I must say that I usually don't, but I've been so worked up about things in general, and now this terrible thing has happened to Craig. I know the doctors haven't said there's anything seriously wrong with him, but I'm still worried to death. I don't know what I'd do if . . ." Rita searched the priest's face for some hint of his intentions, but there was nothing there except his cold, unblinking stare. "Father, I—I'm very concerned about Craig. I feel so helpless when he's just lying there. What should I do?"

"Pray."

"But there must be something else. Isn't there a patron saint I should ask to intercede?"

"I don't think it will matter one way or another in the outcome, signorina. Some things are beyond any power to prevent." Zeffirelli put down his cup and leaned slightly toward her, his eyes willing surrender. "You said Signore Durant had regained consciousness? Did he say anything to you?"

"No, not really. He was just rambling, groggy."

"Did he inquire about anything in particular? Ask you to find anything for him?" Zeffirelli's tone was quiet but insistent.

"No, Father, he didn't. Except for his clothes. He was upset that they weren't in his room. Why?" Rita began to sense that she was losing whatever control she'd had over the situation. She wouldn't be able to delay much longer.

"And where were his clothes, signorina?"

"Cut off him in the emergency room, I suppose. Why do you ask?"

The priest held her in his gaze while he took another sip and let the silence work her fear. "And your father, signorina, is he recovering well?"

Rita felt a chill strike through her, pulling at the flesh on her back. Had she mentioned her father? How would Zeffirelli have known about him? "He's doing much better. No permanent damage, the doctors say." She did her best to smile, but it felt lopsided at best.

"How encouraging." Zeffirelli spoke just above an intense whisper, forcing Rita to concentrate on his words. "I should pray for him, too, if I were you."

Rita kept her cup on the table, gripping it with both her hands to hide their uncontrollable shaking. She turned away to break the priest's stare and fought the impulse to run screaming from the cafeteria. But as she looked toward the doorway, she found herself chuckling.

There, in the serving line, stood Rivette, still in his hospital uniform with the rolled-up legs. He moved along like an avalanche, with the mound of food on his tray swelling as he went. He grabbed a hard roll with one hand and plopped three large scoops of butter on top of it with the other. He swept up a large fruit salad, spilling a trail of heavy syrup down the front of his uniform in the process. His march halted when a wil-

326

lowy hand reached from behind the counter to set out bottles of *acqua minerale*. Rivette craned his neck over the top, then cupped his hand and spoke.

A giggling, startled girl stood up, and Rivette had to lean backward to keep her in view as she rose. She was young and beautiful, with the smooth features that had intrigued Italian sculptors for centuries. She was also more than a head taller than Rivette, but he was not deterred. He stood on tiptoe and kept up the conversation, bringing a blush to her cheeks.

Rita looked away. Her terror was gone now, submerged by exhaustion into the feeling that she was about to collapse into a fit of hysterical laughter. She was sitting across the table from the devil himself, a man from whom Rivette had ordered immediate escape, yet the Frenchman could find time to act the clown. She forced herself to take another gulp of her now-cold coffee, trying to keep Zeffirelli's attention away from the serving line, but it was too late. He was already watching.

The serving girl's supervisor arrived and delivered a stern scolding. With a shrug and a wink, Rivette shoved his tray along until he reached the desserts. He stopped to appraise a large piece of chocolate cake as if it were a sculpture, then held it to his nose, closed his eyes, and sniffed longingly. There was an irritated cough from behind him in line, so Rivette added the cake to his load and moved along. He picked up two glasses of juice, arranging them on opposite sides for ballast. Then he carefully stacked two cups of coffee, one on top of the other, and presented the tray proudly to the supervisor to ring up his bill.

She scowled angrily, despite his best efforts at flirtation and flattery. He gave her a broad smile, pulled out a cheroot, and stuck it in the corner of his mouth. Her icy face went crimson with rage. The supervisor exploded into a storm of Italian, pointing furiously to the sign above the counter that proclaimed "no smoking" in six languages. Rivette nodded politely and touched his finger to the unlit end of his cheroot, an unassailable loophole. Bowing his head in salute, he picked up his tray and left the fuming cashier behind.

His face lit up as he spotted Rita on the other side of the labyrinth of tables. "Mam'selle Chapman! Mam'selle Chapman!" His bellow cut through the hum of the late morning dining, drawing all eyes to him.

Zeffirelli turned back to Rita. "Signorina, who is that man?"

Rita laced her fingers around the cup and gave the priest a benign smile. "I'm afraid I haven't the foggiest idea."

Rivette balanced the tray high on one hand and began to pick his way toward them. He bumped a path through empty chairs, letting the weight of his tray pull him from side to side as he went. He pirouetted through a narrow space between two full tables, drawing appreciative applause from the crowd. He acknowledged it with a slight bow and a cocky smile and moved on.

Two portly women sat back to back in his path, with only a slight separation between them. Rivette sized up the opening and lowered his nearly overflowing tray for equilibrium. It passed only inches above one of the women, whose eyes grew large when she saw the mound of food teetering overhead. The crowd gasped as the tray wobbled back and forth, seemingly out of control, until he slipped through with a flourish and raised his burden high once more. There was more applause, this time accompanied by scattered cries of "bravo!"

The cafeteria manager stood by the astonished cashier, watching in mute disbelief as Rivette broke free of the last of the crowd and danced like a trained bear past one empty table after another, trailing a wake of laughter.

Finally, he arrived at the table where Rita and Zeffirelli sat, and turned to his audience. Another wave of applause washed through the room and he beamed his appreciation.

Zeffirelli sat silently, his eyes suddenly narrowed with malice. Rita gave the priest an innocent toss of her head. With his arms straining from the weight of the tray, Rivette leaned toward her and spoke quietly.

"Mam'selle Chapman, Dr. Fittipaldi told me to inform you that your father is asking for you. You may visit him now."

"Thank you, signore." Rita stood abruptly, a teary smile of relief on her exhausted face. She turned to the priest, who came slowly to his feet._ "Excuse me, Father, but I must go upstairs straight away. Thank you for chatting with me." She grabbed her purse and scurried toward the door.

"Excuse me, signorina, perhaps I could—" Zeffirelli started after her but was blocked by Rivette's tray.

"*Pardon,* Father, but if you have a few moments, could I talk with you?" Rivette hung his head, disgraced.

"I'm sorry. I'm really in a hurry." The priest

329

stepped to the left, but Rivette moved with him, keeping the tray against Zeffirelli's belt.

"It would only take a moment, Father." He looked anxiously around, then lowered his voice confidentially. "You see, I have gotten *une fille* with child."

Zeffirelli waltzed back to the right. The tray followed, tilting dangerously. He glanced toward the door to see Rita vanish through it into the hall. "Signore, I really am not the person to help you. Perhaps if you'll check by the hospital rectory later, someone can—" He stepped back a pace, trying to gain some clearance.

"Oh, no, no, Father." Rivette locked the priest's eyes with his own as he filled the space between them and pushed the tray firmly against him. "I can't wait. My soul is so burdened it will break in two, I confess it. I am lost."

Zeffirelli's cheeks colored with frustration. "See here, imbecile!" Several diners turned to watch, drawn by his outburst. "You work here! Talk to the chaplain!"

"Oh, I couldn't do that, Father. The girl is his niece."

Zeffirelli grabbed the tray and pulled. Rivette pushed.

The crash of breaking glass and crockery cut through the cafeteria's background drone as the load of food tipped up full against the priest, oozing in several colors down his suit.

"Oh! Forgive me, Father! I'm so sorry!" Rivette grabbed a napkin from the table and dabbed futilely at the mess. Zeffirelli's face was a purpling mask of hate.

The cafeteria manager and three busboys closed in, surrounding the priest, and began wiping his suit. *"Disastro!"* the manager clucked as he scrubbed a streak of

330

melted butter off Zeffirelli's sleeve. "I cannot believe this has happened! Mark my words, *Padre*, that man will never come into this cafeteria again so long as I am in charge!"

Zeffirelli stood helplessly, hemmed in, as Rivette backed quietly away and, with a sympathetic shrug, disappeared through the door.

Rita stood at the elevator, nervously pushing the up button every few seconds.

"I don't think that will help, signorina." An elderly man in a baggy sweater gestured reassuringly with his handful of carnations. "It will come, don't worry."

"I know. It's just that I'm anxious to see my father."

"He's lucky to have such a beautiful daughter. Seeing you should make any man feel better."

Rita smiled briefly pleased by the compliment. The elevator arrived and the man with the carnations motioned for her to enter first. As she stepped in, Rivette grabbed her arm, almost knocking her down.

"Come on! The car is outside the hall exit. Hurry!" He yanked her sideways, but she drew back.

"No, not yet. I have to see my father first."

The old man nodded. "She wants to see her father, *amico*. You should leave her alone."

Rivette tugged her arm more forcefully, pulling her back across the threshold. "I've talked with his doctors. He isn't here. Now come with me!"

"But you said—"

"I know what I said." He gently pulled her all the way out of the elevator.

The man in the baggy sweater craned his neck as

the elevator doors began to close. "But she wants to see her—"

"Scusi, signore," Rivette yelled as the elevator shut. "It's all right. I'm her brother." He led Rita into a side corridor. "Zeffirelli will be looking for us any moment. We have no time to waste."

Rita was near tears, exhausted and confused. "But my father . . . I don't understand why—"

"Believe me, Rita. He's safe and well protected. He was moved from here this morning to another facility."

"But where is—"

Rivette held a finger to her lips as Zeffirelli's angry voice floated around the corner, accompanied by hurried footsteps toward the elevator.

"Fool! Out of my way!"

"But, Father," the cafeteria manager wailed. "You can't go about looking like this. I am disgraced! *Per favore,* let me find you something else to wear while I have your suit cleaned."

"Very well! I'd be glad for you to do that. Find me another suit. But I have to visit a very sick patient right now. I'll be back down in a few minutes."

"Gràzie tanto, Father! It will be done."

The elevator door opened and closed, then the manager's footsteps faded quickly down the hall. Rivette inched around the corner to be sure their escape was clear, then pulled Rita into the hall behind him. "Come on! We must leave now!"

The Lancia sat in a no-parking zone, empty except for a large canvas tarpaulin crumpled across the rear seat. Rivette started the engine as Rita slipped into the car beside him.

"Where's Craig? Didn't you bring him?"

There was a muffled groan from the canvas bundle as the car lurched forward. "Can I come out now?" Durant's head emerged from under the tarp. His nose wrinkled in distaste. "This thing smells."

Rita smiled. "Well, Mr. Durant, you seem to be doing all right. Wherever did that canvas come from?"

Durant shut his eyes and rubbed his forehead slowly. "Francois got it from a painter's truck."

"I only borrowed it." Rivette held up a small piece of paper. "I even took down the name and address. Just as soon as we have no more need of it, back it goes." He put the paper back in his shirt pocket and studied Durant's puffy face in the mirror. "You don't look well, *mon ami*. But you'll be in good hands shortly. The Vatican infirmary is one—"

"Oh, no. I'm not going there. I've got to get to Buchmeunster to tell him the Nicodemus Codex is a fake. Besides, I want to find out what the hell is going on! People are dead because of that scroll and now that maniac Zeffirelli is hunting me. I want to know why!"

Rivette chewed his cheroot pensively as he tossed the Lancia through holes in the traffic. "Mam'selle, do you know the way to Buchmeunster's villa?"

Rita looked startled. "Yes, I've been there before with Father. Why?"

"Because you're taking Craig there. I want you to let me out near the Vatican. Piazza Risorgimento."

"That's another thing I want to know." Durant leaned forward, resting against the front seat. "What was all that routine with the cross and the telephone?"

"I'm a deeply religious man, Craig."

"So was my mother, but she couldn't call the Vati-

333

can for help. That's not enough, Francois. Who are you, really? What are you?''

"Only your friend. Rita's. That's how I serve my God.'' Rivette sighed heavily. "Years ago, I fancied myself an adventurer, a soldier of fortune. I was a mercenary, killing people for money and telling myself that I was only doing a job someone else was going to do anyway, so why not? One day in Algeria, my squad was cut off by an overwhelming rebel force. They surrounded us in the desert and picked us off one by one. When darkness came, there were only two of us left, both wounded. Paulo couldn't walk, so I carried him, and by the Grace of God, we slipped through the rebel lines.'' Rivette's eyes took on a faraway look as he spoke; the pain of the memory was etched into his face.

"We had no food, but we did have a canteen. We traveled across the sands at night and hid from our pursuers by day. Paulo got weaker and we ran out of water by the end of the second day. He was near death, and I was near madness. The vultures were circling when I laid him in the shade of some rocks. I watched them come to rest on the stones around us. I didn't care anymore, I just closed my eyes and waited. The next thing I remember is someone shaking me awake and speaking French. I thought it was an apparition, but it turned out I had made my grave within sight of a monastery. The monks took us in and did their best, but their facilities were crude and Paulo . . .'' The Frenchman turned his face away and sighed again. "God gave me to them; they gave me to the cross. If I ever needed help, they said, use it, but only to serve the cause of God. I've done so ever since.''

The sound of chimes floated back into Johann Buchmeunster's study, heralding visitors. He heard the faltering steps of his old servant starting toward the front door. "It's all right, Vittorio," Buchmeunster shouted, "I will go."

"*Gràzie, Dottore,*" came the reply.

Buchmeunster bent over his desk and turned the key, then tugged on the center drawer to be certain it had locked. He straightened up painfully and rubbed his back, hoping the spasm would fade. "Ach, old age," he muttered. "Wonderful for a wine, but not for me."

The chimes came again, and Buchmeunster shuffled past the open bookcase that led to his file room, on out of the study, locking the door behind him. "Coming!" he shouted. "*Un momento, per favore!*" He arrived at the entryway, puffing hard from the effort, and pulled unsteadily on the knob.

Cardinal Frescobaldi stood in the gallery, imposing in his red soutane and a heavy cape. Guglielmo waited deferentially a pace back.

"Eminence," Buchmeunster said warmly with a slight bow. "So good of you to come on such short notice."

Frescobaldi smiled perfunctorily, his eyes trying to read the old scholar's face but finding nothing. "Always a pleasure, Doctor, especially when I am told you have an urgent message for the Holy Father. May I present Father Guglielmo, my secretary?"

The younger priest fixed Buchmeunster with an earnest gaze and shook his hand. "An honor, *Dottore.* I've heard a great deal about you."

"Overblown nonsense, no doubt." Buchmeunster gave an embarrassed chuckle and stepped back from the door. "Come in and give me your coats. Vittorio is laying out lunch for us."

"Lunch?" The cardinal's professional reserve slipped for an instant, letting his pudgy face register a flicker of surprise. "But I thought your message for the Holy Father was urgent."

The scholar laughed easily as he hung the coats away. "Eminence, if there is one thing I have learned in forty years of working in Rome, it is that nothing should interfere with the chance to sample a good table. After two millennia of waiting, what I have to tell you will not be hurt by another hour or two. Come."

Frescobaldi and Guglielmo exchanged anxious glances as they followed Buchmeunster into the formal dining room. A roaring fireplace took up most of one wall, and a long polished table swept across much of the floor. The brocaded drapes had been drawn, and two crystal chandeliers warmed the room with hues of red and gold.

"Be seated, gentlemen." Buchmeunster motioned his guests to opposing chairs at the end of the table and took a seat between them at the head. "Vittorio, Father Guglielmo will be dining with us."

"Sì, Dottore." The old servant hurried over to the massive buffet and began to lay a third place setting.

Guglielmo was drawn to a large tapestry that hung above the buffet. Buchmeunster watched as the priest turned in his chair for a more careful look.

"Do you like my van Aelst, Father?"

"Yes, it's quite impressive. Jacob's betrayal of Esau, isn't it?"

Buchmeunster rose and walked over to the tapestry, with Guglielmo limping behind him. "Yes, from Brussels. Originally done for Pope Leo X, I believe, and quite rare for its subject matter. The Old Testament was not a popular source of themes in the sixteenth century." He stroked his black and grey beard pensively. "You know, I have spent most of my life in study of the Middle East—its history, its origins. Sometimes, I think of this tapestry as a metaphor for that place. Two brothers quarreling bitterly without end over who had the right to their father's land."

"But Jacob and his brother reconciled."

"True, but for Arab and Jew, there are now millions of Jacobs and millions of Esaus, and they will all have to learn to trust each other before the feuding ends." He shook his head and turned to the young priest. "The biblical Jacob could have spared himself and his brother all of that pain if he'd tried to understand Esau and work out a way of living with him. Instead, he tried to steal what was his brother's with a trick. Sometimes, thousands of years of history can be influenced like that, just by one small act."

Chapter Twenty-eight

Rivette smiled as the Swiss Guard hailed him at St. Anne's Gate.

"Your business in the Vatican, sir?" The guard's words frosted in the chill.

"Only to go to mass. I feel the need, especially for the New Year."

The guard looked him up and down. Rivette still wore the hospital uniform with the rolled-up pantlegs, and he had the remains of a soggy cheroot stuck in his mouth. Finally, the guard waved him on.

Rivette hurried through the iron archway and up the steps of the church.

He stood for a moment inside, letting his eyes adjust to the glow of candles at the altar. It was a small church, alive with frescoes across the ceiling. Built in the fifteenth century, it still served the papal community—nuns, workers, and their families—who preferred the smaller church to the packaged glory of St. Peter's, three hundred meters away.

The front pews were filling up. Rivette took a seat at the rear and waited until the confessional nearest him emptied. It was an old booth, in which the priest would sit in secret and the supplicants would whisper anxiously outside at either end. He knelt and spoke quietly into the brass grating.

"Bless me, *Padre*, for I have sinned."

A fatigued sigh floated across the partition as the shriving began anew. "And what are your sins, my son?"

"I have coveted my neighbor's house."

The chair inside the booth creaked as its occupant leaned forward. "And his wife?"

"No, *Padre*, only his cigars."

"Where have you been?" The voice from the confessional was coldly furious. "I have been waiting for two hours!"

"That could not be helped."

"Nothing can be helped with you, can it? When will you learn that y—"

"I have found him, *Padre*. I have found Sayeb."

"What?"

"I know his cover, I know where he lives."

There was a moment of astonished silence from across the partition, then more creaking. "Well. That *is* worth the wait. What did you learn?"

"He's taken the guise of a priest—a Father Zeffirelli—and he lives under your very nose at the *Palazzo Sant' Uffizio.*"

"Impossible!"

"Possible or not, it is true. He's even been hearing confessions at a parish church."

"But . . . why? What is he doing here?"

"I'm not entirely certain. But I believe he's responsible for a number of very brutal murders of women here in Rome. The work of a psychopath."

"There must be more than that. He's a known terrorist."

"There is. He's also involved in something concerning an archaeological find that's being evaluated here, a set of ancient scrolls that it seems may be complete forgeries. I think he's already had a priest killed over this."

"Is he a danger to the Holy Father?" The voice in the confessional was anxious.

"Padre, I have seen Sayeb twice, up close. I've even spoken with him. The first time, there was curiosity in his eyes. The second time, hatred. There's something about him that troubles me deeply." Rivette shook his head slowly. "I can't tell you what he'll do."

The man on the other side of the partition clucked his tongue noisily and creaked his chair several times. "That's not much of an assessment from as practiced a mind as yours."

"It's all I have. What am I to do now that I've found him? I had no other instructions."

"Bring him in."

"Quoi? Alone?"

"Well, we can't very well raise the hue and cry in the Vatican, can we? You'll have to ferret him out and get him yourself. But you'll have to move quickly, before he has time to do anything else. *Periculum in mora—*danger in delay, you know."

"Oui, Padre," Rivette sighed. *"Periculum in mora."* He rose to leave.

"Oh, and Francois?"

"Yes, *Padre?"*

"Assume Sayeb is armed. If he tries to kill you—"

"Which he will."

"—you are dispensed. If necessary, you may kill him, but only to defend yourself or others."

Rivette left the church and stood blinking in the sunlight. He turned and walked down Via di Belvedere toward the inner checkpoint. The Papal Gendarmes, crisp in their blue police uniforms, watched him approach curiously for a moment, then turned their attention back to the steady flow of pedestrians past the barrier.

Rivette idly scanned the passersby, wondering how to get close enough to Sayeb-Zeffirelli to have a safe chance of grabbing him. No doubt the priest, if the hospital events hadn't already forced a change of cover, would at least suspect that his identity was known. Subtlety and stealth would be best, Rivette decided, if time and place allowed. Otherwise, it would have to be *audace* and luck.

An explosion of invective from across the street jolted Rivette from his preoccupation. A heavyset man in a wool cap got up from the pavement and delivered an enraged lecture to another man who was standing nearby. He shook his fist angrily and pointed to the dirt on his suit, the ground, finally spreading his hands skyward in a plea for Divine justice. The target of his abuse reached down to retrieve his sunglasses and gave the man with the cap a frigid stare before resuming his course toward the inner gate.

It was Zeffirelli.

Rivette crossed the cobbled street quickly, moving nimbly through the stream of worshipers on their way to the several churches within the Vatican walls. He came up within hailing distance and cupped his hands to be heard over the street noises.

"Padre! Father! A moment, *per favore."*

The priest paused in midstep and searched for the voice. He saw Rivette and whirled, crossing onto Via del Pellegrino to avoid the gendarmes at their checkpoint.

Rivette glanced quickly through the crowd, hoping Zeffirelli was alone. Nobody was following, so he crossed over and tried again. *"Padre!* Please wait! I'd like to apologize for the accident at the hospital. *Attendez!"*

Zeffirelli didn't turn. He quickened his pace, moving along the street, which was empty except for a few tourists and two cars outside the offices of *L'Osservatore Romano.*

Most of Via del Pellegrino was still in deep shade, and Rivette shivered as he followed. The hospital uniform was only light cotton, and the Mediterranean dampness of January whipped through it to his bones. He wished he'd had time to retrieve his jacket from Durant, but there was nothing to be done about that now. He concentrated on keeping the priest in sight.

Suddenly, Zeffirelli was gone. Rivette moved to the nearest wall and inched along, mindful of the honeycombed doorways and alcoves ahead that could hide a man from view. An elderly couple passed, pointing at him and speaking German, on their way back to St. Anne's Gate. Rivette nodded and smiled nervously, praying Zeffirelli wouldn't use them for a diversion.

There was an alley further on across the street, but that led to the barracks of the Papal Gendarmes. Rivette flattened himself against a building while he considered the possibilities. There was another alleyway just ahead to the left by the Vatican supermarket, the

Anonna. He scooted across the opening and chanced a look. It was empty. Rivette left the street and crept quickly along the passage until it opened into a small courtyard between the buildings. There was no one there.

He ran, hurrying to where the courtyard joined Via della Topigrafico, next to the former stable that housed the Polyglot Press. The Vatican presses were running, churning out Documents of State even on New Year's Day. He cursed his caution as he reached the street and sorted the possible routes: past the central post office to the left, or up the street along the apartments of the Belvedere Palace. There was no sign of Zeffirelli in either direction.

The priest had escaped, vanished into the air. Rivette felt his anger rise, at his own incompetence and at the faceless voice in the confessional who'd decreed that he pursue this terrorist alone. He squeezed his eyes tightly shut and breathed deeply, trying to drive the anger from his mind. When he opened them again, it had subsided to frustration. He shook his head and walked toward Via di Belvedere and the way out. A delivery van rolled past the central post office on its way to St. Anne's Gate. As it passed, Rivette sensed movement where the van had been. He looked again.

There, by a deep archway leading into a complex of buildings, strode Zeffirelli. He walked nonchalantly along, unconcerned about any pursuit.

Rivette concentrated, trying to remember what lay beyond that entrance: the Vatican Museum, the Secret Archives, the hall of the Synod of Bishops.

And the Papal Residence.

Rivette scrambled across Via di Belvedere and trotted along toward a small courtyard that led to the Vatican Bank. He sheltered himself there and watched. When Zeffirelli disappeared into the archway, Rivette hurried to follow.

A gendarme stopped Rivette at the archway while a Vatican limousine lumbered out of it. When the car had passed, the policeman gave Rivette's ill-fitting uniform a curious stare. *"Mi scusi, signore,* but do you have business here?"

Rivette smiled and spread his hands wide, indulgently explaining what he hoped would look obvious. "Painting crew. I missed my truck."

"Painting on New Year's Day, signore? Where?"

Rivette shuffled from one foot to the other in the cold, trying to appear uncaring as he resisted the urge to sprint down the tunnel after Zeffirelli. "In the . . . ah . . . the Art Gallery. *Oui,* the *Pinacoteca.* Fewer tourists to get in the way today. Rush job." He smiled and prayed the gendarme would wave him on.

"But, signore, the *Pinacoteca* is that way." He pointed to another long tunnel that rose to the left, toward the Galleon Fountain and the entrance to the Vatican Museum.

"This way is shorter on foot." Rivette saw the man's eyes grow more skeptical. With the image of Zeffirelli's escape getting stronger in his mind, he decided to take the offensive.

"What is this about, *Officier?* You don't believe me?" Rivette let his voice rise, more with impatience than anger. "Or is it that I'm French, not Italian?"

"Signore, all I want to know is—"

"That *is* it, *n'est-ce pas?* Never mind that the Holy Father is in your care! You're just like the dockworkers

344

and everyone else! Every foreigner who comes here for work is fair game. I have a wife and three children to support, and there's my poor old mother in Marseille and you—"

The ring of a telephone in a kiosk by the entrance cut him off.

"Perdono, signore," the gendarme said coldly. "You will wait here."

The annoyance in the policeman's eyes told Rivette that he'd overstepped his bounds. He waited, pacing as the gendarme talked and watched him from the booth. He could hear another truck grinding its way through the huge Belvedere courtyard on the other side of the building. When it turned into the archway toward him, Rivette strolled across the entrance and stood, scuffing his feet against the pavement. When the truck blocked the gendarme's view, Rivette bolted through the archway into the courtyard.

There were only a few sightseers, seminarians clustered around the central fountain as they took pictures. Rivette ignored them and surveyed the possible exits: the Vatican Museum and the Secret Archives to the right, another tunnel directly across that led out behind the basilica, the Bishops' Synod hall to the left.

A portico lay at the far end, leading to elevators that would go up to the Secretariat of State and the Papal Apartments. There, nearing the entrance, walked Zeffirelli, his back turned in Rivette's direction.

"No! Stop!" Rivette screamed and ran full tilt toward the priest. The shriek of a police whistle reached him from the archway, and he pushed harder, trying to close the distance over the long courtyard before anyone could stop him.

The tall priest walked on, oblivious, but another gendarme appeared at the portico entrance in front of him.

"Assassino!" Rivette yelled. "Stop that man! Warn the Holy Father!"

The guard studied the situation for a second, then drew his pistol and took the priest by the arm as he reached the entrance.

"Oui! Seize him!" Rivette nearly wept with relief.

The police whistle grew louder as Rivette neared the portico. The priest, suddenly aware, turned for a look as the gendarme pulled him into safety.

He was a tall Oriental, and he clutched a small diplomatic pouch to his chest.

Strong arms grabbed Rivette from behind as the officer with the pistol beckoned him.

"I can explain it all, believe me!" He smiled broadly as the police flattened him against a wall and began a thorough search. "I thought this priest was an assassin on his way to murder the Holy Father! A silly thought now, don't you agree?" Rivette laughed, quite a bit too loudly under the circumstances. His captors did not. "Ridiculous, *n'est-ce pas?* You see, I thought that he was another—"

"Be quiet, signore." One gendarme kept his pistol leveled; the other patted his way up to a breast pocket and pulled out three cheroots. "What are these?"

"My cigars. That's all they are."

The gendarme sniffed them and wrinkled his nose in distaste. "If you say so." He put them back in the pocket and continued his search. The Oriental priest stepped out of the portico to watch.

"Now, what is this about?" asked the guard with the pistol.

"You see, there's a man—a killer—who's disguised as a priest. I followed him into the Vatican. I thought I was still following him until now." Rivette winced as the searcher slapped his chest hard, felt something firm, and stopped. The policeman pulled out Rivette's jade cross and peered at it curiously.

"And what is this, signore?"

"I . . . ah . . . a personal memento, nothing more."

"Signore, you are in serious trouble. A more complete explanation would—"

"Release him."

The man with the pistol turned in disbelief to the priest. *"Perdono, Monsignore?"*

"I said release him."

"But, *Monsignore*, this man is a danger. He's—"

"He's nothing of the kind. He's harmless, just thought he was doing the right thing." The priest stared at the cross, then locked his gaze on Rivette's eyes as he spoke. "I'm certain the Holy Father would want him released. It's New Year's Day, after all."

"All right, then. If you insist, *Monsignore.*" The gendarmes let Rivette ease away from the wall. "You're free to go. But try to stay out of trouble, signore."

"Merci, gràzie, I will." Rivette nodded and walked as rapidly as he could, just short of a trot, toward the tunnel that led to the rear of the bacilica.

As soon as he was inside the tunnel walls, Rivette began to run again. It was a long ascent, and he emerged panting into the chilly sunlight. He was in Piazza della Zecca, behind St. Peter's. There was a time when pilgrims would have clustered here at the foot of the Vatican Gardens, but with the increased concern for papal security, the only tourists who came this far into the pope's domain rode through on buses. A fountain murmured in the center of the *piazza*. Rivette strode out toward it for a clearer look around.

The cobblestones exploded in a cascade of rock at his feet. He dove for the ground, hitting it just as another slug whined heavily off the wall behind him. It took a chunk the size of his head out of the masonry.

He rolled along the ground toward the cover of the fountain. There had been no sound of gunfire. The shots had probably come from a silenced pistol close by and, from the look of things, with explosive bullets. There wasn't enough clearance around the *piazza* for a rifle at long range from up in the Gardens. Without the report or a muzzle flash, he'd be hard put to find the sniper.

Another shot crashed into the pavement as he rolled. Rivette lay flat near the fountain, searching for the gunman. There was an open door at the far end of the *piazza*. It slammed shut as he spotted it.

Rivette scrambled over to the building and ran along it toward the door. It pulled open easily. He pressed against the outside wall and waited for a burst of shots.

There was only silence. He dropped to a crouch and slipped in.

He was inside a curious warehouse, illuminated only by windows set high in the wall. It was filled with assorted furniture—chairs, tables, brass beds—and a scattering of art pieces. Busts of former popes kept watch from their vantage points around the room. He glanced at the nearest one, Leo XII frozen in a marble scowl.

There was a flat *pop* from behind him and the bust shattered. Rivette ducked instinctively and pressed himself to the floor. He peered through the forest of furniture legs, scanning for movement but seeing nothing. Nor could he hear anything but his own breathing. He forced himself to take shallow, quick breaths and listened again.

Was there a creak, off to the other side?

Quietly, Rivette picked up one of the larger fragments of the smashed bust and hurled it at a collection of vases on a table twenty meters away. They crashed to the floor, and Zeffirelli's silencer immediately coughed twice from the direction of the creaking. The slugs blew out the back of a stuffed chair in a shower of horsehair and damask.

Rivette grabbed two more chunks of the bust and scuttled along toward the gunfire. He tossed one into the far corner, behind Zeffirelli, and was rewarded by another shot thudding into the wall. He crouched and listened again.

Silence.

He threw his last piece of marble back toward the shattered vases, but there was no reaction.

Rivette concentrated, trying to remember how many shots had been fired. Six. Zeffirelli could be out of ammunition, or he could be conserving it. There was no way to be certain without knowing his weapon. Rivette moved silently, sliding on his belly toward the last firing he'd heard, stopping every few seconds to listen. Finally, after what seemed like an hour, he heard a metallic click two meters away.

He spun just as Zeffirelli fired. The slug crashed into the marble flooring, throwing up a cloud of shards.

Rivette rolled toward the gunman, hoping to throw off his aim, perhaps knock him off balance. Zeffirelli stepped backward, firing again. The bullet exploded into the floor in front of Rivette, its fragments painfully cutting his face. Zeffirelli stepped back for another shot, this time aiming resolutely.

A low table caught the priest in the back of the legs and sent him sprawling. The pistol clattered uselessly off to one side.

Rivette flew at him, hitting Zeffirelli with a force that knocked out his wind with a painful sigh. With surprising strength, Zeffirelli tossed him off and scrambled for the gun.

Rivette picked up a small end table and hurled it toward Zeffirelli, striking him on the head. It slowed the priest down enough for Rivette to reach the pistol first and kick it across the room.

Zeffirelli stood, shaking his head to clear it. His hand flashed to his boot, coming up with a stiletto, and he ran to Rivette with an animal scream.

Rivette ducked just as the priest began his downward stroke. He took the blow of the knife arm full on one shoulder but missed the blade itself. He grabbed the priest's wrist and chopped down hard, but the knife didn't fall loose. He tried again, but Zeffirelli's free hand caught his and they stood locked face to face.

They circled, Zeffirelli's cool blue eyes an icon of rage. He kicked at Rivette's feet and, with the advantage of height, made a solid connection. Rivette felt his ankle erupt in a flash fire of agony and his leg buckled, but he kept his footing. When the priest kicked again, Rivette stepped back and shoved hard. Zeffirelli's unstable stance gave way, and he threw his arms out to break the backward fall. Rivette picked up a chair and hurled it down at the priest's head, but it splintered impotently as Zeffirelli rolled aside and came up in a fighting crouch, the knife still in his hand.

He rushed at Rivette again, slashing broadly. Rivette jabbed at the knife hand and missed, but the blade scored a red furrow across his upper arm. He grabbed the wound reflexively, taking his eyes off the knife, and Zeffirelli came at him full force. Rivette saw the movement begin and lurched aside far enough to throw off his assailant's aim. The knife seared across the side of his chest, grazing his flesh instead of sinking into his heart. With his full weight behind the blow, Zeffirelli crashed into Rivette and the two went sprawling onto the marble. The knife, at last, fell free and slid under a large chest of drawers, beyond reach.

Blinded by blood and pain, Rivette felt Zeffirelli's fingers close on his throat. He struggled, but the grip on his life only tightened. He felt colder, then curiously relaxed as the pain receded. Then he was dimly aware of someone yelling.

The yelling grew suddenly louder, and the vise around his throat was gone. He breathed deeply, trying to force his mind back to awareness. His vision cleared just in time to see the terrorist shove his way past an astonished workman, who was brandishing a broom, and run out the door into the *piazza*.

The workman shook a fist at Rivette. *"Brigante!* This is the Holy Father's storehouse! Attacking a priest, were you! Get out!" He circled and swatted warily at Rivette with the broom.

Rivette pulled himself painfully to his feet, warding off the blows, and shuffled obediently toward the door.

No sense waiting around for another run-in with the gendarmes, he thought, especially the way he looked now. Too many explanations. Must find Zeffirelli.

He stepped out into the sunlight again and wiped his eyes as he tried to get his bearings. There was still no one in the *piazza*, but the warehouseman would be on the telephone by now, alerting the guards. There was an open gate ahead in the wall by St. Peter's. The other routes would lead to the Vatican Museum, the Papal Gardens, or back past the gendarmes in the courtyard. St. Peter's was the most promising. The quickest road to safety, for Zeffirelli and himself, would be through the gate, then across the huge square in front of the church.

His pain faded, replaced by the urgency of pursuit. He trotted through the opening in the wall and into the deep shade by the basilica. The walkway there to the square was barred by a steel gate. He would have to go through a side entrance into the church itself.

St. Peter's was a cavernous place, easily swallowing the dimensions of the world's great cathedrals. In spite of his haste, Rivette found his eyes drawn by the sweep of Bernini's bronze canopy over the High Altar to the great dome above. Mosaic saints and angels, lit only by piercing shafts of sunlight from the windows, kept vigil over the pilgrims who came and went below. Over them all, suspended in the highest recess of the cupola, brooded a sixteenth-century image of God the Father.

Rivette tore his gaze from the splendor of the dome back to the clutter on the basilica floor. Under the imperious direction of several men in swallowtail coats, sextons were aligning phalanxes of chairs and barricades in preparation for the New Year's Pontifical

Mass. He skirted them as inconspicuously as possible and made his way down the left nave toward the main doors out to the square. The marble faces of dead popes loomed on either side, prodding him onward. Zeffirelli had to be caught. Holy Mother Church needed no more monuments to a pontiff dead before his time.

The elevator to the roof began to whine upward as he passed its entrance. But there was no line of waiting sightseers; the entrance had been roped off and the ticket booth by the stairway was closed. The roof would lead to the interior gallery of the dome, with a clear view of the High Altar where the pope would celebrate mass. A workman?

Zeffirelli!

Rivette scrambled up the broad steps, breathing hard as he pushed his battered body. He lost his footing, bouncing painfully off the outside wall and a marble plaque that marked the visit of a nineteenth-century Russian Grand Duke. He landed in a crouch and sprang forward, trying to conserve his momentum.

The stairs spiraled ahead, and Rivette drove himself around the circle, once, twice, a third time. Then the steps narrowed abruptly. He slowed and moved cautiously against the inside wall as he neared the summit.

The elevator car was there, but there was no sign of Zeffirelli.

He crept onto the landing and peered out at the roof of the basilica. Christ and his marbled apostles stood overlooking the square, with a vacant walkway behind them. Rivette stepped out of the landing house into the biting wind and looked again.

The roof was empty.

He swept his gaze toward the huge dome.

The door at its base was open.

Rivette dashed toward the dome, praying to catch Zeffirelli before he could melt into the honeycomb of chambers and passages within its walls.

He stole onto the balustrade that circled over the Papal Altar. There was no one there.

Panic rose inside Rivette like a storm tide with the realization that the terrorist had slipped away. The elevator had been a ruse, sent up while Zeffirelli hid below among the monuments, the open door a coincidence, left by a careless workman. Pain, fatigue, and fear caved in on him and he sagged against the marble wall, slipping down it to the floor. In a few hours, the Pontiff would come down the central nave to celebrate the new year, applauded by the crowd that pressed in toward him. Somewhere in that crowd would be a killer, a man Rivette's incompetence had let slip away. He closed his eyes and let the frustration boil to the surface. With a deep sigh, he gingerly felt his arm and the graze on his chest. Still bleeding, but not much. Satisfied that he was intact, Rivette picked himself back up.

There were rapid footsteps, faint but regular.

Rivette froze.

The sound drifted toward him from the passage up to the top of the dome.

Zeffirelli was there, going for the high ground.

Rivette started up the steps. They were worn stone, set in a narrow, sloping tunnel. He pressed one hand against a wall for support as he went, adding to the grey smudge countless others had built up over the graffiti. The first landing came, a nearly flat stretch flooded with light from a deep-set outside window. He stopped to listen.

Zeffirelli was still ahead of him, moving up.

The steps resumed and the passageway tightened, leaning inward with the profile of the dome. Rivette's legs burned from exhaustion, threatening to give way. Regular breaths, he told himself. Each step was a goal; climb one, then the next.

The footfalls were louder now, a hollow clanking. The stairs would become steel ahead. Unbelievably, Zeffirelli's pace had quickened. The priest was nearly running. Suddenly, the sound stopped.

Rivette slid along the wall until he came to the steel stairs and looked up the three short flights. There was a landing midway, partly hidden. He slipped off his shoes and started noiselessly up. He tensed when he reached the landing, but there was no attack. The terrorist's shoes lay in a corner. The man, his feet silenced, had gone on.

"*Merde!*" Rivette exploded, hating his wariness. He hauled himself up the steps with new strength and ran through the stone tunnel at the top. There was a low door to the right, then a tight corkscrew upward. It had no railing, and his hand slipped on the worn rope that dangled around the stone pillar in the middle.

He braced himself against the wall, ignoring the fire in his arm, and closed his mind to all thoughts except Zeffirelli. He summoned up an image of the old man at the door in St. Susannah's, priest killer and butcher of women, and chased him up the steps.

A frigid gust washed over him, and in the growing light, the scrawl of another spent climber proclaimed "*'E Finita.*" He'd reached the end at last. He turned through another low door and found himself under a series of low arches that ringed the outside of the massive dome.

Even in pursuit, Rivette was dazzled by the panorama below. New apartments clustered on hills to the north, giving way to the blocklike architecture of Mussolini's Imperial Rome reborn. Further south, the Victor Emmanuel monument rose, its white marble gleaming like a beacon amid Rome's downtown clutter. And dwarfing it all in the foreground, St. Peter's Square, already filling with tourists and early worshipers despite the weather.

He was on the balustrade at the foot of the lantern of the dome, one hundred twenty meters above the square. It had once been possible to go further, even up into the golden orb below the cross, but safety now made this walkway the highest point, a magnet for sightseers. They would come up later, after the Papal Mass. For now, the balustrade was empty.

Except for a dead security guard. Rivette crept past the glassed-in booth where the man sat slumped over a newspaper, the back of his head crushed by a heavy blow. The coffee cup on his desk still steamed in the chill.

Just beyond the booth was a barred door at the entrance to a narrow stairway upward. It was open, with a set of keys still in the lock. The worn inscription above it told Rivette the steps would lead to the next platform, the top of the lantern. He listened at the door.

Silence, except for the wind and the street sounds below.

A massive weight crashed onto Rivette's shoulders from the archway overhead, dragging him to the floor.

Steely hands pounded his face into the tile. The pain and shock ripped through him.

The pain flashed into rage, flaring from deep inside, rage born of revulsion at the merciless slaughter of innocents. It coursed through his body, pushing aside every sensation, every thought, except the compulsion to destroy his attacker. Animal need.

Kill Zeffirelli.

He rolled, shoving hard, and tossed the terrorist against the wall. He was on Zeffirelli before the man could regain his feet. Images shimmered in his mind: Richardson lying by the communion rail with his chest blown open, gore dripping off the face of a terrified child, women turned to frozen meat in Manetti's storehouse of death. Rivette locked his fingers around the terrorist's throat and felt the windpipe collapse.

Wheezing, Zeffirelli kicked solidly into Rivette's groin, and the shock broke the hold on his throat. But the respite was only for an instant. Rivette's bulk crashed full against him, pinning him against the sharp edge of an arch. Rivette's left hand, fingers braced into a calloused point, speared at his larynx, but Zeffirelli turned his head and the blow bounced painfully off the neck muscles instead of crushing his airway.

For the first time, the terrorist's eyes went wide with fear. He saw Rivette's hand draw back for another jab.

"*Fratellino,*" he croaked. "*Fratellino.*"

Rivette's wedged blow froze in mid-flight. Confusion flooded his face.

"You have done well for yourself, *fratellino* . . . for the bastard of a Marseille fishwife."

"Pao . . . Paolo. . . ?" Rivette's voice was an

astonished whisper. "No! I saw the monks bury you. It can't be!" His anger was spent, cast out by disbelief.

"You said requiem for an empty box." Zeffirelli massaged his throat as Rivette's hold relaxed. "They told me you were dead, too. I thought you were, until that night in the doorway at St. Susannah's."

"But your face . . ." Rivette dropped his arms.

"They tried to make me one of them, you know, like you." Zeffirelli stepped out from the wall, moving Rivette a pace back. "But it wouldn't take. I left, and the Father Abbot set his hounds on the hunt for me because I knew too much by then. There was a price on my head all over North Africa, so I couldn't stay there." He traced a set of tiny scars by his ear. "The surgeons changed my face and I became a phantom, working for whoever would give me shelter, doing whatever dirty jobs they needed done. It didn't matter who it was. And I've kept running, without a country, without a friend, without a home."

"Paolo, I . . ." Rivette's words trailed off in a mass of conflicting emotion. "The murders, the women . . . why?"

Zeffirelli spat. "Unfaithful sluts, all of them! Slaves to their own flesh, with the morals of a bitch in heat! They don't matter."

"But, Paolo, the police. You have to—"

Zeffirelli clasped his hands together angrily and stepped out from under the arch. "I haven't slept for twenty years without keeping one eye open and a weapon under my pillow." His voice rose sharply. "Why couldn't you have left me to die in the desert? I've hated you for giving me back my life! You condemned me to the hell I've been living! And the hell you're going to now!''

He rushed against Rivette, slamming his back painfully against the steel railing. He grabbed Rivette's legs and hurled him over the edge.

Rivette fell, hitting the slope of the marble dome. He began to pray as he rolled downward. An instant later, his descent stopped, halted by a large cornice five meters below the walkway.

Through a haze of agony, Rivette watched Zeffirelli climb down the handholds. The terrorist reached him and hooked a boot firmly under the small of his back, then began to shove him toward oblivion. Unable to resist any further, Rivette closed his eyes and waited.

"Oh, my God," he whispered, "I am heartily sorry for having offended Thee—''

The sharp crack of a rifle split the air, echoing off the Apostolic Palace across the way. The pressure on Rivette's back ceased, and Zeffirelli fell, his head torn half away. His body whirled, end over end, until it crumpled in a broken heap at the base of the dome.

On the basilica's main roof, the Swiss Guard sharpshooter lowered his rifle and knelt in prayer. Next to him, a thin priest with sparse white hair poking from under his black beret spoke quietly into a hand-held radio.

"Terminatus est. We have taken him.''

Chapter Twenty-nine

Buchmeunster pushed away from the table with a sigh. "Well, so much for the needs of the body. I trust you enjoyed lunch, Eminence?"

Frescobaldi patted a napkin delicately against his mouth. "Magnificent, Doctor. A very pleasant surprise."

Guglielmo nodded. "Excellent. *Gràzie tanto.*"

Buchmeunster smiled. *"Prego.* I was pleased to have you dine with me. Now, I think we'd better get to the business at hand." He stood, and the other two men followed.

They went into the study, where Buchmeunster directed his guests to the wing-backed chairs in front of his desk, then turned the key switch to open his file room. When the bookshelf wall began to move, Frescobaldi and Guglielmo exchanged surprised looks. Buchmeunster disappeared momentarily through the opening and returned with three slim folders. He handed both men a copy, then sat down at his desk.

"Now, gentlemen," Buchmeunster began, "in the interest of saving time, let me ask you to open to page three. That's where the text begins. I think you will find it fascinating."

The cardinal paused in an attempt to clean his glasses. "Excuse me, but how many copies of this are there?"

"I have prepared only four. One goes to Hebrew University, one to the Vatican Archives, one to the Holy Father, and one to my files. There are no more, not even carbons. May we begin?"

Both priests nodded. Buchmeunster read aloud.

"I am old and no longer see. This is not written by my hand, but by my words to a scribe. As a Pharisee and member of the Sanhedrin, I have spent a lifetime telling others of God's law. Now I, Nicodemus, must confess to my own grievous transgression before I die. It is the sin of deception.

I was drawn to Jesus of Nazareth early in his teachings. I, myself, have witnessed the Master perform five miracles. My position made it impossible to be seen approaching him in public. Yet, I could not keep this man from my thoughts, so by night I would come to him.

It has been thirty years, and I grieve for him still. His loving words haunt me.

I knew he was in danger. My warnings went unheeded. One Passover, the soldiers came for him. I spoke for him before the Sanhedrin, but he was condemned.

Even as they crucified him, I was still bound by my pride and by fear. I watched from a distance, weeping as I hid my face from the crowd, until the earth trembled at his passing.

Joseph of Arimathea, a man of great courage, went to Pilate and asked to take the body. We took our Lord and wrapped him in linen, and were to anoint him with spices and ointment as is our custom. However, since the Sabbath was about to begin, we laid him in a new tomb and decided to return for the anointing when it was over.

My shame and grief overtook me that night. I could not sleep, and I longed to be at my Master's feet, listening to his words. I went to the tomb but dared not approach, for guards had been posted.

In anguish, I searched for John, who stood by Jesus even at the end. At a small house where I had met with the Master, I heard voices. I pushed the door slowly open and stepped inside.

Emotion overwhelmed me, for I beheld John and James sitting at the table with Jesus. John rose and brought me a cup of wine. My Lord watched, but his eyes gave no sign of recognition. None of the rest of the Twelve were there.

When I had recovered my senses, John took me on oath that I would never betray the secrets of that night. But as I feel my death approach, I must break the bonds of silence.

His name was Mordecai. He was twin brother to Jesus of Nazareth. At birth, Mordecai had been taken by one of the Magi into the wilderness of Auranitis, where he had lived with shepherds. In the days when Jesus knew his own death was soon to come, he sent for his brother.

John outlined my Master's plan. They would drug the guards and steal Jesus from the tomb. The guards, in fear for their lives, would never admit to falling asleep at their posts.

Mordecai would appear as the risen Jesus and would take on the markings of the crucifixion. He argued with John and James over how long the pretense would continue. Finally, they agreed upon forty days, the span of time of the Great Flood.

Thus it was done. When his time was finished, Mordecai fled back to the wilderness. James, John, and I were the only ones who knew. Peter was not to be told.

I remained in Jerusalem for three years, then I sought out the community of the Essenes in the desert, where I remained to purify for . . .''

Buchmeunster laid down the page and looked at his audience. ''I am afraid the rest of the scroll was too deteriorated to decipher.''

Guglielmo was impassive. Frescobaldi's face was pale and damp as he spoke. "Well, Doctor, what is your opinion? How recently was this heresy forged?"

"Eminence, even though I could not translate parts of the narrative, you will agree that it tells a fascinating story, and it certainly would solve one of the Church's 'sacred mysteries' if it is what it appears to be. Whether it is truth or heresy is not for me to say."

"Let me assure you that there is no question in my mind." Frescobaldi's hands shook as they held the folder. "It is scandalously blatant, another anti-Christian attempt at discrediting the linchpin of our faith, the Blessed Resurrection. Can you pinpoint the date? One hundred, two hundred years? Perhaps farther back, during the Schism?"

Buchmeunster flipped back through the report. "We passed over this because I wanted to get to the text, but there is a summary of my conclusions about the date in the first two pages. The execution of the scroll is historically consistent with other finds in the Qumran area. The linen the manuscript was wrapped in tests correctly. It was written on the hairy side of an animal skin, just as most of the Dead Sea Scrolls were, and the leather shows the proper amount of deterioration and worm damage. I can't speak for the truth of the text, obviously, but I don't have any doubts about its age. And, I think, it is quite possible that Nicodemus, a Pharisee, joined the Essenes. A good number of Pharisees did so."

"Impossible!" the cardinal exploded. "A story such as this, if it were true, could never have been suppressed! How could something like this—this fiction have gone unheard of for two thousand years?"

"Eminence, you must remember that this manuscript was found in the same way the Dead Sea Scrolls were discovered, quite by accident." The scholar tapped his finger on the typed translation. "In a cave, sealed up centuries ago and reopened by the chance occurrence of an earthquake. Assuming that this is the only copy and that the scribe who penned it kept his own counsel, it is quite possible that this document is genuine."

Frescobaldi shook his head and sputtered, unable to find his words.

"Excuse me, *Dottore*." The cardinal's secretary hefted the folder up and down in one hand, as though testing its weight. "What about the parchment, the skin itself? Has it been tested for age?"

Buchmeunster nodded. "Usually, the document itself would not be tested if there is other material found at the site which provides a date reference. We try to conserve as much of it as possible. In this case, however, because of what the preliminary textual analysis revealed, my colleagues at Hebrew University did run a radiodating test on a small piece of it. The best conclusion is that this scroll was most likely written no earlier than 20 A.D., no later than the year 80 A.D. There might be some slippage, but it's certainly first century."

There was a knock on the door, and Vittorio entered with an announcement. "His Holiness, Lucas I."

All three men rose as the Pontiff came into the room.

"Johann, it's kind of you to receive me on such short notice."

"Not kindness, Holy Father, a pleasure always." He bowed slightly.

"And for me." The Pope turned to Buchmeunster's guests. "Eminence, Father, it's good to see you."

The cardinal and his secretary knelt to kiss the Fisherman's ring.

"Holiness," Frescobaldi began earnestly, "I had no idea you were planning to visit Dr. Buchmeunster this afternoon. You should have told me."

"My apologies. A change in plans." The Pope flashed a professional smile at Frescobaldi and let it fade while the cardinal watched.

"Please, Holy Father." Buchmeunster beckoned toward the chair Frescobaldi had vacated. "May I get you anything to drink? Coffee? Some wine?"

"No, thank you."

Vittorio nodded and left, closing the door behind him. Lucas I glided across the rug, barely wrinkling his white cassock as he went. "Thank you again, Johann, for coming to see me when I called this morning. I hope I didn't wake you."

"No matter. I am always glad to be of service, Holiness."

The Pope smiled as he sat.

"This morning?" Confusion clouded Frescobaldi's face as he sank into the other empty chair. Guglielmo remained standing behind him.

"Yes, I had something important to give Dr. Buchmeunster, and I did not think it could wait."

"But Holy Father," said Frescobaldi, "we spoke of this conference yesterday. You didn't mention anything about—"

"The situation developed overnight, Eminence. Has Dr. Buchmeunster told you of his findings about the

Nicodemus Codex? He was kind enough to brief me this morning. Remarkable, isn't it? A letter from a man who lived when Christ walked the earth. Incredible!"

His voice was filled with wonder.

Frescobaldi cleared his throat as he tested the Pontiff's mood. "Forgive me, Holiness, but it seems the issue is more than the effect of the storyteller's art. It's rank heresy!"

"Not the first, and it won't be the last." Lucas I shook his head slowly. "There will always be doubters among us, as Christ knew. 'Blessed are those who have not seen and yet believe.' " He turned his gaze squarely toward the cardinal and his secretary, and chuckled softly. "It's almost as if we've stumbled onto a two-thousand-year-old disinformation campaign, don't you think?"

"Disinformation?" Guglielmo asked. "I realize that you haven't had much time to study this, Holy Father, but is that how Holy Mother Church will explain this discovery to the world? Disinformation?"

"You're right, Father, and I share your concern. I've had very little time." He picked up one of the folders and rapped it gently. "But we don't know who really wrote this letter, even if it actually is from the dawn of Christianity. Certainly, Jesus had enemies who would have worked to discredit him then, as they do even today. Perhaps this was the product of such efforts. But we must remember that salvation remains a matter of faith, and faith alone, as it always has been, no matter what may be found in a crumbling scroll. And in any case, what is written is not always what it seems. Johann, did you evaluate the material I gave you?''

Buchmeunster unlocked a desk drawer, then pulled out Muller's hardbound journal and handed it to the Pope.

The Pontiff stroked the tattered cover. "This is an extremely valuable book. During the past weeks, innocent people have been terrified, maimed, even killed in the attempts of desperate men to obtain it. Yet still, it found its way to us." He smiled as he turned back in Frescobaldi's direction. "As always, God protects his Church. Johann, would you share with us your reading of this book?''

"Certainly." Buchmeunster pulled a sheaf of note paper from the same drawer and consulted it as he spoke. "It's a diary of sorts, written in the hand of Dr. Andrew Muller, an archivist at the Vatican Library until his death this past autumn. Over a span of decades, it tells how he formulated a plan, then carried it out with the help of an Arab extremist and the KGB, to fabricate the Nicodemus Codex."

"What!" echoed Frescobaldi and Guglielmo in unison.

"Muller tells of being expelled from the seminary as a young man and swearing vengeance. In minute detail, he describes the development of his project of revenge. He even sets out the text of Nicodemus's account itself accurately in this journal. It was a bold plan and quite workable, at least in theory, given access to materials of the right age and enough scientific resources. He was a man of considerable genius."

"But how could he accomplish such a thing?" Frescobaldi's jowls shook with the violence of his speech. "The facility of language, the mechanics of the task?"

Buchmeunster nodded. "You must remember, Eminence, that we are talking about a man whose entire life was the scholarly review of historical documents. He had the background and certainly the time to draft an accurate rendering of what such a document should contain, in correct Masoretic Hebrew, and the precise cultural fabric."

"Johann," the Pontiff interrupted, "we come now to the central point. Is the journal a fraud? Or is our Nicodemus the hoax?"

Buchmeunster leaned back and wove his fingers into a triangle of pronouncement before speaking. "In my opinion, the journal is Muller's work. It is certainly consistent with what we know of him, and everything written in it is certainly plausible. But it is precisely because this journal is Muller's work that I find it difficult to reconcile the glaring errors that appear in it."

"Errors?" Lucas trained his dark brown eyes on the Austrian's face.

Buchmeunster shrugged nervously. "Oh, they would not be evident to a casual reader, even to a moderately competent Middle East historian. But for any scholar who knows, really knows, the other finds at Qumran. . . It's as if Muller claimed that he'd found a scroll in which the Judeans had written in Basque."

"But the Nicodemus Codex," Frescobaldi protested. "Your report says it's in the proper Hebrew dialect, historically correct, and there are no references to anything but Jesus and the story about a twin brother. What possible contradictions could you find in the other Qumran scrolls?"

"Not in the words, Eminence, but in the writing of them." Buchmeunster took the journal from the Pope and flipped through it until he found a particular page, then ran his finger down it. "In the Dead Sea Scrolls, scholars have found that each scribe had a particular identifying script, as distinctive as a signature. Muller writes that he planned to model the Nicodemus script after that used by the scribe who penned the 'Scroll of the Thanksgiving Hymns,' found in cave one at Qumran. Yet we know, and so did he, that the Thanksgiving scroll was the work of two scribes, one with elegant calligraphy and another who seemed barely able to write at all. To which did Muller refer?"

"An oversight?" offered Guglielmo.

"No, he was too careful a scholar for that to be accidental. And the writing that does appear in the Nicodemus Codex doesn't match either of them." Buchmeunster referred again to his notes. "The script is the same as we find in the 'Commentary on the Psalms,' which came from cave four. That is the scroll which caused all of the furor because of its mention of a 'Teacher of Righteousness' and the practice of 'hanging men up alive,' which some read as a reference to crucifixion." He closed the journal and looked up. "I ask you, if Andrew Muller were planning a forgery of this magnitude, and if he had the resources to produce a document that would pass all the current tests for dating, would a man with his fidelity to historical fact make such mistakes unintentionally? I can't think that possible."

Lucas I stared wordlessly at the other two priests while they mulled over Buchmeunster's conclusions. It was Frescobaldi who finally broke the silence. "But why

370

would anyone go to the trouble of making an authentic manuscript of this age appear to be a fraud?''

"An interesting question, with an obvious answer," said the Pope. "But the obvious is not always the correct." He rose and paced the floor as he spoke. "Let's start with the assumption that the Nicodemus Codex is genuine. Let's also assume that Dr. Muller felt compelled to protect Christendom from the upheaval which was certain to result when the manuscript was revealed to the world. So, he penned this journal. Makes sense, doesn't it?''

The others nodded.

The Pope raised a finger to underscore the flaws. "But would Muller, a meticulous scholar, have made such glaring errors if he hoped to be convincing? And his journal has the complete text of what Johann translated, word for word. Where did he get that? He wasn't involved in evaluating the Codex.''

"Leaks, Holy Father?'' The cardinal fingered his pectoral cross nervously. "We've always had a Vatican riddled with wagging tongues.''

"I agree that's possible, Eminence, but not at all likely. There was only one copy of that manuscript sent to Rome, and it's been in the custody of my learned friend, Dr. Buchmeunster, whom I would trust with my life. When he didn't have control of it, my Swiss Guards did, and their loyalty is beyond question. No, I think his copy came from outside of Rome, before the Vatican copy ever arrived.''

He turned to the cardinal's secretary. "Indulge me, Father. Play the devil's advocate while we pursue this mystery together. Let's assume that Muller's motive was to fuel the fires of controversy that were certain to rage over this find, settling believers and non-believers at each others' throats. Who would benefit from such a situation?''

Guglielmo cleared his throat as though weighing his words. "I suppose the first who come to mind are some extremist Moslem groups and, of course, Moscow. It could help undermine Catholic influence in the Warsaw Pact countries.''

"Exactly! And in order to accomplish this, Muller would need the help of such people. But again, we have the deliberate mistakes in his journal. So, we have to consider yet another possibility. Muller was coerced into writing the journal, but he had too much loyalty to the truth to do so without striking back. And he did, by planting subtle errors that another scholar would spot in an instant. So, it was not Muller who was the prime mover, it was the group who supplied him with the manuscript.''

Guglielmo shook his head vigorously. "But they must have recognized that the Codex itself would be extremely disruptive, Holiness. Why try to make it appear a fake? Wouldn't that hurt its effectiveness?''

"Father, that is the most intriguing question of all. So, we must look more deeply." Lucas I folded his arms and sat on the edge of Buchmeunster's massive desk. "Whoever revealed this letter to be a fraud would be extremely popular with conservative Catholics, to say the least, and probably with most of the mainstream church as well. There'd be worldwide publicity for this Champion of the Faith, and the thanks of all Christendom for exposing a horrible lie. Agreed?''

"Certainly." Guglielmo's eyes followed the Pontiff like a predator scouting its prey.

"Good. Now, if that person were an eminent member of the clergy—a prominent cardinal—he'd be almost unbeatable in the next papal conclave."

Frescobaldi exhaled decisively. "Forgive me, Holiness, but there's the flaw. You are Pontiff and you are, *Deo Gratias*, young and in the pink of health."

"Indeed, for which I am most thankful." The Pope rose and talked to the broad window behind the desk, peering out as he spoke. "But life is such a precarious condition, isn't it, Giacomo? None of us is here forever."

"Excuse me, Holiness, but what is gained by all of this?" The cardinal clapped his hands against his abdomen in puzzled irritation. "I thought your thesis was that this was a scheme to destroy Holy Mother Church, not provide it with a strong leader!"

Lucas I gave Frescobaldi a withering glare. "There is destruction from without and destruction from within, Eminence. Suppose there were an election and this man became Pontiff. His entire credibility, all his temporal and theological power base, is bound up in this pronouncement that the Nicodemus Codex is a terrible hoax." He walked toward the cardinal as he spoke. "Then, just as the new pope solidifies his position, his benefactors, the people who arranged for the Muller journal to fall into his hands, come by the Apostolic Palace for a quiet chat. They suggest he make a few concessions, a few changes in the Church's views on liberation theology, Israel's position, the role of Catholicism in Eastern Europe. In return, they offer not to tell the world that the Vicar of Christ lied his way to election with a diary that was itself a lie." He laid a firm hand on the cardinal's shoulder. "Put yourself in that man's place. Don't you see it now? Not the complete destruction of the Church; something far better—its complete control."

"That's ridiculous!" Frescobaldi sounded less than convinced of his own response. "What man of God would submit to such manipulation?"

"You're a practical man, Giacomo. It would take someone of considerable personal strength to resist it under those circumstances. I'm not certain I could do it."

"But don't you have to assume a high-level infiltration of the Vatican?" Guglielmo's voice was insistent. "Surely you can't believe—"

"There's no leap of faith required for that, Father. My envoys to the Communist world are invariably met with opposition that's well prepared, if my proposals had been made known in advance. Even the last two conclaves may have been bugged. Can't you believe there could be an agent in the Vatican?"

"I've heard rumors, yes."

"And so has everyone else!" The Pope strode around behind the chairs, his presence commanding the attention of all three men. "I propose that there is such an agent—a mole—and that he heard about the Nicodemus Codex and then hit upon this entire plan as a means to rise above being a mere conduit of information. He went to his KGB masters and told them he could practically guarantee the election of the next Pontiff."

"But he would still remain a lackey, Holy Father." The cardinal's secretary left his seat and began to pace, dragging one foot slightly. "What would that gain this mole, as you call him?"

"As a confidant of the new pope, he would certainly get a red hat, perhaps become Pope himself in time. And as the man who controls the Vatican, his stock in Moscow would certainly increase. For a young man of ambition, there could be a few quicker routes to power."

"Forgive me, Holiness, but I still have trouble with this entire argument." Guglielmo shrugged in dismay. "It assumes too much." Lucas I stood within arm's reach of the young priest and spoke quietly. "Not for someone who has been privy to his cardinal's most intimate secrets for years, someone who knew his very thoughts."

Frescobaldi paled and he searched his secretary's face anxiously.

Guglielmo was suddenly contrite. "Excuse me, Holy Father? I don't understand."

The Pontiff moved steadily toward Guglielmo as he spoke, forcing the younger man toward a corner of the study. "Your Moscow friends weren't content to wait for old age to deliver me from this life. They ordered my assassination to clear the way for Frescobaldi's reign—their reign—and you sheltered my killer. You were Abdul Sayeb's only contact, his control. You are the Judas."

The young priest stepped beyond reach of the taller man's advance. "I don't know what you're talking about, Holiness. There must be some other explanation."

Lucas I shook his head. "There isn't any. It's time to retire the field, Guglielmo. Sayeb was captured at the Vatican this morning as he was setting up an ambush for me in the basilica. He has already told us a great deal about you."

"Some story this man concocted to save himself!" Guglielmo turned to the cardinal, pleading for support. "Eminence, surely you can't believe this!"

Frescobaldi sat mute, his eyes wide with shock.

"You'll get a fair hearing." The Pope's voice turned persuasive. "Come. There are men waiting for you."

"Then we certainly shouldn't keep them any longer!" Guglielmo pulled a small Steyr automatic from inside his jacket and motioned the Pontiff back to a chair. "Why don't you have a seat, Holiness, with your friends."

"Carlo . . . Carlo . . . How could it be?" Frescobaldi's voice quavered as he turned to Lucas I. "Holy Father, I had no idea. I didn't know."

The Pope smiled sadly. "Neither did I, Giacomo. I told them it couldn't be true. They warned me not to confront him, but I didn't believe what I was hearing, so I had to put him to the test myself. What a fool I am." He shook his head ruefully. "Guglielmo, you're too trusting. You should have kept silent. I lied to you. Sayeb died before he could even tell us the time of day."

"Isn't that ironic?" the cardinal's secretary chortled bitterly. "Can't even trust a Pope. How many men are outside?"

"Six."

"Fine. *Dottore,* please call your manservant. I may need him between here and the airport."

"You only need me, you know." The Pontiff's voice was calm, reassuring. "I'll do whatever you ask."

"Ring for him!"

Buchmeunster pushed a button on the side of his desk.

Guglielmo waved the gun. "I don't expect to say things twice!" He stepped over next to the study door. "Now, nobody moves. Nobody makes a sound!"

It opened and Vittorio took two steps in before Guglielmo shoved him forward, slammed the door shut, and locked it. The old man whirled, bristling with sudden anger. The priest leveled the pistol at his head and whispered with the hiss of a threatened cobra, "Relax! I'm telling you! Don't move!"

Vittorio's face purpled as his gaze shifted around the room. "What's going on here? It's not right! You can't do this to *Il Dottore* and the Holy Fa—"

The pistol slashed across his face, clubbing the old man to the floor. He tottered slowly back to his feet.

Guglielmo aimed the gun barrel at Vittorio's chest. "I warned you. Now be silent!"

"*Il Dottore* won't tolerate this!" the servant persisted. "I won't tolerate it!"

"Vittorio, calm yourself!" Buchmeunster started out of the chair to restrain him. Guglielmo saw the movement and spun, bringing the pistol to bear.

The old buttler leaped for the gun and crashed against the priest.

Thrown off balance, he fell to the floor with Vittorio on top of him. Both had a grip on the weapon, the old man on the barrel, Guglielmo on the handle. The servant coiled his body around the priest, blocking his line of fire toward anyone else.

They rolled across the floor knocking over an end table, pushing the chairs. Guglielmo pinned the old man under him and fought to break his hold on the gun barrel.

Slowly, the pistol tilted downward. Guglielmo smiled as the muzzle neared Vittorio's face. ''Soon, old man, soon!''

Frescobaldi sat frozen in horror, his jaws clamped tightly shut. Buchmeunster banged his fist on the desk, livid with frustration.

Lucas I put a restraining arm on his sleeve. ''Don't, Johann. Stay where you are.'' The Pontiff crossed himself and closed his eyes in prayer. Two brown-robed monks entered unnoticed from Buchmeunster's hidden file room. One, with a jagged scar across his cheek, trained a pistol at the wrestling pair on the floor but couldn't get a clear shot.

Suddenly, Guglielmo jerked the gun toward himself in a new effort to wrench it free. The old man followed the motion, tucking the barrel between them. Vittorio's bony hand closed over the priest's trigger finger. Guglielmo screamed.

The weapon fired, its explosion muffled by the flesh over its muzzle. Both bodies jerked, then were still.

After a moment, Vittorio groaned and pushed the priest off him. Guglielmo rolled over with a gaping hole in his chest, landing in a limp heap. His eyes stared emptily at the ceiling. One of the monks knelt and checked for a carotid pulse, but shook his head and closed the dead man's eyes.

The Pope knelt by the body and moved his lips in prayer as he made the sign of the cross.

Vittorio clutched at his heart and gasped for breath. The cardinal, now out of his chair, looked down at him with contempt. "Old fool! You could have gotten the Holy Father killed! You could have gotten us all killed!"

Lucas I reached over and grasped the old man's shoulder firmly. "You are not so foolish, *cavaliere*. Brave, valiant, but not foolish." He motioned to the other monk. "Please put him in the helicopter. Radio ahead to Gemelli Hospital."

Frescobaldi turned his attention to the monks, seemingly aware of their presence for the first time. "Where did you come from? Who are you? I don't recognize your Order."

The Pope waved the brown-clad men away. "That, Eminence, is for me to know and for me to decide who else will know. You are not on that list, nor do I think you will be."

"Surely, Holiness, you can't believe that I had anything to do—"

"No, I don't," said the Pontiff angrily. "But you are vain and self-indulgent, and those are grievous flaws in a Prince of the Church. You would have been easy prey, soaring like a falcon but always returning to your master's tether. If you ever want my trust again, then pray for the strength to realize that you are no higher in the sight of God than the lowest beggar on the streets of Rome."

Rita and Durant parked the Lancia where the driveway widened in front of the villa and ran toward the steps. They stopped at the sight of the two monks bearing Vittorio on a stretcher, heading down a walk that led behind the house. Buchmeunster followed with a folder and Muller's red leather-bound book under his arm.

"Look, Rita! The journal!" Durant started after Buchmeunster, but she grabbed him and pointed toward the front door.,

"Good god!" Durant drew in his breath sharply. "The Pope!"

"Perhaps we could just tell him?"

They walked toward the white figure of Lucas I and met him at the bottom of the steps. Lucas I smiled and extended his hand. "Ah, Mr. Durant. A pleasure to meet you at last. And you, Miss Chapman."

"But—but—" Rita stammered. I don't recall ever—"

"We haven't. But I have heard much about you both." He fingered the red jade cross that hung over his breast, a *tau* with a band of gold at its junction. "We have a mutual friend."

Durant cleared his throat nervously. "Holy Father, we have to speak to Doctor Buchmeunster. It's about a manuscript that he was evaluating."

"You'll have that chance, but not just now."

A jet turbine began to whine from the meadow behind the villa. Durant raised his voice to be heard. "Excuse me, Holiness, but what's going on? What are you doing here, and who are those guys in the brown robes?"

"We'll talk about that, too, Mr. Durant. The manuscript, Andrew Muller's journal, all of it. I'm afraid I have to return to St. Peter's now and say mass. Come to my apartments tomorrow and bring your cameraman."

"An interview? An exclusive story?"

"The interview of your lifetime, Mr. Durant. And of mine."

THE FINEST IN SUSPENSE!

THE URSA ULTIMATUM (2130, $3.95)
by Terry Baxter

In the dead of night, twelve nuclear warheads are smuggled north across the Mexican border to be detonated simultaneously in major cities throughout the U.S. And only a small-town desert lawman stands between a face-less Russian superspy and World War Three!

THE LAST ASSASSIN (1989, $3.95)
by Daniel Easterman

From New York City to the Middle East, the devastating flames of revolution and terrorism sweep across a world gone mad . . . as the most terrifying conspiracy in the history of mankind is born!

FLOWERS FROM BERLIN (2060, $4.50)
by Noel Hynd

With the Earth on the brink of World War Two, the Third Reich's deadliest professional killer is dispatched on the most heinous assignment of his murderous career: the assassination of Franklin Delano Roosevelt!

THE BIG NEEDLE (1921, $2.95)
by Ken Follett

All across Europe, innocent people are being terrorized, homes are destroyed, and dead bodies have become an unnervingly common sight. And the horrors will continue until the most powerful organization on Earth finds Chadwell Carstairs—and kills him!

DOMINATOR (2118, $3.95)
by James Follett

Two extraordinary men, each driven by dangerously ambiguous loyalties, play out the ultimate nuclear endgame miles above the helpless planet—aboard a hijacked space shuttle called DOMINATOR!